"A sudden wild, fierce shout pealed up to the vaulted ceiling."
[*Frontispiece. See page 196*]

SIR NIGEL

A NOVEL OF THE HUNDRED YEARS' WAR

SIR ARTHUR CONAN DOYLE

DOVER PUBLICATIONS, INC.
Mineola, New York

Bibliographical Note

This Dover edition, first published in 2009, is an unabridged republication of the work originally published by Smith, Elder & Co., London, in 1906.

Library of Congress Cataloging-in-Publication Data

Doyle, Arthur Conan, Sir, 1859–1930.
    Sir Nigel : a novel of the Hundred Years' War / Arthur Conan Doyle. — Dover ed.
      p. cm.
   ISBN-13: 978-0-486-47144-0
   ISBN-10: 0-486-47144-6
   1. Great Britain—History—Edward III, 1327–1377—Fiction. 2. Hundred Years' War, 1339–1453—Fiction. 3. Knights and knighthood—Fiction. I. Title.

PR4622.S46 2009
823'.8—dc22

2008044797

Manufactured in the United States of America
Dover Publications, Inc., 31 East 2nd Street, Mineola, N.Y. 11501

Introduction

DAME HISTORY IS so austere a lady that if one has been so ill-advised as to take a liberty with her one should hasten to make amends by repentance and confession. Events have been transposed to the extent of some few months in this narrative in order to preserve the continuity and evenness of the story. I hope so small a divergence may seem a venial error after so many centuries. For the rest it is as accurate as a good deal of research and hard work could make it.

The matter of diction is always a question of taste and discretion in a historical reproduction. In the year 1350 the upper classes still spoke Norman-French, though they were just beginning to condescend to English. The lower classes spoke the English of the original Piers Plowman text, which would be considerably more obscure than their superiors' French if the two were now reproduced or imitated. The most which the chronicler can do is to catch the cadence and style of their talk, and to infuse here and there such a dash of the archaic as may indicate their fashion of speech.

I am aware that there are incidents which may strike the modern reader as brutal and repellent. It is useless, however, to draw the Twentieth Century and label it the Fourteenth. It was a sterner age, and men's code of morality, especially in matters of cruelty, was very different. There is no incident in the text for which very good warrant may not be given. The fantastic graces of chivalry lay upon the surface of life, but beneath it was a half-savage population, fierce and animal, with little ruth or mercy. It was a raw, rude England, full of elemental passions, and redeemed only by elemental virtues. Such I have tried to draw it.

For good or bad, many books have gone to the building of this one. I look round my study table and I survey those which lie with me at the moment, before I happily disperse them for ever. I see La Croix's "Middle Ages," Oman's "Art of War," Rietstap's "Armorial Général," De la Borderie's "Histoire de Bretagne," Dame Berners' "Boke of St. Albans," "The Chronicle of Jocelyn of Brakelond," "The Old Road," Hewitt's "Ancient Armour," Coussan's "Heraldry," Boutell's "Arms," Browne's "Chaucer's England," Cust's "Scenes of the Middle Ages," Jusserand's "Wayfaring Life," Ward's "Canterbury Pilgrims," Cornish's "Chivalry," Hastings' "British Archer," Strutt's "Sports," Johnes "Froissart," Hargrove's "Archery," Longman's "Edward III," Wright's "Domestic Manners." With these and many others I have lived for months. If I have been unable to combine and transfer their effect the fault is mine.

ARTHUR CONAN DOYLE.

UNDERSHAW
October 1906

Contents

I. THE HOUSE OF LORING

IN THE MONTH of July of the year 1348, between the feasts of St. Benedict and of St. Swithin, a strange thing came upon England, for out of the east there drifted a monstrous cloud, purple and piled, heavy with evil, climbing slowly up the hushed heaven. In the shadow of that strange cloud the leaves drooped in the trees, the birds ceased their calling, and the cattle and the sheep gathered cowering under the hedges. A gloom fell upon all the land, and men stood with their eyes upon the strange cloud and a heaviness upon their hearts. They crept into the churches, where the trembling people were blessed and shriven by the trembling priests. Outside no bird flew, and there came no rustling from the woods, nor any of the homely sounds of Nature. All was still, and nothing moved, save only the great cloud which rolled up and onward, with fold on fold from the black horizon. To the west was the light summer sky, to the east this brooding cloud-bank, creeping ever slowly across, until the last thin blue gleam faded away and the whole vast sweep of the heavens was one great leaden arch.

Then the rain began to fall. All day it rained, and all the night and all the week and all the month, until folk had forgotten the blue heavens and the gleam of the sunshine. It was not heavy, but it was steady and cold and unceasing, so that the people were weary of its hissing and its splashing, with the slow drip from the eaves. Always the same thick evil cloud flowed from east to west with the rain beneath it. None could see for more than a bow-shot from their dwellings for the drifting veil of the rain-storms. Every morning the folk looked upward for a break, but their eyes rested always upon the same endless cloud, until at last they ceased to look up, and their hearts despaired of ever seeing the change. It was raining at Lammas-tide and raining at the Feast of the Assumption and still raining at Michaelmas. The crops and the hay, sodden and black, had rotted in the fields, for they were not worth the garnering. The sheep had died, and the calves also, so there was little to kill when Martinmas came and it was time to salt the meat for the winter. They feared a famine, but it was worse than famine which was in store for them.

For the rain had ceased at last, and a sickly autumn sun shone upon a land which was soaked and sodden with water. Wet and rotten leaves reeked and festered under the foul haze which rose from the woods. The fields were spotted with monstrous fungi of a size and color never matched before—scarlet and mauve and liver and black. It was as though the sick earth had burst into foul pustules; mildew and lichen mottled the walls, and with that filthy crop Death sprang also from the water-soaked earth. Men died, and women and children, the baron of the castle, the franklin on the farm, the monk in the abbey, and the villein in his wattle-and-daub cottage. All breathed the same polluted reek and all died the same death of corruption. Of those who were stricken none recovered, and the illness was ever the same—gross boils, raving, and the black blotches which gave its name to the disease. All through the winter the dead rotted by the wayside for want of some one to bury them. In many a village no single man was left alive. Then at last the spring came, with sunshine and health and lightness and laugh-ter—the greenest, sweetest, tenderest spring that England had ever known. But only half of England could know it—the other half had passed away with the great purple cloud.

Yet it was there, in that stream of death, in that reek of cor-ruption, that the brighter and freer England was born. There in that dark hour the first streak of the new dawn was seen. For in no way save by a great upheaval and change could the nation break away from that iron feudal system which held her limbs. But now it was a new country which came out from that year of death. The barons were dead in swaths. No high turret nor cun-ning moat could keep out that black commoner who struck them down. Oppressive laws slackened for want of those who could enforce them, and once slackened could never be enforced again. The laborer would be a slave no longer. The bondsman snapped his shackles. There was much to do and few left to do it. Therefore the few should be free men, name their own price, and work where and for whom they would. It was the black death which cleared the way for that great rising thirty years later which left the English peasant the freest of his class in Europe.

But there were few so far-sighted that they could see that here as ever good was coming out of evil. At the moment misery and ruin were brought into every family. The dead cattle, the ungarnered crops, the untilled lands—every spring of wealth had dried up at the same moment. Those who were rich became poor; but those who were poor already, and especially those who were poor with the burden of gentility upon their shoulders, found themselves in a perilous state. All through England the smaller gentry were ruined, for they had no trade save war, and they drew their living from the work of others. On many a manor-house there came evil times, and on none more than on the Manor of Tilford, where for many generations the noble family of the Lorings had held their home.

There was a time when the Lorings had held the country from the North Downs to the Lakes of Frensham, and when their grim castle-keep rising above the green meadows which border the River Wey had been the strongest fortalice between Guildford Castle in the east and Winchester in the west. But there came that Barons' War, in which the King used his Saxon subjects as a whip with which to scourge his Norman barons, and Castle Loring, like so many other great strongholds, was swept from the face of the land. From that time the Lorings, with estates sadly curtailed, lived in what had been the dower-house, with enough for their needs, but shorn of all their splendor.

And then came their lawsuit with Waverley Abbey, and the Cistercians laid claim to their richest land, with peccary, turbary, and feudal rights over the remainder. It straggled on for years, this great lawsuit, and when it was finished the men of the

Church and the men of the Law had divided all that was richest of the estate between them. There was still left the old manor-house, from which with each generation there came a soldier to uphold the credit of the name, and to show the five scarlet roses on the silver shield where it had always been shown—in the van. There were twelve bronzes in the little chapel where Matthew the priest said mass every morning, all of men of the house of Loring. Two lay with their legs crossed, as being from the Crusades. Six others rested their feet upon lions, as having died in war. Four only lay with the effigy of their hounds to show that they had passed in peace.

Of this famous but impoverished family, doubly impoverished by law and by pestilence, two members were living in the year of grace 1349—Lady Ermyntrude Loring and her grandson Nigel. Lady Ermyntrude's husband had fallen before the Scottish spearsmen at Stirling, and her son Eustace, Nigel's father, had found a glorious death, nine years before this chronicle opens, upon the poop of a Norman galley at the sea-fight of Sluys. The lonely old woman, fierce and brooding like the falcon mewed in her chamber, was soft only toward the lad whom she had brought up. All the tenderness and love of her nature, so hidden from others that they could not imagine their existence, were lavished upon him. She could not bear him away from her, and he, with that respect for authority which the age demanded, would not go without her blessing and consent.

So it came about that Nigel, with his lion heart and with the blood of a hundred soldiers thrilling in his veins, still at the age of two-and-twenty, wasted the weary days reclaiming his hawks with leash and lure or training the alans and spaniels who shared with the family the big earthen-floored hall of the manor-house.

Day by day the aged Lady Ermyntrude had seen him wax in strength and in manhood, small of stature, it is true, but with muscles of steel and a soul of fire. From all parts, from the warden of Guildford Castle, from the tilt-yard of Farnham, tales of his prowess were brought back to her, of his daring as a rider, of his debonair courage, of his skill with all weapons; but still she, who had both husband and son torn from her by a bloody death, could not bear that this, the last of the Lorings, the final bud of so famous an old tree, should share the same fate. With a weary heart, but with a smiling face, he bore with his uneventful days, while she would ever put off the evil time, until the harvest was better, until the monks of Waverley should give up what they had taken, until his uncle should die and leave money for his outfit, or any other excuse with which she could hold him to her side.

And, indeed, there was need for a man at Tilford, for the strife betwixt the Abbey and the manor-house had never been appeased, and still on one pretext or another the monks would clip off yet one more slice of their neighbor's land. Over the winding river, across the green meadows, rose the short square tower and the high gray walls of the grim Abbey, with its bell tolling by day and night, a voice of menace and of dread to the little household.

It is in the heart of the great Cistercian monastery that this chronicle of old days must take its start, as we trace the feud betwixt the monks and the house of Loring with those events to which it gave birth, ending with the coming of Chandos, the strange spear-running of Tilford Bridge, and the deeds with which Nigel won fame in the wars. Elsewhere, in the chronicle of the White Company, it has been set forth what manner of man was Nigel Loring. Those who love him may read herein the things which went to his making. Let us go back together and gaze upon this green stage of England, the scenery, hill, plain and river even as now, the actors in much our very selves, in much also so changed in thought and act that they might be dwellers in another world to ours.

II. HOW THE DEVIL CAME
TO WAVERLEY

THE DAY WAS the first of May, which was the Festival of the Blessed Apostles Philip and James. The year was the 1349th from man's salvation.

From tierce to sext, and then again from sext to nones, Abbot John of the House of Waverley had been seated in his study while he conducted the many high duties of his office. All around for many a mile on every side stretched the fertile and flourishing estate of which he was the master. In the center lay the broad Abbey buildings, with church and cloisters, hospitium, chapter-house and frater-house, all buzzing with a busy life. Through the open window came the low hum of the voices of the brethren as they walked in pious converse in the ambulatory below. From across the cloister there rolled the distant rise and fall of a Gregorian chant, where the precentor was hard at work upon the choir, while down in the chapter-house sounded the strident voice of Brother Peter, expounding the rule of Saint Bernard to the novices.

Abbot John rose to stretch his cramped limbs. He looked out at the greensward of the cloister, and at the graceful line of open Gothic arches which skirted a covered walk for the brethren within. Two and two in their black-and-white garb, with slow step and heads inclined, they paced round and round. Several of the more studious had brought their illuminating work from the scriptorium, and sat in the warm sunshine, with their little platters of pigments and packets of gold-leaf before them, their shoulders rounded and their faces sunk low over the white sheets of vellum. There, too, was the copper-worker with his burin and graver. Learning and art were not traditions with the

Cistercians as with the parent Order of the Benedictines, and yet the library of Waverley was well filled both with precious books and with pious students.

But the true glory of the Cistercian lay in his outdoor work, and so ever and anon there passed through the cloister some sunburned monk, soiled mattock or shovel in hand, with his gown looped to his knee, fresh from the fields or the garden. The lush green water-meadows speckled with the heavy-fleeced sheep, the acres of corn-land reclaimed from heather and bracken, the vineyards on the southern slope of Crooksbury Hill, the rows of Hankley fish-ponds, the Frensham marshes drained and sown with vegetables, the spacious pigeon-cotes, all circled the great Abbey round with the visible labors of the Order.

The Abbot's full and florid face shone with a quiet content as he looked out at his huge but well-ordered household. Like every head of a prosperous Abbey, Abbot John, the fourth of the name, was a man of varied accomplishments. Through his own chosen instruments he had to minister a great estate, and to keep order and decorum among a large body of men living a celibate life. He was a rigid disciplinarian toward all beneath him, a supple diplomatist to all above. He held high debate with neighboring abbots and lords, with bishops, with papal legates, and even on occasion with the King's majesty himself. Many were the subjects with which he must be conversant. Questions of doctrine, questions of building, points of forestry, of agriculture, of drainage, of feudal law, all came to the Abbot for settlement. He held the scales of Justice in all the Abbey banlieue which stretched over many a mile of Hampshire and of Surrey. To the monks his displeasure might mean fasting, exile to some sterner community, or even imprisonment in chains. Over the layman also he could hold any punishment save only corporeal death, instead of which he had in hand the far more dreadful weapon of spiritual excommunication.

Such were the powers of the Abbot, and it is no wonder that there were masterful lines in the ruddy features of Abbot John, or that the brethren, glancing up, should put on an even meeker carriage and more demure expression as they saw the watchful face in the window above them.

A knock at the door of his study recalled the Abbot to his immediate duties, and he returned to his desk. Already he had spoken with his cellarer and prior, almoner, chaplain, and lector, but now in the tall and gaunt monk who obeyed his summons to enter he recognized the most important and also the most importunate of his agents, Brother Samuel the sacrist, whose office, corresponding to that of the layman's bailiff, placed the material interests of the monastery and its dealings with the outer world entirely under his control, subject only to the check of the Abbot. Brother Samuel was a gnarled and stringy old monk, whose stern and sharp-featured face reflected no light from above, but only that sordid workaday world toward which it was for ever turned. A huge book of accounts was tucked under one of his arms, while a great bunch of keys hung from the other hand, a badge of his office, and also, on occasion of impatience, a weapon of offense, as many a scarred head among rustics and lay brothers could testify.

The Abbot sighed wearily, for he suffered much at the hands of his strenuous agent.

"Well, Brother Samuel, what is your will?" he asked.

"Holy father, I have to report that I have sold the wool to Master Baldwin of Winchester at two shillings a bale more than it fetched last year, for the murrain among the sheep has raised the price."

"You have done well, brother."

"I have also to tell you that I have distrained Wat the warrener from his cottage; for his Christmas rent is still unpaid, nor the hen-rents of last year."

"He has a wife and four children, brother." He was a good, easy man, the Abbot, though liable to be overborne by his sterner subordinate.

"It is true, holy father; but if I should pass him, then how am I to ask the rent of the foresters of Puttenham, or the hinds in the village? Such a thing spreads from house to house, and where then is the wealth of Waverley?"

"What else, Brother Samuel?"

"There is the matter of the fish-ponds."

The Abbot's face brightened. It was a subject upon which he

was an authority. If the rule of his Order had robbed him of the softer joys of life, he had the keener zest for those which remained.

"How have the char prospered, brother?"

"They have done well, holy father; but the carp have died in the Abbot's pond."

"Carp prosper only upon a gravel bottom. They must be put in also in their due proportion, three milters to one spawner, brother sacrist, and the spot must be free from wind, stony and sandy, an ell deep, with willows and grass upon the banks. Mud for tench, brother, gravel for carp."

The sacrist leaned forward with the face of one who bears tidings of woe.

"There are pike in the Abbot's pond," said he.

"Pike!" cried the Abbot, in horror. "As well shut up a wolf in our sheepfold. How came a pike in the pond? There were no pike last year, and a pike does not fall with the rain nor rise in the springs. The pond must be drained, or we shall spend next Lent upon stock-fish, and have the brethren down with the great sickness ere Easter Sunday has come to absolve us from our abstinence."

"The pond shall be drained, holy father; I have already ordered it. Then we shall plant pot-herbs on the mud bottom, and after we have gathered them in, return the fish and water once more from the lower pond, so that they may fatten among the rich stubble."

"Good!" cried the Abbot. "I would have three fish-stews in every well-ordered house—one dry for herbs, one shallow for the fry and the yearlings, and one deep for the breeders and the table-fish. But still, I have not heard you say how the pike came in the Abbot's pond?"

A spasm of anger passed over the fierce face of the sacrist, and his keys rattled as his bony hand clasped them more tightly.

"Young Nigel Loring!" said he. "He swore that he would do us scathe, and in this way he has done it."

"How know you this?"

"Six weeks ago he was seen day by day fishing for pike at the great Lake of Frensham. Twice at night he has been met with a bundle of straw under his arm on the Hankley Down. Well, I wot that the straw was wet and that a live pike lay within it."

The Abbot shook his head. "I have heard much of this youth's wild ways; but now, indeed, he has passed all bounds if what you say be truth. It was bad enough when it was said that he slew the king's deer in Woolmer Chase, or broke the head of Hobbs the chapman, so that he lay for seven days betwixt life and death in our infirmary, saved only by Brother Peter's skill in the pharmacies of herbs; but to put pike in the Abbot's pond—why should he play such a devil's prank?"

"Because he hates the House of Waverley, holy father; because he swears that we hold his father's land."

"In which there is surely some truth."

"But, holy father, we hold no more than the law has allowed."

"True, brother, and yet, between ourselves, we may admit that the heavier purse may weigh down the scales of Justice. When I have passed the old house and have seen that aged woman with her ruddled cheeks and her baleful eyes look the curses she dare not speak, I have many a time wished that we had other neighbors."

"That we can soon bring about, holy father. Indeed, it is of it that I wished to speak to you. Surely it is not hard for us to drive them from the country-side. There are thirty years' claims of escuage unsettled, and there is Sergeant Wilkins, the lawyer of Guildford, whom I will warrant to draw up such arrears of dues and rents and issues of hidage and fodder-corn that these folk, who are as beggarly as they are proud, will have to sell the roof-tree over them ere they can meet them. Within three days I will have them at our mercy."

"They are an ancient family and of good repute. I would not treat them too harshly, brother."

"Bethink you of the pike in the carp pond!"

The Abbot hardened his heart at the thought. "It was indeed a devil's deed—when we had but newly stocked it with char and with carp. Well, well, the law is the law, and if you can use it to hurt it is still lawful to do so. Have these claims been advanced?"

"Deacon, the bailiff, with his two varlets went down to the Hall yesternight on the matter of the escuage, and came screaming back with this young hot-head raging at their heels. He is small and slight, yet he has the strength of many men in the hour of his wrath. The bailiff swears that he will go no more, save with half a score of archers to uphold him."

The Abbot was red with anger at this new offense. "I will teach him that the servants of Holy Church, even though we of the rule of Saint Bernard be the lowliest and humblest of her children, can still defend their own against the froward and the violent! Go, cite this man before the Abbey court. Let him appear in the chapter-house after tierce to-morrow."

But the wary sacrist shook his head. "Nay, holy father, the times are not yet ripe. Give me three days, I pray you, that my case against him may be complete. Bear in mind that the father and the grandfather of this unruly squire were both famous men of their day and the foremost knights in the king's own service, living in high honor and dying in their knightly duty. The Lady Ermyntrude Loring was first lady to the king's mother. Roger Fitz-Allan of Farnham and Sir Hugh Walcott of Guildford Castle were each old comrades-in-arms of Nigel's father, and sib to him on the distaff side. Already there has been talk that we have dealt harshly with them. Therefore, my rede is that we be wise and wary and wait until his cup be indeed full."

The Abbot had opened his mouth to reply, when the consultation was interrupted by a most unwonted buzz of excitement from among the monks in the cloister below. Questions and answers in excited voices sounded from one side of the ambulatory to the other. Sacrist and Abbot were gazing at each other in amazement at such a breach of the discipline and decorum of their well-trained flock, when there came a swift step upon the stair, and a white-faced brother flung open the door and rushed into the room.

"Father Abbot!" he cried. "Alas, alas! Brother John is dead, and the holy sub-prior is dead, and the Devil is loose in the five-virgate field!"

III. THE YELLOW HORSE
OF CROOKSBURY

IN THOSE SIMPLE times there was a great wonder and mystery in life. Man walked in fear and solemnity, with Heaven very close above his head, and Hell below his very feet. God's visible hand was everywhere, in the rainbow and the comet, in the thunder and the wind. The Devil, too, raged openly upon the earth; he skulked behind the hedgerows in the gloaming; he laughed loudly in the night-time; he clawed the dying sinner, pounced on the unbaptized babe, and twisted the limbs of the epileptic. A foul fiend slunk ever by a man's side and whispered villainies in his ear, while above him there hovered an angel of grace who pointed to the steep and narrow track. How could one doubt these things, when Pope and priest and scholar and king were all united in believing them, with no single voice of question in the whole wide world?

Every book read, every picture seen, every tale heard from nurse or mother, all taught the same lesson. And as a man traveled through the world his faith would grow the firmer, for go where he would there were the endless shrines of the saints, each with its holy relic in the center, and around it the tradition of incessant miracles, with stacks of deserted crutches and silver votive hearts to prove them. At every turn he was made to feel how thin was the veil, and how easily rent, which screened him from the awful denizens of the unseen world.

Hence the wild announcement of the frightened monk seemed terrible rather than incredible to those whom he addressed. The Abbot's ruddy face paled for a moment, it is true, but he plucked the crucifix from his desk and rose valiantly to his feet.

"Lead me to him!" said he. "Show me the foul fiend who dares to lay his grip upon brethren of the holy house of Saint Bernard! Run down to my chaplain, brother! Bid him bring the exorcist with him, and also the blessed box of relics, and the bones of Saint James from under the altar! With these and a contrite and humble heart we may show front to all the powers of darkness."

But the sacrist was of a more critical turn of mind. He clutched the monk's arm with a grip which left its five purple spots for many a day to come.

"Is this the way to enter the Abbot's own chamber without knock or reverence, or so much as a '*Pax vobiscum*'?" said he, sternly. "You were wont to be our gentlest novice, of lowly carriage in chapter, devout in psalmody, and strict in the cloister. Pull your wits together and answer me straightly. In what form has the foul fiend appeared, and how has he done this grievous scathe to our brethren? Have you seen him with your own eyes, or do you repeat from hearsay? Speak, man, or you stand on the penance-stool in the chapter-house this very hour!"

Thus adjured, the frightened monk grew calmer in his bearing, though his white lips and his startled eyes, with the gasping of his breath, told of his inward tremors.

"If it please you, holy father, and you, reverend sacrist, it came about in this way. James the sub-prior, and Brother John and I had spent our day from sext onward on Hankley cutting bracken for the cow-houses. We were coming back over the five-virgate field, and the holy sub-prior was telling us a saintly tale from the life of Saint Gregory, when there came a sudden sound like a rushing torrent, and the foul fiend sprang over the high wall which skirts the water-meadow and rushed upon us with the speed of the wind. The lay brother he struck to the ground and trampled into the mire. Then, seizing the good sub-prior in his teeth, he rushed round the field, swinging him as though he were a fardel of old clothes.

"Amazed at such a sight, I stood without movement, and had said a credo and three aves, when the Devil dropped the sub-prior and sprang upon me. With the help of Saint Bernard I clambered over the wall, but not before his teeth had found my leg, and he had torn away the whole back skirt of my gown."

As he spoke he turned and gave corroboration to his story by the hanging ruins of his long trailing garment.

"In what shape, then, did Satan appear?" the Abbot demanded.

"As a great yellow horse, holy father—a monster horse, with eyes of fire and the teeth of a griffin."

"A yellow horse!" The sacrist glared at the scared monk. "You foolish brother! How will you behave when you have indeed to face the King of Terrors himself if you can be so frightened by the sight of a yellow horse? It is the horse of Franklin Aylward, my father, which has been distrained by us because he owes the Abbey fifty good shillings, and can never hope to pay it. Such a horse, they say, is not to be found between this and the king's stables at Windsor, for his sire was a Spanish destrier, and his dam an Arab mare of the very breed which Saladin kept for his own use, and even, it has been said, under the shelter of his own tent. I took him in discharge of the debt, and I ordered the varlets who had haltered him to leave him alone in the water-meadow, for I have heard that the beast has indeed a most evil spirit, and has killed more men than one."

"It was an ill day for Waverley that you brought such a monster within its bounds," said the Abbot. "If the sub-prior and Brother John be indeed dead, then it would seem that if the horse be not the devil, he is at least the devil's instrument."

"Horse or devil, holy father, I heard him shout with joy as he trampled upon Brother John, and had you seen him tossing the sub-prior as a dog shakes a rat, you would perchance have felt even as I did."

"Come, then," cried the Abbot, "let us see with our own eyes what evil has been done."

And the three monks hurried down the stair which led to the cloisters.

They had no sooner descended than their more pressing fears were set at rest, for at that very moment, limping, disheveled and mud-stained, the two sufferers were being led in amid a crowd of sympathizing brethren. Shouts and cries from outside showed, however, that some further drama was in progress, and both Abbot and sacrist hastened onward as fast as the dignity of their office would permit, until they had passed the gates and gained the wall of the meadow. Looking over it, a remarkable sight presented itself to their eyes.

Fetlock deep in the lush grass there stood a magnificent horse, such a horse as a sculptor or a soldier might thrill to see. His color was a light chestnut, with mane and tail of a more tawny tint. Seventeen hands high, with a barrel and haunches which bespoke tremendous strength, he fined down to the most delicate lines of dainty breed in neck and crest and shoulder. He was indeed a glorious sight as he stood there, his beautiful body leaning back from his wide-spread and propped forelegs, his head craned high, his ears erect, his mane bristling, his red nostrils opening and shutting with wrath, and his flashing eyes turning from side to side in haughty menace and defiance.

Scattered round in a respectful circle, six of the Abbey lay servants and foresters, each holding a halter, were creeping toward him. Every now and then, with a beautiful toss and swerve and plunge, the great creature would turn upon one of his would-be captors, and with outstretched head, flying mane and flashing teeth, would chase him screaming to the safety of the wall, while the others would close swiftly in behind, and cast their ropes in the hope of catching neck or leg, but only in their turn to be chased to the nearest refuge.

Had two of these ropes settled upon the horse, and had their throwers found some purchase of stump or boulder by which they could hold them, then the man's brain might have won its wonted victory over swiftness and strength. But the brains were themselves at fault which imagined that one such rope would serve any purpose save to endanger the thrower.

Yet so it was, and what might have been foreseen occurred at the very moment of the arrival of the monks. The horse, having chased one of his enemies to the wall, remained so long snorting his contempt over the coping that the others were able to creep upon him from behind. Several ropes were flung, and one noose settled over the proud crest and lost itself in the waving mane. In an instant the creature had turned, and the men were flying for their lives; but he who had cast the rope lingered, uncertain what use to make of his own success. That moment of doubt was fatal. With a yell of dismay, the man saw the great creature rear above him. Then with a crash the fore-feet fell upon him and dashed him to the ground. He rose screaming, was hurled over once more, and lay a quivering, bleeding heap, while the savage horse, the most cruel and terrible in its anger of all creatures on earth, bit and shook and trampled the writhing body.

A loud wail of horror rose from the lines of tonsured heads which skirted the high wall—a wail which suddenly died away into a long, hushed silence, broken at last by a rapturous cry of thanksgiving and of joy.

On the road which led to the old dark manor-house upon the side of the hill a youth had been riding. His mount was a sorry one, a weedy, shambling, long-haired colt, and his patched tunic of faded purple with stained leather belt presented no very smart appearance; yet in the bearing of the man, in the poise of his head, in his easy, graceful carriage, and in the bold glance of his large blue eyes, there was that stamp of distinction and of breed which would have given him a place of his own in any assembly. He was of small stature, but his frame was singularly elegant and graceful. His face, though tanned with the weather, was delicate in features, and most eager and alert in expression. A thick fringe of crisp yellow curls broke from under the dark flat cap which he was wearing, and a short golden beard hid the outline of his strong, square chin. One white osprey feather thrust through a gold brooch in the front of his cap gave a touch of grace to his somber garb. This and other points of his attire, the short hanging mantle, the leather-sheathed hunting-knife, the cross-belt which sustained a brazen horn, the soft doe-skin boots and the prick spurs, would all disclose themselves to an observer; but at the first glance the brown face set in gold, and the dancing light of the quick, reckless, laughing eyes, were the one strong memory left behind.

Such was the youth who, cracking his whip joyously, and followed by half a score of dogs, cantered on his rude pony down the Tilford Lane, and thence it was that, with a smile of amused contempt upon his face, he observed the comedy in the field and the impotent efforts of the servants of Waverley.

Suddenly, however, as the comedy turned swiftly to black tragedy, this passive spectator leaped into quick strenuous life. With a spring he was off his pony, and with another he was over the stone wall and flying swiftly across the field. Looking up from his victim, the great yellow horse saw this other enemy approach, and spurning the prostrate but still writhing body with his heels, dashed at the newcomer.

But this time there was no hasty flight, no rapturous pursuit to the wall. The little man braced himself straight, flung up his metal-headed whip, and met the horse with a crashing blow upon the head, repeated again and again with every attack. In vain the horse reared and tried to overthrow its enemy with swooping shoulders and pawing hoofs. Cool, swift, and alert, the man sprang swiftly aside from under the very shadow of death, and then again came the swish and thud of the unerring blow from the heavy handle.

The horse drew off, glared with wonder and fury at this masterful man, and then trotted round in a circle, with mane bristling, tail streaming, and ears on end, snorting in its rage and pain. The man, hardly deigning to glance at his fell neighbor, passed on to the wounded forester, raised him in his arms with a strength which could not have been expected in so slight a body, and carried him, groaning, to the wall, where a dozen hands were outstretched to help him over. Then, at his leisure, the young man also climbed the wall, smiling back with cool contempt at the yellow horse, which had come raging after him once more.

As he sprang down, a dozen monks surrounded him to thank him or to praise him; but he would have turned sullenly away without a word had he not been stopped by Abbot John in person.

"Nay, Squire Loring," said he, "if you be a bad friend to our Abbey, yet we must needs own that you have played the part of a good Christian this day, for if there be breath left in our servant's body it is to you next to our blessed patron Saint Bernard that we owe it."

"By Saint Paul! I owe you no good-will, Abbot John," said the young man. "The shadow of your Abbey has ever fallen across the house of Loring. As to any small deed that I may have done this day, I ask no thanks for it. It is not for you nor for your house that I have done it, but only because it was my pleasure so to do."

The Abbot flushed at the bold words, and bit his lip with vexation.

It was the sacrist, however, who answered: "It would be more fitting and more gracious," said he, "if you were to speak to the holy Father Abbot in a manner suited to his high rank and to the respect which is due to a Prince of the Church."

The youth turned his bold blue eyes upon the monk, and his sunburned face darkened with anger.

"Were it not for the gown upon your back, and for your silvering hair, I would answer you in another fashion," said he. "You are the lean wolf which growls ever at our door, greedy for the little which hath been left to us. Say and do what you will with me, but by Saint Paul! if I find that Dame Ermyntrude is baited by your ravenous pack I will beat them off with this whip from the little patch which still remains of all the acres of my fathers."

"Have a care, Nigel Loring, have a care!" cried the Abbot, with finger upraised. "Have you no fears of the law of England?"

"A just law I fear and obey."

"Have you no respect for Holy Church?"

"I respect all that is holy in her. I do not respect those who grind the poor or steal their neighbor's land."

"Rash man, many a one has been blighted by her ban for less than you have now said! And yet it is not for us to judge you harshly this day. You are young and hot words come easily to your lips. How fares the forester?"

"His hurt is grievous, Father Abbot, but he will live," said a brother, looking up from the prostrate form. "With a blood-letting and an electuary, I will warrant him sound within a month."

"Then bear him to the hospital. And now, brother, about this terrible beast who still gazes and snorts at us over the top of the wall as though his thoughts of Holy Church were as uncouth as those of Squire Nigel himself, what are we to do with him?"

"Here is Franklin Aylward," said one of the brethren. "The horse was his, and doubtless he will take it back to his farm."

But the stout red-faced farmer shook his head at the proposal. "Not I, in faith!" said he. "The beast hath chased me twice round the paddock; it has nigh slain my boy Samkin. He would never be happy till he had ridden it, nor has he ever been happy since. There is not a hind in my employ who will enter his stall. Ill fare the day that ever I took the beast from the Castle stud at Guildford, where they could do nothing with it and no rider could be found bold enough to mount it! When the sacrist here took it for a fifty-shilling debt he made his own bargain and must abide by it. He comes no more to the Crooksbury farm."

"And he stays no more here," said the Abbot. "Brother sacrist, you have raised the Devil, and it is for you to lay it again."

"That I will most readily," cried the sacrist. "The pittance-master can stop the fifty shillings from my very own weekly dole, and so the Abbey be none the poorer. In the mean time here is Wat with his arbalist and a bolt in his girdle. Let him drive it to the head through this cursed creature, for his hide and his hoofs are of more value than his wicked self."

A hard brown old woodman who had been shooting vermin in the Abbey groves stepped forward with a grin of pleasure. After a lifetime of stoats and foxes, this was indeed a noble quarry which was to fall before him. Fitting a bolt on the nut of his taut crossbow, he had raised it to his shoulder and leveled it at the fierce, proud, disheveled head which tossed in savage freedom at the other side of the wall. His finger was crooked on the spring, when a blow from a whip struck the bow upward and the bolt flew harmless over the Abbey orchard, while the woodman shrank abashed from Nigel Loring's angry eyes.

"Keep your bolts for your weasels," said he. "Would you take life from a creature whose only fault is that its spirit is so high that it has met none yet who dare control it? You would slay such a horse as a king might be proud to mount, and all because a country franklin, or a monk, or a monk's varlet, has not the wit nor the hands to master him?"

The sacrist turned swiftly on the Squire. "The Abbey owes you an offering for this day's work, however rude your words may be," said he. "If you think so much of the horse, you may desire to own it. If I am to pay for it, then with the holy Abbot's permission it is in my gift, and I bestow it freely upon you."

The Abbot plucked at his subordinate's sleeve. "Bethink you, brother sacrist," he whispered, "shall we not have this man's blood upon our heads?"

"His pride is as stubborn as the horse's, holy father," the sacrist answered, his gaunt face breaking into a malicious smile. "Man or beast, one will break the other, and the world will be the better for it. If you forbid me——"

"Nay, brother, you have bought the horse, and you may have the bestowal of it."

"Then I give it—hide and hoofs, tail and temper—to Nigel Loring, and may it be as sweet and as gentle to him as he hath been to the Abbot of Waverley!"

The sacrist spoke aloud amid the tittering of the monks, for the man concerned was out of earshot. At the first words which had shown him the turn which affairs had taken he had run swiftly to the spot where he had left his pony. From its mouth he removed the bit and the stout bridle which held it. Then leaving the creature to nibble the grass by the wayside, he sped back whence he came.

"I take your gift, monk," said he, "though I know well why it is that you give it. Yet I thank you, for there are two things upon earth for which I have ever yearned, and which my thin purse could never buy. The one is a noble horse, such a horse as my father's son should have betwixt his thighs, and here is the one of all others which I would have chosen, since some small deed is to be done in the winning of him, and some honorable advancement to be gained. How is the horse called?"

"Its name," said the franklin, "is Pommers. I warn you, young sir, that none may ride him, for many have tried, and the luckiest is he who has only a staved rib to show for it."

"I thank you for your rede," said Nigel, "and now I see that this is indeed a horse which I would journey far to meet. I am your man, Pommers, and you are my horse, and this night you shall own it, or I will never need horse again. My spirit against thine, and God hold thy spirit high, Pommers, so that the greater be the adventure, and the more hope of honor gained!"

While he spoke the young Squire had climbed on to the top of the wall and stood there balanced, the very image of grace and spirit and gallantry, his bridle hanging from one hand and his whip grasped in the other. With a fierce snort, the horse made for him instantly, and his white teeth flashed as he snapped; but again a heavy blow from the loaded whip caused him to swerve, and even at the instant of the swerve, measuring the distance with steady eyes, and bending his supple body for the spring, Nigel bounded into the air and fell with his legs astride the broad back of the yellow horse. For a minute, with neither saddle nor stirrups to help him, and the beast ramping and rearing like a mad thing beneath him, he was hard pressed to hold his own. His legs were like two bands of steel welded on to the swelling arches of the great horse's ribs, and his left hand was buried deep in the tawny mane.

Never had the dull round of the lives of the gentle brethren of Waverley been broken by so fiery a scene. Springing to right and swooping to left, now with its tangled wicked head between its fore-feet, and now pawing eight feet high in the air, with scarlet, furious nostrils and maddened eyes, the yellow horse was a thing of terror and of beauty. But the lithe figure on his back, bending like a reed in the wind to every movement, firm below, pliant above, with calm inexorable face, and eyes which danced and gleamed with the joy of contest, still held its masterful place for all that the fiery heart and the iron muscles of the great beast could do.

Once a long drone of dismay rose from the monks, as rearing higher and higher yet, a last mad effort sent the creature toppling over backward upon its rider. But, swift and cool, he had writhed from under it ere it fell, spurned it with his foot as it rolled upon the earth, and then seizing its mane as it rose, swung himself lightly on to its back once more. Even the grim

"With neither saddle nor stirrups to help him, . . .
he was hard pressed to hold his own." [*page 21*]

sacrist could not but join the cheer, as Pommers, amazed to find the rider still upon his back, plunged and curveted down the field.

But the wild horse only swelled into a greater fury. In the sullen gloom of its untamed heart there rose the furious resolve to dash the life from this clinging rider, even if it meant destruction to beast and man. With red, blazing eyes it looked round for death. On three sides the five-virgate field was bounded by a high wall, broken only at one spot by a heavy four-foot wooden gate. But on the fourth side was a low gray building, one of the granges of the Abbey, presenting a long flank unbroken by door or window. The horse stretched itself into a gallop, and headed straight for that craggy thirty-foot wall. He would break in red ruin at the base of it if he could but dash for ever the life of this man, who claimed mastery over that which had never found its master yet.

The great haunches gathered under it, the eager hoofs drummed the grass, as faster and still more fast the frantic horse bore himself and his rider toward the wall. Would Nigel spring off? To do so would be to bend his will to that of the beast beneath him. There was a better way than that. Cool, quick and decided, the man swiftly passed both whip and bridle into the left hand which still held the mane. Then with the right he slipped his short mantle from his shoulders, and lying forward along the creature's strenuous, rippling back, he cast the flapping cloth over the horse's eyes.

The result was but too successful, for it nearly brought about the downfall of the rider. When those red eyes, straining for death, were suddenly shrouded in unexpected darkness, the amazed horse propped on its fore-feet and came to so dead a stop that Nigel was shot forward on to its neck and hardly held himself by his hair-entwined hand. Ere he had slid back into position the moment of danger had passed, for the horse, its purpose all blurred in its mind by this strange thing which had befallen, wheeled round once more, trembling in every fiber, and tossing its petulant head until at last the mantle had been slipped from its eyes and the chilling darkness had melted into the homely circle of sunlit grass once more.

But what was this new outrage which had been inflicted upon it? What was this defiling bar of iron which was locked hard against its mouth? What were these straps which galled the tossing neck, this band which spanned its brow? In those instants of stillness ere the mantle had been plucked away Nigel had lain forward, had slipped the snaffle between the champing teeth, and had deftly secured it.

Blind, frantic fury surged in the yellow horse's heart once more at this new degradation, this badge of serfdom and infamy. His spirit rose high and menacing at the touch. He loathed this place, these people, all and everything which threatened his freedom. He would have done with them for ever; he would see them no more! Let him away to the uttermost parts of the earth, to the great plains where freedom is! Anywhere over the far horizon where he could get away from the defiling bit and the insufferable mastery of man!

He turned with a rush, and one magnificent deer-like bound carried him over the four-foot gate. Nigel's hat had flown off, and his yellow curls streamed behind him as he rose and fell in the leap. They were in the water-meadow now, and the rippling stream twenty feet wide gleamed in front of them, running down to the main current of the Wey. The yellow horse gathered his haunches under him and flew over like an arrow. He took off from behind a boulder and cleared a furze-bush on the farther side. Two stones still mark the leap from hoof-mark to hoof-mark, and they are eleven good paces apart. Under the hanging branch of the great oak tree on the farther side (that *Quercus Tilfordiensis* still shown as the bound of the Abbey's immediate precincts) the great horse passed. He had hoped to sweep off his rider, but Nigel sank low on the heaving back, with his face buried in the flying mane. The rough bough rasped him rudely, but never shook his spirit nor his grip. Rearing, plunging and struggling, Pommers broke through the sapling grove and was out on the broad stretch of Hankley Down.

And now came such a ride as still lingers in the gossip of the lowly country folk, and forms the rude jingle of that old Surrey ballad, now nearly forgotten, save for the refrain—

The Doe that sped on Hinde Head,
The Kestril on the winde,
And Nigel on the Yellow Horse
Can leave the world behinde.

Before them lay a rolling ocean of dark heather, knee-deep, swelling in billow on billow up to the clear-cut hill before them. Above stretched one unbroken arch of peaceful blue, with a sun which was sinking down towards the Hampshire hills. Through the deep heather, down the gullies, over the watercourses, up the broken slopes, Pommers flew, his great heart bursting with rage, and every fiber quivering at the indignities which he had endured.

And still, do what he would, the man clung fast to his heaving sides and to his flying mane, silent, motionless, inexorable, letting him do what he would, but fixed as Fate upon his purpose. Over Hankley Down, through Thursley Marsh, with the reeds up to his mud-splashed withers, onward up the long slope of the Headland of the Hinds, down by the Nutcombe Gorge, slipping, blundering, bounding, but never slackening his fearful speed, on went the great yellow horse. The villagers of Shottermill heard the wild clatter of hoofs, but ere they could swing the ox-hide curtains of their cottage doors, horse and rider were lost amid the high bracken of the Haslemere Valley. On he went, and on, tossing the miles behind his flying hoofs. No marsh-land could clog him, no hill could hold him back. Up the slope of Linchmere and the long ascent of Fernhurst he thundered as on the level, and it was not until he had flown down the incline of Henley Hill, and the gray castle tower of Midhurst rose over the coppice in front, that at last the eager outstretched neck sank a little on the breast, and the breath came quick and fast. Look where he would, in woodland and on down, his straining eyes could catch no sign of those plains of freedom which he sought.

And yet another outrage! It was bad that this creature should still cling so tight upon his back, but now he would even go to the intolerable length of checking him and guiding him on the way that he would have him go. There was a sharp pluck at his mouth, and his head was turned north once more. As well go that way as another; but the man was mad indeed if he thought that such a horse as Pommers was at the end of his spirit or his strength. He would soon show him that he was unconquered, if it strained his sinews or broke his heart to do so. Back, then, he flew up the long, long ascent. Would he ever get to the end of it? Yet he would not own that he could go no farther while the man still kept his grip. He was white with foam and caked with mud. His eyes were gorged with blood, his mouth open and gasping, his nostrils expanded, his coat stark and reeking. On he flew down the long Sunday Hill, until he reached the deep Kingsley Marsh at the bottom. No, it was too much! Flesh and blood could go no farther. As he struggled out from the reedy slime, with the heavy black mud still clinging to his fetlocks, he at last eased down with sobbing breath, and slowed the tumultuous gallop to a canter.

Oh, crowning infamy! Was there no limit to these degradations? He was no longer even to choose his own pace. Since he had chosen to gallop so far at his own will he must now gallop farther still at the will of another. A spur struck home on either flank. A stinging whip-lash fell across his shoulder. He bounded his own height in the air at the pain and the shame of it. Then, forgetting his weary limbs, forgetting his panting, reeking sides, forgetting everything save this intolerable insult and the burning spirit within, he plunged off once more upon his furious gallop. He was out on the heather slopes again, and heading for Weydown Common. On he flew and on. But again his brain failed him, and again his limbs trembled beneath him, and yet again he strove to ease his pace, only to be driven onward by the cruel spur and the falling lash. He was blind and giddy with fatigue.

He saw no longer where he placed his feet, he cared no longer whither he went, but his one mad longing was to get away from this dreadful thing, this torture which clung to him and would not let him go. Through Thursley village he passed, his eyes straining in his agony, his heart bursting within him, and he had won his way to the crest of Thursley Down, still stung forward by stab and blow, when his spirit weakened, his giant strength ebbed out of him, and with one deep sob of agony the yellow horse sank among the heather. So sudden was the fall that Nigel flew forward over his shoulder, and beast and man lay prostrate and gasping, while the last red rim of the sun sank behind Butser and the first stars gleamed in a violet sky.

The young Squire was the first to recover, and kneeling by the panting, overwrought horse, he passed his hand gently over the tangled mane and down the foam-flecked face. The red eye rolled up at him; but it was wonder, not hatred, a prayer and not a threat, which he could read in it. As he stroked the reeking muzzle, the horse whinnied gently and thrust his nose into the hollow of his hand. It was enough. It was the end of the contest, the acceptance of new conditions by a chivalrous foe from a chivalrous victor.

"You are my horse, Pommers," Nigel whispered, and he laid his cheek against the craning head. "I know you, Pommers, and you know me, and with the help of Saint Paul we shall teach some other folk to know us both. Now let us walk together as far as this moorland pond, for indeed I wot not whether it is you or I who need the water most."

And so it was that some belated monks of Waverley, passing homeward from the outer farms, saw a strange sight, which they carried on with them so that it reached that very night the ears both of sacrist and of Abbot. For, as they passed through Tilford, they had seen horse and man walking side by side and head by head up the manor-house lane. And when they had raised their lanterns on the pair, it was none other than the young Squire himself who was leading home, as a shepherd leads a lamb, the fearsome yellow horse of Crooksbury.

IV. HOW THE SUMMONER CAME
TO THE MANOR-HOUSE OF TILFORD

By THE DATE of this chronicle, the ascetic sternness of the old Norman castles had been humanized and refined, so that the new dwellings of the nobility, if less imposing in appearance, were much more comfortable as places of residence. A gentle race had built their houses rather for peace than for war. He who compares the savage bareness of Pevensey or Guildford with the piled grandeur of Bodmin or Windsor cannot fail to understand the change in manners which they represent.

The earlier castles had a set purpose, for they were built that the invaders might hold down the country; but when the Conquest was once firmly established, a castle had lost its meaning, save as a refuge from justice or as a center for civil strife. On the marches of Wales and of Scotland the castle might continue to be a bulwark to the kingdom, and there still grew and flourished; but in all other places they were rather a menace to the King's majesty, and as such were discouraged and destroyed. By the reign of the third Edward the greater part of the old fighting castles had been converted into dwelling-houses or had been ruined in the civil wars, and left where their grim gray bones are still littered upon the brows of our hills. The new buildings were either great country-houses, capable of defense, but mainly residential, or they were manor-houses with no military significance at all.

Such was the Tilford Manor-house, where the last survivors of the old and magnificent house of Loring still struggled hard to keep a footing and to hold off the monks and the lawyers from the few acres which were left to them. The mansion was a two-storied one, framed in heavy beams of wood, the interstices filled with rude blocks of stone. An outside staircase led up to several sleeping-rooms above. Below, there were only two apartments, the smaller of which was the bower of the aged Lady Ermyntrude. The other was the hall, a very large room, which served as the living-room of the family and as the common dining-room of themselves and of their little group of servants and retainers. The dwellings of these servants, the kitchens, the offices, and the stables were all represented by a row of penthouses and sheds behind the main building. Here lived Charles, the page; Peter, the old falconer; Red Swire, who had followed Nigel's grandfather to the Scottish wars; Weathercote, the broken minstrel; John, the cook, and other survivors of more prosperous days, who still clung to the old house as the barnacles to some wrecked and stranded vessel.

One evening, about a week after the breaking of the yellow horse, Nigel and his grandmother sat on either side of the large empty fireplace in this spacious apartment. The supper had been removed, and so had the trestle tables upon which it had been served, so that the room seemed bare and empty. The stone floor was strewed with a thick layer of green rushes, which was swept out every Saturday, and carried with it all the dirt and debris of the week. Several dogs were now crouched among these rushes, gnawing and cracking the bones which had been thrown from the table. A long wooden buffet loaded with plates and dishes filled one end of the room, but there was little other furniture, save some benches against the walls, two dorseret chairs, one small table littered with chessmen, and a great iron coffer. In one corner was a high wickerwork stand, and on it two stately falcons were perched, silent and motionless, save for an occasional twinkle of their fierce yellow eyes.

But if the actual fittings of the room would have appeared scanty to one who had lived in a more luxurious age, he would have been surprised on looking up to see the multitude of objects which were suspended above his head. Over the fireplace were the coats-of-arms of a number of houses allied by blood or by marriage to the Lorings. The two cresset-lights which flared upon each side gleamed upon the blue lion of the Percies, the red birds of de Valence, the black engrailed cross of de Mohun, the silver star of de Vere, and the ruddy bars of FitzAlan, all grouped round the famous red roses on the silver shield which the Lorings had borne to glory upon many a bloody field. Then from side to side the room was spanned by heavy oaken beams, from which a great number of objects were hanging. There were mail-shirts of obsolete pattern, several shields, one or two rusted and battered helmets, bow-staves, lances, otter-spears, harness, fishing-rods, and other implements of war or of the chase, while higher still amid the black shadows could be seen rows of hams, flitches of bacon, salted geese, and those other forms of pre- served meat which played so great a part in the housekeeping of the Middle Ages.

Dame Ermyntrude Loring, daughter, wife, and mother of warriors, was herself a formidable figure. Tall and gaunt, with hard craggy features and intolerant dark eyes, even her snow- white hair and stooping back could not entirely remove the sense of fear which she inspired in those around her. Her thoughts and memories went back to harsher times, and she looked upon the England around her as a degenerate and ef- feminate land which had fallen away from the old standard of knightly courtesy and valor.

The rising power of the people, the growing wealth of the Church, the increasing luxury in life and manners, and the gen- tler tone of the age were all equally abhorrent to her, so that the dread of her fierce face, and even of the heavy oak staff with which she supported her failing limbs, was widespread through all the country round.

Yet if she was feared she was also respected, for in days when books were few and readers scarce, a long memory and a ready tongue were of the more value; and where, save from Dame Ermyntrude, could the young unlettered Squires of Surrey and Hampshire hear of their grandfathers and their battles, or learn that lore of heraldry and chivalry which she handed down from a ruder but a more martial age? Poor as she was, there was no one in Surrey whose guidance would be more readily sought upon a question of precedence or of conduct than the Dame Ermyntrude Loring.

She sat now with bowed back by the empty fireplace, and

looked across at Nigel with all the harsh lines of her old ruddled face softening into love and pride. The young Squire was busy cutting bird-bolts for his crossbow, and whistling softly as he worked. Suddenly he looked up and caught the dark eyes which were fixed upon him. He leaned forward and patted the bony hand.

"What hath pleased you, dear dame? I read pleasure in your eyes."

"I have heard to-day, Nigel, how you came to win that great war-horse which stamps in our stable."

"Nay, dame; I had told you that the monks had given it to me."

"You said so, fair son, but never a word more. Yet the horse which you brought home was a very different horse, I wot, to that which was given you. Why did you not tell me?"

"I should think it shame to talk of such a thing."

"So would your father before you, and his father no less. They would sit silent among the knights when the wine went round and listen to every man's deeds; but if perchance there was any one who spoke louder than the rest and seemed to be eager for honor, then afterwards your father would pluck him softly by the sleeve and whisper in his ear to learn if there was any small vow of which he could relieve him, or if he would deign to perform some noble deed of arms upon his person. And if the man were a braggart and would go no further, your father would be silent and none would know it. But if he bore himself well, your father would spread his fame far and wide, but never make mention of himself."

Nigel looked at the old woman with shining eyes. "I love to hear you speak of him," said he. "I pray you to tell me once more of the manner of his death."

"He died as he had lived, a very courtly gentleman. It was at the great sea-battle upon the Norman coast, and your father was in command of the after-guard in the King's own ship. Now the French had taken a great English ship the year before when they came over and held the narrow seas and burned the town of Southampton. This ship was the *Christopher,* and they placed it in the front of their battle; but the English closed upon it and stormed over its side, and slew all who were upon it."

"But your father and Sir Lorredan of Genoa, who commanded the *Christopher,* fought upon the high poop, so that all the fleet stopped to watch it, and the king himself cried aloud at the sight, for Sir Lorredan was a famous man-at-arms and bore himself very stoutly that day, and many a knight envied your father that he should have chanced upon so excellent a person. But your father bore him back and struck him such a blow with a mace that he turned the helmet half round on his head, so that he could no longer see through the eyeholes, and Sir Lorredan threw down his sword and gave himself to ransom. But your father took him by the helmet and twisted it until he had it straight upon his head. Then, when he could see once again, he handed him his sword, and prayed him that he would rest himself and then continue, for it was great profit and joy to see any gentleman carry himself so well. So they sat together and rested by the rail of the poop; but even as they raised their hands again your father was struck by a stone from a mangonel and so died."

"And this Sir Lorredan," cried Nigel, "he died also, as I understand?"

"I fear that he was slain by the archers, for they loved your father, and they do not see these things with our eyes."

"It was a pity," said Nigel; "for it is clear that he was a good knight and bore himself very bravely."

"Time was, when I was young, when commoners dared not have laid their grimy hands upon such a man. Men of gentle blood and coat-armor made war upon each other, and the others, spearmen or archers, could scramble amongst themselves. But now all are of a level, and only here and there one like yourself, fair son, who reminds me of the men who are gone."

Nigel leaned forward and took her hands in his. "What I am you have made me," said he.

"It is true, Nigel. I have indeed watched over you as the gardener watches his most precious blossom, for in you alone are all the hopes of our ancient house, and soon—very soon—you will be alone."

"Nay, dear lady, say not that."

"I am very old, Nigel, and I feel the shadow closing in upon me. My heart yearns to go, for all whom I have known and loved have gone before me. And you—it will be a blessed day for you, since I have held you back from that world into which your brave spirit longs to plunge."

"Nay, nay, I have been happy here with you at Tilford."

"We are very poor, Nigel. I do not know where we may find the money to fit you for the wars. Yet we have good friends. There is Sir John Chandos, who has won such credit in the French wars and who rides ever by the King's bridle-arm. He was your father's friend, and they were squires together. If I sent you to court with a message to him he would do what he could."

Nigel's fair face flushed. "Nay, dame Ermyntrude, I must find my own gear, even as I have found my own horse, for I had rather ride into battle in this tunic than owe my suit to another."

"I feared that you would say so, Nigel; but indeed I know not how else we may get the money," said the old woman, sadly. "It was different in the days of my father. I can remember that a suit of mail was but a small matter in those days, for in every English town such things could be made. But year by year, since men have come to take more care of their bodies, there have been added a plate of proof here and a cunning joint there, and all must be from Toledo or Milan, so that a knight must have much metal in his purse ere he puts any on his limbs."

Nigel looked up wistfully at the old armor which was slung on the beams above him. "The ash spear is good," said he, "and so is the oaken shield with facings of steel. Sir Roger FitzAlan handled them and said that he had never seen better. But the armor——"

Lady Ermyntrude shook her old head and laughed. "You have your father's great soul, Nigel, but you have not his mighty breadth of shoulder and length of limb. There was not in all the King's great host a taller or a stronger man. His harness would be little use to you. No, fair son, I rede you that when the time comes you sell this crumbling house and the few acres which are still left, and so go forth to the wars in the hope that with your own right hand you will plant the fortunes of a new house of Loring."

A shadow of anger passed over Nigel's fresh young face. "I know not if we may hold off these monks and their lawyers much longer. This very day there came a man from Guildford with claims from the Abbey extending back before my father's death."

"Where are they, fair son?"

"They are flapping on the furze-bushes of Hankley, for I sent his papers and parchments down wind as fast as ever falcon flew."

"Nay! you were mad to do that, Nigel. And the man, where is he?"

"Red Swire and old George the Archer threw him into the Thursley bog."

"Alas! I fear me such things cannot be done in these days, though my father or my husband would have sent the rascal back to Guildford without his ears. But the Church and the Law are too strong now for us who are of gentler blood. Trouble will come of it, Nigel, for the Abbot of Waverley is not one who will hold back the shield of the Church from those who are her servants."

"The Abbot would not hurt us. It is that gray lean wolf of a sacrist who hungers for our land. Let him do his worst. I fear him not."

"He has such an engine at his back, Nigel, that even the bravest must fear him. The ban which blasts a man's soul is in the keeping of his Church, and what have we to place against it? I pray you to speak him fair, Nigel."

"Nay, dear lady, it is both my duty and my pleasure to do what you bid me; but I would die ere I ask as a favor that which we can claim as a right. Never can I cast my eyes from yonder window that I do not see the swelling down-lands and the rich meadows, glade and dingle, copse and wood, which have been ours since Norman William gave them to that Loring who bore his shield at Senlac. Now by trick and fraud they have passed away from us, and many a franklin is a richer man than I; but

never shall it be said that I saved the rest by bending my neck
to their yoke. Let them do their worst, and let me endure it or
fight it as best I may."

The old lady sighed and shook her head. "You speak as a
Loring should, and yet I fear that some great trouble will befall
us. But let us talk no more of such matters, since we cannot
mend them. Where is your citole, Nigel? Will you not play and
sing to me?"

The gentleman of those days could scarce read and write; but
he spoke in two languages, played at least one musical instrument as a matter of course, and possessed a number of other
accomplishments, from the imping of hawk's feathers, to the
mystery of venery, with knowledge of every beast and bird, its
time of grace and when it was seasonable. As far as physical feats
went, to vault barebacked upon a horse, to hit a running hare
with a crossbow-bolt, or to climb the angle of a castle courtyard,
were feats which had come by nature to the young Squire; but
it was very different with music, which had called for many a
weary hour of irksome work. Now at last he could master the
strings, but both his ear and his voice were not of the best, so
that it was well, perhaps, that there was so small and so preju-
diced an audience to the Norman-French chanson, which he
sang in a high reedy voice with great earnestness of feeling, but
with many a slip and quaver, waving his yellow head in cadence
to the music—

> "A sword! A sword! Ah, give me a sword!
>   For the world is all to win.
> Though the way be hard and the door be barred,
>   The strong man enters in.
> If Chance and Fate still hold the gate,
>   Give me the iron key,
> And turret high my plume shall fly,
>   Or you may weep for me!
>
> "A horse! A horse! Ah, give me a horse!
>   To bear me out afar,
> Where blackest need and grimmest deed
>   And sweetest perils are.
> Hold thou my ways from glutted days

Where poisoned leisure lies,
And point the path of tears and wrath
Which mounts to high emprise!

"A heart! A heart! Ah, give me a heart
To rise to circumstance!
Serene and high and bold to try
The hazard of the chance,
With strength to wait, but fixed as fate
To plan and dare and do,
The peer of all, and only thrall,
Sweet lady mine, to you!"

It may have been that the sentiment went for more than the music, or it may have been the nicety of her own ears had been dulled by age, but old Dame Ermyntrude clapped her lean hands together and cried out in shrill applause.

"Weathercote has indeed had an apt pupil!" she said. "I pray you that you will sing again."

"Nay, dear dame, it is turn and turn betwixt you and me. I beg that you will recite a romance, you who know them all. For all the years that I have listened I have never yet come to the end of them, and I dare swear that there are more in your head than in all the great books which they showed me at Guildford Castle. I would fain hear 'Doon of Mayence,' or 'The Song of Roland,' or 'Sir Isumbras.'"

So the old dame broke into a long poem, slow and dull in the inception, but quickening as the interest grew, until with darting hands and glowing face she poured forth the verses which told of the emptiness of sordid life, the beauty of heroic death, the high sacredness of love and the bondage of honor. Nigel, with set, still features and brooding eyes, drank in the fiery words, until at last they died upon the old woman's lips and she sank back weary in her chair. Nigel stooped over her and kissed her brow.

"Your words will ever be as a star upon my path," said he. Then carrying over the small table and the chessmen, he proposed that they should play their usual game before they sought their rooms for the night.

But a sudden and rude interruption broke in upon their

gentle contest. A dog pricked its ears and barked. The others ran growling to the door. And then there came a sharp clash of arms, a dull heavy blow as from a club or sword pommel, and a deep voice from without summoned them to open in the king's name. The old dame and Nigel had both sprung to their feet, their table overturned and their chessmen scattered among the rushes. Nigel's hand had sought his crossbow, but the Lady Ermyntrude grasped his arm.

"Nay, fair son! Have you not heard that it is in the King's name?" said she. "Down, Talbot! Down, Bayard! Open the door and let his messenger in!"

Nigel undid the bolt, and the heavy wooden door swung outward upon its hinges. The light from the flaring cressets beat upon steel caps and fierce bearded faces, with the glimmer of drawn swords and the yellow gleam of bowstaves. A dozen armed archers forced their way into the room. At their head were the gaunt sacrist of Waverley and a stout elderly man clad in a red-velvet doublet and breeches, much stained and mottled with mud and clay. He bore a great sheet of parchment with a fringe of dangling seals, which he held aloft as he entered.

"I call on Nigel Loring!" he cried. "I, the officer of the King's law and the lay summoner of Waverley, call upon the man named Nigel Loring!"

"I am he."

"Yes, it is he!" cried the sacrist. "Archers, do as you were ordered!"

In an instant the band threw themselves upon him like the hounds on a stag. Desperately Nigel strove to gain his sword which lay upon the iron coffer. With the convulsive strength which comes from the spirit rather than from the body, he bore them all in that direction, but the sacrist snatched the weapon from its place, and the rest dragged the writhing Squire to the ground and swathed him in a cord.

"Hold him fast, good archers! Keep a stout grip on him!" cried the summoner. "I pray you, one of you, prick off these great dogs which snarl at my heels. Stand off, I say, in the name of the king! Watkin, come betwixt me and these creatures who have as little regard for the law as their master."

"Desperately Nigel strove to gain his sword." [*page* 37]

One of the archers kicked off the faithful dogs. But there were others of the household who were equally ready to show their teeth in defense of the old house of Loring. From the door which led to their quarters there emerged the pitiful muster of Nigel's threadbare retainers. There was a time when ten knights, forty men-at-arms and two hundred archers would march behind the scarlet roses. Now at this last rally, when the young head of the house lay bound in his own hall, there mustered at his call the page Charles with a cudgel, John the cook with his longest spit, Red Swire the aged man-at-arms with a formidable axe swung over his snowy head, and Weathercote the minstrel with a boar-spear. Yet this motley array was fired with the spirit of the house, and under the lead of the fierce old soldier they would certainly have flung themselves upon the ready swords of the archers, had the Lady Ermyntrude not swept between them.

"Stand back, Swire!" she cried. "Back, Weathercote! Charles, put a leash on Talbot, and hold Bayard back!" Her black eyes blazed upon the invaders until they shrank from that baleful gaze. "Who are you, you rascal robbers, who dare to misuse the king's name and to lay hands upon one whose smallest drop of blood has more worth than all your thrall and caitiff bodies?"

"Nay, not so fast, dame, not so fast, I pray you!" cried the stout summoner, whose face had resumed its natural color, now that he had a woman to deal with. "There is a law of England, mark you, and there are those who serve and uphold it, who are the true men and the king's own lieges. Such a one am I. Then, again, there are those who take such as me and transfer, carry or convey us into a bog or morass. Such a one is this graceless old man with the axe, whom I have seen already this day. There are also those who tear, destroy, or scatter the papers of the law, of which this young man is the chief. Therefore I would rede you, dame, not to rail against us, but to understand that we are the king's men on the king's own service."

"What, then, is your errand in this house at this hour of the night?"

The summoner cleared his throat pompously, and turning his parchment to the light of the cressets he read out a long document in Norman-French, couched in such a style and such a language that the most involved and foolish of our forms were simplicity itself compared to those by which the men of the long gown made a mystery of that which of all things on earth should be the plainest and the most simple. Despair fell cold upon Nigel's heart and blanched the face of the old dame as they listened to the dread catalogue of claims and suits and issues, questions of peccary and turbary, of house-bote and fire-bote, which ended by a demand for all the lands, hereditaments, tenements, messuages and curtilages, which made up their worldly all.

Nigel, still bound, had been placed with his back against the iron coffer, whence he heard with dry lips and moist brow this doom of his house. Now he broke in on the recital with a vehemence which made the summoner jump—

"You shall rue what you have done this night!" he cried. "Poor as we are, we have our friends who will not see us wronged, and I will plead my cause before the king's own majesty at Windsor, that he, who saw the father die, may know what things are done in his royal name against the son. But these matters are to be settled in course of law in the king's courts, and how will you excuse yourself for this assault upon my house and person?"

"Nay, that is another matter," said the sacrist. "The question of debt may indeed be an affair of a civil court. But it is a crime against the law and an act of the Devil which comes within the jurisdiction of the Abbey Court of Waverley when you dare to lay hands upon the summoner or his papers."

"Indeed, he speaks truth," cried the official. "I know no blacker sin."

"Therefore," said the stern monk, "it is the order of the holy father Abbot that you sleep this night in the Abbey cell, and that to-morrow you be brought before him at the court held in the chapter-house so that you receive the fit punishment for this and the many other violent and froward deeds which you have wrought upon the servants of Holy Church. Enough is now said, worthy master summoner. Archers, remove your prisoner!"

As Nigel was lifted up by four stout archers, the Dame

Ermyntrude would have rushed to his aid, but the sacrist thrust her back.

"Stand off, proud woman! Let the law take its course, and learn to humble your heart before the power of Holy Church. Has your life not taught its lesson, you, whose horn was exalted among the highest and will soon not have a roof above your gray hairs? Stand back, I say, lest I lay a curse upon you!"

The old dame flamed suddenly into white wrath as she stood before the angry monk—

"Listen to me while I lay a curse upon you and yours!" she cried as she raised her shriveled arms and blighted him with her flashing eyes: "As you have done to the house of Loring, so may God do to you, until your power is swept from the land of England, and of your great Abbey of Waverley there is nothing left but a pile of gray stones in a green meadow! I see it! I see it! With my old eyes I see it! From scullion to abbot and from cellar to tower, may Waverley and all within it droop and wither from this night on!"

The monk, hard as he was, quailed before the frantic figure and the bitter, burning words. Already the summoner and the archers with their prisoner were clear of the house. He turned, and with a clang he shut the heavy door behind him.

V. HOW NIGEL WAS TRIED
BY THE ABBOT OF WAVERLEY

THE LAW OF the Middle Ages, shrouded as it was in old Norman-French dialect, and abounding in uncouth and incomprehensible terms, in deodands and heriots, in infang and outfang, was a fearsome weapon in the hands of those who knew how to use it. It was not for nothing that the first act of the rebel commoners was to hew off the head of the Lord Chancellor. In an age when few knew how to read or to write, these mystic phrases and intricate forms, with the parchments and seals which were their outward expression, struck cold terror into hearts which were steeled against mere physical danger.

Even young Nigel Loring's blithe and elastic spirit was chilled as he lay that night in the penal cell of Waverley, and pondered over the absolute ruin which threatened his house from a source against which all his courage was of no avail. As well take up sword and shield to defend himself against the black death, as against this blight of Holy Church. He was powerless in the grip of the Abbey. Already they had shorn off a field here and a grove there, and now in one sweep they would take in the rest, and where then was the home of the Lorings, and where should Lady Ermyntrude lay her aged head, or his old retainers, broken and spent, eke out the balance of their days. He shivered as he thought of it.

It was very well for him to threaten to carry the matter before the king, but it was years since Royal Edward had heard the name of Loring, and Nigel knew that the memory of princes was a short one. Besides, the Church was the ruling power in the palace as well as in the cottage, and it was only for very good cause that a king could be expected to cross the purposes of so high a prelate as the Abbot of Waverley, as long as they came within the scope of the law. Where, then, was he to look for help? With the simple and practical piety of the age, he prayed for the aid of his own particular saints: of Saint Paul, whose adventures by land and sea had always endeared him; of Saint George, who had gained much honorable advancement from the Dragon; and of Saint Thomas, who was a gentleman of coat-armor, who would understand and help a person of gentle blood. Then, much comforted by his naïve orisons, he enjoyed the sleep of youth and health until the entrance of the lay brother with the bread and small beer, which served as breakfast in the morning.

The Abbey court sat in the chapter-house at the canonical hour of tierce, which was nine in the forenoon. At all times the function was a solemn one, even when the culprit might be a villain who was taken poaching on the Abbey estate, or a chapman who had given false measure from his biased scales. But now, when a man of noble birth was to be tried, the whole legal and ecclesiastical ceremony was carried out with every detail, grotesque or impressive, which the full ritual prescribed. Mid the distant roll of church music and the slow tolling of the Abbey bell, the white-robed brethren, two and two, walked thrice round the hall singing the *Benedicite* and the *Veni, Creator* before they settled in their places at the desks on either side. Then in turn each high officer of the Abbey from below upward, the almoner, the lector, the chaplain, the sub-prior and the prior, swept to their wonted places.

Finally there came the grim sacrist, with demure triumph upon his downcast features, and at his heels Abbot John himself, slow and dignified, with pompous walk and solemn, composed face, his iron-beaded rosary swinging from his waist, his breviary in his hand, and his lips muttering as he hurried through his office for the day. He knelt at his high prie-dieu; the brethren, at a signal from the prior, prostrated themselves upon the floor, and the low deep voices rolled in prayer, echoed back from the arched and vaulted roof like the wash of waves from an ocean cavern. Finally the monks resumed their seats; there entered clerks in seemly black with pens and parchment; the redvelveted summoner appeared to tell his tale; Nigel was led in with archers pressing close around him; and then, with much calling of old French and much legal incantation and mystery, the court of the Abbey was open for business.

It was the sacrist who first advanced to the oaken desk reserved for the witnesses and expounded in hard, dry, mechanical fashion the many claims which the House of Waverley had against the family of Loring. Some generations back, in return for money advanced or for spiritual favor received, the Loring of the day had admitted that his estate had certain feudal duties toward the Abbey. The sacrist held up the crackling yellow parchment with swinging leaden seals on which the claim was based. Amid the obligations was that of escuage, by which the price of a knight's fee should be paid every year. No such price had been paid, nor had any service been done. The accumulated years came now to a greater sum than the fee-simple of the estate. There were other claims also. The sacrist called for his books, and with thin, eager forefinger he tracked them down: dues for this, and tallage for that, so many shillings this year, and so many marks that one. Some of it occurred before Nigel was born; some of it when he was but a child. The accounts had been checked and certified by the sergeant of the law.

Nigel listened to the dread recital, and felt like some young stag who stands at bay with brave pose and heart of fire, but who sees himself compassed round and knows clearly that there is no escape. With his bold young face, his steady blue eyes, and the proud poise of his head, he was a worthy scion of the old house, and the sun, shining through the high oriel window, and showing up the stained and threadbare condition of his once rich doublet, seemed to illuminate the fallen fortunes of his family.

The sacrist had finished his exposition, and the sergeant-at-law was about to conclude a case which Nigel could in no way controvert, when help came to him from an unexpected quarter. It may have been a certain malignity with which the sacrist urged his suit, it may have been a diplomatic dislike to driving matters to extremes, or it may have been some genuine impulse of kindliness, for Abbot John was choleric but easily appeased.

Whatever the cause, the result was that a white plump hand, raised in the air with a gesture of authority, showed that the case was at an end.

"Our brother sacrist hath done his duty in urging this suit," said he, "for the worldly wealth of this Abbey is placed in his pious keeping, and it is to him that we should look if we suffered in such ways, for we are but the trustees of those who come after us. But to my keeping has been consigned that which is more precious still, the inner spirit and high repute of those who follow the rule of Saint Bernard. Now, it has ever been our endeavor, since first our saintly founder went down into the valley of Clairvaux and built himself a cell there, that we should set an example to all men in gentleness and humility. For this reason it is that we built our houses in lowly places, that we have no tower to our Abbey churches, and that no finery and no metal, save only iron or lead, come within our walls. A brother shall eat from a wooden platter, drink from an iron cup, and light himself from a leaden sconce. Surely it is not for such an order who await the exaltation which is promised to the humble, to judge their own case and so acquire the lands of their neighbor! If our cause be just, as indeed I believe that it is, then it were better that it be judged at the king's assizes at Guildford, and so I decree that the case be now dismissed from the Abbey court so that it can be heard elsewhere."

Nigel breathed a prayer to the three sturdy saints who had stood by him so manfully and well in the hour of his need.

"Abbot John," said he, "I never thought that any man of my name would utter thanks to a Cistercian of Waverley; but, by Saint Paul! you have spoken like a man this day, for it would indeed be to play with cogged dice if the Abbey's case is to be tried in the Abbey court."

The eighty white-clad brethren looked with half-resentful, half-amused eyes as they listened to this frank address to one who, in their small lives, seemed to be the direct vice-regent of Heaven. The archers had stood back from Nigel, as though he was at liberty to go, when the loud voice of the summoner broke in upon the silence—

"If it please you, holy father Abbot," cried the voice, "this decision of yours is indeed *secundum legem* and *intra vires* so far as the civil suit is concerned which lies between this person and the Abbey. That is your affair; but it is I, Joseph the summoner, who have been grievously and criminally mishandled, my writs, papers and indentures destroyed, my authority flouted, and my person dragged through a bog, quagmire or morass, so that my velvet gabardine and silver badge of office were lost and are, as I verily believe, in the morass, quagmire or bog aforementioned, which is the same bog, morass——"

"Enough!" cried the Abbot sternly. "Lay aside this foolish fashion of speech, and say straitly what you desire."

"Holy father, I have been the officer of the king's law no less than the servant of Holy Church, and I have been let, hindered and assaulted in the performance of my lawful and proper duties, whilst my papers, drawn in the king's name, have been shended and rended and cast to the wind. Therefore I demand justice upon this man in the Abbey court, the said assault having been committed within the banlieue of the Abbey's jurisdiction."

"What have you to say to this, brother sacrist?" asked the Abbot in some perplexity.

"I would say, father, that it is within our power to deal gently and charitably with all that concerns ourselves, but that where the king's officer is concerned, we are wanting in our duty if we give him less than the protection that he demands. I would remind you also, holy father, that this is not the first of this man's violence, but that he has before now beaten our servants, defied our authority, and put pike in the Abbot's own fish-pond."

The prelate's heavy cheeks flushed with anger as this old grievance came fresh into his mind. His eyes hardened as he looked at the prisoner. "Tell me, Squire Nigel, did you indeed put pike in the pond?"

The young man drew himself proudly up. "Ere I answer such a question, father Abbot, do you answer one from me, and tell me what the monks of Waverley have ever done for me that I should hold my hand when I could injure them?"

A low murmur ran round the room, partly wonder at his frankness, and partly anger at his boldness.

The Abbot settled down in his seat as one who has made up

his mind. "Let the case of the summoner be laid before me," said he. "Justice shall be done, and the offender shall be punished, be he noble or simple. Let the plaint be brought before the court."

The tale of the summoner, though rambling and filled with endless legal reiteration, was only too clear in its essence. Red Swire, with his angry face framed in white bristles, was led in, and confessed to his ill-treatment of the official. A second culprit, a little wiry, nut-brown archer from Churt, had aided and abetted in the deed. Both of them were ready to declare that young Squire Nigel Loring knew nothing of the matter. But then there was the awkward incident of the tearing of the writs. Nigel, to whom a lie was an impossibility, had to admit that with his own hands he had shredded those august documents. As to an excuse or an explanation, he was too proud to advance any. A cloud gathered over the brow of the Abbot, and the sacrist gazed with an ironical smile at the prisoner, while a solemn hush fell over the chapter-house as the case ended and only judgment remained.

"Squire Nigel," said the Abbot, "it was for you, who are, as all men know, of ancient lineage in this land, to give a fair example by which others should set their conduct. Instead of this, your manor-house has ever been a center for the stirring up of strife, and now not content with your harsh showing toward us, the Cistercian monks of Waverley, you have even marked your contempt for the king's law, and through your servants have mishandled the person of his messenger. For such offenses it is in my power to call the spiritual terrors of the Church upon your head, and yet I would not be harsh with you, seeing that you are young, and that even last week you saved the life of a servant of the Abbey when in peril. Therefore it is by temporal and carnal means that I will use my power to tame your overbold spirit, and to chasten that headstrong and violent humor which has caused such scandal in your dealings with our Abbey. Bread and water for six weeks from now to the Feast of Saint Benedict, with a daily exhortation from our chaplain, the pious Father Ambrose, may still avail to bend the stiff neck and to soften the hard heart."

At this ignominious sentence, by which the proud heir of the house of Loring would share the fate of the meanest village poacher, the hot blood of Nigel rushed to his face, and his eye glanced round him with a gleam which said more plainly than words that there could be no tame acceptance of such a doom. Twice he tried to speak, and twice his anger and his shame held the words in his throat.

"I am no subject of yours, proud Abbot!" he cried at last. "My house has ever been vavasor to the king. I deny the power of you and your court to lay sentence upon me. Punish these your own monks, who whimper at your frown, but do not dare to lay your hand upon him who fears you not, for he is a free man, and the peer of any save only the king himself."

The Abbot seemed for an instant taken aback by these bold words, and by the high and strenuous voice in which they were uttered. But the sterner sacrist came as ever to stiffen his will. He held up the old parchment in his hand.

"The Lorings were indeed vavasors to the king," said he; "but here is the very seal of Eustace Loring, which shows that he made himself vassal to the Abbey, and held his land from it."

"Because he was gentle," cried Nigel, "because he had no thought of trick or guile."

"Nay!" said the summoner. "If my voice may be heard, father Abbot, upon a point of the law, it is of no weight what the causes may have been why a deed is subscribed, signed or confirmed, but a court is concerned only with the terms, articles, covenants, and contracts of the said deed."

"Besides," said the sacrist, "sentence is passed by the Abbey court, and there is an end of its honor and good name if it be not upheld."

"Brother sacrist," said the Abbot angrily, "methinks you show overmuch zeal in this case, and certes, we are well able to uphold the dignity and honor of the Abbey court without any rede of thine. As to you, worthy summoner, you will give your opinion when we crave for it, and not before, or you may yourself get some touch of the power of our tribunal. But your case hath been tried, Squire Loring, and judgment given. I have no more to say."

He motioned with his hand, and an archer laid his grip upon the shoulder of the prisoner. But that rough plebeian touch woke every passion of revolt in Nigel's spirit. Of all his high line of ancestors, was there one who had been subjected to such ignominy as this? Would they not have preferred death? And should he be the first to lower their spirit or their traditions? With a quick, lithe movement, he slipped under the arm of the archer, and plucked the short, straight sword from the soldier's side as he did so. The next instant he had wedged himself into the recess of one of the narrow windows, and there were his pale, set face, his burning eyes, and his ready blade turned upon the assembly.

"By Saint Paul!" said he, "I never thought to find honorable advancement under the roof of an abbey, but, perchance, there may be some room for it ere you hale me to your prison."

The chapter-house was in an uproar. Never in the long and decorous history of the Abbey had such a scene been witnessed within its walls. The monks themselves seemed for an instant to be infected by this spirit of daring revolt. Their own lifelong fetters hung more loosely as they viewed this unheard-of defiance of authority. They broke from their seats on either side, and huddled half-scared, half-fascinated, in a large half-circle round the defiant captive, chattering, pointing, grimacing, a scandal for all time. Scourges should fall and penance be done for many a long week before the shadow of that day should pass from Waverley. But meanwhile there was no effort to bring them back to their rule. Everything was chaos and disorder. The Abbot had left his seat of justice and hurried angrily forward, to be engulfed and hustled in the crowd of his own monks like a sheep-dog who finds himself entangled amid a flock.

Only the sacrist stood clear. He had taken shelter behind the half-dozen archers, who looked with some approval and a good deal of indecision at this bold fugitive from justice.

"On him!" cried the sacrist. "Shall he defy the authority of the court, or shall one man hold six of you at bay? Close in upon him and seize him. You, Baddlesmere, why do you hold back?"

The man in question, a tall bushy-bearded fellow, clad like the others in green jerkin and breeches, with high brown boots, advanced slowly, sword in hand, against Nigel. His heart was not in the business, for these clerical courts were not popular, and every one had a tender heart for the fallen fortunes of the house of Loring and wished well to its young heir.

"Come, young sir, you have caused scathe enough," said he. "Stand forth and give yourself up!"

"Come and fetch me, good fellow," said Nigel, with a dangerous smile.

The archer ran in. There was a rasp of steel, a blade flickered like a swift dart of flame, and the man staggered back, with blood running down his forearm and dripping from his fingers. He wrung them and growled a Saxon oath.

"By the black rood of Bromeholm!" he cried, "I had as soon put my hand down a fox's earth to drag up a vixen from her cubs."

"Standoff!" said Nigel, curtly. "I would not hurt you; but, by Saint Paul! I will not be handled, or some one will be hurt in the handling."

So fierce was his eye and so menacing his blade as he crouched in the narrow bay of the window that the little knot of archers were at a loss what to do. The Abbot had forced his way through the crowd, and stood, purple with outraged dignity, at their side.

"He is outside the law," said he. "He hath shed blood in a court of justice, and for such a sin there is no forgiveness. I will not have my court so flouted and set at naught. He who draws the sword, by the sword also let him perish. Forester Hugh, lay a shaft to your bow!"

The man, who was one of the Abbey's lay servants, put his weight upon his long bow and slipped the loose end of the string into the upper notch. Then, drawing one of the terrible three-foot arrows, steel-tipped and gaudily winged, from his waist, he laid it to the string.

"Now draw your bow and hold it ready!" cried the furious Abbot. "Squire Nigel, it is not for Holy Church to shed blood, but there is naught but violence which will prevail against the violent, and on your head be the sin. Cast down the sword which you hold in your hand!"

"Will you give me freedom to leave your Abbey?"

"When you have abided your sentence and purged your sin."

"Then I had rather die where I stand than give up my sword."

A dangerous flame lit in the Abbot's eyes. He came of a fighting Norman stock, like so many of those fierce prelates who, bearing a mace lest they should be guilty of effusion of blood, led their troops into battle, ever remembering that it was one of their own cloth and dignity who, crosier in hand, had turned the long-drawn bloody day of Hastings. The soft accent of the churchman was gone, and it was the hard voice of a soldier which said—

"One minute I give you, and no more. Then when I cry 'Loose!' drive me an arrow through his body."

The shaft was fitted, the bow was bent, and the stern eyes of the woodman were fixed on his mark. Slowly the minute passed, while Nigel breathed a prayer to his three soldier saints, not that they should save his body in this life, but that they should have a kindly care for his soul in the next. Some thought of a fierce wildcat sally crossed his mind, but once out of his corner he was lost indeed. Yet at the last he would have rushed among his enemies, and his body was bent for the spring, when with a deep sonorous hum, like a breaking harp-string, the cord of the bow was cloven in twain, and the arrow tinkled upon the tiled floor. At the same moment a young curly-headed bowman, whose broad shoulders and deep chest told of immense strength, as clearly as his frank, laughing face and honest hazel eyes did of good humor and courage, sprang forward sword in hand and took his place by Nigel's side.

"Nay, comrades!" said he. "Samkin Aylward cannot stand by and see a gallant man shot down like a bull at the end of a baiting. Five against one is long odds, but two against four is better; and by my finger-bones! Squire Nigel and I leave this room together, be it on our feet or no."

The formidable appearance of this ally and his high reputation among his fellows gave a further chill to the lukewarm ardor of the attack. Aylward's left arm was passed through his strung bow, and he was known from Woolmer Forest to the Weald as the quickest, surest archer that ever dropped a running deer at ten-score paces.

"Nay, Baddlesmere, hold your fingers from your string-case, or I may chance to give your drawing hand a two months' rest," said Aylward. "Swords, if you will, comrades, but no man strings his bow till I have loosed mine."

Yet the angry hearts of both Abbot and sacrist rose higher with a fresh obstacle.

"This is an ill day for your father, Franklin Aylward, who holds the tenancy of Crooksbury," said the sacrist. "He will rue it that ever he begot a son who will lose him his acres and his steading."

"My father is a bold yeoman, and would rue it even more that ever his son should stand by while foul work was afoot," said Aylward, stoutly. "Fall on, comrades! We are waiting."

Encouraged by promises of reward if they should fall in the service of the Abbey, and by threats of penalties if they should hold back, the four archers were about to close, when a singular interruption gave an entirely new turn to the proceedings.

At the door of the chapter-house, while these fiery doings had been afoot, there had assembled a mixed crowd of lay brothers, servants and varlets who had watched the development of the drama with the interest and delight with which men hail a sudden break in a dull routine. Suddenly there was an agitation at the back of this group, then a swirl in the center, and finally the front rank was violently thrust aside, and through the gap there emerged a strange and whimsical figure, who from the instant of his appearance dominated both chapter-house and Abbey, monks, prelates, and archers, as if he were their owner and their master.

He was a man somewhat above middle age, with thin lemon-colored hair, a curling mustache, a tufted chin of the same hue, and a high craggy face, all running to a great hook of the nose, like the beak of an eagle. His skin was tanned a brown-red by much exposure to the wind and sun. In height he was tall, and his figure was thin and loose-jointed, but stringy and hard-bitten. One eye was entirely covered by its lid, which lay flat over an empty socket, but the other danced and sparkled with a most roguish light, darting here and there with a twinkle of humor and criticism and intelligence, the whole fire of his soul bursting through that one narrow cranny.

His dress was as noteworthy as his person. A rich purple doublet and cloak was marked on the lapels with a strange scarlet device shaped like a wedge. Costly lace hung round his shoulders, and amid its soft folds there smoldered the dull red of a

SIR NIGEL

53

heavy golden chain. A knight's belt at his waist and a knight's golden spurs twinkling from his doeskin riding-boots proclaimed his rank, and on the wrist of his left gauntlet there sat a demure little hooded falcon of a breed which in itself was a mark of the dignity of the owner. Of weapons he had none, but a mandolin was slung by a black silken band over his back, and the high brown end projected above his shoulder. Such was the man, quaint, critical, masterful, with a touch of what is formidable behind it, who now surveyed the opposing groups of armed men and angry monks with an eye which commanded their attention.

"*Excusez!*" said he, in a lisping French. "*Excusez, mes amis!* I had thought to arouse you from prayer or meditation, but never have I seen such a holy exercise as this under an abbey's roof, with swords for breviaries and archers for acolytes. I fear that I have come amiss, and yet I ride on an errand from one who permits no delay."

The Abbot, and possibly the sacrist also, had begun to realize that events had gone a great deal farther than they had intended, and that without an extreme scandal it was no easy matter for them to save their dignity and the good name of Waverley. Therefore, in spite of the debonair, not to say disrespectful, bearing of the newcomer, they rejoiced at his appearance and intervention.

"I am the Abbot of Waverley, fair son," said the prelate. "If your message deal with a public matter it may be fitly repeated in the chapter-house; if not I will give you audience in my own chamber; for it is clear to me that you are a gentleman of blood and coat-armor who would not lightly break in upon the business of our court—a business which, as you have remarked, is little welcome to men of peace like myself and the brethren of the rule of Saint Bernard."

"*Pardieu!* Father Abbot," said the stranger. "One had but to glance at you and your men to see that the business was indeed little to your taste, and it may be even less so when I say that rather than see this young person in the window, who hath a noble bearing, further molested by these archers, I will adventure my person on his behalf."

The Abbot's smile turned to a frown at these frank words. "It would become you better, sir, to deliver the message of which you say that you are the bearer, than to uphold a prisoner against the rightful judgment of a court."

The stranger swept the court with his questioning eye. "The message is not for you, good father Abbot. It is for one I know not. I have been to his house, and they have sent me hither. The name is Nigel Loring."

"It is for me, fair sir."

"I had thought as much. I knew your father, Eustace Loring, and though he would have made two of you, yet he has left his stamp plain enough upon your face."

"You know not the truth of this matter," said the Abbot. "If you are a loyal man, you will stand aside, for this young man hath grievously offended against the law, and it is for the king's lieges to give us their support."

"And you have haled him up for judgment," cried the stranger, with much amusement. "It is as though a rookery sat in judgment upon a falcon. I warrant that you have found it easier to judge than to punish. Let me tell you, father Abbot, that this standeth not aright. When powers such as these were given to the like of you, they were given that you might check a brawling underling or correct a drunken woodman, and not that you might drag the best blood in England to your bar and set your archers on him if he questioned your findings."

The Abbot was little used to hear such words of reproof uttered in so stern a voice under his own abbey roof and before his listening monks.

"You may perchance find that an Abbey court has more powers than you wot of, Sir Knight," said he, "if knight indeed you be who are so uncourteous and short in your speech. Ere we go further, I would ask your name and style?"

The stranger laughed. "It is easy to see that you are indeed men of peace," said he proudly. "Had I shown this sign," and he touched the token upon his lapels, "whether on shield or pennon, in the marches of France or Scotland, there is not a cavalier but would have known the red pile of Chandos."

Chandos, John Chandos, the flower of English chivalry, the

pink of knight-errantry, the hero already of fifty desperate enterprises, a man known and honored from end to end of Europe! Nigel gazed at him as one who sees a vision. The archers stood back abashed, while the monks crowded closer to stare at the famous soldier of the French wars. The Abbot abated his tone, and a smile came to his angry face.

"We are indeed men of peace, Sir John, and little skilled in warlike blazonry," said he; "yet stout as are our Abbey walls, they are not so thick that the fame of your exploits has not passed through them and reached our ears. If it be your pleasure to take an interest in this young and misguided squire, it is not for us to thwart your kind intention or to withhold such grace as you request. I am glad indeed that he hath one who can set him so fair an example for a friend."

"I thank you for your courtesy, good father Abbot," said Chandos, carelessly. "This young squire has, however, a better friend than myself, one who is kinder to those he loves and more terrible to those he hates. It is from him I bear a message."

"I pray you, fair and honored sir," said Nigel, "that you will tell me what is the message that you bear."

"The message, *mon ami*, is that your friend comes into these parts and would have a night's lodging at the manor-house of Tilford for the love and respect that he bears your family."

"Nay, he is most welcome," said Nigel, "and yet I hope that he is one who can relish a soldier's fare and sleep under a humble roof, for indeed we can but give our best, poor as it is."

"He is indeed a soldier and a good one," Chandos answered, laughing, "and I warrant he has slept in rougher quarters than Tilford Manor-house."

"I have few friends, fair sir," said Nigel, with a puzzled face. "I pray you give me this gentleman's name."

"His name is Edward."

"Sir Edward Mortimer of Kent, perchance, or is it Sir Edward Brocas of whom the Lady Ermyntrude talks?"

"Nay, he is known as Edward only, and if you ask a second name it is Plantagenet, for he who comes to seek the shelter of your roof is your liege lord and mine, the King's high majesty, Edward of England."

VI. IN WHICH LADY ERMYNTRUDE OPENS THE IRON COFFER

As in a dream Nigel heard these stupendous and incredible words. As in a dream also he had a vision of a smiling and conciliatory Abbot, of an obsequious sacrist, and of a band of archers who cleared a path for him and for the king's messenger through the motley crowd who had choked the entrance of the Abbey court. A minute later he was walking by the side of Chandos through the peaceful cloister, and in front, in the open archway of the great gate, was the broad yellow road between its borders of green meadow-land. The spring air was the sweeter and the more fragrant for that chill dread of dishonor and captivity which had so recently frozen his ardent heart. He had already passed the portal when a hand plucked at his sleeve and he turned to find himself confronted by the brown honest face and hazel eyes of the archer who had interfered in his behalf.

"Well," said Aylward, "what have you to say to me, young sir?"

"What can I say, my good fellow, save that I thank you with all my heart? By Saint Paul! if you had been my blood brother you could not have stood by me more stoutly."

"Nay! but this is not enough."

Nigel colored with vexation, and the more so as Chandos was listening with his critical smile to their conversation.

"If you had heard what was said in the court," said he, "you will understand that I am not blessed at this moment with much of this world's gear. The black death and the monks have between them been heavy upon our estate. Willingly would I give you a handful of gold for your assistance, since that is what you seem to crave; but indeed I have it not, and so once more I say that you must be satisfied with my thanks."

"Your gold is nothing to me," said Aylward, shortly, "nor would you buy my loyalty if you filled my wallet with rose nobles, so long as you were not a man after my own heart. But I have seen you back the yellow horse, and I have seen you face the Abbot of Waverley, and you are such a master as I would very gladly serve if you have by chance a place for such a man. I have seen your following, and I doubt not that they were stout fellows in your grandfather's time; but which of them now would draw a bow-string to his ear? Through you I have left the service of the Abbey of Waverley, and where can I look now for a post? If I stay here I am all undone like a fretted bow-string."

"Nay, there can be no difficulty there," said Chandos. "*Pardieu!* a roistering, swaggering dare-devil archer is worth his price on the French border. There are two hundred such who march behind my own person, and I would ask nothing better than to see you among them."

"I thank you, noble sir, for your offer," said Aylward, "and I had rather follow your banner than many another one, for it is well-known that it goes ever forward, and I have heard enough of the wars to know that there are small pickings for the man who lags behind. Yet, if the squire will have me, I would choose to fight under the five roses of Loring, for though I was born in the hundred of Easebourne and the rape of Chichester, yet I have grown up and learned to use the longbow in these parts, and as the free son of a free franklin I had rather serve my own neighbor than a stranger."

"My good fellow," said Nigel, "I have told you that I could in no wise reward you for such service."

"If you will but take me to the wars I will see to my own reward," said Aylward. "Till then I ask for none, save a corner of your table and six feet of your floor, for it is certain that the only reward I would get from the Abbey for this day's work would be the scourge for my back and the stocks for my ankles. Samkin Aylward is your man, Squire Nigel, from this hour on, and by these ten finger-bones he trusts the Devil will fly away with him if ever he gives you cause to regret it!" So saying he raised his hand to his steel cap in salute, slung his great yellow bow over his back, and followed on some paces in the rear of his new master.

"*Pardieu!* I have arrived *à la bonne heure*," said Chandos. "I rode from Windsor and came to your manor-house, to find it empty save for a fine old dame, who told me of your troubles. From her I walked across to the Abbey, and none too soon, for what with cloth-yard shafts for your body, and bell, book, and candle for your soul, it was no very cheerful outlook. But here is the very dame herself, if I mistake not."

It was indeed the formidable figure of the Lady Ermyntrude, gaunt, bowed, and leaning on her staff, which had emerged from the door of the manor-house and advanced to greet them. She croaked with laughter, and shook her stick at the great building as she heard of the discomfiture of the Abbey court. Then she led the way into the hall, where the best which she could provide had been laid out for their illustrious guest. There was Chandos blood in her own veins, traceable back through the de Greys, de Multons, de Valences, de Montagues, and other high and noble strains, so that the meal had been eaten and cleared before she had done tracing the network of intermarriages and connections, with quarterings, impalements, lozenges and augmentations by which the blazonry of the two families might be made to show a common origin. Back to the Conquest and before it there was not a noble family-tree every twig and bud of which was not familiar to the Dame Ermyntrude.

And now, when the trestles were cleared and the three were left alone in the hall, Chandos broke his message to the lady. "King Edward hath ever borne in mind that noble knight, your son, Sir Eustace," said he. "He will journey to Southampton next week, and I am his harbinger. He bade me say, noble and honored lady, that he would come from Guildford in any easy stage so that he might spend one night under your roof."

The old dame flushed with pleasure, and then turned white with vexation at the words.

"It is in truth great honor to the house of Loring," said she, "yet our roof is now humble and, as you have seen, our fare is plain. The king knows not that we are so poor. I fear lest we seem churlish and niggard in his eyes."

But Chandos reasoned away her fears. The king's retinue would journey on to Farnham Castle. There were no ladies in his party. Though he was king, still he was a hardy soldier, and cared little for his ease. In any case, since he had declared his coming, they must make the best of it. Finally, with all delicacy, Chandos offered his own purse if it would help in the matter. But already the Lady Ermyntrude had recovered her composure.

"Nay, fair kinsman, that may not be," said she. "I will make such preparation as I may for the king. He will bear in mind that if the house of Loring can give nothing else, they have always held their blood and their lives at his disposal."

Chandos was to ride on to Farnham Castle and beyond, but he expressed his desire to have a warm bath ere he left Tilford, for, like most of his fellow-knights, he was much addicted to simmering in the hottest water that he could possibly endure. The bath therefore, a high hooped arrangement like a broader but shorter churn, was carried into the privacy of the guest-chamber, and thither it was that Nigel was summoned to hold him company while he stewed and sweltered in his tub.

Nigel perched himself upon the side of the high bed, swinging his legs over the edge and gazing with wonder and amusement at the quaint face, the ruffled yellow hair, and the sinewy shoulders of the famous warrior, dimly seen amid a pillar of steam. He was in a mood for talk; so Nigel, with eager lips, plied him with a thousand questions about the wars, hanging upon every word which came back to him, like those of the ancient oracles, out of the mist and the cloud. To Chandos himself, the old soldier for whom war had lost its freshness, it was a renewal of his own ardent youth to listen to Nigel's rapid questions and to mark the rapt attention with which he listened.

"Tell me of the Welsh, honored sir?" asked the squire. "What manner of soldiers are the Welsh?"

"They are very valiant men of war," said Chandos, splashing about in his tub. "There is good skirmishing to be had in their valleys if you ride with a small following. They flare up like a furze-bush in the flames, but if for a short space you may abide the heat of it, then there is a chance that it may be cooler."

"And the Scotch?" asked Nigel. "You have made war upon them also, as I understand."

"The Scotch knights have no masters in the world, and he who can hold his own with the best of them, be it a Douglas, a Murray, or a Seaton, has nothing more to learn. Though you be a hard man, you will always meet as hard a one if you ride northward. If the Welsh be like the furze-fire, then, *pardieu!* the Scotch are the peat, for they will smolder and you will never come to the end of them. I have had many happy hours on the marches of Scotland, for even if there be no war the Percies of Alnwick or the Governor of Carlisle can still raise a little bickering with the border clans."

"I bear in mind that my father was wont to say that they were very stout spearmen."

"No better in the world, for the spears are twelve foot long and they hold them in very thick array; but their archers are weak, save only the men of Ettrick and Selkirk, who come from the forest. I pray you to open the lattice, Nigel, for the steam is overthick. Now, in Wales it is the spearmen who are weak, and there are no archers in these islands like the men of Gwent with their bows of elm, which shoot with such power that I have known a cavalier to have his horse killed when the shaft had passed through his mail breeches, his thigh, and his saddle. And yet, what is the most strongly shot arrow to these new balls of iron driven by the fire-powder which will crush a man's armor as an egg is crushed by a stone? Our fathers knew them not."

"Then the better for us," cried Nigel, "since there is at least one honorable venture which is all our own."

Chandos chuckled and turned upon the flushed youth a twinkling and sympathetic eye. "You have a fashion of speech which carries me back to the old men whom I met in my boyhood," said he. "There were some of the real old knight-errants left in those days, and they spoke as you do. Young as you are, you belong to another age. Where got you that trick of thought and word?"

"I have had only one to teach me, the Lady Ermyntrude."

"*Pardieu!* she has trained a proper young hawk ready to stoop at a lordly quarry," said Chandos. "I would that I had the first unhooding of you. Will you not ride with me to the wars?"

The tears brimmed over from Nigel's eyes, and he wrung the gaunt hand extended from the bath. "By Saint Paul! what could I ask better in the world? I fear to leave her, for she has none other to care for her. But if it can in any way be arranged——"

"The king's hand may smooth it out. Say no more until he is here. But if you wish to ride with me——"

"What could man wish for more? Is there a squire in England who would not serve under the banner of Chandos! Whither do you go, fair sir? And when do you go? Is it to Scotland? Is it to Ireland? Is it to France? But alas, alas!"

The eager face had clouded. For the instant he had forgotten that a suit of armor was as much beyond his means as a service of gold plate. Down in a twinkling came all his high hopes to the ground. Oh, these sordid material things, which come between our dreams and their fulfilment! The squire of such a knight must dress with the best. Yet all the fee simple of Tilford would scarce suffice for one suit of plate.

Chandos, with his quick wit and knowledge of the world, had guessed the cause of this sudden change.

"If you fight under my banner it is for me to find the weapons," said he. "Nay, I will not be denied."

But Nigel shook his head sadly. "It may not be. The Lady Ermyntrude would sell this old house and every acre round it, ere she would permit me to accept this gracious bounty which you offer. Yet I do not despair, for only last week I won for myself a noble war-horse for which I paid not a penny, so perchance a suit of armor may also come my way."

"And how won you the horse?"

"It was given me by the monks of Waverley."

"This is wonderful. *Pardieu!* I should have expected, from what I have seen, that they would have given you little save their malediction."

"They had no use for the horse, and they gave it to me."

"Then we have only to find some one who has no use for a suit of armor and will give it to you. Yet I trust that you will think better of it and let me, since that good lady proves that I am your kinsman, fit you for the wars."

"I thank you, noble sir, and if I should turn to anyone it would indeed be to you; but there are other ways which I would try first. But I pray you, good Sir John, to tell me of some of your noble spear-runnings against the French, for the whole land rings with the tale of your deeds, and I have heard that in one morning three champions have fallen before your lance. Was it not so?"

"That it was indeed so these scars upon my body will prove; but these were the follies of my youth."

"How can you call them follies? Are they not the means by which honorable advancement may be gained and one's lady exalted?"

"It is right that you should think so, Nigel. At your age a man should have a hot head and a high heart. I also had both, and fought for my lady's glove or for my vow or for the love of fighting. But as one grows older and commands men one has other things to think of. One thinks less of one's own honor and more of the safety of the army. It is not your own spear, your own sword, your own arm, which will turn the tide of fight; but a cool head may save a stricken field. He who knows when his horsemen should charge and when they should fight on foot, he who can mix his archers with his men-at-arms in such a fashion that each can support the other, he who can hold up his reserve and pour it into the battle when it may turn the tide, he who has a quick eye for boggy land and broken ground—that is the man who is of more worth to an army than Roland, Oliver, and all the paladins."

"Yet if his knights fail him, honored sir, all his head-work will not prevail."

"True enough, Nigel; so may every squire ride to the wars with his soul on fire, as yours is now. But I must linger no longer, for the king's service must be done. I will dress, and when I have bid farewell to the noble Dame Ermyntrude I will on to Farnham; but you will see me here again on the day that the king comes."

So Chandos went his way that evening, walking his horse

through the peaceful lanes and twanging his citole as he went, for he loved music and was famous for his merry songs. The cottagers came from their huts and laughed and clapped as the rich full voice swelled and sank to the cheery tinkling of the strings. There were few who saw him pass that would have guessed that the quaint one-eyed man with the yellow hair was the toughest fighter and craftiest man of war in Europe. Once only, as he entered Farnham, an old broken man-at-arms ran out in his rags and clutched at his horse as a dog gambols round his master. Chandos threw him a kind word and a gold coin as he passed on to the castle.

In the mean while young Nigel and the Lady Ermyntrude, left alone with their difficulties, looked blankly in each other's faces.

"The cellar is well-nigh empty," said Nigel. "There are two firkins of small beer and a tun of canary. How can we set such drink before the king and his court?"

"We must have some wine of Bordeaux. With that and the mottled cow's calf and the fowls and a goose, we can set forth a sufficient repast if he stays only for the one night. How many will be with him?"

"A dozen, at the least."

The old dame wrung her hands in despair.

"Nay, take it not to heart, dear lady!" said Nigel. "We have but to say the word and the king would stop at Waverley, where he and his court would find all that they could wish."

"Never!" cried the Lady Ermyntrude. "It would be shame and disgrace to us for ever if the king were to pass our door when he has graciously said that he was fain to enter in. Nay, I will do it. Never did I think that I would be forced to this, but I know that he would wish it, and I will do it."

She went to the old iron coffer, and taking a small key from her girdle she unlocked it. The rusty hinges, screaming shrilly as she threw back the lid, proclaimed how seldom it was that she had penetrated into the sacred recesses of her treasure-chest. At the top were some relics of old finery: a silken cloak spangled with golden stars, a coif of silver filigree, a roll of Venetian lace. Beneath were little packets tied in silk which the old lady handled with tender care; a man's hunting-glove, a child's shoe, a love-knot done in faded-green ribbon, some letters in rude rough script, and a vernicle of Saint Thomas. Then from the very bottom of the box she drew three objects, swathed in silken cloth, which she uncovered and laid upon the table. The one was a bracelet of rough gold studded with uncut rubies, the second was a gold salver, and the third was a high goblet of the same metal.

"You have heard me speak of these, Nigel, but never before have you seen them, for indeed I have not opened the hutch for fear that we might be tempted in our great need to turn them into money. I have kept them out of my sight and even out of my thoughts. But now it is the honor of the house which calls, and even these must go. This goblet was that which my husband, Sir Nele Loring, won after the intaking of Belgrade, when he and his comrades held the lists from matins to vespers against the flower of the French chivalry. The salver was given him by the Earl of Pembroke in memory of his valor upon the field of Falkirk."

"And the bracelet, dear lady?"

"You will not laugh, Nigel?"

"Nay, why should I laugh?"

"The bracelet was the prize for the Queen of Beauty which was given to me before all the high-born ladies of England by Sir Nele Loring a month before our marriage. The Queen of Beauty, Nigel—I, old and twisted, as you see me. Five strong men went down before his lance ere he won that trinket for me. And now in my last years——"

"Nay, dear and honored lady, we will not part with it."

"Yes, Nigel, he would have it so. I can hear his whisper in my ear. Honor to him was everything—the rest nothing. Take it from me, Nigel, ere my heart weakens. To-morrow you will ride with it to Guildford; you will see Thorold the goldsmith; and you will raise enough money to pay for all that we shall need for the king's coming."

She turned her face away to hide the quivering of her wrinkled features, and the crash of the iron lid covered the sob which burst from her overwrought soul.

VII. HOW NIGEL WENT MARKETING TO GUILDFORD

IT WAS ON a bright June morning that young Nigel, with youth and springtime to make his heart light, rode upon his errand from Tilford to Guildford town. Beneath him was his great yellow war-horse, caracoling and curveting as he went, as blithe and free of spirit as his master. In all England one would scarce have found upon that morning so high-mettled and so debonair a pair. The sandy road wound through groves of fir, where the breeze came soft and fragrant with resinous gums, or over heathery downs, which rolled away to north and to south, vast and untenanted, for on the uplands the soil was poor and water scarce. Over Crooksbury Common he passed, and then across the great Heath of Puttenham, following a sandy path which wound amid the bracken and the heather, for he meant to strike the Pilgrim's Way where it turned eastward from Farnham and from Seale. As he rode he continually felt his saddle-bag with his hand, for in it, securely strapped, he had placed the precious treasures of the Lady Ermyntrude. As he saw the grand tawny neck tossing before him, and felt the easy heave of the great horse and heard the muffled drumming of his hoofs, he could have sung and shouted with the joy of living.

Behind him, upon the little brown pony which had been Nigel's former mount, rode Samkin Aylward, the bowman, who had taken upon himself the duties of personal attendant and body-guard. His great shoulders and breadth of frame seemed dangerously top-heavy upon the tiny steed, but he ambled along, whistling a merry lilt, and as lighthearted as his master. There was no countryman who had not a nod and no woman who had not a smile for the jovial bowman, who rode for the most part with his face over his shoulder, staring at the last pet-ticoat which had passed him. Once only he met with a harsher greeting. It was from a tall, white-headed, red-faced man whom they met upon the moor.

"Good morrow, dear father!" cried Aylward. "How is it with you at Crooksbury? And how are the new black cow and the ewes from Alton, and Mary the dairymaid, and all your gear?"

"It ill becomes you to ask, you ne'er-do-weel," said the old man. "You have angered the monks of Waverley, whose tenant I am, and they would drive me out of my farm. Yet there are three more years to run, and do what they may I will bide till then. But little did I think that I should lose my homestead through you, Samkin, and big as you are I would knock the dust out of that green jerkin with a good hazel switch if I had you at Crooksbury."

"Then you shall do it to-morrow morning, good father, for I will come and see you then. But indeed I did not do more at Waverley than you would have done yourself. Look me in the eye, old hot-head, and tell me if you would have stood by while the last Loring—look at him as he rides with his head in the air and his soul in the clouds—was shot down before your very eyes at the bidding of that fat monk! If you would, then I disown you as my father."

"Nay, Samkin, if it was like that, then perhaps what you did was not so far amiss. But it is hard to lose the old farm when my heart is buried deep in the good brown soil."

"Tut, man! there are three years to run, and what may not happen in three years? Before that time I shall have gone to the wars, and when I have opened a French strong box or two you can buy the good brown soil and snap your fingers at Abbot John and his bailiffs. Am I not as proper a man as Tom Withstaff of Churt? And yet he came back after six months with his pockets full of rose nobles and a French wench on either arm."

"God preserve us from the wenches, Samkin! But indeed I think that if there is money to be gathered you are as likely to get your fist full as any man who goes to the war. But hasten, lad, hasten! Already your young master is over the brow."

Thus admonished, the archer waved his gauntleted hand to

his father, and digging his heels into the sides of his little pony soon drew up with the squire. Nigel glanced over his shoulder and slackened speed until the pony's head was up to his saddle.

"Have I not heard, archer," said he, "that an outlaw has been loose in these parts?"

"It is true, fair sir. He was villein to Sir Peter Mandeville, but he broke his bonds and fled into the forests. Men call him the 'Wild Man of Puttenham.'"

"How comes it that he has not been hunted down? If the man be a draw-latch and a robber it would be an honorable deed to clear the country of such an evil."

"Twice the sergeants-at-arms from Guildford have come out against him, but the fox has many earths, and it would puzzle you to get him out of them."

"By Saint Paul! were my errand not a pressing one I would be tempted to turn aside and seek him. Where lives he, then?"

"There is a great morass beyond Puttenham, and across it there are caves in which he and his people lurk."

"His people? He hath a band?"

"There are several with him."

"It sounds a most honorable enterprise," said Nigel. "When the king hath come and gone we will spare a day for the outlaws of Puttenham. I fear there is little chance for us to see them on this journey."

"They prey upon the pilgrims who pass along the Winchester Road, and they are well loved by the folk in these parts, for they rob none of them and have an open hand for all who will help them."

"It is right easy to have an open hand with the money that you have stolen," said Nigel; "but I fear that they will not try to rob two men with swords at their girdles like you and me, so we shall have no profit from them."

They had passed over the wild moors and had come down now into the main road by which the pilgrims from the west of England made their way to the national shrine at Canterbury. It passed from Winchester, and up the beautiful valley of the Itchen until it reached Farnham, where it forked into two branches, one of which ran along the Hog's Back, while the second wound to the south and came out at Saint Catharine's Hill, where stands the Pilgrim shrine, a gray old ruin now, but once so august, so crowded, and so affluent. It was this second branch upon which Nigel and Aylward found themselves as they rode to Guildford.

No one, as it chanced, was going the same way as themselves, but they met one large drove of pilgrims returning from their journey with pictures of Saint Thomas and snails' shells or little leaden ampullæ in their hats and bundles of purchases over their shoulders. They were a grimy, ragged, travel-stained crew, the men walking, the women borne on asses. Man and beast, they limped along as if it would be a glad day when they saw their homes once more. These and a few beggars or minstrels, who crouched among the heather on either side of the track in the hope of receiving an occasional farthing from the passer-by, were the only folk they met until they had reached the village of Puttenham. Already there, was a hot sun and just breeze enough to send the dust flying down the road, so they were glad to clear their throats with a glass of beer at the ale-stake in the village, where the fair alewife gave Nigel a cold farewell because he had no attentions for her, and Aylward a box on the ear because he had too many.

On the farther side of Puttenham the road runs through thick woods of oak and beech, with a tangled undergrowth of fern and bramble. Here they met a patrol of sergeants-at-arms, tall fellows, well-mounted, clad in studded-leather caps and tunics, with lances and swords. They walked their horses slowly on the shady side of the road, and stopped as the travelers came up, to ask if they had been molested on the way.

"Have a care," they added, "for the 'Wild Man' and his wife are out. Only yesterday they slew a merchant from the west and took a hundred crowns."

"His wife, you say?"

"Yes, she is ever at his side, and has saved him many a time, for if he has the strength it is she who has the wit. I hope to see their heads together upon the green grass one of these mornings."

The patrol passed downward toward Farnham, and so, as it proved, away from the robbers, who had doubtless watched them closely from the dense brushwood which skirted the road. Coming round a curve, Nigel and Aylward were aware of a tall and graceful woman who sat, wringing her hands and weeping bitterly, upon the bank by the side of the track. At such a sight of beauty in distress Nigel pricked Pommers with the spur and in three bounds was at the side of the unhappy lady.

"What ails you, fair dame?" he asked. "Is there any small matter in which I may stand your friend, or is it possible that any one hath so hard a heart as to do you an injury."

She rose and turned upon him a face full of hope and entreaty.

"Oh, save my poor, poor father!" she cried. "Have you perchance seen the way-wardens? They passed us, and I fear they are beyond call."

"Yes, they have ridden onward, but we may serve as well."

"Then, hasten, hasten, I pray you! Even now they may be doing him to death. They have dragged him into yonder grove and I have heard his voice growing ever weaker in the distance. Hasten, I implore you!"

Nigel sprang from his horse and tossed the rein to Aylward.

"Nay, let us go together. How many robbers were there, lady?"

"Two stout fellows."

"Then I come also."

"Nay, it is not possible," said Nigel. "The wood is too thick for horses, and we cannot leave them in the road."

"I will guard them," cried the lady.

"Pommers is not so easily held. Do you bide here, Aylward, until you hear from me. Stir not, I command you!"

So saying, Nigel, with the light, of adventure gleaming in his joyous eyes, drew his sword and plunged swiftly into the forest.

Far and fast he ran, from glade to glade, breaking through the bushes, springing over the brambles, light as a young deer, peering this way and that, straining his ears for a sound, and catching only the cry of the wood-pigeons. Still on he went, with the constant thought of the weeping woman behind and of the captured man in front. It was not until he was footsore and out of breath that he stopped with his hand to his side, and considered that his own business had still to be done, and that it was time once more that he should seek the road to Guildford.

Meantime Aylward had found his own rough means of consoling the woman in the road, who stood sobbing with her face against the side of Pommers' saddle.

"Nay, weep not, my pretty one," said he. "It brings the tears to my own eyes to see them stream from thine."

"Alas! good archer, he was the best of fathers, so gentle and so kind! Had you but known him, you must have loved him."

"Tut, tut! he will suffer no scathe. Squire Nigel will bring him back to you anon."

"No, no, I shall never see him more. Hold me, archer, or I fall!"

Aylward pressed his ready arm round the supple waist. The fainting woman leaned with her hand upon his shoulder. Her pale face looked past him, and it was some new light in her eyes, a flash of expectancy, of triumph, of wicked joy, which gave him sudden warning of his danger.

He shook her off and sprang to one side, but only just in time to avoid a crashing blow from a great club in the hands of a man even taller and stronger than himself. He had one quick vision of great white teeth clenched in grim ferocity, a wild flying beard and blazing wild-beast eyes. The next instant he had closed, ducking his head beneath another swing of that murderous cudgel.

With his arms round the robber's burly body and his face buried in his bushy beard, Aylward gasped and strained and heaved. Back and forward in the dusty road the two men stamped and staggered, a grim wrestling-match, with life for the prize. Twice the great strength of the outlaw had Aylward nearly down, and twice with his greater youth and skill the archer restored his grip and his balance. Then at last his turn came. He slipped his leg behind the other's knee, and, giving a mighty wrench, tore him across it. With a hoarse shout the outlaw toppled backward, and had hardly reached the ground before

Aylward had his knee upon his chest and his short sword deep in his beard and pointed to his throat.

"By these ten finger-bones!" he gasped, "one more struggle and it is your last!"

The man lay still enough, for he was half-stunned by the crashing fall. Aylward looked round him, but the woman had disappeared. At the first blow struck she had vanished into the forest. He began to have fears for his master, thinking that he perhaps had been lured into some death-trap; but his forebodings were soon at rest, for Nigel himself came hastening down the road, which he had struck some distance from the spot where he left it.

"By Saint Paul!" he cried, "who is this man on whom you are perched, and where is the lady who has honored us so far as to crave our help? Alas, that I have been unable to find her father!"

"As well for you, fair sir," said Aylward, "for I am of opinion that her father was the Devil. This woman is, as I believe, the wife of the 'Wild Man of Puttenham,' and this is the 'Wild Man' himself who set upon me and tried to brain me with his club."

The outlaw, who had opened his eyes, looked with a scowl from his captor to the newcomer.

"You are in luck, archer," said he, "for I have come to grips with many a man, but I cannot call to mind any who have had the better of me."

"You have indeed the grip of a bear," said Aylward; "but it was a coward deed that your wife should hold me while you dashed out my brains with a stick. It is also a most villainous thing to lay a snare for wayfarers by asking for their pity and assistance, so that it was our own soft hearts which brought us into such danger. The next who hath real need of our help may suffer for your sins."

"When the hand of the whole world is against you," said the outlaw, in a surly voice, "you must fight as best you can."

"You well deserve to be hanged, if only because you have brought this woman, who is fair and gentle-spoken, to such a life," said Nigel. "Let us tie him by the wrist to my stirrup leather, Aylward, and we will lead him into Guildford."

The archer drew a spare bowstring from his case and had bound the prisoner as directed, when Nigel gave a sudden start and cry of alarm.

"Holy Mary!" he cried. "Where is the saddle-bag?"

It had been cut away by a sharp knife. Only the two ends of a strap remained. Aylward and Nigel stared at each other in blank dismay. Then the young squire shook his clenched hands and pulled at his yellow curls in his despair.

"The Lady Ermyntrude's bracelet! My grandfather's cup!" he cried. "I would have died ere I lost them! What can I say to her? I dare not return until I have found them. Oh, Aylward, Aylward! how came you to let them be taken?"

The honest archer had pushed back his steel cap and was scratching his tangled head.

"Nay, I know nothing of it. You never said that there was aught of price in the bag, else had I kept a better eye upon it. Certes! it was not this fellow who took it, since I have never had my hands from him. It can only be the woman who fled with it while we fought."

Nigel stamped about the road in his perplexity. "I would follow her to the world's end if I knew where I could find her, but to search these woods for her is to look for a mouse in a wheatfield. Good Saint George, thou who didst overcome the Dragon, I pray you by that most honorable and knightly achievement that you will be with me now! And you also, great Saint Julian, patron of all wayfarers in distress! Two candles shall burn before your shrine at Godalming, if you will but bring me back my saddle-bag. What would I not give to have it back?"

"Will you give me my life?" asked the outlaw. "Promise that I go free, and you shall have it back, if it be indeed true that my wife has taken it."

"Nay, I cannot do that," said Nigel. "My honor would surely be concerned, since my loss is a private one; but it would be to the public scathe that you should go free. By Saint Paul! it would be an ungentle deed if in order to save my own I let you loose upon the gear of a hundred others."

"I will not ask you to let me loose," said the "Wild Man." "If you will promise that my life be spared I will restore your bag."

"I cannot give such a promise, for it will lie with the sheriff and reeves of Guildford."

"Shall I have your word in my favor?"

"That I could promise you, if you will give back the bag, though I know not how far my word may avail. But your words are vain, for you cannot think that we will be so fond as to let you go in the hope that you return?"

"I would not ask it," said the "Wild Man," "for I can get your bag and yet never stir from the spot where I stand. Have I your promise upon your honor and all that you hold dear that you will ask for grace?"

"You have."

"And that my wife shall be unharmed?"

"I promise it."

The outlaw laid back his head and uttered a long shrill cry like the howl of a wolf. There was a silent pause, and then, clear and shrill, there rose the same cry no great distance away in the forest. Again the "Wild Man" called, and again his mate replied. A third time he summoned, as the deer bells to the doe in the greenwood. Then with a rustle of brushwood and snapping of twigs the woman was before them once more, tall, pale, graceful, wonderful. She glanced neither at Aylward nor Nigel, but ran to the side of her husband.

"Dear and sweet lord," she cried, "I trust they have done you no hurt. I waited by the old ash, and my heart sank when you came not."

"I have been taken at last, wife."

"Oh, cursed, cursed day! Let him go, kind, gentle sirs, do not take him from me!"

"They will speak for me at Guildford," said the "Wild Man." "They have sworn it. But hand them first the bag that you have taken."

She drew it out from under her loose cloak. "Here it is, gentle sir. Indeed it went to my heart to take it, for you had mercy upon me in my trouble. But now I am, as you see, in real and very sore distress. Will you not have mercy now? Take ruth on us, fair sir! On my knees I beg it of you, most gentle and kindly squire!"

Nigel had clutched his bag, and right glad he was to feel that the treasures were all safe within it.

"My promise is given," said he. "I will say what I can; but the issue rests with others. I pray you to stand up, for indeed I cannot promise more."

"Then I must be content," said she, rising, with a composed face. "I have prayed you to take ruth, and indeed I can do no more; but ere I go back to the forest I would rede you to be on your guard lest you lose your bag once more. Wot you how I took it, archer? Nay, it was simple enough, and may happen again, so I make it clear to you. I had this knife in my sleeve, and though it is small it is very sharp. I slipped it down like this. Then, when I seemed to weep with my face against the saddle, I cut down like this——"

In an instant she had shorn through the stirrup leather which bound her man, and he, diving under the belly of the horse, had slipped like a snake into the brushwood. In passing he had struck Pommers from beneath, and the great horse, enraged and insulted, was rearing high, with two men hanging to his bridle. When at last he had calmed there was no sign left of the "Wild Man" or of his wife. In vain did Aylward, an arrow on his string, run here and there among the great trees and peer down the shadowy glades. When he returned he and his master cast a shame-faced glance at each other.

"I trust that we are better soldiers than jailers," said Aylward, as he climbed on his pony.

But Nigel's frown relaxed into a smile. "At least we have gained back what we lost," said he. "Here I place it on the pommel of my saddle, and I shall not take my eyes from it until we are safe in Guildford town."

So they jogged on together until passing Saint Catharine's shrine they crossed the winding Wey once more, and so found themselves in the steep high street with its heavy-eaved gabled houses, its monkish hospitium upon the left, where good ale may still be quaffed, and its great square-keeped castle upon the right, no gray and grim skeleton of ruin, but very quick and alert, with blazoned banner flying free, and steel caps twinkling from the battlement. A row of booths extended from the castle gate to the high street, and two doors from the Church of the Trinity was that of Thorold the goldsmith, a rich burgess and Mayor of the town.

He looked long and lovingly at the rich rubies and at the fine work upon the goblet. Then he stroked his flowing gray beard as he pondered whether he should offer fifty nobles or sixty, for he knew well that he could sell them again for two hundred. If he offered too much his profit would be reduced. If he offered too little the youth might go as far as London with them, for they were rare and of great worth. The young man was ill-clad, and his eyes were anxious. Perchance he was hard pressed and was ignorant of the value of what he bore. He would sound him.

"These things are old and out of fashion, fair sir," said he. "Of the stones I can scarce say if they are of good quality or not, but they are dull and rough. Yet, if your price be low I may add them to my stock, though indeed this booth was made to sell and not to buy. What do you ask?"

Nigel bent his brows in perplexity. Here was a game in which neither his bold heart nor his active limbs could help him. It was the new force mastering the old: the man of commerce conquering the man of war—wearing him down and weakening him through the centuries until he had him as his bond-servant and his thrall.

"I know not what to ask, good sir," said Nigel. "It is not for me, nor for any man who bears my name, to chaffer and to haggle. You know the worth of these things, for it is your trade to do so. The Lady Ermyntrude lacks money, and we must have it against the king's coming, so give me that which is right and just, and we will say no more."

The goldsmith smiled. The business was growing more simple and more profitable. He had intended to offer fifty, but surely it would be sinful waste to give more than twenty-five.

"I shall scarce know what to do with them when I have them," said he. "Yet I should not grudge twenty nobles if it is a matter in which the king is concerned."

Nigel's heart turned to lead. This sum would not buy one-half what was needful. It was clear that the Lady Ermyntrude had overvalued her treasures. Yet he could not return empty-handed, so if twenty nobles was the real worth, as this good old man assured him, then he must be thankful and take it.

"I am concerned by what you say," said he. "You know more of these things than I can do. However, I will take——"

"A hundred and fifty," whispered Aylward's voice in his ear.

"A hundred and fifty," said Nigel, only too relieved to have found the humblest guide upon these unwonted paths.

The goldsmith started. This youth was not the simple soldier that he had seemed. That frank face, those blue eyes, were traps for the unwary. Never had he been more taken aback in a bargain.

"This is fond talk and can lead to nothing, fair sir," said he, turning away and fiddling with the keys of his strong boxes. "Yet I have no wish to be hard on you. Take my outside price, which is fifty nobles."

"And a hundred," whispered Aylward.

"And a hundred," said Nigel, blushing at his own greed.

"Well, well, take a hundred!" cried the merchant. "Fleece me, skin me, leave me a loser, and take for your wares the full hundred!"

"I should be shamed for ever if I were to treat you so badly," said Nigel. "You have spoken me fair, and I would not grind you down. Therefore, I will gladly take one hundred——"

"And fifty," whispered Aylward.

"And fifty," said Nigel.

"By Saint John of Beverley!" cried the merchant. "I came hither from the North Country, and they are said to be shrewd at a deal in those parts; but I had rather bargain with a synagogue full of Jews than with you, for all your gentle ways. Will you indeed take no less than a hundred and fifty? Alas! you pluck from me my profits of a month. It is a fell morning's work for me. I would I had never seen you!" With groans and lamentations he paid the gold pieces across the counter, and Nigel, hardly able to credit his own good fortune, gathered them into the leather saddle-bag.

A moment later with flushed face he was in the street and pouring out his thanks to Aylward.

"Alas, my fair lord! the man has robbed us now," said the archer. "We could have had another twenty had we stood fast."

"How know you that, good Aylward?"

"By his eyes, Squire Loring. I wot I have little store of reading where the parchment of a book or the pricking of a blazon is concerned, but I can read men's eyes, and I never doubted that he would give what he has given."

The two travelers had dinner at the monk's hospitium, Nigel at the high table and Aylward among the commonalty. Then again they roamed the high street on business intent. Nigel bought taffeta for hangings, wine, preserves, fruit, damask table linen and many other articles of need. At last he halted before the armorer's shop at the castle-yard, staring at the fine suits of plate, the engraved pectorals, the plumed helmets, the cunningly jointed gorgets, as a child at a sweet-shop.

"Well, Squire Loring," said Wat the armorer, looking sidewise from the furnace where he was tempering a sword blade, "what can I sell you this morning? I swear to you by Tubal Cain, the father of all workers in metal, that you might go from end to end of Cheapside and never see a better suit than that which hangs from yonder hook!"

"And the price, armorer?"

"To any one else, two hundred and fifty rose nobles. To you two hundred."

"And why cheaper to me, good fellow?"

"Because I fitted your father also for the wars, and a finer suit never went out of my shop. I warrant that it turned many an edge before he laid it aside. We worked in mail in those days, and I had as soon have a well-made thick-meshed mail as any plates; but a young knight will be in the fashion like any dame of the court, and so it must be plate now, even though the price be trebled."

"Your rede is that the mail is as good?"

"I am well sure of it."

"Hearken then, armorer! I cannot at this moment buy a suit of plate, and yet I sorely need steel harness on account of a small deed which it is in my mind to do. Now I have at my home at

Tilford that very suit of mail of which you speak, with which my father first rode to the wars. Could you not so alter it that it should guard my limbs also?"

The armorer looked at Nigel's small upright figure and burst out laughing.

"You jest, Squire Loring! The suit was made for one who was far above the common stature of man."

"Nay, I jest not. If it will but carry me through one spear-running it will have served its purpose."

The armorer leaned back on his anvil and pondered while Nigel stared anxiously at his sooty face.

"Right gladly would I lend you a suit of plate for this one venture, Squire Loring, but I know well that if you should be overthrown your harness becomes prize to the victor. I am a poor man with many children, and I dare not risk the loss of it. But as to what you say of the old suit of mail, is it indeed in good condition?"

"Most excellent, save only at the neck, which is much frayed."

"To shorten the limbs is easy. It is but to cut out a length of the mail and then loop up the links. But to shorten the body—nay, that is beyond the armorer's art."

"It was my last hope. Nay, good armorer, if you have indeed served and loved my gallant father, then I beg you by his memory that you will help me now."

The armorer threw down his heavy hammer with a crash upon the floor.

"It is not only that I loved your father, Squire Loring, but it is that I have seen you, half armed as you were, ride against the best of them at the Castle tilt-yard. Last Martinmas my heart bled for you when I saw how sorry was your harness, and yet you held your own against the stout Sir Oliver with his Milan suit. When go you to Tilford?"

"Even now."

"Heh, Jenkin, fetch out the cob!" cried the worthy Wat. "May my right hand lose its cunning if I do not send you into battle in your father's suit! To-morrow I must be back in my booth, but to-day I give to you without fee and for the sake of the good-will which I bear to your house. I will ride with you to Tilford, and before night you shall see what Wat can do."

So it came about that there was a busy evening at the old Tilford Manor-house, where the Lady Ermyntrude planned and cut and hung the curtains for the hall, and stocked her cupboards with the good things which Nigel had brought from Guildford.

Meanwhile the squire and the armorer sat with their heads touching and the old suit of mail with its gorget of overlapping plates laid out across their knees. Again and again old Wat shrugged his shoulders, as one who has been asked to do more than can be demanded from mortal man. At last, at a suggestion from the squire, he leaned back in his chair and laughed long and loudly in his bushy beard, while the Lady Ermyntrude glared her black displeasure at such plebeian merriment. Then taking his fine chisel and his hammer from his pouch of tools, the armorer, still chuckling at his own thoughts, began to drive a hole through the center of the steel tunic.

VIII. HOW THE KING HAWKED
ON CROOKSBURY HEATH

THE KING AND his attendants had shaken off the crowd who had
followed them from Guildford along the Pilgrim's Way, and
now, the mounted archers having beaten off the more persistent
of the spectators, they rode at their ease in a long, straggling,
glittering train over the dark undulating plain of heather.

In the van was the king himself, for his hawks were with him
and he had some hope of sport. Edward at that time was a well-
grown, vigorous man in the very prime of his years, a keen
sportsman, an ardent gallant and a chivalrous soldier. He was a
scholar too, speaking Latin, French, German, Spanish, and even
a little English.

So much had long been patent to the world, but only of recent years had he shown other and more formidable characteristics: a restless ambition which coveted his neighbor's throne,
and a wise foresight in matters of commerce, which engaged
him now in transplanting Flemish weavers and sowing the seeds
of what for many years was the staple trade of England. Each of
these varied qualities might have been read upon his face. The
brow, shaded by a crimson cap of maintenance, was broad and
lofty. The large brown eyes were ardent and bold. His chin was
clean-shaven, and the close-cropped dark mustache did not
conceal the strong mouth, firm, proud, and kindly, but capable
of setting tight in merciless ferocity. His complexion was tanned
to copper by a life spent in field sports or in war, and he rode his
magnificent black horse carelessly and easily, as one who has
grown up in the saddle. His own color was black also, for his
active, sinewy figure was set off by close-fitting velvet of that
hue, broken only by a belt of gold, and by a golden border of
open pods of the broom-plant.

With his high and noble bearing, his simple yet rich attire and his splendid mount, he looked every inch a king. The picture of gallant man on gallant horse was completed by the noble Falcon of the Isles which fluttered along some twelve feet above his head, "waiting on," as it was termed, for any quarry which might arise. The second bird of the cast was borne upon the gauntleted wrist of Raoul the chief falconer in the rear.

At the right side of the monarch and a little behind him rode a youth some twenty years of age, tall, slim, and dark, with noble aquiline features and keen penetrating eyes which sparkled with vivacity and affection as he answered the remarks of the king. He was clad in deep crimson diapered with gold, and the trappings of his white palfrey were of a magnificence which proclaimed the rank of its rider. On his face, still free from mustache or beard, there sat a certain gravity and majesty of expression which showed that, young as he was, great affairs had been in his keeping, and that his thoughts and interests were those of the statesman and the warrior. That great day when, little more than a schoolboy, he had led the van of the victorious army which had crushed the power of France at Crécy had left this stamp upon his features; but stern as they were they had not assumed that tinge of fierceness which in after years was to make "The Black Prince" a name of terror on the marches of France. Not yet had the first shadow of fell disease come to poison his nature ere it struck at his life, as he rode that spring day, light and debonair, upon the heath of Crooksbury.

On the left of the king, and so near to him that great intimacy was implied, rode a man about his own age, with the broad face, the projecting jaw, and the flattish nose which are often the outward indications of a pugnacious nature. His complexion was crimson, his large blue eyes somewhat prominent, and his whole appearance full-blooded and choleric. He was short, but massively built, and evidently possessed of immense strength. His voice, however, when he spoke was gentle and lisping, while his manner was quiet and courteous. Unlike the king or the prince, he was clad in light armor and carried a sword by his side and a mace at his saddle-bow, for he was acting as captain of the king's guard, and a dozen other knights in steel followed in the escort.

No hardier soldier could Edward have at his side, if, as was always possible in those lawless times, sudden danger was to threaten, for this was the famous knight of Hainault, now naturalized as an Englishman, Sir Walter Manny, who bore as high a reputation for chivalrous valor and for gallant temerity as Chandos himself.

Behind the knights, who were forbidden to scatter and must always follow the king's person, there was a body of twenty or thirty hobelers or mounted bowmen, together with several squires, unarmed themselves but leading spare horses upon which the heavier part of their knights' equipment was carried. A straggling tail of falconers, harbingers, varlets, body-servants and huntsmen holding hounds in leash completed the long and many-colored train which rose and dipped on the low undulations of the moor.

Many weighty things were on the mind of Edward the King. There was truce for the moment with France, but it was a truce broken by many small deeds of arms, raids, surprises, and ambushes upon either side, and it was certain that it would soon dissolve again into open war. Money must be raised, and it was no light matter to raise it, now that the Commons had once already voted the tenth lamb and the tenth sheaf. Besides, the Black Death had ruined the country, the arable land was all turned to pasture, the laborer, laughing at statutes, would not work under fourpence a day, and all society was chaos. In addition, the Scotch were growling over the border, there was the perennial trouble in half-conquered Ireland, and his allies abroad in Flanders and in Brabant were clamoring for the arrears of their subsidies.

All this was enough to make even a victorious monarch full of care; but now Edward had thrown it all to the winds and was as light-hearted as a boy upon a holiday. No thought had he for the dunning of Florentine bankers or the vexatious conditions of those busybodies at Westminster. He was out with his hawks, and his thoughts and his talk should be of nothing else. The varlets beat the heather and bushes as they passed, and whooped loudly as the birds flew out.

"A magpie! A magpie!" cried the falconer.

"Nay, nay, it is not worthy of your talons, my brown-eyed queen," said the king, looking up at the great bird which flapped from side to side above his head, waiting for the whistle which should give her the signal. "The tercels, falconer—a cast of tercels! Quick, man, quick! Ha! the rascal makes for wood! He puts in! Well flown, brave peregrine! He makes his point. Drive him out to thy comrade. Serve him, varlets! Beat the bushes! He breaks! He breaks! Nay, come away then! You will see master magpie no more."

The bird had indeed, with the cunning of its race, flapped its way through brushwood and bushes to the thicker woods beyond, so that neither the hawk amid the cover nor its partner above nor the clamorous beaters could harm it. The king laughed at the mischance and rode on. Continually birds of various sorts were flushed, and each was pursued by the appropriate hawk, the snipe by the tercel, the partridge by the goshawk, even the lark by the little merlin. But the king soon tired of this petty sport and went slowly on his way, still with the magnificent silent attendant flapping above his head.

"Is she not a noble bird, fair son?" he asked, glancing up as her shadow fell upon him.

"She is indeed, sire. Surely no finer ever came from the isles of the north."

"Perhaps not, and yet I have had a hawk from Barbary as good a footer and a swifter flyer. An Eastern bird in yarak has no peer."

"I had one once from the Holy Land," said de Manny. "It was fierce and keen and swift as the Saracens themselves. They say of old Saladin that in his day his breed of birds, of hounds, and of horses had no equal on earth."

"I trust, dear father, that the day may come when we shall lay our hands on all three," said the prince, looking with shining eyes upon the king. "Is the Holy Land to lie for ever in the grasp of these unbelieving savages, or the Holy Temple to be defiled by their foul presence? Ah! my dear and most sweet lord, give to me a thousand lances with ten thousand bowmen like those I led at Crécy, and I swear to you by God's soul that within a year

I will have done homage to you for the Kingdom of Jerusalem!"

The king laughed as he turned to Walter Manny. "Boys will still be boys," said he.

"The French do not count me such!" cried the young prince, flushing with anger.

"Nay, fair son, there is no one sets you at a higher rate than your father. But you have the nimble mind and quick fancy of youth, turning over from the thing that is half done to a further task beyond. How would we fare in Brittany and Normandy while my young paladin, with his lances and his bowmen, was besieging Ascalon or battering at Jerusalem?"

"Heaven would help in Heaven's work."

"From what I have heard of the past," said the king dryly, "I cannot see that Heaven has counted for much as an ally in these wars of the East. I speak with reverence, and yet it is but sooth to say that Richard of the Lion Heart, or Louis of France, might have found the smallest earthly principality of greater service to him than all the celestial hosts. How say you to that, my lord bishop?"

A stout churchman, who had ridden behind the king on a solid, bay cob, well suited to his weight and dignity, jogged up to the monarch's elbow.

"How say you, sire? I was watching the goshawk on the partridge, and heard you not."

"Had I said that I would add two manors to the See of Chichester, I warrant that you would have heard me, my lord bishop."

"Nay, fair lord, test the matter by saying so," cried the jovial bishop.

The king laughed aloud. "A fair counter, your reverence. By the rood! you broke your lance that passage. But the question I debated was this: How is it that since the Crusades have manifestly been fought in God's quarrel, we Christians have had so little comfort or support in fighting them? After all our efforts and the loss of more men than could be counted, we are at last driven from the country, and even the military orders, which were formed only for that one purpose, can scarce hold a footing in the islands of the Greek sea. There is not one seaport nor one fortress in Palestine over which the flag of the Cross still waves. Where, then, was our ally?"

"Nay, sire, you open a great debate which extends far beyond this question of the Holy Land, though that may, indeed, be chosen as a fair example. It is the question of all sin, of all suffering, of all injustice—why it should pass without the rain of fire and the lightnings of Sinai. The wisdom of God is beyond our understanding."

The king shrugged his shoulders. "This is an easy answer, my lord bishop. You are a prince of the Church. It would fare ill with an earthly prince who could give no better answer to the affairs which concerned his realm."

"There are other considerations which might be urged, most gracious sire. It is true that the Crusades were a holy enterprise which might well expect the immediate blessing of God; but the Crusaders—is it certain that they deserved such a blessing? Have I not heard that their camp was the most dissolute ever seen?"

"Camps are camps all the world over, and you cannot in a moment change a bowman into a saint. But the holy Louis was a crusader after your own heart. Yet his men perished at Mansurah, and he himself at Tunis."

"Bethink you also that this world is but the antechamber of the next," said the prelate. "By suffering and tribulation the soul is cleansed, and the true victor may be he who, by the patient endurance of misfortune, merits the happiness to come."

"If that be the true meaning of the Church's blessing, then I hope that it will be long before it rests upon our banners in France," said the king. "But methinks that when one is out with a brave horse and a good hawk, one might find some other subject than theology. Back to the birds, bishop, or Raoul, the falconer, will come to interrupt thee in thy cathedral."

Straightway the conversation came back to the mystery of the woods and the mystery of the rivers, to the dark-eyed hawks and the yellow-eyed, to hawks of the lure and hawks of the fist. The bishop was as steeped in the lore of falconry as the king, and the others smiled as the two wrangled hard over disputed and technical questions: if an eyas trained in the mews can ever emulate the passage hawk taken wild, or how long the young hawks should be placed at hack, and how long weathered before they are fully reclaimed.

Monarch and prelate were still deep in this learned discussion, the bishop speaking with a freedom and assurance which he would never have dared to use in affairs of Church and state, for in all ages there is no such leveler as sport. Suddenly, however, the prince, whose keen eyes had swept from time to time over the great blue heaven, uttered a peculiar call and reined up his palfrey, pointing at the same time into the air.

"A heron!" he cried. "A heron on passage!"

To gain the full sport of hawking, a heron must not be put up from its feeding-ground, where it is heavy with its meal, and has no time to get its pace on before it is pounced upon by the more active hawk, but it must be aloft, traveling from point to point, probably from the fish-stream to the heronry. Thus, to catch the bird on passage was the prelude of all good sport. The object to which the prince had pointed was but a black dot in the southern sky, but his strained eyes had not deceived him, and both bishop and king agreed that it was indeed a heron, which grew larger every instant as it flew in their direction.

"Whistle him off, sire! Whistle off the gerfalcon!" cried the bishop.

"Nay, nay, he is overfar. She would fly at check."

"Now, sire, now!" cried the prince, as the great bird, with the breeze behind him, came sweeping down the sky.

The king gave the shrill whistle, and the well-trained hawk raked out to the right and to the left to make sure which quarry she was to follow. Then, spying the heron, she shot up in a swift, ascending curve to meet him.

"Well flown, Margot! Good bird!" cried the king, clapping his hands to encourage the hawk, while the falconers broke into the shrill whoop peculiar to the sport.

Going on her curve, the hawk would soon have crossed the path of the heron; but the latter, seeing the danger in his front, and confident in his own great strength of wing and lightness of body, proceeded to mount higher in the air, flying in such small rings that, to the spectators, it almost seemed as if the bird was going perpendicularly upward.

"He takes the air!" cried the king. "But strong as he flies, he cannot outfly Margot. Bishop, I lay you ten gold pieces to one that the heron is mine."

"I cover your wager, sire," said the bishop. "I may not take gold so won, and yet I warrant that there is an altar-cloth somewhere in need of repairs."

"You have good store of altar-cloths, bishop, if all the gold I have seen you win at tables goes to the mending of them," said the king. "Ah! by the rood, rascal, rascal! See how she flies at check!"

The quick eyes of the bishop had perceived a drift of rooks which on their evening flight to the rookery were passing along the very line which divided the hawk from the heron. A rook is a hard temptation for a hawk to resist. In an instant the inconstant bird had forgotten all about the great heron above her, and was circling over the rooks, flying westward with them as she singled out the plumpest for her stoop.

"There is yet time, sire! Shall I cast off her mate?" cried the falconer.

"Or shall I show you, sire, how a peregrine may win where a gerfalcon fails?" said the bishop. "Ten golden pieces to one upon my bird."

"Done with you, bishop!" cried the king, his brow dark with vexation. "By the rood! if you were as learned in the fathers as you are in hawks, you would win to the throne of Saint Peter! Cast off your peregrine, and make your boasting good."

Smaller than the royal gerfalcon, the bishop's bird was none the less a swift and beautiful creature. From her perch upon his wrist she had watched with fierce, keen eyes the birds in the heaven, mantling herself from time to time in her eagerness. Now, when the button was undone, and the leash uncast, the peregrine dashed off with a whir of her sharp-pointed wings, whizzing round in a great ascending circle which mounted swiftly upward, growing ever smaller as she approached that lofty point where, a mere speck in the sky, the heron sought escape from its enemies. Still higher and higher the two birds mounted, while the horsemen, their faces upturned, strained their eyes in their efforts to follow them.

"She rings! She still rings!" cried the bishop. "She is above him! She has gained her pitch."

"Nay, nay, she is far below," said the king.

"By my soul, my lord bishop is right!" cried the prince. "I believe she is above. See! See! She swoops!"

"She binds! She binds!" cried a dozen voices as the two dots blended suddenly into one.

There could be no doubt that they were falling rapidly. Already they grew larger to the eye. Presently the heron disengaged himself and flapped heavily away, the worse for that deadly embrace, while the peregrine, shaking her plumage, ringed once more so as to get high above the quarry and deal it a second and more fatal blow. The bishop smiled, for nothing, as it seemed, could hinder his victory.

"Thy gold pieces shall be well spent, sire," said he. "What is lost to the Church is gained by the loser."

But a most unlooked-for chance deprived the bishop's altar cloth of its costly mending. The king's gerfalcon having struck down a rook, and finding the sport but tame, bethought herself suddenly of that noble heron, which she still perceived fluttering over Crooksbury Heath. How could she have been so weak as to allow these silly, chattering rooks to entice her away from that lordly bird? Even now it was not too late to atone for her mistake. In a great spiral she shot upward until she was over the heron. But what was this? Every fiber of her, from her crest to her deck feathers, quivered with jealousy and rage at the sight of this creature, a mere peregrine, who had dared to come between a royal gerfalcon and her quarry. With one sweep of her great wings she shot up until she was above her rival. The next instant——

"They crab! They crab!" cried the king, with a roar of laughter, following them with his eyes as they hurtled down through the air.

"Mend thy own altar-cloths, bishop. Not a groat shall you have from me this journey. Pull them apart, falconer, lest they do each other an injury. And now, masters, let us on, for the sun sinks toward the west."

The two hawks, which had come to the ground interlocked with clutching talons and ruffled plumes, were torn apart and brought back bleeding and panting to their perches, while the heron, after its perilous adventure, flapped its way heavily onward to settle safely in the heronry of Waverley. The *cortége*, who had scattered in the excitement of the chase, came together again, and the journey was once more resumed.

A horseman who had been riding toward them across the moor now quickened his pace and closed swiftly upon them. As he came nearer, the king and the prince cried out joyously and waved their hands in greeting.

"It is good John Chandos!!" cried the king. "By the rood, John, I have missed your merry songs this week or more! Glad I am to see that you have your citole slung to your back. Whence come you, then?"

"I come from Tilford, sire, in the hope that I should meet your majesty."

"It was well thought of. Come, ride here between the prince and me, and we will believe that we are back in France with our war harness on our backs once more. What is your news, Master John?"

Chandos's quaint face quivered with suppressed amusement and his one eye twinkled like a star.

"Have you had sport, my liege?"

"Poor sport, John. We flew two hawks on the same heron. They crabbed, and the bird got free. But why do you smile so?"

"Because I hope to show you better sport ere you come to Tilford."

"For the hawk? For the hound?"

"A nobler sport than either."

"Is this a riddle, John? What mean you?"

"Nay, to tell all would be to spoil all. I say again that there is rare sport betwixt here and Tilford, and I beg you, dear lord, to mend your pace that we make the most of the daylight."

Thus adjured, the king set spurs to his horse, and the whole cavalcade cantered over the heath in the direction which Chandos showed. Presently as they came over a slope they saw beneath them a winding river with an old high-backed bridge across it. On the farther side was a village-green with a fringe of cottages and one dark manor-house upon the side of the hill.

"This is Tilford," said Chandos. "Yonder is the house of the Lorings."

The king's expectations had been aroused and his face showed his disappointment.

"Is this the sport that you have promised us, Sir John? How can you make good your words?"

"I will make them good, my liege."

"Where, then, is the sport?"

On the high crown of the bridge a rider in armor was seated, lance in hand, upon a great yellow steed. Chandos touched the king's arm and pointed.

"That is the sport," said he.

IX. HOW NIGEL HELD THE BRIDGE AT TILFORD

THE KING LOOKED at the motionless figure, at the little crowd of hushed expectant rustics beyond the bridge, and finally at the face of Chandos, which shone with amusement.

"What is this, John?" he asked.

"You remember Sir Eustace Loring, sire?"

"Indeed I could never forget him nor the manner of his death."

"He was a knight-errant in his day."

"That indeed he was—none better have I known."

"So is his son Nigel, as fierce a young war-hawk as ever yearned to use beak and claws; but held fast in the mews up to now. This is his trial fight. There he stands at the bridge-head, as was the wont in our fathers' time, ready to measure himself against all comers."

Of all Englishmen there was no greater knight-errant than the king himself, and none so steeped in every quaint usage of chivalry; so that the situation was after his own heart.

"He is not yet a knight?"

"No, sire, only a squire."

"Then he must bear himself bravely this day if he is to make good what he has done. Is it fitting that a young untried squire should venture to couch his lance against the best in England?"

"He hath given me his cartel and challenge," said Chandos, drawing a paper from his tunic. "Have I your permission, sire, to issue it?"

"Surely, John, we have no cavalier more versed in the laws of chivalry than yourself. You know this young man, and you are aware how far he is worthy of the high honor which he asks. Let us hear his defiance."

The knights and squires of the escort, most of whom were veterans of the French war, had been gazing with interest and some surprise at the steel-clad figure in front of them. Now at a call from Sir Walter Manny they assembled round the spot where the king and Chandos had halted. Chandos cleared his throat and read from his paper—

"'*A tous seigneurs, chevaliers et escuyers*,' so it is headed, gentlemen. It is a message from the good Squire Nigel Loring of Tilford, son of Sir Eustace Loring, of honorable memory. Squire Loring awaits you in arms, gentlemen, yonder upon the crown of the old bridge. Thus says he: 'For the great desire that I, a most humble and unworthy squire, entertain, that I may come to the knowledge of the noble gentlemen who ride with my royal master, I now wait on the Bridge of the Way in the hope that some of them may condescend to do some small deed of arms upon me, or that I may deliver them from any vow which they may have taken. This I say out of no esteem for myself, but solely that I may witness the noble bearing of these famous cavaliers and admire their skill in the handling of arms. Therefore, with the help of Saint George, I will hold the bridge with sharpened lances against any or all who may deign to present themselves while daylight lasts.'"

"What say you to this, gentlemen?" asked the king, looking round with laughing eyes.

"Truly it is issued in very good form," said the prince. "Neither Claricieux nor Red Dragon nor any herald that ever wore tabard could better it. Did he draw it of his own hand?"

"He hath a grim old grandmother who is one of the ancient breed," said Chandos. "I doubt not that the Dame Ermyntrude hath drawn a challenge or two before now. But hark ye, sire, I would have a word in your ear—and yours too, most noble prince."

Leading them aside, Chandos whispered some explanations, which ended by them all three bursting into a shout of laughter.

"By the rood! no honorable gentleman should be reduced to such straits," said the king. "It behoves me to look to it. But how now, gentlemen? This worthy cavalier still waits his answer."

The soldiers had all been buzzing together; but now Walter Manny turned to the king with the result of their counsel.

"If it please your majesty," said he, "we are of opinion that this squire hath exceeded all bounds in desiring to break a spear with a belted knight ere he has given his proofs. We do him sufficient honor if a squire ride against him, and with your consent I have chosen my own body-squire, John Widdicombe, to clear the path for us across the bridge."

"What you say, Walter, is right and fair," said the king. "Master Chandos, you will tell our champion yonder what hath been arranged. You will advise him also that it is our royal will that this contest be not fought upon the bridge, since it is very clear that it must end in one or both going over into the river, but that he advance to the end of the bridge and fight upon the plain. You will tell him also that a blunted lance is sufficient for such an encounter, but that a hand-stroke or two with sword or mace may well be exchanged, if both riders should keep their saddles. A blast upon Raoul's horn shall be the signal to close."

Such ventures as these where an aspirant for fame would wait for days at a cross-road, a ford, or a bridge, until some worthy antagonist should ride that way, were very common in the old days of adventurous knight errantry, and were still familiar to the minds of all men, because the stories of the romancers and the songs of the trouvères were full of such incidents. Their actual occurrence, however, had become rare. There was the more curiosity, not unmixed with amusement, in the thoughts of the courtiers as they watched Chandos ride down to the bridge and commented upon the somewhat singular figure of the challenger. His build was strange, and so also was his figure, for the limbs were short for so tall a man. His head also was sunk forward as if he were lost in thought or overcome with deep dejection.

"This is surely the Cavalier of the Heavy Heart," said Manny. "What trouble has he, that he should hang his head?"

"Perchance he hath a weak neck," said the king.

"At least he hath no weak voice," the prince remarked, as Nigel's answer to Chandos came to their ears. "By our lady, he booms like a bittern."

As Chandos rode back again to the king, Nigel exchanged the old ash spear which had been his father's for one of the blunted tournament lances which he took from the hands of a stout archer in attendance. He then rode down to the end of the bridge where a hundred-yard stretch of greensward lay in front of him. At the same moment the squire of Sir Walter Manny, who had been hastily armed by his comrades, spurred forward and took up his position.

The king raised his hand; there was a clang from the falconer's horn, and the two riders, with a thrust of their heels and a shake of their bridles, dashed furiously at each other. In the center the green strip of marshy meadowland, with the water squirting from the galloping hoofs, and the two crouching men, gleaming bright in the evening sun; on one side the half circle of motionless horsemen, some in steel, some in velvet, silent and attentive, dogs, hawks, and horses all turned to stone; on the other the old peaked bridge, the blue lazy river, the group of open-mouthed rustics, and the dark old manor-house with one grim face which peered from the upper window.

A good man was John Widdicombe, but he had met a better that day. Before that yellow whirlwind of a horse and that rider who was welded and riveted to his saddle his knees could not hold their grip. Nigel and Pommers were one flying missile, with all their weight and strength and energy centered on the steady end of the lance. Had Widdicombe been struck by a thunderbolt he could not have flown faster or farther from his saddle. Two full somersaults did he make, his plates clanging like cymbals, ere he lay prone upon his back.

For a moment the king looked grave at that prodigious fall. Then smiling once more as Widdicombe staggered to his feet, he clapped his hands loudly in applause. "A fair course and fairly run!" he cried. "The five scarlet roses bear themselves in peace even as I have seen them in war. How now, my good Walter? Have you another squire, or will you clear a path for us yourself?"

Manny's choleric face had turned darker as he observed the mischance of his representative. He beckoned now to a tall knight, whose gaunt and savage face looked out from his open bassinet as an eagle might from a cage of steel.

"Had Widdicombe been struck by a thunderbolt, he could not have flown faster or farther from his saddle." [*page 94*]

"Sir Hubert," said he, "I bear in mind the day when you over-bore the Frenchman at Caen. Will you not be our champion now?"

"When I fought the Frenchman, Walter, it was with naked weapons," said the knight, sternly. "I am a soldier and I love a soldier's work, but I care not for these tilt-yard tricks which were invented for nothing but to tickle the fancies of foolish women."

"Oh, most ungallant speech!" cried the king. "Had my good consort heard you she would have arraigned you to appear at a Court of Love with a jury of virgins to answer for your sins. But I pray you to take a tilting spear, good Sir Hubert!"

"I had as soon take a peacock's feather, my fair lord; but I will do it, if you ask me. Here, page, hand me one of those sticks, and let me see what I can do."

But Sir Hubert de Burgh was not destined to test either his skill or his luck. The great bay horse which he rode was as un-used to this warlike play as was its master, and had none of its master's stoutness of heart; so that when it saw the leveled lance, the gleaming figure and the frenzied yellow horse rushing down upon it, it swerved, turned and galloped furiously down the river-bank. Amid roars of laughter from the rustics on the one side and from the courtiers on the other, Sir Hubert was seen tugging vainly at his bridle, and bounding onward, clearing gorse-bushes and heather clumps, until he was but a shimmer-ing, quivering gleam upon the dark hillside. Nigel, who had pulled Pommers on to his very haunches at the instant that his opponent turned, saluted with his lance and trotted back to the bridge-head, where he awaited his next assailant.

"The ladies would say that a judgment hath fallen upon our good Sir Hubert for his impious words," said the king.

"Let us hope that his charger may be broken in ere they ven-ture to ride out between two armies," remarked the prince. "They might mistake the hardness of his horse's mouth for a softness of the rider's heart. See where he rides, still clearing every bush upon his path."

"By the rood!" said the king, "if the bold Hubert has not in-creased his repute as a jouster he has gained great honor as a horseman. But the bridge is still closed, Walter. How say you now? Is this young squire never to be unhorsed, or is your king himself to lay lance in rest ere the way can be cleared? By the head of Saint Thomas! I am in the very mood to run a course with this gentle youth."

"Nay, nay, sire, too much honor hath already been done him!" said Manny, looking angrily at the motionless horseman. "That this untried boy should be able to say that in one evening he has unhorsed my squire, and seen the back of one of the bravest knights in England, is surely enough to turn his foolish head. Fetch me a spear, Robert! I will see what I can make of him."

The famous knight took the spear when it was brought to him as a master-workman takes a tool. He balanced it, shook it once or twice in the air, ran his eyes down it for a flaw in the wood, and then finally, having made sure of its poise and weight, laid it carefully in rest under his arm. Then, gathering up his bridle so as to have his horse under perfect command, and covering himself with the shield, which was slung round his neck, he rode out to do battle.

Now, Nigel, young and inexperienced, all Nature's aid will not help you against the mixed craft and strength of such a warrior. The day will come when neither Manny nor even Chandos could sweep you from your saddle; but now, even had you some less cumbrous armor, your chance were small. Your downfall is near; but as you see the famous black chevrons on a golden ground, your gallant heart, which never knew fear, is only filled with joy and amazement at the honor done you. Your downfall is near, and yet in your wildest dreams you would never guess how strange your downfall is to be.

Again, with a dull thunder of hoofs, the horses gallop over the soft water-meadow. Again, with a clash of metal, the two riders meet. It is Nigel now, taken clean in the face of his helmet with the blunted spear, who flies backward off his horse and falls clanging on the grass.

But, good heavens! what is this? Manny has thrown up his hands in horror, and the lance has dropped from his nerveless fingers. From all sides, with cries of dismay, with oaths and shouts and ejaculations to the saints, the horsemen ride wildly in. Was ever so dreadful, so sudden, so complete, an end to a gentle passage at arms? Surely their eyes must be at fault? Some wizard's trick has been played upon them to deceive their senses. But no, it was only too clear. There on the greensward lay the trunk of the stricken cavalier, and there, a good dozen yards beyond, lay his helmeted head.

"By the Virgin!" cried Manny, wildly, as he jumped from his horse, "I would give my last gold piece that the work of this evening should be undone! How came it? What does it mean? Hither, my lord bishop, for surely it smacks of witchcraft and the Devil."

With a white face the bishop had sprung down beside the prostrate body, pushing through the knot of horrified knights and squires.

"I fear that the last offices of the Holy Church come too late," said he in a quivering voice. "Most unfortunate young man! How sudden an end! *In medio vitæ,* as the Holy Book has it— one moment in the pride of his youth, the next his head torn from his body. Now God and his saints have mercy upon me and guard me from evil!"

The last prayer was shot out of the bishop with an energy and earnestness unusual in his orisons. It was caused by the sudden outcry of one of the squires who, having lifted the helmet from the ground, cast it down again with a scream of horror.

"It is empty!" he cried. "It weighs as light as a feather."

"'Fore God, it is true!" cried Manny, laying his hand on it. "There is no one in it. With what have I fought, father bishop? Is it of this world or of the next?"

The bishop had clambered on his horse the better to consider the point.

"If the foul fiend is abroad," said he, "my place is over yonder by the king's side. Certes that sulphur-colored horse hath a very devilish look. I could have sworn that I saw both smoke and flame from its nostrils. The beast is fit to bear a suit of armor which rides and fights, and yet hath no man within it."

"Nay, not too fast, father bishop," said one of the knights. "It may be all that you say and yet come from a human workshop. When I made a campaign in South Germany I have seen at Nuremberg a cunning figure, devised by an armorer, which could both ride and wield a sword. If this be such a one——"

"I thank you all for your very gentle courtesy," said a booming voice from the figure upon the ground.

At the words even the valiant Manny sprang into his saddle.

Some rode madly away from the horrid trunk. A few of the boldest lingered.

"Most of all," said the voice, "would I thank the most noble knight, Sir Walter Manny, that he should deign to lay aside his greatness and condescend to do a deed of arms upon so humble a squire."

"'Fore God!" said Manny, "if this be the Devil, then the Devil hath a very courtly tongue. I will have him out of his armor, if he blast me!"

So saying, he sprang once more from his horse and plunging his hand down the slit in the collapsed gorget, he closed it tightly upon a fistful of Nigel's yellow curls. The groan that came forth was enough to convince him that it was indeed a man who lurked within. At the same time his eyes fell upon the hole in the mail corselet which had served the squire as a visor, and he burst into deep-chested mirth. The king, the prince and Chandos, who had watched the scene from a distance, too much amused by it to explain or interfere, rode up weary with laughter, now that all was discovered.

"Let him out!" said the king, with his hand to his side. "I pray you to unlace him and let him out! I have shared in many a spear-running, but never have I been nearer falling from my horse than as I watched this one. I feared the fall had struck him senseless, since he lay so still."

Nigel had indeed lain with all the breath shaken from his body, and as he was unaware that his helmet had been carried off, he had not understood either the alarm or the amusement that he had caused. Now, freed from the great hauberk in which he had been shut like a pea in a pod, he stood blinking in the light, blushing deeply with shame that the shifts to which his poverty had reduced him should be exposed to all these laughing courtiers. It was the king who brought him comfort.

"You have shown that you can use your father's weapons," said he, "and you have proved also that you are the worthy bearer of his name and his arms, for you have within you that spirit for which he was famous. But I wot that neither he nor you would suffer a train of hungry men to starve before your door; so lead on, I pray you, and if the meat be as good as this grace before it, then it will be a feast indeed."

X. HOW THE KING GREETED
HIS SENESCHAL OF CALAIS

IT WOULD HAVE fared ill with the good name of Tilford Manor-house and with the housekeeping of the aged Dame Ermyntrude had the king's whole retinue, with his outer and inner marshal, his justiciar, his chamberlain, and his guard, all gathered under the one roof. But by the foresight and the gentle management of Chandos this calamity was avoided, so that some were quartered at the great Abbey and others passed on to enjoy the hospitality of Sir Roger FitzAlan at Farnham Castle. Only the king himself, the prince, Manny, Chandos, Sir Hubert de Burgh, the bishop, and two or three more remained behind as the guests of the Lorings.

But small as was the party, and humble the surroundings, the king in no way relaxed that love of ceremony, of elaborate form and of brilliant coloring which was one of his characteristics. The sumpter-mules were unpacked, squires ran hither and thither, baths smoked in the bed-chambers, silks and satins were unfolded, gold chains gleamed and clinked, so that when, at last, to the long blast of two court trumpeters, the company took their seats at the board, it was the brightest, fairest scene which those old black rafters had ever spanned.

The great influx of foreign knights who had come in their splendor from all parts of Christendom to take part in the opening of the Round Tower of Windsor six years before, and to try their luck and their skill at the tournament connected with it, had deeply modified the English fashions of dress. The old tunic, over-tunic, and cyclas were too sad and simple for the new fashions, so now strange and brilliant cote-hardies, pourpoints, courtepies, paltocks, hanselines, and many other wondrous garments, party-colored or diapered, with looped, embroidered or escalloped edges, flamed and glittered round the king. He himself, in black velvet and gold, formed a dark rich center to the finery around him. On his right sat the prince, on his left the bishop, while Dame Ermyntrude marshaled the forces of the household outside, alert and watchful, pouring in her dishes and her flagons at the right moment, rallying her tired servants, encouraging the van, hurrying the rear, hastening up her reserves, the tapping of her oak stick heard wherever the pressure was the greatest.

Behind the king, clad in his best, but looking drab and sorry amid the brilliant costumes round him, Nigel himself, regardless of an aching body and a twisted knee, waited upon his royal guests, who threw many a merry jest at him over their shoulders as they still chuckled at the adventure of the bridge.

"By the rood!" said King Edward, leaning back, with a chicken bone held daintily between the courtesy fingers of his left hand, "the play is too good for this country stage. You must to Windsor with me, Nigel, and bring with you this great suit of harness in which you lurk. There you shall hold the lists with your eyes in your midriff, and unless some one cleave you to the waist I see not how any harm can befall you. Never have I seen so small a nut in so great a shell."

The prince, looking back with laughing eyes, saw by Nigel's flushed and embarrassed face that his poverty hung heavily upon him.

"Nay," said he kindly, "such a workman is surely worthy of better tools."

"And it is for his master to see that he has them," added the king. "The court armorer will look to it that the next time your helmet is carried away, Nigel, your head shall be inside it."

Nigel, red to the roots of his flaxen hair, stammered out some words of thanks.

John Chandos, however, had a fresh suggestion, and he cocked a roguish eye as he made it—

"Surely, my liege, your bounty is little needed in this case. It is the ancient law of arms that if two cavaliers start to joust, and one either by maladdress or misadventure fail to meet the shock, then his arms become the property of him who still holds the lists. This being so, methinks, Sir Hubert de Burgh, that the fine hauberk of Milan and the helmet of Bordeaux steel in which you rode to Tilford should remain with our young host as some small remembrance of your visit."

The suggestion raised a general chorus of approval and laughter, in which all joined, save only Sir Hubert himself, who, flushed with anger, fixed his baleful eyes upon Chandos's mischievous and smiling face.

"I said that I did not play that foolish game, and I know nothing of its laws," said he; "but you know well, John, that if you would have a bout with sharpened spear or sword, where two ride to the ground, and only one away from it, you have not far to go to find it."

"Nay, nay, would you ride to the ground? Surely you had best walk, Hubert," said Chandos. "On your feet I know well that I should not see your back as we have seen it to-day. Say what you will, your horse has played you false, and I claim your suit of harness for Nigel Loring."

"Your tongue is overlong, John, and I am weary of its endless clack!" said Sir Hubert, his yellow mustache bristling from a scarlet face. "If you claim my harness, do you yourself come and take it. If there is a moon in the sky you may try this very night when the board is cleared."

"Nay, fair sirs," cried the king, smiling from one to the other, "this matter must be followed no further. Do you fill a bumper of Gascony, John, and you also, Hubert. Now pledge each other, I pray you, as good and loyal comrades who would scorn to fight save in your king's quarrel. We can spare neither of you while there is so much work for brave hearts over the sea. As to this matter of the harness, John Chandos speaks truly where it concerns a joust in the lists, but we hold that such a law is scarce binding in this, which was but a wayside passage and a gentle trial of arms. On the other hand, in the case of your squire, Master Manny, there can be no doubt that his suit is forfeit."

"It is a grievous hearing for him, my liege," said Walter Manny; "for he is a poor man, and hath been at sore pains to fit himself for the wars. Yet what you say shall be done, fair sire. So, if you will come to me in the morning, Squire Loring, John Widdicombe's suit will be handed over to you."

"Then, with the king's leave, I will hand it back to him," said Nigel, troubled and stammering; "for indeed I had rather never ride to the wars than take from a brave man his only suit of plate."

"There spoke your father's spirit!" cried the king. "By the rood! Nigel, I like you full well. Let the matter bide in my hands. But I marvel much that Sir Aymery the Lombard hath not come to us yet from Windsor."

From the moment of his arrival at Tilford, again and again King Edward had asked most eagerly whether Sir Aymery had come, and whether there was any news of him, so that the courtiers glanced at each other in wonder. For Aymery was known to all of them as a famous mercenary of Italy, lately appointed Governor of Calais, and this sudden and urgent summons from the king might well mean some renewal of the war with France, which was the dearest wish of every soldier. Twice the king had stopped his meal and sat with sidelong head, his wine-cup in his hand, listening attentively when some sound like the clatter of hoofs was heard from outside; but the third time there could be no mistake. The tramp and jingle of the horses broke loud upon the ear, and ended in hoarse voices calling out of the darkness, which were answered by the archers posted as sentries without the door.

"Some traveler has indeed arrived, my liege," said Nigel. "What is your royal will?"

"It can be but Aymery," the king answered, "for it was only to him that I left the message that he should follow me hither. Bid him come in, I pray you, and make him very welcome at your board."

Nigel cast open the door, plucking a torch from its bracket as he did so. Half a dozen men-at-arms sat on their horses outside, but one had dismounted, a short, squat, swarthy man with a rat face and quick, restless brown eyes, which peered eagerly past Nigel into the red glare of the well-lit hall.

"I am Sir Aymery of Pavia," he whispered. "For God's sake, tell me! is the king within?"

"He is at table, fair sir, and he bids you to enter."

"One moment, young man, one moment, and a secret word in your ear. Wot you why it is that the king has sent for me?"

Nigel read terror in the dark cunning eyes which glanced in sidelong fashion into his.

"Nay, I know not."

"I would I knew—I would I was sure ere I sought his presence."

"You have but to cross the threshold, fair sir, and doubtless you will learn from the king's own lips."

Sir Aymery seemed to gather himself as one who braces for a spring into ice-cold water. Then he crossed with a quick stride from the darkness into the light. The king stood up and held out his hand with a smile upon his long handsome face, and yet it seemed to the Italian that it was the lips which smiled but not the eyes.

"Welcome!" cried Edward. "Welcome to our worthy and faithful Seneschal of Calais! Come, sit here before me at the board, for I have sent for you that I may hear your news from over the sea, and thank you for the care that you have taken of that which is as dear to me as wife or child. Set a place for Sir Aymery there, and give him food and drink, for he has ridden fast and far in our service to-day."

Throughout the long feast which the skill of the Lady Ermyntrude had arranged, Edward chatted lightly with the Italian as well as with the barons near him. Finally, when the last dish was removed and the gravy-soaked rounds of coarse bread which served as plates had been cast to the dogs, the wine-flagons were passed round, and old Weathercote the minstrel entered timidly with his harp in the hope that he might be allowed to play before the king's majesty. But Edward had other sport afoot.

"I pray you, Nigel, to send out the servants so that we may be alone. I would have two men-at-arms at every door lest we be disturbed in our debate, for it is a matter of privacy. And now, Sir Aymery, these noble lords as well as I, your master, would fain hear from your own lips how all goes forward in France."

The Italian's face was calm, but he looked restlessly from one to another along the line of his listeners.

"So far as I know, my liege, all is quiet on the French marches," said he.

"You have not heard, then, that they have mustered or gathered to a head with the intention of breaking the truce and making some attempt upon our dominions?"

"Nay, sire, I have heard nothing of it."

"You set my mind much at ease, Aymery," said the king; "for if nothing has come to your ears, then surely it cannot be. It was said that the wild Knight de Chargny had come down to St. Omer with his eyes upon my precious jewel and his mailed hands ready to grasp it."

"Nay, sire, let him come. He will find the jewel safe in its strong box, with a goodly guard over it."

"You are the guard over my jewel, Aymery."

"Yes, sire, I am the guard."

"And you are a faithful guard and one whom I can trust, are you not? You would not barter away that which is so dear to me when I have chosen you out of all my army to hold it for me?"

"Nay, sire, what reasons can there be for such questions? They touch my honor very nearly. You know that I would part with Calais only when I parted with my soul."

"Then you know nothing of de Chargny's attempt?"

"Nothing sire."

"Liar and villain!" yelled the king, springing to his feet and dashing his fist upon the table until the glasses rattled again. "Seize him, archers! Seize him this instant! Stand close by either elbow, lest he do himself a mischief! Now, do you dare to tell me to my face, you perjured Lombard, that you know nothing of de Chargny and his plans?"

"As God is my witness, I know nothing of him!"

The man's lips were white, and he spoke in a thin, sighing, reedy voice, his eyes wincing away from the fell gaze of the angry king.

Edward laughed bitterly, and drew a paper from his breast.

"You are the judges in this case, you, my fair son, and you,

Chandos, and you, Manny, and you, Sir Hubert, and you also, my lord bishop. By my sovereign power I make you a court that you may deal justice upon this man, for by God's eyes I will not stir from this room until I have sifted the matter to the bottom. And first I would read you this letter. It is superscribed to Sir Aymery of Pavia, *nommé* Le Lombard, Château de Calais. Is not that your name and style, you rogue?"

"It is my name, sire; but no such letter has come to me."

"Else had your villainy never been disclosed. It is signed 'Isidore de Chargny.' What says my enemy de Chargny to my trusted servant? Listen! 'We could not come with the last moon, for we have not gathered sufficient strength, nor have we been able to collect the twenty thousand crowns which are your price. But with the next turn of the moon in the darkest hour, we will come, and you will be paid your money at the small postern gate with the rowan bush beside it.' Well, rogue, what say you now?"

"It is a forgery!" gasped the Italian.

"I pray you that you will let me see it, sire," said Chandos. "De Chargny was my prisoner, and so many letters passed ere his ransom was paid that his script is well-known to me. Yes, yes, I will swear that this is indeed his. If my salvation were at stake I could swear it."

"If it were indeed written by de Chargny it was to dishonor me," cried Sir Aymery.

"Nay, nay!" said the young prince. "We all know de Chargny and have fought against him. Many faults he has, a boaster and a brawler, but a braver man and one of greater heart and higher of enterprise does not ride beneath the lilies of France. Such a man would never stoop to write a letter for the sake of putting dishonor upon one of knightly rank. I, for one, will never believe it."

A gruff murmur from the others showed that they were of one mind with the prince. The light of the torches from the walls beat upon the line of stern faces at the high table. They had sat like flint, and the Italian shrank from their inexorable eyes. He looked swiftly round, but armed men choked every entrance. The shadow of death had fallen athwart his soul.

"This letter," said the king, "was given by de Chargny to one Dom Beauvais, a priest of St. Omer, to carry into Calais. The said priest, smelling a reward, brought it to one who is my faithful servant, and so it came to me. Straightway I sent for this man that he should come to me. Meanwhile the priest has returned so that de Chargny may think that his message is indeed delivered."

"I know nothing of it," said the Italian doggedly, licking his dry lips.

A dark flush mounted to the king's forehead, and his eyes were gorged with his wrath.

"No more of this, for God's dignity!" he cried. "Had we this fellow at the Tower, a few turns of the rack would tear a confession from his craven soul. But why should we need his word for his own guilt? You have seen, my lords, you have heard? How say you, fair son? Is the man guilty?"

"Sire, he is guilty."

"And you, John? And you, Walter? And you, Hubert? And you, my lord bishop? You are all of one mind, then. He is guilty of the betrayal of his trust. And the punishment?"

"It can only be death," said the prince, and each in turn the others nodded their agreement.

"Aymery of Pavia, you have heard your doom," said Edward, leaning his chin upon his hand and glooming at the cowering Italian. "Step forward, you archer at the door—you with the black beard. Draw your sword! Nay, you white-faced rogue, I would not dishonor this roof-tree by your blood. It is your heels, not your head, that we want. Hack off these golden spurs of knighthood with your sword, archer! 'Twas I who gave them, and I who take them back. Ha! they fly across the hall, and with them every bond betwixt you and the worshipful order whose sign and badge they are! Now lead him out on the heath afar from the house where his carrion can best lie, and hew his scheming head from his body as a warning to all such traitors!"

The Italian, who had slipped from his chair to his knees, uttered a cry of despair, as an archer seized him by either shoulder. Writhing out of their grip, he threw himself upon the floor and clutched at the king's feet.

"Spare me, my most dread lord, spare me, I beseech you! In the name of Christ's passion, I implore your grace and pardon! Bethink you, my good and dear lord, how many years I have served under your banners and how many services I have rendered. Was it not I who found the ford upon the Seine two days before the great battle? Was it not I also who marshaled the attack at the intaking of Calais? I have a wife and four children in Italy, great king, and it was the thought of them which led me to fall from my duty, for this money would have allowed me to leave the wars and to see them once again. Mercy, my liege, mercy, I implore!"

The English are a rough race, but not a cruel one. The king sat with a face of doom; but the others looked askance and fidgeted in their seats.

"Indeed, my fair liege," said Chandos, "I pray you that you will abate somewhat of your anger."

Edward shook his head curtly. "Be silent, John. It shall be as I have said."

"I pray you, my dear and honored liege, not to act with over-much haste in the matter," said Manny. "Bind him and hold him until the morning, for other counsels may prevail."

"Nay, I have spoken. Lead him out!"

But the trembling man clung to the king's knees in such a fashion that the archers could not disengage his convulsive grip.

"Listen to me a moment, I implore you! Give me but one minute to plead with you, and then do what you will."

The king leaned back in his chair. "Speak and have done," said he.

"You must spare me, my noble liege. For your own sake I say that you must spare me, for I can set you in the way of such a knightly adventure as will gladden your heart. Bethink you, sire, that this de Chargny and his comrades know nothing of their plans having gone awry. If I do but send them a message they will surely come to the postern gate. Then, if we have placed our bushment with skill, we shall have such a capture and such a ransom as will fill your coffers. He and his comrades should be worth a good hundred thousand crowns."

Edward spurned the Italian away from him with his foot until he sprawled among the rushes, but even as he lay there like a wounded snake his dark eyes never left the king's face.

"You double traitor! You would sell Calais to de Chargny, and then in turn you would sell de Chargny to me. How dare you suppose that I or any noble knight had such a huckster's soul as to think only of ransoms where honor is to be won? Could I or any true man be so caitiff and so thrall? You have sealed your own doom. Lead him out!"

"One instant, I pray you, my fair and most sweet lord," cried the prince. "Assuage your wrath yet a little while, for this man's rede deserves, perhaps, more thought than we have given it. He has turned your noble soul sick with his talk of ransoms; but look at it, I pray you, from the side of honor, and where could we find such hope of worshipfully winning worship? I pray you to let me put my body in this adventure, for it is one from which, if rightly handled, much advancement is to be gained."

Edward looked with sparkling eyes at the noble youth at his side.

"Never was hound more keen on the track of a stricken hart than you on the hope of honor, fair son," said he. "How do you conceive the matter in your mind?"

"De Chargny and his men will be such as are worth going far to meet, for he will have the pick of France under his banner that night. If we did as this man says and awaited him with the same number of lances, then I cannot think that there is any spot in Christendom where one would rather be than in Calais that night."

"By the rood, fair son, you are right!" cried the king, his face shining with the thought. "Now, which of you, John Chandos or Walter Manny, will take the thing in charge?" He looked mischievously from one to the other, like a master who dangles a bone between two fierce old hounds. All they had to say was in their burning, longing eyes. "Nay, John, you must not take it amiss; but it is Walter's turn, and he shall have it."

"Shall we not all go under your banner, sire, or that of the prince?"

"Nay, it is not fitting that the royal banners of England should be advanced in so small an adventure. And yet, if you have space in your ranks for two more cavaliers, both the prince and I would ride with you that night."

The young man stooped and kissed his father's hand.

"Take this man in your charge, Walter, and do with him as you will. Guard well, lest he betray us once again. Take him from my sight, for his breath poisons the room. And now, Nigel, if that worthy graybeard of thine would fain twang his harp or sing to us—but what in God's name would you have?"

He had turned, to find his young host upon his knee and his flaxen head bent in entreaty.

"What is it, man? What do you crave?"

"A boon, fair liege!"

"Well, well, am I to have no peace to-night, with a traitor kneeling to me in front, and a true man on his knees behind? Out with it, Nigel. What would you have?"

"To come with you to Calais."

"By the rood! your request is fair enough, seeing that our plot is hatched beneath your very roof. How say you, Walter? Will you take him, armor and all?" asked King Edward.

"Say rather will you take me?" said Chandos. "We are two rivals in honor, Walter, but I am very sure that you would not hold me back."

"Nay, John, I will be proud to have the best lance in Christendom beneath my banner."

"And I to follow so knightly a leader. But Nigel Loring is my squire, and so he comes with us also."

"Then that is settled," said the king, "and now there is no need for hurry, since there can be no move until the moon has changed. So I pray you to pass the flagon once again, and to drink with me to the good knights of France. May they be of great heart and high of enterprise when we all meet once more within the castle wall of Calais!"

XI. IN THE HALL OF THE KNIGHT OF DUPPLIN

THE KING HAD come and had gone. Tilford Manor-house stood once more dark and silent, but joy and contentment reigned within its walls. In one night every trouble had fallen away like some dark curtain which had shut out the sun. A princely sum of money had come from the king's treasurer, given in such fashion that there could be no refusal. With a bag of gold pieces at his saddle-bow, Nigel rode once more into Guildford, and not a beggar on the way who had not cause to bless his name.

There he had gone first to the goldsmith and had bought back cup and salver and bracelet, mourning with the merchant over the evil chance that gold and gold-work had for certain reasons which only those in the trade could fully understand gone up in value during the last week, so that already fifty gold pieces had to be paid more than the price which Nigel had received. In vain the faithful Aylward fretted and fumed and muttered a prayer that the day would come when he might feather a shaft in the merchant's portly paunch. The money had to be paid.

Thence Nigel hurried to Wat the armorer's, and there he bought that very suit for which he had yearned so short a time before. Then and there he tried it on in the booth, Wat and his boy walking round him with spanner and wrench, fixing bolts and twisting rivets.

"How is that, my fair sir?" cried the armorer as he drew the bassinet over the head and fastened it to the camail which extended to the shoulders. "I swear by Tubal Cain that it fits you as the shell fits the crab! A finer suit never came from Italy or Spain."

Nigel stood in front of a burnished shield which served as a mirror, and he turned this way and that, preening himself like a little shining bird. His smooth breastplate, his wondrous joints with their deft protection by the disks at knee and elbow and shoulder, the beautifully flexible gauntlets and sollerets, the shirt of mail and the close-fitting greave-plates were all things of joy and of beauty in his eyes. He sprang about the shop to show his lightness, and then, running out, he placed his hand on the pommel and vaulted into Pommers' saddle, while Wat and his boy applauded in the doorway.

Then, springing off and running into the shop again he clanked down upon his knees before the image of the Virgin upon the smithy wall. There from his heart he prayed that no shadow or stain should come upon his soul or his honor while these arms incased his body, and that he might be strengthened to use them for noble and godly ends. A strange turn this to a religion of peace, and yet for many a century the sword and the faith had upheld each other, and in a darkened world the best ideal of the soldier had turned in some dim groping fashion toward the light. *"Benedictus dominus deus meus qui docet manus meas ad Praelium et digitos meos ad bellum!"* There spoke the soul of the knightly soldier.

So the armor was trussed upon the armorer's mule and went back with them to Tilford, where Nigel put it on once more for the pleasure of the Lady Ermyntrude, who clapped her skinny hands and shed tears of mingled pain and joy—pain that she should lose him, joy that he should go so bravely to the wars. As to her own future, it had been made easy for her, since it was arranged that a steward should look to the Tilford estate while she had at her disposal a suite of rooms in royal Windsor, where, with other venerable dames of her own age and standing, she could spend the twilight of her days discussing long-forgotten scandals and whispering sad things about the grandfathers and grandmothers of the young courtiers all around them. There Nigel might leave her with an easy mind when he turned his face to France.

But there was one more visit to be paid, and one more farewell to be spoken ere Nigel could leave the moorlands where he had dwelt so long. That evening he donned his brightest tunic, dark purple velvet of Genoa, with trimming of miniver, his hat with the snow-white feather curling round the front, and his belt of embossed silver round his loins. Mounted on lordly Pommers, with his hawk upon wrist and his sword by his side, never did fairer young gallant or one more modest in mind set forth upon such an errand. It was but the old Knight of Dupplin to whom he would say farewell; but the Knight of Dupplin had two daughters, Edith and Mary, and Edith was the fairest maid in all the heather-country.

Sir John Buttesthorn, the Knight of Dupplin, was so called because he had been present at that strange battle, some eighteen years before, when the full power of Scotland had been for a moment beaten to the ground by a handful of adventurers and mercenaries, marching under the banner of no nation, but fighting in their own private quarrel. Their exploit fills no pages of history, for it is to the interest of no nation to record it, and yet the rumor and fame of the great fight bulked large in those times, for it was on that day when the flower of Scotland was left dead upon the field, that the world first understood that a new force had arisen in war, and that the English archer, with his robust courage and his skill with the weapon which he had wielded from his boyhood, was a power with which even the mailed chivalry of Europe had seriously to reckon.

Sir John after his return from Scotland had become the king's own head huntsman, famous through all England for his knowledge of venery, until at last, getting overheavy for his horses, he had settled in modest comfort into the old house of Cosford upon the eastern slope of the Hindhead hill. Here, as his face grew redder, and his beard more white, he spent the evening of his days amid hawks and hounds, a flagon of spiced wine ever at his elbow, and his swollen foot perched upon a stool before him. There it was that many an old comrade broke his journey as he passed down the rude road which led from London to Portsmouth, and thither also came the young gallants of the country to hear the stout knight's tales of old wars, or to learn from him that lore of the forest and the chase which none could teach so well as he.

But sooth to say, whatever the old knight might think, it was

not merely his old tales and older wine which drew the young
men to Cosford, but rather the fair face of his younger daughter,
or the strong soul and wise counsel of the elder. Never had two
more different branches sprung from the same trunk. Both
were tall and of a queenly graceful figure. But there all resem-
blance began and ended.

Edith was yellow as the ripe corn, blue-eyed, winning, mischievous, with a chattering tongue, a merry laugh, and a smile
which a dozen of young gallants, Nigel of Tilford at their head,
could share equally among them. Like a young kitten she played
with all the things that she found in life, and some there were
who thought that already the claws could be felt amid the pat-
ting of her velvet touch.

Mary was dark as night, grave-featured, plain-visaged, with
steady brown eyes looking bravely at the world from under a
strong black arch of brows. None could call her beautiful, and
when her fair sister cast her arm round her and placed her
cheek against hers, as was her wont when company was there,
the fairness of the one and the plainness of the other leaped vis-
ibly to the eyes of all, each the clearer for that hard contrast.
And yet, here and there, there was one who, looking at her
strange, strong face, and at the passing gleams far down in her
dark eyes, felt that this silent woman, with her proud bearing
and her queenly grace, had in her something of strength, of reserve, and of mystery which was more to them than all the
dainty glitter of her sister.

Such were the ladies of Cosford toward whom Nigel Loring
rode that night with doublet of Genoan velvet and the new
white feather in his cap.

He had ridden over Thursley Ridge past that old stone where
in days gone by at the place of Thor the wild Saxons worshiped
their war-god. Nigel looked at it with a wary eye and spurred
Pommers onward as he passed it, for still it was said that wild
fires danced round it on the moonless nights, and they who had
ears for such things could hear the scream and sob of those
whose lives had been ripped from them that the fiend might be
honored. Thor's Stone, Thor's Jumps, Thor's Punch-bowl—the
whole countryside was one grim monument to the God of

Battles, though the pious monks had changed his uncouth name for that of the Devil his father, so that it was the Devil's Jumps and the Devil's Punch-bowl of which they spoke. Nigel glanced back at the old gray boulder, and he felt for an instant a shudder pass through his stout heart. Was it the chill of the evening air, or was it that some inner voice had whispered to him of the day when he also might lie bound on such a rock and have such a bloodstained pagan crew howling around him?

An instant later the rock and his vague fear and all things else had passed from his mind, for there, down the yellow sandy path, the setting sun gleaming on her golden hair, her lithe figure bending and swaying with every heave of the cantering horse, was none other than the same fair Edith, whose face had come so often between him and his sleep. His blood rushed hot to his face at the sight, for fearless of all else, his spirit was attracted and yet daunted by the delicate mystery of woman. To his pure and knightly soul not Edith alone, but every woman, sat high and aloof, enthroned and exalted, with a thousand mystic excellencies and virtues which raised her far above the rude world of man. There was joy in contact with them; and yet there was fear, fear lest his own unworthiness, his untrained tongue or rougher ways should in some way break rudely upon this delicate and tender thing. Such was his thought as the white horse cantered toward him; but a moment later his vague doubts were set at rest by the frank voice of the young girl, who waved her whip in merry greeting.

"Hail and well met, Nigel!" she cried. "Whither away this evening? Sure I am that it is not to see your friends of Cosford, for when did you ever don so brave a doublet for us? Come, Nigel, her name, that I may hate her for ever!"

"Nay, Edith," said the young squire, laughing back at the laughing girl. "I was indeed coming to Cosford."

"Then we shall ride back together, for I will go no farther. How think you that I am looking?"

Nigel's answer was in his eyes as he glanced at the fair flushed face, the golden hair, the sparkling eyes, and the daintily graceful figure set off in a scarlet-and-black riding-dress.

"You are as fair as ever, Edith."

"Oh cold of speech! Surely you were bred for the cloisters and not for a lady's bower, Nigel. Had I asked such a question from young Sir George Brocas or the Squire of Fernhurst, he would have raved from here to Cosford. They are both more to my taste than you are, Nigel."

"It is the worse for me, Edith," said Nigel ruefully.

"Nay, but you must not lose heart."

"Have I not already lost it?" said he.

"That is better," she cried, laughing. "You can be quick enough when you choose, Master Malapert. But you are more fit to speak of high and weary matters with my sister Mary. She will have none of the prattle and courtesy of Sir George, and yet I love them well. But tell me, Nigel, why do you come to Cosford to-night?"

"To bid you farewell."

"Me alone?"

"Nay, Edith, you and your sister Mary and the good knight, your father."

"Sir George would have said that he had come for me alone. Indeed you are but a poor courtier beside him. But is it true, Nigel, that you go to France?"

"Yes, Edith."

"It was so rumored after the king had been to Tilford. The story goes that the king goes to France and you in his train. Is that true?"

"Yes, Edith, it is true."

"Tell me, then, to what part you go, and when?"

"That, alas! I may not say."

"Oh, in sooth!" She tossed her fair head and rode onward in silence, with compressed lips and angry eyes.

Nigel glanced at her in surprise and dismay. "Surely, Edith," said he, at last, "you have overmuch regard for my honor that you should wish me to break the word that I have given?"

"Your honor belongs to you, and my likings belong to me," said she. "You hold fast to the one, and I will do the same by the other."

They rode in silence through Thursley village. Then a thought came to her mind, and in an instant her anger was forgotten and she was hot on a new scent.

"What would you do if I were injured, Nigel? I have heard my father say that, small as you are, there is no man in these parts could stand against you. Would you be my champion if I suffered wrong?"

"Surely I or any man of gentle blood would be the champion of any woman who had suffered wrong."

"You or any and I or any—what sort of speech is that? Is it a compliment, think you, to be mixed with a drove in that fashion? My question was of you and me. If I were wronged would you be my man?"

"Try me and see, Edith!"

"Then I will do so, Nigel. Either Sir George Brocas or the Squire of Fernhurst would gladly do what I ask, and yet I am of a mind, Nigel, to turn to you."

"I pray you to tell me what it is."

"You know Paul de la Fosse of Shalford?"

"You mean the small man with the twisted back?"

"He is no smaller than yourself, Nigel, and as to his back there are many folk that I know who would be glad to have his face."

"Nay, I am no judge of that, and I spoke out of no discourtesy. What of the man?"

"He has flouted me, Nigel, and I would have revenge."

"What—on that poor twisted creature?"

"I tell you that he has flouted me!"

"But how?"

"I should have thought that a true cavalier would have flown to my aid, withouten all these questions. But I will tell you, since I needs must. Know then that he was one of those who came around me and professed to be my own. Then, merely because he thought that there were others who were as dear to me as himself he left me, and now he pays court to Maude Twynham, the little freckle-faced hussy in his village."

"But how has this hurt you, since he was no man of thine?"

"He was one of my men, was he not? And he has made game of me to his wench. He has told her things about me. He has made me foolish in her eyes. Yes, yes, I can read it in her saffron face and in her watery gaze when we meet at the church door on Sundays. She smiles—yes, smiles at me! Nigel, go to him! Do not slay him, nor even wound him, but lay his face open with thy riding-whip, and then come back to me and tell me how I can serve you."

Nigel's face was haggard with the strife within, for desire ran hot in every vein, and yet reason shrank with horror.

"By Saint Paul! Edith," he cried, "I see no honor nor advancement of any sort in this thing which you have asked me to do. Is it for me to strike one who is no better than a cripple? For my manhood I could not do such a deed, and I pray you, dear lady, that you will set me some other task."

Her eyes flashed at him in contempt. "And you are a man-at-arms!" she cried, laughing in bitter scorn. "You are afraid of a little man who can scarce walk. Yes, yes, say what you will, I shall ever believe that you have heard of his skill at fence, and of his great spirit, and that your heart has failed you! You are right, Nigel. He is indeed a perilous man. Had you done what I asked he would have slain you, and so you have shown your wisdom."

Nigel flushed and winced under the words, but he said no more, for his mind was fighting hard within him, striving to keep that high image of woman which seemed for a moment to totter on the edge of a fall. Together in silence, side by side, the little man and the stately woman, the yellow charger and the white jennet, passed up the sandy winding track with the gorse and the bracken head-high on either side. Soon a path branched off through a gateway marked with the boar-heads of the Buttesthorns, and there was the low widespread house heavily timbered, loud with the barking of dogs. The ruddy knight limped forth with outstretched hand and roaring voice—

"What how, Nigel! Good welcome and all hail! I had thought that you had given over poor friends like us, now that the king had made so much of you. The horses, varlets, or my crutch will be across you! Hush, Lydiard! Down, Pelamon! I can scarce hear my voice for your yelping. Mary, a cup of wine for young Squire Loring!"

She stood framed in the doorway, tall, mystic, silent, with

strange, wistful face and deep soul shining in her dark questioning eyes. Nigel kissed the hand that she held out, and all his faith
in woman and his reverence came back to him as he looked at
her. Her sister had slipped behind her, and her, fair elfish face
smiled her forgiveness of Nigel over Mary's shoulder.

The Knight of Dupplin leaned his weight upon the young
man's arm and limped his way across the great high-roofed hall
to his capacious oaken chair.

"Come, come, the stool, Edith!" he cried. "As God is my help,
that girl's mind swarms with gallants as a granary with rats. Well,
Nigel, I hear strange tales of your spear-running at Tilford and
of the visit of the king. How seemed he? And my old friend
Chandos—many happy hours in the woodlands have we had
together—and Manny too, he was ever a bold and a hard
rider—what news of them all?"

Nigel told the old knight all that had occurred, saying little of
his own success and much of his own failure, yet the eyes of the
dark woman burned the brighter as she sat at her tapestry and
listened.

Sir John followed the story with a running fire of oaths,
prayers, thumps with his great fist, and flourishes of his crutch.

"Well, well, lad, you could scarce expect to hold your saddle
against Manny, and you have carried yourself well. We are
proud of you, Nigel, for you are our own man, reared in the
heather-country. But indeed I take shame that you are not more
skilled in the mystery of the woods, seeing that I have had the
teaching of you, and that no one in broad England is my master
at the craft. I pray you to fill your cup again whilst I make use of
the little time that is left to us."

And straightway the old knight began a long and weary lecture upon the times of grace and when each beast and bird was
seasonable, with many anecdotes, illustrations, warnings and
exceptions, drawn from his own great experience. He spoke also
of the several ranks and grades of the chase: how the hare, hart,
and boar must ever take precedence over the buck, the doe, the
fox, the marten and the roe, even as a knight banneret does over
a knight, while these in turn are of a higher class to the badger,
the wildcat, or the otter, who are but the common populace of

the world of beasts. Of blood-stains also he spoke—how the skilled hunter may see at a glance if blood be dark and frothy, which means a mortal hurt, or thin and clear, which means that the arrow has struck a bone.

"By such signs," said he, "you will surely know whether to lay on the hounds and cast down the blinks which hinder the stricken deer in its flight. But above all I pray you, Nigel, to have a care in the use of the terms of the craft, lest you should make some blunder at table, so that those who are wiser may have the laugh of you, and we who love you may be shamed."

"Nay, Sir John," said Nigel. "I think that after your teaching I can hold my place with the others."

The old knight shook his white head doubtfully. "There is so much to be learned that there is no one who can be said to know all," said he. "For example, Nigel, it is sooth that for every collection of beasts of the forest, and for every gathering of birds of the air, there is their own private name so that none may be confused with another."

"I know it, fair sir."

"You know it, Nigel, but you do not know each separate name, else are you a wiser man than I had thought you. In truth none can say that they know all, though I have myself pricked off eighty and six for a wager at court, and it is said that the chief huntsman of the Duke of Burgundy has counted over a hundred—but it is in my mind that he may have found them as he went, for there was none to say him nay. Answer me now, lad, how would you say if you saw ten badgers together in the forest?"

"A cete of badgers, fair sir."

"Good, Nigel—good, by my faith! And if you walk in Woolmer Forest and see a swarm of foxes, how would you call it?"

"A skulk of foxes."

"And if they be lions?"

"Nay, fair sir, I am not like to meet several lions in Woolmer Forest."

"Aye, lad, but there are other forests besides Woolmer, and other lands besides England, and who can tell how far afield such a knight errant as Nigel of Tilford may go, when he sees

worship to be won? We will say that you were in the deserts of
Nubia, and that afterward at the court of the great Sultan you
wished to say that you had seen several lions, which is the first
beast of the chase, being the king of all animals. How then
would you say it?"

Nigel scratched his head. "Surely, fair sir, I would be content
to say that I had seen a number of lions, if indeed I could say
aught after so wondrous an adventure."

"Nay, Nigel, a huntsman would have said that he had seen a
pride of lions, and so proved that he knew the language of the
chase. Now, had it been boars instead of lions?"

"One says a singular of boars."

"And if they be swine?"

"Surely it is a herd of swine."

"Nay, nay, lad, it is indeed sad to see how little you know.
Your hands, Nigel, were always better than your head. No man
of gentle birth would speak of a herd of swine; that is the peasant speech. If you drive them it is a herd. If you hunt them it is
other. What call you them, then, Edith?"

"Nay, I know not," said the girl, listlessly. A crumpled note
brought in by a varlet was clinched in her right hand and her
blue eyes looked afar into the deep shadows of the roof.

"But you can tell us, Mary?"

"Surely, sweet sir, one talks of a sounder of swine."

The old knight laughed exultantly. "Here is a pupil who never
brings me shame!" he cried. "Be it lore of chivalry or heraldry or
woodcraft or what you will, I can always turn to Mary. Many a
man can she put to the blush."

"Myself among them," said Nigel.

"Ah, lad, you are a Solomon to some of them. Hark ye! only
last week that jack-fool, the young Lord of Brocas, was here
talking of having seen a covey of pheasants in the wood. One
such speech would have been the ruin of a young squire at the
court. How would you have said it, Nigel?"

"Surely, fair sir, it should be a nye of pheasants."

"Good, Nigel—a nye of pheasants, even as it is a gaggle of
geese or a badling of ducks, a fall of woodcock or a wisp of snipe.
But a covey of pheasants! What sort of talk is that? I made him

sit even where you are sitting, Nigel, and I saw the bottom of two pots of Rhenish ere I let him up. Even then I fear that he had no great profit from his lesson, for he was casting his foolish eyes at Edith when he should have been turning his ears to her father. But where is the wench?"

"She hath gone forth, father."

"She ever doth go forth when there is a chance of learning aught that is useful indoors. But supper will soon be ready, and there is a boar's ham fresh from the forest with which I would ask your help, Nigel, and a side of venison from the king's own chase. The tinemen and verderers have not forgotten me yet, and my larder is ever full. Blow three moots on the horn, Mary, that the varlets may set the table, for the growing shadow and my loosening belt warn me that it is time."

XII. HOW NIGEL FOUGHT
THE TWISTED MAN OF SHALFORD

IN THE DAYS of which you read all classes, save perhaps the very poor, fared better in meat and in drink than they have ever done since. The country was covered with woodlands—there were seventy separate forests in England alone, some of them covering half a shire. Within these forests the great beasts of the chase were strictly preserved, but the smaller game, the hares, the rabbits, the birds, which swarmed round the coverts, found their way readily into the poor man's pot. Ale was very cheap, and cheaper still was the mead which every peasant could make for himself out of the wild honey in the tree trunks. There were many tea-like drinks also, which were brewed by the poor at no expense: mallow tea, tansy tea, and others the secret of which has passed.

Amid the richer classes there was rude profusion, great joints ever on the sideboard, huge pies, beasts of the field and beasts of the chase, with ale and rough French or Rhenish wines to wash them down. But the very rich had attained to a high pitch of luxury in their food, and cookery was a science in which the ornamentation of the dish was almost as important as the dressing of the food. It was gilded, it was silvered, it was painted, it was surrounded with flame. From the boar and the peacock down to such strange food as the porpoise and the hedgehog, every dish had its own setting and its own sauce, very strange and very complex, with flavorings of dates, currants, cloves, vinegar, sugar and honey, of cinnamon, ground ginger, sandalwood, saffron, brawn and pines. It was the Norman tradition to eat in moderation, but to have a great profusion of the best and of the most delicate from which to choose. From them came this complex cookery, so unlike the rude and often gluttonous simplicity of the old Teutonic stock.

Sir John Buttesthorn was of that middle class who fared in the old fashion, and his great oak supper-table groaned beneath the generous pasties, the mighty joints and the great flagons. Below were the household, above on a raised daïs the family table, with places ever ready for those frequent guests who dropped in from the high road outside. Such a one had just come, an old priest, journeying from the Abbey of Chertsey to the Priory of Saint John at Midhurst. He passed often that way, and never without breaking his journey at the hospitable board of Cosford.

"Welcome again, good Father Athanasius!" cried the burly knight. "Come sit here on my right and give me the news of the countryside, for there is never a scandal but the priests are the first to know it."

The priest, a kindly, quiet man, glanced at an empty place upon the farther side of his host.

"Mistress Edith?" said he.

"Aye, aye, where is the hussy?" cried her father, impatiently. "Mary, I beg you to have the horn blown again, that she may know that the supper is on the table. What can the little owlet do abroad at this hour of the night?"

There was trouble in the priest's gentle eyes as he touched the knight upon the sleeve. "I have seen Mistress Edith within this hour," said he. "I fear that she will hear no horn that you may blow, for she must be at Milford ere now."

"At Milford? What does she there?"

"I pray you, good Sir John, to abate your voice somewhat, for indeed this matter is for our private discourse, since it touches the honor of a lady."

"Her honor?" Sir John's ruddy face had turned redder still, as he stared at the troubled features of the priest. "Her honor, say you—the honor of my daughter? Make good those words, or never set your foot over the threshold of Cosford again!"

"I trust that I have done no wrong, Sir John, but indeed I must say what I have seen, else would I be a false friend and an unworthy priest."

"Haste man, haste! What in the Devil's name have you seen?"

"Know you a little man, partly misshapen, named Paul de la Fosse?"

"I know him well. He is a man of noble family and coat-armor, being the younger brother of Sir Eustace de la Fosse of Shalford. Time was when I had thought that I might call him son, for there was never a day that he did not pass with my girls, but I fear that his crooked back sped him ill in his wooing."

"Alas, Sir John! It is his mind that is more crooked than his back. He is a perilous man with women, for the Devil hath given him such a tongue and such an eye that he charms them even as the basilisk. Marriage may be in their mind, but never in his, so that I could count a dozen and more whom he has led to their undoing. It is his pride and his boast over the whole country-side."

"Well, well, and what is this to me or mine?"

"Even now, Sir John, as I rode my mule up the road I met this man speeding toward his home. A woman rode by his side, and though her face was hooded I heard her laugh as she passed me. That laugh I have heard before, and it was under this very roof, from the lips of Mistress Edith."

The knight's knife dropped from his hand. But the debate had been such that neither Mary nor Nigel could fail to have heard it. Mid the rough laughter and clatter of voices from below the little group at the high table had a privacy of their own.

"Fear not, father," said the girl—"indeed, the good Father Athanasius hath fallen into error, and Edith will be with us anon. I have heard her speak of this man many times of late, and always with bitter words."

"It is true, sir," cried Nigel, eagerly. "It was only this very evening as we rode over Thursley Moor that Mistress Edith told me that she counted him not a fly, and that she would be glad if he were beaten for his evil deeds."

But the wise priest shook his silvery locks. "Nay, there is ever danger when a woman speaks like that. Hot hate is twin brother to hot love. Why should she speak so if there were not some bond between them?"

"And yet," said Nigel, "what can have changed her thoughts in three short hours? She was here in the hall with us since I came. By Saint Paul, I will not believe it!"

Mary's face darkened. "I call to mind," said she, "that a note was brought her by Hannekin the stable varlet when you were talking to us, fair sir, of the terms of the chase. She read it and went forth."

Sir John sprang to his feet, but sank into his chair again with a groan.

"Would that I were dead," he cried, "ere I saw dishonor come upon my house, and am so tied with this accursed foot that I can neither examine if it be true, nor yet avenge it! If my son Oliver were here, then all would be well. Send me this stable varlet that I may question him."

"I pray you, fair and honored sir," said Nigel, "that you will take me for your son this night, that I may handle this matter in the way which seems best. On jeopardy of my honor I will do all that a man may."

"Nigel, I thank you. There is no man in Christendom to whom I would sooner turn."

"But I would learn your mind in one matter, fair sir. This man, Paul de la Fosse, owns broad acres, as I understand, and comes of noble blood. There is no reason, if things be as we fear, that he should not marry your daughter?"

"Nay, she could not wish for better."

"It is well. And first I would question this Hannekin; but it shall be done in such a fashion that none shall know, for indeed it is not a matter for the gossip of servants. But if you will show me the man, Mistress Mary, I will take him out to tend my own horse, and so I shall learn all that he has to tell."

Nigel was absent for some time, and when he returned the shadow upon his face brought little hope to the anxious hearts at the high table.

"I have locked him in the stable-loft, lest he talk too much," said he, "for my questions must have shown him whence the wind blew. It was indeed from this man that the note came, and he had brought with him a spare horse for the lady."

The old knight groaned, and his face sank upon his hands.

"Nay, father, they watch you!" whispered Mary. "For the honor of our house let us keep a bold face to all." Then, raising her young clear voice, so that it sounded through the room: "If you ride eastward, Nigel, I would fain go with you, that my sister may not come back alone."

"We will ride together, Mary," said Nigel, rising; then, in a lower voice: "But we cannot go alone, and if we take a servant all is known. I pray you to stay at home and leave the matter with me."

"Nay, Nigel, she may sorely need a woman's aid, and what woman should it be save her own sister? I can take my tire-woman with us."

"Nay, I shall ride with you myself if your impatience can keep within the powers of my mule," said the old priest.

"But it is not your road, father?"

"The only road of a true priest is that which leads to the good of others. Come, my children, and we will go together."

And so it was that stout Sir John Buttesthorn, the aged Knight of Dupplin, was left alone at his own high table, pretending to eat, pretending to drink, fidgeting in his seat, trying hard to seem unconcerned with his mind and body in a fever, while below him his varlets and handmaids laughed and jested, clattering their cups and clearing their trenchers, all unconscious of the dark shadow which threw its gloom over the lonely man upon the daïs above.

Meantime the Lady Mary upon the white jennet which her sister had ridden on the same evening, Nigel on his war-horse, and the priest on the mule, clattered down the rude winding road which led to London. The country on either side was a wilderness of heather moors and of morasses from which came the strange crying of night-fowl. A half-moon shone in the sky between the rifts of hurrying clouds. The lady rode in silence, absorbed in the thought of the task before them, the danger and the shame.

Nigel chatted in a low tone with the priest. From him he learned more of the evil name of this man whom they followed. His house at Shalford was a den of profligacy and vice. No woman could cross that threshold and depart unstained. In some strange fashion, inexplicable and yet common, the man, with all his evil soul and his twisted body, had yet some strange fascination for women, some mastery over them which compelled them to his will. Again and again he had brought ruin to a household, again and again his adroit tongue and his cunning wit had in some fashion saved him from the punishment of his deeds. His family was great in the county, and his kinsmen held favor with the king, so that his neighbors feared to push things too far against him. Such was the man, malignant and ravenous, who had stooped like some foul night-hawk, and borne away to his evil nest the golden beauty of Cosford. Nigel said little as he listened, but he raised his hunting-dagger to his tightened lips, and thrice he kissed the cross of its handle.

They had passed over the moors, and through the village of Milford and the little township of Godalming, until their path turned southward over the Pease marsh, and crossed the meadows of Shalford. There on the dark hillside glowed the red points of light which marked the windows of the house which they sought. A somber arched avenue of oak trees led up to it, and then they were in the moon-silvered clearing in front.

From the shadow of the arched door there sprang two rough serving-men, bearded and gruff, great cudgels in their hands, to ask them who they were and what their errand. The Lady Mary had slipped from her horse, and was advancing to the door, but they rudely barred her way.

"Nay, nay, our master needs no more!" cried one, with a hoarse laugh. "Stand back, mistress, whoever you be! The house is shut, and our lord sees no guests to-night."

"Fellow," said Nigel, speaking low and clear, "stand back from us! Our errand is with your master."

"Bethink you, my children," cried the old priest, "would it not be best, perchance, that I go in to him, and see whether the voice of the Church may not soften this hard heart? I fear bloodshed if you enter."

"Nay, father, I pray you to stay here for the nonce," said Nigel. "And you, Mary, do you bide with the good priest, for we know not what may be within."

Again he turned to the door, and again the two men barred his passage.

"Stand back, I say, back for your lives!" said Nigel. "By Saint Paul! I should think it shame to soil my sword with such as you, but my soul is set, and no man shall bar my path this night."

The men shrank from the deadly menace of that gentle voice.

"Hold!" said one of them, peering through the darkness, "is it not Squire Loring of Tilford?"

"That is indeed my name."

"Had you spoken it, I for one would not have stopped your way. Put down your staff, Wat, for this is no stranger, but the Squire of Tilford."

"As well for him," grumbled the other, lowering his cudgel with an inward prayer of thanksgiving. "Had it been otherwise I should have had blood upon my soul to-night. But our master said nothing of neighbors when he ordered us to hold the door. I will enter and ask him what is his will."

But already Nigel was past them, and had pushed open the outer door. Swift as he was, the Lady Mary was at his very heels, and the two passed together into the hall beyond.

It was a great room, draped and curtained with black shadows, with one vivid circle of light in the center, where two oil lamps shone upon a small table. A meal was laid upon the table, but only two were seated at it, and there were no servants in the room. At the near end was Edith, her golden hair loose and streaming down over the scarlet and black of her riding-dress.

At the farther end the light beat strongly upon the harsh face and the high-drawn misshapen shoulders of the lord of the house. A tangle of black hair surmounted a high rounded forehead, the forehead of a thinker, with two deep-set, cold, gray eyes twinkling sharply from under tufted brows. His nose was curved and sharp, like the beak of some cruel bird, but below the whole of his clean-shaven, powerful face was marred by the loose, slabbing mouth and the round folds of the heavy chin. His knife in one hand and a half-gnawed bone in the other, he looked fiercely up, like some beast disturbed in his den, as the two intruders broke in upon his hall.

Nigel stopped midway between the door and the table. His eyes and those of Paul de la Fosse were riveted upon each other. But Mary, with her woman's soul flooded over with love and pity, had rushed forward and cast her arms round her younger sister. Edith had sprung up from her chair, and with averted face tried to push the other away from her.

"Edith, Edith! By the virgin, I implore you to come back with us, and to leave this wicked man!" cried Mary. "Dear sister, you would not break our father's heart, nor bring his gray head in dishonor to the grave! Come back! Edith, come back and all is well."

But Edith pushed her away, and her fair cheeks were flushed with her anger.

"What right have you over me, Mary, you who are but two years older, that you should follow me over the countryside as though I were a runagate villein and you my mistress? Do you yourself go back, and leave me to do that which seems best in my own eyes."

But Mary still held her in her arms, and still strove to soften the hard and angry heart.

"Our mother is dead, Edith. I thank God that she died ere she saw you under this roof! But I stand for her, as I have done all my life, since I am indeed your elder. It is with her voice that I beg and pray you that you will not trust this man further, and that you will come back ere it be too late!"

Edith writhed from her grasp, and stood flushed and defiant, with gleaming, angry eyes fixed upon her sister.

"You may speak evil of him now," said she, "but there was a time when Paul de la Fosse came to Cosford, and who so gentle and soft-spoken to him then as wise, grave, sister Mary? But he has learned to love another; so now he is the wicked man, and it is shame to be seen under his roof! From what I see of my good, pious sister and her cavalier, it is sin for another to ride at night with a man at your side, but it comes easy enough to you. Look at your own eye, good sister, ere you would take the speck from that of another."

Mary stood irresolute and greatly troubled, holding down her pride and her anger, but uncertain how best to deal with this strong, wayward spirit.

"It is not a time for bitter words, dear sister," said she, and again she laid her hand upon her sister's sleeve. "All that you say may be true. There was, indeed, a time when this man was friend to us both, and I know even as you do the power which he may have to win a woman's heart. But I know him now, and you do not. I know the evil that he has wrought, the dishonor that he has brought, the perjury that lies upon his soul, the confidence betrayed, the promise unfulfilled—all this I know. Am I to see my own sister caught in the same well-used trap? Has it shut upon you, child? Am I, indeed, already too late? For God's sake, tell me, Edith, that it is not so!"

Edith plucked her sleeve from her sister, and made two swift steps to the head of the table. Paul de la Fosse still sat silent with his eyes upon Nigel. Edith laid her hand upon his shoulder.

"This is the man I love, and the only man that I have ever loved. This is my husband," said she.

At the word Mary gave a cry of joy.

"And is it so?" she cried. "Nay, then all is in honor, and God will see to the rest. If you are man and wife before the altar, then, indeed, why should I, or any other, stand between you? Tell me that it is indeed so, and I return this moment to make your father a happy man."

Edith pouted like a naughty child. "We are man and wife in the eyes of God. Soon also we shall be wedded before all the world. We do but wait until next Monday, when Paul's brother, who is a priest at Saint Albans, will come to wed us. Already a messenger has sped for him, and he will come, will he not, dear love?"

"He will come," said the master of Shalford, still with his eyes fixed upon the silent Nigel.

"It is a lie; he will not come," said a voice from the door.

It was the old priest, who had followed the others as far as the threshold.

"He will not come," he repeated as he advanced into the room. "Daughter, my daughter, hearken to the words of one who is indeed old enough to be your earthly father. This lie has served before. He has ruined others before you with it. The man has no brother at Saint Albans. I know his brothers well, and there is no priest among them. Before Monday, when it is all too late, you will have found the truth as others have done before you. Trust him not, but come with us!"

Paul de la Fosse looked up at her with a quick smile and patted the hand upon his shoulder.

"Do you speak to them, Edith," said he.

Her eyes flashed with scorn as she surveyed them each in turn, the woman, the youth, and the priest.

"I have but one word to say to them," said she. "It is that they go hence and trouble us no more. Am I not a free woman? Have I not said that this is the only man I ever loved? I have loved him long. He did not know it, and in despair he turned to another. Now he knows all, and never again can doubt come between us. Therefore I will stay here at Shalford and come to Cosford no more save upon the arm of my husband. Am I so weak that I would believe the tales you tell against him? Is it hard for a jealous woman and a wandering priest to agree upon a lie? No, no, Mary, you can go hence and take your cavalier and your priest with you, for here I stay, true to my love and safe in my trust upon his honor!"

"Well spoken, on my faith, my golden bird!" said the little master of Shalford. "Let me add my own word to that which has been said. You would not grant me any virtue in your unkindly speech, good Lady Mary, and yet you must needs confess that at least I have good store of patience, since I have not set my dogs upon your friends who have come between me and my ease. But even to the most virtuous there comes at last a time when poor human frailty may prevail, and so I pray you to remove both yourself, your priest and your valiant knight errant, lest perhaps there be more haste and less dignity when at last you do take your leave. Sit down, my fair love, and let us turn once more to our supper." He motioned her to her chair, and he filled her wine-cup as well as his own.

Nigel had said no word since he had entered the room, but his look had never lost its set purpose, nor had his brooding eyes

ever wandered from the sneering face of the deformed master
of Shalford. Now he turned with swift decision to Mary and to
the priest.

"That is over," said he, in a low voice. "You have done all that
you could, and now it is for me to play my part as well as I am
able. I pray you, Mary, and you, good father, that you will await
me outside."

"Nay, Nigel, if there is danger——"

"It is easier for me, Mary, if you are not there. I pray you to
go. I can speak to this man more at my ease."

She looked at him with questioning eyes and then obeyed.

Nigel plucked at the priest's gown. "I pray you, father, have
you your book of offices with you?"

"Surely, Nigel, it is ever in my breast."

"Have it ready, father!"

"For what, my son?"

"There are two places you may mark: there is the service of
marriage, and there is the prayer for the dying. Go with her,
father, and be ready at my call."

He closed the door behind them and was alone with this ill-
matched couple. They both turned in their chairs to look at him,
Edith with a defiant face, the man with a bitter smile upon his
lips and malignant hatred in his eyes.

"What," said he, "the knight errant still lingers? Have we not
heard of his thirst for glory? What new venture does he see that
he should tarry here?"

Nigel walked to the table. "There is no glory and little venture," said he; "but I have come for a purpose and I must do it.
I learn from your own lips, Edith, that you will not leave this
man."

"If you have ears you have heard it."

"You are, as you have said, a free woman, and who can gainsay
you? But I have known you, Edith, since we played as boy and
girl on the heather-hills together. I will save you from this man's
cunning and from your own foolish weakness."

"What would you do?"

"There is a priest without. He will marry you now. I will see
you married ere I leave this hall."

"Or else?" sneered the man.

"Or else you never leave this hall alive. Nay, call not for your servants or your dogs! By Saint Paul! I swear to you that this matter lies between us three, and that if any fourth comes at your call, you, at least, shall never live to see what comes of it! Speak then, Paul of Shalford! Will you wed this woman now, or will you not?"

Edith was on her feet with outstretched arms between them.

"Stand back, Nigel! He is small and weak. You would not do him a hurt! Did you not say so this very day? For God's sake, Nigel, do not look at him so! There is death in your eyes."

"A snake may be small and weak, Edith, yet every honest man would place his heel upon it. Do you stand back yourself, for my purpose is set."

"Paul!" She turned her eyes to the pale sneering face. "Bethink you, Paul! Why should you not do what he asks? What matter to you whether it be now or on Monday? I pray you, dear Paul, for my sake let him have his way! Your brother can read the service again if it so please him. Let us wed now, Paul, and then all is well."

He had risen from his chair, and he dashed aside her appealing hands.

"You foolish woman," he snarled, "and you, my savior of fair damsels, who are so bold against a cripple, you have both to learn that if my body be weak, there is the soul of my breed within it! To marry because a boasting, ranting, country squire would have me do so—no, by the soul of God, I will die first! On Monday I will marry, and no day sooner, so let that be your answer."

"It is the answer that I wished," said Nigel, "for indeed I see no happiness in this marriage, and the other may well be the better way. Stand aside, Edith!" He gently forced her to one side and drew his sword.

De la Fosse cried aloud at the sight. "I have no sword. You would not murder me?" said he, leaning back with haggard face and burning eyes against his chair. The bright steel shone in the lamp-light. Edith shrank back, her hand over her face.

"Take this sword!" said Nigel, and he turned the hilt to the cripple. "Now!" he added, as he drew his hunting-knife. "Kill me if you can, Paul de la Fosse, for as God is my help I will do as much for you!"

The woman, half swooning and yet spellbound and fascinated, looked on at that strange combat. For a moment the cripple stood with an air of doubt, the sword grasped in his nerveless fingers. Then, as he saw the tiny blade in Nigel's hand, the greatness of the advantage came home to him, and a cruel smile tightened his loose lips. Slowly, step by step he advanced, his chin sunk upon his chest, his eyes glaring from under the thick tangle of his brows like fires through the brushwood. Nigel waited for him, his left hand forward, his knife down by his hip, his face grave, still, and watchful.

Nearer and nearer yet, with stealthy step, and then with a bound and a cry of hatred and rage, Paul de la Fosse had sped his blow. It was well judged and well swung, but point would have been wiser than edge against that supple body and those active feet. Quick as a flash, Nigel had sprung inside the sweep of the blade, taking a flesh wound on his left forearm, as he pressed it under the hilt. The next instant the cripple was on the ground and Nigel's dagger was at his throat.

"You dog!" he whispered. "I have you at my mercy! Quick ere I strike, and for the last time! Will you marry or no?"

The crash of the fall and the sharp point upon his throat had cowed the man's spirit. He looked up with a white face, and the sweat gleamed upon his forehead. There was terror in his eyes.

"Nay, take your knife from me!" he cried. "I cannot die like a calf in the shambles."

"Will you marry?"

"Yes, yes; I will wed her! After all, she is a good wench, and I might do worse. Let me up! I tell you I will marry her! What more would you have?"

Nigel stood above him with his foot upon his misshapen body. He had picked up his sword, and the point rested upon the cripple's breast.

"Nay, you will bide where you are! If you are to live—and my conscience cries loud against it—at least your wedding will be such as your sins have deserved. Lie there, like the crushed worm that you are!" Then he raised his voice. "Father Athanasius!" he cried. "What ho! Father Athanasius!"

The old priest ran to the cry, and so did the Lady Mary. A strange sight it was that met them now in the circle of light, the frightened girl, half-unconscious against the table, the prostrate cripple, and Nigel with foot and sword upon his body.

"Your book, father!" cried Nigel. "I know not if what we do is good or ill; but we must wed them, for there is no way out."

But the girl by the table had given a great cry, and she was clinging and sobbing with her arms round her sister's neck.

"Oh, Mary, I thank the Virgin that you have come! I thank the Virgin that it is not too late! What did he say? He said that he was a de la Fosse, and that he would not be married at the sword-point. My heart went out to him when he said it. But I, am I not a Buttesthorn, and shall it be said that I would marry a man who could be led to the altar with a knife at his throat? No, no; I see him as he is! I know him now, the mean spirit, the lying tongue! Can I not read in his eyes that he has indeed deceived me, that he would have left me as you say that he has left others? Take me home, Mary, my sister, for you have plucked me back this night from the very mouth of Hell!"

And so it was that the master of Shalford, livid and brooding, was left with his wine at his lonely table, while the golden beauty of Cosford, hot with shame and anger, her fair face wet with tears, passed out safe from the house of infamy into the great calm and peace of the starry night.

"A strange sight it was that met them now in the circle of light."
[*page 136.*]

XIII. HOW THE COMRADES JOURNEYED DOWN THE OLD, OLD ROAD

AND NOW THE season of the moonless nights was drawing nigh and the king's design was ripe. Very secretly his preparations were made. Already the garrison of Calais, which consisted of five hundred archers and two hundred men-at-arms, could, if forewarned, resist any attack made upon it. But it was the king's design not merely to resist the attack, but to capture the attackers. Above all it was his wish to find the occasion for one of those adventurous passages of arms which had made his name famous throughout Christendom as the very pattern and leader of knight-errant chivalry.

But the affair wanted careful handling. The arrival of any reinforcements, or even the crossing of any famous soldier, would have alarmed the French and warned them that their plot had been discovered. Therefore it was in twos and threes in the creyers and provision ships which were continually passing from shore to shore that the chosen warriors and their squires were brought to Calais. There they were passed at night through the water-gate into the castle where they could lie hidden, unknown to the townsfolk, until the hour for action had come.

Nigel had received word from Chandos to join him at "The Sign of the Broom-Pod" in Winchelsea. Three days beforehand he and Aylward rode from Tilford all armed and ready for the wars. Nigel was in hunting-costume, blithe and gay, with his precious armor and his small baggage trussed upon the back of a spare horse which Aylward led by the bridle. The archer had himself a good black mare, heavy and slow, but strong enough to be fit to carry his powerful frame. In his brigandine of chain mail and his steel cap, with straight strong sword by his side, his

yellow long-bow jutting over his shoulder, and his quiver of arrows supported by a scarlet baldric, he was such a warrior as any
knight might well be proud to have in his train. All Tilford
trailed behind them, as they rode slowly over the long slope of
heath land which skirts the flank of Crooksbury Hill.

At the summit of the rise Nigel reined in Pommers and
looked back at the little village behind him. There was the old
dark manor-house, with one bent figure leaning upon a stick
and gazing dimly after him from beside the door. He looked at
the high-pitched roof, the timbered walls, the long trail of swirling blue smoke which rose from the single chimney, and the
group of downcast old servants who lingered at the gate—John
the cook, Weathercote the minstrel, and Red Swire the broken
soldier. Over the river amid the trees he could see the grim, gray
tower of Waverley, and even as he looked, the iron bell, which
had so often seemed to be the hoarse threatening cry of an
enemy, clanged out its call to prayer. Nigel doffed his velvet cap
and prayed also—prayed that peace might remain at home, and
good warfare, in which honor and fame should await him, might
still be found abroad. Then, waving his hand to the people, he
turned his horse's head and rode slowly eastward. A moment
later Aylward broke from the group of archers and laughing girls
who clung to his bridle and his stirrup straps, and rode on, blowing kisses over his shoulder. So at last the two comrades, gentle
and simple, were fairly started on their venture.

There are two seasons of color in those parts: the yellow,
when the countryside is flaming with the gorse-blossoms, and
the crimson, when all the long slopes are smoldering with the
heather. So it was now. Nigel looked back from time to time, as
he rode along the narrow track where the ferns and the ling
brushed his feet on either side, and as he looked it seemed to
him that, wander where he might, he would never see a fairer
scene than that of his own home. Far to the westward, glowing
in the morning light, rolled billow after billow of ruddy heather
land, until they merged into the dark shadows of Woolmer
Forest and the pale clear green of the Butser chalk downs.
Never in his life had Nigel wandered far beyond these limits,
and the woodlands, the down, and the heather were dear to his

soul. It gave him a pang in his heart now as he turned his face away from them; but if home lay to the westward, out there to the east and south was the great world of adventure, the noble stage where each of his kinsmen in turn had played his manly part and left a proud name behind.

How often he had longed for this day! And now it had come with no shadow cast behind it. Dame Ermyntrude was under the king's protection. The old servants had their future assured. The strife with the monks of Waverley had been assuaged. He had a noble horse under him, the best of weapons, and a stout follower at his back. Above all he was bound on a gallant errand with the bravest knight in England as his leader. All these thoughts surged together in his mind, and he whistled and sang, as he rode, out of the joy of his heart, while Pommers sidled and curveted in sympathy with the mood of his master. Presently, glancing back, he saw from Aylward's downcast eyes and puckered brow that the archer was clouded with trouble. He reined his horse to let him come abreast of him.

"How now, Aylward?" said he. "Surely of all men in England you and I should be the most blithe this morning, since we ride forward with all hopes of honorable advancement. By Saint Paul! ere we see these heather hills once more we shall either worshipfully win worship, or we shall venture our persons in the attempt. These be glad thoughts, and why should you be downcast?"

Aylward shrugged his broad shoulders, and a wry smile dawned upon his rugged face.

"I am indeed as limp as a wetted bowstring," said he. "It is the nature of a man that he should be sad when he leaves the woman he loves."

"In truth, yes!" cried Nigel, and in a flash the dark eyes of Mary Buttesthorn rose before him, and he heard her low, sweet, earnest voice as he had heard it that night when they brought her frailer sister back from Shalford Manor, a voice which made all that was best and noblest in a man thrill within his soul. "Yet, bethink you, archer, that what a woman loves in man is not his gross body, but rather his soul, his honor, his fame, the deeds with which he has made his life beautiful. Therefore you are winning love as well as glory when you turn to the wars."

"It may be so," said Aylward; "but indeed it goes to my heart to see the pretty dears weep, and I would fain weep as well to keep them company. When Mary—or was it Dolly?—nay, it was Martha, the red-headed girl from the Mill—when she held tight to my baldric it was like snapping my heart-string to pluck myself loose."

"You speak of one name and then of another," said Nigel. "How is she called, then, this maid whom you love?"

Aylward pushed back his steel cap and scratched his bristling head with some embarrassment.

"Her name," said he, "is Mary Dolly Martha Susan Jane Cicely Theodosia Agnes Johanna Kate."

Nigel laughed as Aylward rolled out this prodigious title.

"I had no right to take you to the wars," said he; "for by Saint Paul! it is very clear that I have widowed half the parish. But I saw your aged father the franklin. Bethink you of the joy that will fill his heart when he hears that you have done some small deed in France, and so won honor in the eyes of all."

"I fear that honor will not help him to pay his arrears of rent to the sacrist of Waverley," said Aylward. "Out he will go on the roadside, honor and all, if he does not find ten nobles by next Epiphany. But if I could win a ransom or be at the storming of a rich city, then indeed the old man would be proud of me. 'Thy sword must help my spade, Samkin,' said he as he kissed me good-bye. Ah! it would indeed be a happy day for him and for all if I could ride back with a saddle-bag full of gold pieces, and please God, I shall dip my hand in somebody's pocket before I see Crooksbury Hill once more!"

Nigel shook his head, for indeed it seemed hopeless to try to bridge the gulf between them. Already they had made such good progress along the bridle-path through the heather that the little hill of Saint Catharine and the ancient shrine upon its summit loomed up before them. Here they crossed the road from the south to London, and at the crossing two wayfarers were waiting who waved their hands in greeting, the one a tall, slender, dark woman upon a white jennet, the other a very thick and red-faced old man, whose weight seemed to curve the back of the stout gray cob which he bestrode.

"What how, Nigel!" he cried. "Mary has told me that you make a start this morning, and we have waited here this hour and more on the chance of seeing you pass. Come, lad, and have a last stoup of English ale, for many a time amid the sour French wines you will long for the white foam under your nose, and the good homely twang of it."

Nigel had to decline the draught, for it meant riding into Guildford town, a mile out of his course, but very gladly he agreed with Mary that they should climb the path to the old shrine and offer a last orison together. The knight and Aylward waited below with the horses; and so it came about that Nigel and Mary found themselves alone under the solemn old Gothic arches, in front of the dark shadowed recess in which gleamed the golden reliquary of the saint. In silence they knelt side by side in prayer, and then came forth once more out of the gloom and the shadow into the fresh sunlit summer morning. They stopped ere they descended the path, and looked to right and left at the fair meadows and the blue Wey curling down the valley.

"What have you prayed for, Nigel?" said she.

"I have prayed that God and His saints will hold my spirit high and will send me back from France in such a fashion that I may dare to come to you and to claim you for my own."

"Bethink you well what it is that you say, Nigel," said she. "What you are to me only my own heart can tell; but I would never set eyes upon your face again rather than abate by one inch that height of honor and worshipful achievement to which you may attain."

"Nay, my dear and most sweet lady, how should you abate it, since it is the thought of you which will nerve my arm and up-hold my heart?"

"Think once more, my fair lord, and hold yourself bound by no word which you have said. Let it be as the breeze which blows past our faces and is heard of no more. Your soul yearns for honor. To that has it ever turned. Is there room in it for love also? or is it possible that both shall live at their highest in one mind? Do you not call to mind that Galahad and other great knights of old have put women out of their lives that they might ever give their whole soul and strength to the winning of honor? May it not be that I shall be a drag upon you, that your heart may shrink from some honorable task, lest it should bring risk and pain to me? Think well before you answer, my fair lord, for indeed my very heart would break if it should ever happen that through love of me your high hopes and great promise should miss fulfilment."

Nigel looked at her with sparkling eyes. The soul which shone through her dark face had transformed it for the moment into a beauty, more lofty and more rare than that of her shallow sister. He bowed before the majesty of the woman, and pressed his lips to her hand.

"You are like a star upon my path which guides me on the upward way," said he. "Our souls are set together upon the finding of honor, and how shall we hold each other back when our purpose is the same?"

She shook her proud head. "So it seems to you now, fair lord, but it may be otherwise as the years pass. How shall you prove that I am indeed a help and not a hindrance?"

"I will prove it by my deeds, fair and dear lady," said Nigel. "Here at the shrine of the holy Catharine, on this, the Feast of Saint Margaret, I take my oath that I will do three deeds in your honor as a proof of my high love before I set eyes upon your face again, and these three deeds shall stand as a proof to you that if I love you dearly, still I will not let the thought of you stand betwixt me and honorable achievement!"

Her face shone with her love and her pride. "I also make my oath," said she, "and I do it in the name of the holy Catharine whose shrine is hard by. I swear that I will hold myself for you until these three deeds be done and we meet once more; also that if—which may dear Christ forfend!—you fall in doing them then I shall take the veil in Shalford nunnery and look upon no man's face again! Give me your hand, Nigel."

She had taken a little bangle of gold filigree work from her arm and fastened it upon his sunburnt wrist, reading aloud to him the engraved motto in old French: *"Fais ce que dois, ad-viegne que pourra—c'est commandé au chevalier."* Then for one moment they fell into each other's arms and with kiss upon kiss, a loving man and a tender woman, they swore their troth to each other. But the old knight was calling impatiently from below, and together they hurried down the winding path to where the horses waited under the sandy bluff.

As far as the Shalford crossing Sir John rode by Nigel's arm, and many were the last injunctions which he gave him concerning woodcraft, and great his anxiety lest he confuse a spay with a brocket, or either with a hind. At last, when they came to the reedy edge of the Wey, the old knight and his daughter reined up their horses. Nigel looked back at them ere he entered the dark Chantry woods, and saw them still gazing after him and waving their hands. Then the path wound amongst the trees and they were lost to sight; but long afterwards when a clearing exposed once more the Shalford meadows Nigel saw that the old man upon the gray cob was riding slowly toward Saint Catharine's Hill, but that the girl was still where he had seen her last, leaning forward in her saddle and straining her eyes to pierce the dark forest which screened her lover from her view. It was but a fleeting glance through a break in the foliage, and yet in after days of stress and toil in far distant lands it was that one little picture—the green meadow, the reeds, the slow blue winding river, and the eager bending graceful figure upon the white horse—which was the clearest and the dearest image of that England which he had left behind him.

But if Nigel's friends had learned that this was the morning of his leaving, his enemies too were on the alert. The two comrades had just emerged from the Chantry woods and were beginning the ascent of that curving path which leads upward to the old Chapel of the Martyr, when, with a hiss like an angry snake a long white arrow streaked under Pommers and struck quivering in the grassy turf. A second whizzed past Nigel's ear, as he tried to turn, but Aylward struck the great war-horse a sharp blow over the haunches, and it had galloped some hundreds of yards before its rider could pull it up. Aylward followed as hard as he could ride, bending low over his horse's neck, while arrows whizzed all around him.

"By Saint Paul!" said Nigel, tugging at his bridle and white with anger, "they shall not chase me across the country as though I was a frighted doe. Archer, how dare you to lash my horse when I would have turned and ridden in upon them?"

"It is well that I did so," said Aylward, "or by these ten finger-bones! our journey would have begun and ended on the same day. As I glanced round I saw a dozen of them at the least amongst the brushwood. See now how the light glimmers upon their steel caps yonder in the bracken under the great beech-tree. Nay, I pray you, my fair lord, do not ride forward. What chance has a man in the open against all these who lie at their ease in the underwood? If you will not think of yourself, then consider your horse, which would have a cloth-yard shaft feathered in its hide ere it could reach the wood."

Nigel chafed in impotent anger. "Am I to be shot at like a popinjay at a fair, by any reaver or outlaw that seeks a mark for his bow?" he cried. "By Saint Paul! Aylward, I will put on my harness and go further into the matter. Help me to untruss, I pray you!"

"Nay, my fair lord, I will not help you to your own downfall. It is a match with cogged dice betwixt a horseman on the moor and archers amid the forest. But these men are no outlaws, or they would not dare to draw their bows within a league of the sheriff of Guildford."

"Indeed, Aylward, I think that you speak truth," said Nigel. "It may be that these are the men of Paul de la Fosse of Shalford, whom I have given little cause to love me. Ah! there is indeed the very man himself."

They sat their horses with their backs to the long slope which leads up to the old chapel on the hill. In front of them was the dark ragged edge of the wood, with a sharp twinkle of steel here and there in its shadows which spoke of these lurking foes. But now there was a long moot upon a horn, and at once a score of russet-clad bowmen ran forward from amid the trees, spreading out into a scattered line and closing swiftly in upon the travelers.

In the midst of them, upon a great gray horse, sat a small mis-shapen man, waving and cheering as one sets hounds on a badger, turning his head this way and that as he whooped and pointed, urging his bowmen onward up the slope.

"Draw them on, my fair lord! Draw them on until we have them out on the down!" cried Aylward, his eyes shining with joy. "Five hundred paces more, and then we may be on terms with them. Nay, linger not, but keep them always just clear of arrow-shot until our turn has come."

Nigel shook and trembled with eagerness, as with his hand on his sword-hilt he looked at the line of eager hurrying men. But it flashed through his mind what Chandos had said of the cool head which is better for the warrior than the hot heart. Aylward's words were true and wise. He turned Pommers' head therefore, and amid a cry of derision from behind them the comrades trotted over the down. The bowmen broke into a run, while their leader screamed and waved more madly than before. Aylward cast many a glance at them over his shoulder.

"Yet a little farther! Yet a little farther still!" he muttered. "The wind is towards them and the fools have forgot that I can overshoot them by fifty paces. Now, my good lord, I pray you for one instant to hold the horses, for my weapon is of more avail this day than thine can be. They may make sorry cheer ere they gain the shelter of the wood once more."

He had sprung from his horse, and with a downward wrench of his arm and a push with his knee he slipped the string into the upper nock of his mighty war-bow. Then in a flash he notched his shaft and drew it to the pile, his keen blue eyes glowing fiercely behind it from under his knotted brows. With thick legs planted sturdily apart, his body laid to the bow, his left arm motionless as wood, his right bunched into a double curve of swelling muscles as he stretched the white well-waxed string, he looked so keen and fierce a fighter that the advancing line stopped for an instant at the sight of him. Two or three loosed off their arrows, but the shafts flew heavily against the head wind, and snaked along the hard turf some score of paces short of the mark. One only, a short bandy-legged man, whose squat figure spoke of enormous muscular strength, ran swiftly in and then drew so strong a bow that the arrow quivered in the ground at Aylward's very feet.

"It is Black Will of Lynchmere," said the bowman. "Many a match have I shot with him, and I know well that no other man on the Surrey marches could have sped such a shaft. I trust that you are houseled and shriven, Will, for I have known you so long that I would not have your damnation upon my soul."

He raised his bow as he spoke, and the string twanged with a rich, deep musical note. Aylward leaned upon his bow-stave as he keenly watched the long swift flight of his shaft, skimming smoothly down the wind.

"On him, on him! No, over him, by my hilt!" he cried. "There is more wind than I had thought. Nay, nay, friend, now that I have the length of you, you can scarce hope to loose again."

Black Will had notched an arrow and was raising his bow when Aylward's second shaft passed through the shoulder of his drawing arm. With a shout of anger and pain he dropped his weapon, and dancing in his fury he shook his fist and roared curses at his rival.

"I could slay him; but I will not, for good bowmen are not so common," said Aylward. "And now, fair sir, we must on, for they are spreading round on either side, and if once they get behind us, then indeed our journey has come to a sudden end. But ere we go I would send a shaft through yonder horseman who leads them on."

"Nay, Aylward, I pray you to leave him," said Nigel. "Villain as he is, he is none the less a gentleman of coat-armor, and should die by some other weapon than thine."

"As you will," said Aylward, with a clouded brow. "I have been told that in the late wars many a French prince and baron has not been too proud to take his death-wound from an English yeoman's shaft, and that nobles of England have been glad enough to stand by and see it done."

Nigel shook his head sadly. "It is sooth you say, archer, and indeed it is no new thing, for that good knight Richard of the Lion Heart met his end in such a lowly fashion, and so also did Harold the Saxon. But this is a private matter, and I would not have you draw your bow against him. Neither can I ride at him myself, for he is weak in body, though dangerous in spirit. Therefore, we will go upon our way, since there is neither profit nor honor to be gained, nor any hope of advancement."

Aylward, having unstrung his bow, had remounted his horse during this conversation, and the two rode swiftly past the little squat Chapel of the Martyr and over the brow of the hill. From the summit they looked back. The injured archer lay upon the ground, with several of his comrades gathered in a knot around him. Others ran aimlessly up the hill, but were already far behind. The leader sat motionless upon his horse, and as he saw them look back he raised his hand and shrieked his curses at them. An instant later the curve of the ground had hid them from view. So, amid love and hate, Nigel bade adieu to the home of his youth.

And now the comrades were journeying upon that old, old road which runs across the south of England and yet never turns toward London, for the good reason that the place was a poor hamlet when first the road was laid. From Winchester, the Saxon capital, to Canterbury, the holy city of Kent, ran that ancient highway, and on from Canterbury to the narrow straits where, on a clear day, the farther shore can be seen. Along this track as far back as history can trace the metals of the west have been carried and passed the pack-horses which bore the goods which Gaul sent in exchange. Older than the Christian faith, and older than the Romans, is the old road. North and south are the woods and the marshes, so that only on the high dry turf of the chalk land could a clear track be found. The Pilgrim's Way, it still is called; but the pilgrims were the last who ever trod it, for it was already of immemorial age before the death of Thomas a Becket gave a new reason why folk should journey to the scene of his murder.

From the hill of Weston Wood the travelers could see the long white band which dipped and curved and rose over the green downland, its course marked even in the hollows by the line of the old yew-trees which flanked it. Neither Nigel nor Aylward had wandered far from their own country, and now they rode with light hearts and eager eyes taking note of all the varied pictures of nature and of man which passed before them. To their left was a hilly country, a land of rolling heaths and woods, broken here and there into open spaces round the occasional farmhouse of a franklin. Hackhurst Down, Dunley Hill, and Ranmore Common swelled and sank, each merging into the other. But on the right, after passing the village of Shere and the old church of Gomshall, the whole south country lay like a map at their feet. There was the huge wood of the Weald, one unbroken forest of oak-trees stretching away to the South Downs, which rose olive-green against the deep blue sky. Under this great canopy of trees strange folk lived and evil deeds were done. In its recesses were wild tribes, little changed from their heathen ancestors, who danced round the altar of Thor, and well was it for the peaceful traveler that he could tread the high open road of the chalk land with no need to wander into so dangerous a tract, where soft clay, tangled forest, and wild men all barred his progress.

But apart from the rolling country upon the left and the great forest-hidden plain upon the right, there was much upon the road itself to engage the attention of the wayfarers. It was crowded with people. As far as their eyes could carry they could see the black dots scattered thickly upon the thin white band, sometimes single, sometimes several abreast, sometimes in moving crowds, where a drove of pilgrims held together for mutual protection, or a nobleman showed his greatness by the number of retainers who trailed at his heels. At that time the main roads were very crowded, for there were many wandering people in the land. Of all sorts and kinds, they passed in an unbroken stream before the eyes of Nigel and of Aylward, alike only in the fact that one and all were powdered from their hair to their shoes with the gray dust of the chalk.

There were monks journeying from one cell to another, Benedictines with their black gowns looped up to show their white skirts, Carthusians in white, and pied Cistercians. Friars also of the three wandering orders—Dominicans in black, Carmelites in white, and Franciscans in gray. There was no love lost between the cloistered monks and the free friars, each looking on the other as a rival who took from him the oblations of the faithful; so they passed on the high road as cat passes dog, with eyes askance and angry faces.

Then, besides the men of the Church, there were the men of trade, the merchant in dusty broadcloth and Flanders hat riding at the head of his line of pack-horses. He carried Cornish tin, Welt-country wool, or Sussex iron if he traded eastward, or if his head should be turned westward then he bore with him the velvets of Genoa, the ware of Venice, the wine of France, or the armor of Italy and Spain. Pilgrims were everywhere, poor people for the most part, plodding wearily along with trailing feet and bowed heads, thick staves in their hands and bundles over their shoulders. Here and there on a gaily caparisoned palfrey, or in the greater luxury of a horse-litter, some West-country lady might be seen making her easy way to the shrine of Saint Thomas.

Besides all these a constant stream of strange vagabonds drifted along the road; minstrels who wandered from fair to fair, a foul and pestilent crew; jugglers and acrobats, quack doctors and tooth-drawers, students and beggars, free workmen in search of better wages, and escaped bondsmen who would welcome any wages at all. Such was the throng which set the old road smoking in a haze of white dust from Winchester to the narrow sea.

But of all the wayfarers those which interested Nigel most were the soldiers. Several times they passed little knots of archers or men-at-arms, veterans from France, who had received their discharge and were now making their way to their southland homes. They were half drunk all of them, for the wayfarers treated them to beer at the frequent inns and ale-stakes which lined the road, so that they cheered and sang lustily as they passed. They roared rude pleasantries at Aylward, who turned in his saddle and shouted his opinion of them until they were out of hearing.

Once, late in the afternoon, they overtook a body of a hundred archers all marching together with two knights riding at their head. They were passing from Guildford Castle to Reigate Castle, where they were in garrison. Nigel rode with the knights for some distance, and hinted that if either was in search of honorable advancement, or wished to do some small deed, or to relieve himself of any vow, it might be possible to find some means of achieving it. They were both, however, grave and elderly men, intent upon their business and with no mind for fond wayside adventures, so Nigel quickened his pace and left them behind.

They had left Boxhill and Headley Heath upon the left, and the towers of Reigate were rising amid the trees in front of them when they overtook a large, cheery, red-faced man, with a forked beard, riding upon a good horse and exchanging a nod or a merry word with all who passed him. With him they rode nearly as far as Bletchingley, and Nigel laughed much to hear him talk; but always under the raillery there was much earnestness and much wisdom in all his words. He rode at his ease about the country, he said, having sufficient money to keep him from want and to furnish him for the road. He could speak all the three languages of England, the north, the middle, and the south, so that he was at home with the people of every shire and could hear their troubles and their joys. In all parts in town and in country there was unrest, he said; for the poor folk were weary of their masters both of the Church and State, and soon there would be such doings in England as had never been seen before.

But above all this man was earnest against the Church: its enormous wealth, its possession of nearly one-third of the whole land of the country, its insatiable greed for more at the very time when it claimed to be poor and lowly. The monks and friars, too, he lashed with his tongue: their roguish ways, their laziness, and their cunning. He showed how their wealth and that of the haughty lord must always be founded upon the toil of poor humble Peter the Plowman, who worked and strove in rain and cold out in the fields, the butt and laughing-stock of every one, and still bearing up the whole world upon his weary shoulders. He had set it all out in a fair parable; so now as he rode he repeated some of the verses, chanting them and marking time with his forefinger, while Nigel and Aylward on either side of him with their heads inclined inward listened with the same attention but with very different feelings—Nigel shocked at such an attack upon authority, and Aylward chuckling as he heard the sentiments of his class so shrewdly expressed. At last the stranger halted his horse outside the "Five Angels" at Gatton.

"It is a good inn, and I know the ale of old," said he. "When I had finished that 'Dream of Piers the Plowman,' from which I have recited to you, the last verses were thus:

"'Now have I brought my little booke to an ende
    God's blessing be on him who a drinke will me sende'—

I pray you come in with me and share it."

"Nay," said Nigel, "we must on our way, for we have far to go. But give me your name, my friend, for indeed we have passed a merry hour listening to your words."

"Have a care!" the stranger answered, shaking his head. "You and your class will not spend a merry hour when these words are turned into deeds, and Peter the Plowman grows weary of swinking in the fields and takes up his bow and his staff in order to set this land in order."

"By Saint Paul! I expect that we shall bring Peter to reason, and also those who have put such evil thoughts into his head," said Nigel. "So once more I ask your name, that I may know it if ever I chance to hear that you have been hanged?"

The stranger laughed good-humoredly. "You can call me Thomas Lackland," said he. "I should be Thomas Lack-brain if I were indeed to give my true name, since a good many robbers, some in black gowns and some in steel, would be glad to help me upward in the way you speak of. So good-day to you, squire, and to you also, archer; and may you find your way back with whole bones from the wars!"

That night the comrades slept in Godstone Priory, and early next morning they were well upon their road down the Pilgrim's Way. At Titsey it was said that a band of villains were out in Westerham Wood and had murdered three men the day before; so that Nigel had high hopes of an encounter; but the brigands showed no sign, though the travelers went out of their way to ride their horses along the edges of the forest. Farther on they found traces of their work, for the path ran along the hillside at

the base of a chalk quarry, and there in the cutting a man was
lying dead. From his twisted limbs and shattered frame it was
easy to see that he had been thrown over from above, while his
pockets turned outward showed the reason for his murder. The
comrades rode past without too close a survey, for dead men
were no very uncommon objects on the king's highway, and if
sheriff or bailiff should chance upon you near the body you
might find yourself caught in the meshes of the law.

Near Sevenoaks their road turned out of the old Canterbury
way and pointed south toward the coast, leaving the chalk lands
and coming down into the clay of the Weald. It was a wretched,
rutted mule-track running through thick forests with occasional
clearings in which lay the small Kentish villages, where rude
shock-headed peasants with smocks and galligaskins stared with
bold, greedy eyes at the travelers. Once on the right they caught
a distant view of the Towers of Penshurst, and once they heard
the deep tolling of the bells of Bayham Abbey, but for the rest
of their day's journey savage peasants and squalid cottages were
all that met their eyes, with endless droves of pigs who fed upon
the litter of acorns. The throng of travelers who crowded the old
road were all gone, and only here and there did they meet or
overtake some occasional merchant or messenger bound for
Battle Abbey, Pevensey Castle or the towns of the south.

That night they slept in a sordid inn, overrun with rats and
with fleas, one mile south of the hamlet of Mayfield. Aylward
scratched vigorously and cursed with fervor. Nigel lay without
movement or sound. To the man who had learned the old rule
of chivalry there were no small ills in life. It was beneath the
dignity of his soul to stoop to observe them. Cold and heat, hunger and thirst, such things did not exist for the gentleman. The
armor of his soul was so complete that it was proof not only
against the great ills of life but even against the small ones; so
the flea-bitten Nigel lay grimly still while Aylward writhed upon
his couch.

They were now but a short distance from their destination;
but they had hardly started on their journey through the forest
next morning, when an adventure befell them which filled Nigel
with the wildest hopes.

Along the narrow winding path between the great oak-trees there rode a dark sallow man in a scarlet tabard who blew so loudly upon a silver trumpet that they heard the clanging call long before they set eyes on him. Slowly he advanced, pulling up every fifty paces to make the forest ring with another warlike blast. The comrades rode forward to meet him.

"I pray you," said Nigel, "to tell me who you are and why you blow upon this trumpet."

The fellow shook his head, so Nigel repeated the question in French, the common language of chivalry, spoken at that age by every gentleman in Western Europe.

The man put his lips to the trumpet and blew another long note before he answered.

"I am Gaston de Castrier," said he, "the humble squire of the most worthy and valiant knight Raoul de Tubiers, de Pestels, de Grimsard, de Mersac, de Leoy, de Bastanac, who also writes himself Lord of Pons. It is his order that I ride always a mile in front of him to prepare all to receive him, and he desires me to blow upon a trumpet not out of vainglory, but out of greatness of spirit, so that none may be ignorant of his coming should they desire to encounter him."

Nigel sprang from his horse with a cry of joy, and began to unbutton his doublet.

"Quick, Aylward, quick!" he said. "He comes, a knight errant comes! Was there ever such a chance of worshipfully winning worship? Untruss the harness while I loose my clothes! Good sir, I beg you to warn your noble and valiant master that a poor squire of England would implore him to take notice of him and to do some small deed upon him as he passes."

But already the Lord of Pons had come in sight. He was a huge man upon an enormous horse, so that together they seemed to fill up the whole long dark archway under the oaks. He was clad in full armor of a brazen hue, with only his face exposed, and of this face there was little visible save a pair of arrogant eyes and a great black beard, which flowed through the open visor and down over his breastplate. To the crest of his helmet was tied a small brown glove, nodding and swinging above him. He bore a long lance with a red square banner at the end, charged with a black boar's head, and the same symbol was engraved upon his shield. Slowly he rode through the forest, ponderous, menacing, with dull thudding of his charger's hoofs and constant clank of metal, while always in front of him came the distant peal of the silver trumpet calling all men to admit his majesty and to clear his path ere they be cleared from it.

Never in his dreams had so perfect a vision come to cheer Nigel's heart, and as he struggled with his clothes, glancing up continually at this wondrous traveler, he pattered forth prayers of thanksgiving to the good Saint Paul who had shown such loving-kindness to his unworthy servant and thrown him in the path of so excellent and debonair a gentleman.

But alas! how often at the last instant the cup is dashed from the lips! This joyful chance was destined to change suddenly to unexpected and grotesque disaster—disaster so strange and so complete that through all his life Nigel flushed crimson when he thought of it. He was busily stripping his hunting-costume, and with feverish haste he had doffed boots, hat, hose, doublet and cloak, so that nothing remained save a pink jupon and pair of silken drawers. At the same time Aylward was hastily unbuckling the load with the intention of handing his master his armor piece by piece, when the squire gave one last challenging peal from his silver trumpet into the very ear of the spare horse.

In an instant it had taken to its heels, the precious armor upon its back, and thundered away down the road which they had traversed. Aylward jumped upon his mare, drove his prick spurs into her sides, and galloped after the runaway as hard as he could ride. Thus it came about that in an instant Nigel was shorn of all his little dignity, had lost his two horses, his attendant, and his outfit, and found himself a lonely and unarmed man standing in his shirt and drawers upon the pathway down which the burly figure of the Lord of Pons was slowly advancing.

The knight errant, whose mind had been filled by the thought of the maiden whom he had left behind at St. Jean—the same whose glove dangled from his helmet—had observed nothing that had occurred. Hence, all that met his eyes was a noble yellow horse, which was tethered by the track, and a small young man, who appeared to be a lunatic, since he had undressed hastily in the heart of the forest, and stood now with an eager anxious face clad in his underlinen amid the scattered debris of his garments. Of such a person the high Lord of Pons could take no notice, and so he pursued his inexorable way, his arrogant eyes looking out into the distance and his thoughts set intently upon the maiden of St. Jean. He was dimly aware that the little crazy man in the undershirt ran a long way beside him in his stockings, begging, imploring and arguing.

"Just one hour, most fair sir, just one hour at the longest, and a poor squire of England shall ever hold himself your debtor! Do but condescend to rein your horse until my harness comes back to me! Will you not stoop to show me some small deed of arms? I implore you, fair sir, to spare me a little of your time and a handstroke or two ere you go upon your way!"

Lord de Pons motioned impatiently with his gauntleted hand, as one might brush away an importunate fly, but when at last Nigel became desperate in his clamor he thrust his spurs into his great war-horse, and clashing like a pair of cymbals, he thundered off through the forest. So he rode upon his majestic way, until two days later he was slain by Lord Reginald Cobham in a field near Weybridge.

When after a long chase Aylward secured the spare horse and brought it back, he found his master seated upon a fallen tree, his face buried in his hands and his mind clouded with humiliation and grief. Nothing was said, for the matter was beyond words, and so in moody silence they rode upon their way.

But soon they came upon a scene which drew Nigel's thoughts away from his bitter trouble, for in front of them there rose the towers of a great building with a small gray sloping village around it, and they learned from a passing hind that this was the hamlet and Abbey of Battle. Together they drew rein upon the low ridge and looked down into that valley of death from which even now the reek of blood seems to rise. Down beside that sinister lake and amid those scattered bushes sprinkled over the naked flank of the long ridge was fought that long-drawn struggle between two most noble foes with broad England as the prize of victory. Here, up and down the low hill, hour by hour the grim struggle had waxed and waned, until the Saxon army had died where it stood, king, court, house-carl and fyrdsman, each in their ranks even as they had fought. And now, after all the stress and toil, the tyranny, the savage revolt, the fierce suppression, God had made His purpose complete, for here were Nigel the Norman and Aylward the Saxon with good-fellowship in their hearts and a common respect in their minds, with the same banner and the same cause, riding forth to do battle for their old mother England.

And now the long ride drew to an end. In front of them was the blue sea, flecked with the white sails of ships. Once more the road passed upward from the heavy-wooded plain to the springy turf of the chalk downs. Far to the right rose the grim fortalice of Pevensey, squat and powerful, like one great block of rugged stone, the parapet twinkling with steel caps and crowned by the royal banner of England. A flat expanse of reeded marshland lay before them, out of which rose a single wooded hill, crowned with towers, with a bristle of masts rising out of the green plain some distance to the south of it. Nigel looked at it with his hand shading his eyes, and then urged Pommers to a trot. The town was Winchelsea, and there amid that cluster of houses on the hill the gallant Chandos must be awaiting him.

XIV. HOW NIGEL CHASED
THE RED FERRET

THEY PASSED A ferry, wound upward by a curving path, and then, having satisfied a guard of men-at-arms, were admitted through the frowning arch of the Pipewell Gate. There waiting for them, in the middle of the main street, the sun gleaming upon his lemon-colored beard, and puckering his single eye, stood Chandos himself, his legs apart, his hands behind his back, and a welcoming smile upon his quaint high-nosed face. Behind him a crowd of little boys were gazing with reverent eyes at the famous soldier.

"Welcome, Nigel!" said he, "and you also, good archer! I chanced to be walking on the city wall, and I thought from the color of your horse that it was indeed you upon the Udimore Road. How have you fared, young squire errant? Have you held bridges or rescued damsels or slain oppressors on your way from Tilford?"

"Nay, my fair lord, I have accomplished nothing; but I once had hopes——" Nigel flushed at the remembrance.

"I will give you more than hopes, Nigel. I will put you where you can dip both arms to the elbow into danger and honor, where peril will sleep with you at night and rise with you in the morning, and the very air you breathe be laden with it. Are you ready for that, young sir?"

"I can but pray, fair lord, that my spirit will rise to it."

Chandos smiled his approval and laid his thin brown hand on the youth's shoulder.

"Good!" said he. "It is the mute hound which bites the hardest. The babbler is ever the hang-back. Bide with me here, Nigel, and walk upon the ramparts. Archer, do you lead the horses to the Sign of the Broom Pod in the high street, and tell my varlets to see them aboard the cog Thomas before nightfall. We sail at the second hour after curfew. Come hither, Nigel, to the crest of the corner turret, for from it I will show you what you have never seen."

It was but a dim and distant white cloud upon the blue water seen far off over the Dungeness Point, and yet the sight of it flushed the young squire's cheeks and sent the blood hot through his veins. It was the fringe of France, that land of chivalry and glory, the stage where name and fame were to be won. With burning eyes he gazed across at it, his heart rejoicing to think that the hour was at hand when he might tread that sacred soil. Then his gaze crossed the immense stretch of the blue sea, dotted over with the sails of fishing-boats, until it rested upon the double harbor beneath packed with vessels of every size and shape, from the pessoners and creyers which plied up and down the coast to the great cogs and galleys which were used either as war-ships or merchantmen as the occasion served. One of them was at that instant passing out to sea, a huge galleass, with trumpets blowing and nakers banging, the flag of Saint George flaunting over the broad purple sail, and the decks sparkling from end to end with steel. Nigel gave a cry of pleasure at the splendor of the sight.

"Aye, lad," said Chandos, "it is the Trinity of Rye, the very ship on which I fought at Sluys. Her deck ran blood from stem to stern that day. But turn your eyes this way, I beg you, and tell me if you see aught strange about this town."

Nigel looked down at the noble straight street, at the Roundel Tower, at the fine church of Saint Thomas, and the other fair buildings of Winchelsea.

"It is all new," said he—"church, castle, houses, all are new."

"You are right, fair son. My grandfather can call to mind the time when only the conies lived upon this rock. The town was down yonder by the sea, until one night the waves rose upon it and not a house was left. See, yonder is Rye, huddling also on a hill, the two towns like poor sheep when the waters are out. But down there under the blue water and below the Camber Sand lies the true Winchelsea—tower, cathedral, walls and all, even as my grandfather knew it, when the first Edward was young upon the throne."

For an hour or more Chandos paced upon the ramparts with his young squire at his elbow, and talked to him of his duties and of the secrets and craft of warfare, Nigel drinking in and storing in his memory every word from so revered a teacher. Many a time in after life, in stress and in danger, he strengthened himself by the memory of that slow walk with the blue sea on one side and the fair town on the other, when the wise soldier and noble-hearted knight poured forth his precept and advice as the master-workman to the apprentice.

"Perhaps, fair son," said he, "you are like so many other lads who ride to the wars, and know so much already that it is waste of breath to advise them?"

"Nay, my fair lord, I know nothing save that I would fain do my duty and either win honorable advancement or die worshipful on the field."

"You are wise to be humble," said Chandos; "for indeed he who knows most of war knows best that there is much to learn. As there is a mystery of the rivers and a mystery of woodcraft, even so there is a mystery of warfare by which battles may be lost and gained; for all nations are brave, and where the brave meets the brave, it is he who is crafty and war-wise who will win the day. The best hound will run at fault if he be ill laid on, and the best hawk will fly at check if he be badly loosed, and even so the bravest army may go awry if it be ill handled. There are not in Christendom better knights and squires than those of the French, and yet we have had the better of them, for in our Scottish wars and elsewhere we have learned more of this same mystery of which I speak."

"And wherein lies our wisdom, honored sir?" asked Nigel. "I also would fain be war-wise, and learn to fight with my wits as well as with my sword."

Chandos shook his head and smiled. "It is in the forest and on the down that you learn to fly the hawk and loose the hound," said he. "So also it is in camp and on the field that the mystery of war can be learned. There only has every great captain come to be its master. To start he must have a cool head, quick to think, soft as wax before his purpose is formed, hard as steel when once he sees it before him. Ever alert he must be, and cautious also, but with judgment to turn his caution into rashness where a large gain may be put against a small stake. An eye for country also, for the trend of the rivers, the slope of the hills, the cover of the woods, and the light green of the bog-land."

Poor Nigel, who had trusted to his lance and to Pommers to break his path to glory, stood aghast at this list of needs.

"Alas!" he cried. "How am I to gain all this?—I, who could scarce learn to read or write, though the good Father Matthew broke a hazel stick a day across my shoulders?"

"You will gain it, fair son, where others have gained it before you. You have that which is the first thing of all, a heart of fire from which other colder hearts may catch a spark. But you must have knowledge also of that which warfare has taught us in olden times. We know, par exemple, that horsemen alone cannot hope to win against good foot-soldiers. Has it not been tried at Courtrai, at Stirling, and again under my own eyes at Crécy, where the chivalry of France went down before our bowmen?"

Nigel stared at him with a perplexed brow. "Fair sir, my heart grows heavy as I hear you. Do you then say that our chivalry can make no head against archers, billmen, and the like?"

"Nay, Nigel, for it has also been very clearly shown that the best foot-soldiers unsupported cannot hold their own against the mailed horsemen."

"To whom, then, is the victory?" asked Nigel.

"To him who can mix his horse and foot, using each to strengthen the other. Apart they are weak. Together they are strong. The archer who can weaken the enemy's line, the horseman who can break it when it is weakened, as was done at Falkirk and Dupplin, there is the secret of our strength. Now, touching this same battle of Falkirk, I pray you for one instant to give it your attention."

With his whip he began to trace a plan of the Scottish battle upon the dust, and Nigel, with knitted brows, was trying hard to muster his small stock of brains, and to profit by the lecture, when their conversation was interrupted by a strange new arrival.

It was a very stout little man, wheezy and purple with haste, who scudded down the rampart as if he were blown by the wind, his grizzled hair flying, and his long black gown floating behind him. He was clad in the dress of a respectable citizen, a black jerkin trimmed with sable, a black velvet beaver hat and a white feather. At the sight of Chandos he gave a cry of joy, and quickened his pace, so that when he did at last reach him he could only stand gasping and waving his hands.

"Give yourself time, good Master Wintersole, give yourself time!" said Chandos, in a soothing voice.

"The papers!" gasped the little man. "Oh, my Lord Chandos, the papers!"

"What of the papers, my worthy sir?"

"I swear by our good patron Saint Leonard, it is no fault of mine! I had locked them in my coffer. But the lock was forced and the coffer rifled."

A shadow of anger passed over the soldier's keen face.

"How now, Master Mayor? Pull your wits together, and do not stand there babbling like a three-year child. Do you say that some one hath taken the papers?"

"It is sooth, fair sir! Thrice I have been mayor of the town, and fifteen years burgess and jurat, but never once has any public matter gone awry through me. Only last month there came an order from Windsor on a Tuesday for a Friday banquet, a thousand soles, four thousand plaice, two thousand mackerel, five hundred crabs, a thousand lobsters, five thousand whiting——"

"I doubt not, Master Mayor, that you are an excellent fishmonger; but the matter concerns the papers I gave into your keeping. Where are they?"

"Taken, fair sir—gone!"

"And who hath dared to take them?"

"Alas! I know not. It was but for as long as you would say an angelus that I left the chamber, and when I came back there was the coffer, broken and empty, upon my table."

"Do you suspect no one?"

"There was a varlet who hath come with the last few days into my employ. He is not to be found, and I have sent horsemen along both the Udimore Road and that to Rye, that they may seize him. By the help of Saint Leonard they can scarce miss him, for one can tell him a bow-shot off by his hair."

"Is it red?" asked Chandos eagerly. "Is it fox-red, and the man a small man pocked with sun spots, and very quick in his movements?"

"It is the man himself."

Chandos shook his clinched hand with annoyance, and then set off swiftly down the street.

"It is Peter the Red Ferret once more!" said he. "I knew him of old in France, where he has done us more harm than a company of men-at-arms. He speaks English as he speaks French, and he is of such daring and cunning that nothing is secret from him. In all France there is no more dangerous man, for though he is a gentleman of blood and coat-armor, he takes the part of a spy, because it hath the more danger and therefore the more honor."

"But, my fair lord," cried the mayor, as he hurried along, keeping pace with the long strides of the soldier, "I knew that you warned me to take all care of the papers; but surely there was no matter of great import in it? It was but to say what stores were to be sent after you to Calais?"

"Is that not everything?" cried Chandos, impatiently. "Can you not see, oh foolish Master Wintersole, that the French suspect we are about to make some attempt, and that they have sent Peter the Red Ferret, as they have sent him many times before, to get tidings of whither we are bound? Now that he knows that the stores are for Calais, then the French near Calais will take his warning, and so the king's whole plan come to nothing."

"Then he will fly by water. We can stop him yet. He has not an hour's start."

"It may be that a boat awaits him at Rye or Hythe; but it is more like that he has all ready to depart from here. Ah, see yonder! I'll warrant that the Red Ferret is on board!"

Chandos had halted in front of his inn, and now he pointed down to the outer harbor, which lay two miles off across the green plain. It was connected by a long winding canal with the inner dock at the base of the hill, upon which the town was built.

Between the two horns formed by the short curving piers a small schooner was running out to sea, dipping and rising before a sharp southerly breeze.

"It is no Winchelsea boat," said the Mayor. "She is longer and broader in the beam than ours."

"Horses! bring horses!" cried Chandos. "Come, Nigel, let us go further into the matter."

A busy crowd of varlets, archers, and men-at-arms swarmed round the gateway of the Sign of the Broom Pod, singing, shouting, and jostling in rough good-fellowship. The sight of the tall thin figure of Chandos brought order among them, and a few minutes later the horses were ready and saddled. A breakneck ride down a steep declivity, and then a gallop of two miles over the sedgy plain carried them to the outer harbor. A dozen vessels were lying there, ready to start for Bordeaux or Rochelle, and the quay was thick with sailors, laborers, and townsmen, and heaped with wine-barrels and wool-packs.

"Who is warden here?" asked Chandos, springing from his horse.

"Badding! Where is Cock Badding? Badding is warden!" shouted the crowd.

A moment later a short swarthy man, bull-necked and deep-chested, pushed through the people. He was clad in rough russet wool with a scarlet cloth tied round his black curly head. His sleeves were rolled up to his shoulders, and his brown arms, all stained with grease and tar, were like two thick gnarled branches from an oaken stump. His savage brown face was fierce and frowning, and was split from chin to temple with the long white wale of an ill-healed wound.

"How now, gentles, will you never wait your turn?" he rumbled, in a deep angry voice. "Can you not see that we are warping the *Rose of Guienne* into midstream for the ebb-tide? Is this a time to break in upon us? Your goods will go aboard in due season, I promise you; so ride back into the town and find such pleasure as you may, while I and my mates do our work without let or hindrance."

"It is the gentle Chandos!" cried some one in the crowd. "It is the good Sir John."

The rough harbor-master changed his gruffness to smiles in an instant.

"Nay, Sir John, what would you? I pray you to hold me excused if I was short of speech, but we port-wardens are sore plagued with foolish young lordlings, who get betwixt us and our work and blame us because we do not turn an ebb-tide into a flood, or a south wind into a north. I pray you to tell me how I can serve you."

"That boat!" said Chandos, pointing to the already distant sail rising and falling on the waves. "What is it?"

Cock Badding shaded his keen eyes with his strong brown hand.

"She has but just gone out," said he. "She is *La Pucelle*, a small wine-sloop from Gascony, home-bound and laden with barrel-staves."

"I pray you did any man join her at the very last?"

"Nay, I know not. I saw no one."

"But I know," cried a seaman in the crowd. "I was standing at the wharf-side and was nigh knocked into the water by a little red-headed fellow, who breathed as though he had run from the town. Ere I had time to give him a cuff he had jumped aboard, the ropes were cast off, and her nose was seaward."

In a few words Chandos made all clear to Badding, the crowd pressing eagerly round.

"Ay, ay!" cried a seaman, "the good Sir John is right. See how she points. It is Picardy and not Gascony that she will fetch this journey in spite of her wine-staves."

"Then we must lay her aboard!" cried Cock Badding. "Come, lads, here is my own *Marie Rose* ready to cast off. Who's for a trip with a fight at the end of it?"

There was a rush for the boat; but the stout little seaman picked his men. "Go back, Jerry! Your heart is good, but you are overfat for the work. You, Luke, and you, Thomas, and the two Deedes, and William of Sandgate. You will work the boat. And now we need a few men of their hands. Do you come, little sir?"

"I pray you, my dear lord, to let me go!" cried Nigel.

"Yes, Nigel, you can go, and I will bring your gear over to Calais this night."

"I will join you there, fair sir, and with the help of Saint Paul I will bring this Red Ferret with me."

"Aboard, aboard! Time passes!" cried Badding, impatiently, while already his seamen were hauling on the line and raising the mainsail. "Now then, sirrah! who are you?"

It was Aylward, who had followed Nigel, and was pushing his way aboard.

"Where my master goes I go also," cried Aylward, "so stand clear, master-shipman, or you may come by a hurt."

"By Saint Leonard! archer," said Cock Badding, "had I more time I would give you a lesson ere I leave land. Stand back and give place to others!"

"Nay, stand back and give place to me!" cried Aylward, and seizing Badding round the waist he slung him into the dock.

There was a cry of anger from the crowd, for Badding was the hero of all the Cinque Ports and had never yet met his match in manhood. The epitaph still lingers in which it was said that he "could never rest until he had foughten his fill." When, therefore, swimming like a duck, he reached a rope and pulled himself hand over hand up to the quay, all stood aghast to see what fell fate would befall this bold stranger. But Badding laughed loudly, dashing the salt water from his eyes and hair.

"You have fairly won your place, archer," said he. "You are the very man for our work. Where is Black Simon of Norwich?"

A tall dark young man with a long, stern, lean face came forward. "I am with you, Cock," said he, "and I thank you for my place."

"You can come, Hugh Baddlesmere, and you, Hal Masters, and you, Dicon of Rye. That is enough. Now off, in God's name, or it will be night ere we can come up with them!"

Already the head-sails and the mainsail had been raised, while a hundred willing hands poled her off from the wharf. Now the wind caught her; heeling over, and quivering with eagerness like an unleashed hound she flew through the opening and out into the Channel. She was a famous little schooner, the *Marie Rose* of Winchelsea, and under her daring owner Cock Badding, half trader and half pirate, had brought back into port many a rich cargo taken in mid-Channel, and paid for in blood rather than money. Small as she was, her great speed and the fierce character of her master had made her a name of terror along the French coast, and many a bulky Eastlander or Fleming as he passed the narrow seas had scanned the distant Kentish shore, fearing lest that ill-omened purple sail with a gold Christopher upon it should shoot out suddenly from the dim gray cliffs. Now she was clear of the land, with the wind on her larboard quarter, every inch of canvas set, and her high sharp bows smothered in foam, as she dug through the waves.

Cock Badding trod the deck with head erect and jaunty bearing, glancing up at the swelling sails and then ahead at the little tilted white triangle, which stood out clear and hard against the bright blue sky. Behind was the lowland of the Camber marshes, with the bluffs of Rye and Winchelsea, and the line of cliffs behind them. On the larboard bow rose the great white walls of Folkestone and of Dover, and far on the distant sky-line the gray shimmer of those French cliffs for which the fugitives were making.

"By Saint Paul!" cried Nigel, looking with eager eyes over the tossing waters, "it seems to me, Master Badding, that already we draw in upon them."

The master measured the distance with his keen steady gaze, and then looked up at the sinking sun. "We have still four hours of daylight," said he; "but if we do not lay her aboard ere darkness falls she will save herself, for the nights are as black as a wolf's mouth, and if she alter her course I know not how we may follow her."

"Unless, indeed, you might guess to which port she was bound and reach it before her."

"Well thought of, little master!" cried Badding. "If the news be for the French outside Calais, then Ambleteuse would be nearest to Saint Omer. But my sweeting sails three paces to that lubber's two, and if the wind holds we shall have time and to spare. How now, archer? You do not seem so eager as when you made your way aboard this boat by slinging me into the sea."

Aylward sat on the upturned keel of a skiff which lay upon the deck. He groaned sadly and held his green face between his two hands.

"I would gladly sling you into the sea once more, master-shipman," said he, "if by so doing I could get off this most accursed vessel of thine. Or if you would wish to have your turn, then I would thank you if you would lend me a hand over the side, for indeed I am but a useless weight upon your deck. Little did I think that Samkin Aylward could be turned into a weakling by an hour of salt water. Alas the day that ever my foot wandered from the good red heather of Crooksbury!"

Cock Badding laughed loud and long. "Nay, take it not to heart, archer," he cried; "for better men than you or I have groaned upon this deck. The prince himself with ten of his chosen knights crossed with me once, and eleven sadder faces I never saw. Yet within a month they had shown at Crécy that they were no weaklings, as you will do also, I dare swear, when the time comes. Keep that thick head of thine down upon the planks, and all will be well anon. But we raise her, we raise her with every blast of the wind!"

It was indeed evident, even to the inexperienced eyes of Nigel, that the *Marie Rose* was closing in swiftly upon the stranger. She was a heavy, bluff-bowed, broad-sterned vessel which labored clumsily through the seas. The swift, fierce little Winchelsea boat swooping and hissing through the waters behind her was like some keen hawk whizzing down wind at the back of a flapping heavy-bodied duck. Half an hour before *La Pucelle* had been a distant patch of canvas. Now they could see the black hull, and soon the cut of her sails and the lines of her bulwarks. There were at least a dozen men upon her deck, and the twinkle of weapons from among them showed that they were preparing to resist. Cock Badding began to muster his own forces.

He had a crew of seven rough, hardy mariners, who had been at his back in many a skirmish. They were armed with short swords, but Cock Badding carried a weapon peculiar to himself, a twenty-pound blacksmith's hammer, the memory of which, as "Badding's cracker," still lingers in the Cinque Ports. Then there were the eager Nigel, the melancholy Aylward, Black Simon, who was a tried swordsman, and three archers, Baddlesmere, Masters and Dicon of Rye, all veterans of the French

War. The numbers in the two vessels might be about equal; but Badding as he glanced at the bold harsh faces which looked to him for orders had little fear for the result.

Glancing round, however, he saw something which was more dangerous to his plans than the resistance of the enemy. The wind, which had become more fitful and feebler, now fell suddenly away, until the sails hung limp and straight above them. A belt of calm lay along the horizon, and the waves around had smoothed down into a long oily swell on which the two little vessels rose and fell. The great boom of the *Marie Rose* rattled and jarred with every lurch, and the high thin prow pointed skyward one instant and seaward the next in a way that drew fresh groans from the unhappy Aylward. In vain Cock Badding pulled on his sheets and tried hard to husband every little wandering gust which ruffled for an instant the sleek rollers. The French master was as adroit a sailor, and his boom swung round also as each breath of wind came up from astern.

At last even these fitful puffs died finally away, and a cloudless sky overhung a glassy sea. The sun was almost upon the horizon behind Dungeness Point, and the whole western heaven was bright with the glory of the sunset, which blended sea and sky in one blaze of ruddy light. Like rollers of molten gold, the long swell heaved up Channel from the great ocean beyond. In the midst of the immense beauty and peace of nature the two little dark specks with the white sail and the purple rose and fell, so small upon the vast shining bosom of the waters, and yet so charged with all the unrest and the passion of life.

The experienced eye of the seaman told him that it was hopeless to expect a breeze before nightfall. He looked across at the Frenchman, which lay less than a quarter of a mile ahead, and shook his gnarled fist at the line of heads which could be seen looking back over her stern. One of them waved a white kerchief in derision, and Cock Badding swore a bitter oath at the sight.

"By Saint Leonard of Winchelsea," he cried, "I will rub my side up against her yet! Out with the skiff, lads, and two of you to the oars. Make fast the line to the mast, Will. Do you go in the boat, Hugh, and I'll make the second. Now if we bend our backs to it we may have them yet ere night cover them."

The little skiff was swiftly lowered over the side and the slack end of the cable fastened to the after thwart. Cock Badding and his comrades pulled as if they would snap their oars, and the little vessel began slowly to lurch forward over the rollers. But the next moment a larger skiff had splashed over the side of the Frenchman, and no less than four seamen were hard at work under her bows. If the *Marie Rose* advanced a yard the Frenchman was going two. Again Cock Badding raved and shook his fist. He clambered aboard, his face wet with sweat and dark with anger.

"Curse them! they have had the best of us!" he cried. "I can do no more. Sir John has lost his papers, for indeed now that night is at hand I can see no way in which we can gain them."

Nigel had leaned against the bulwark during these events, watching with keen attention the doings of the sailors, and praying alternately to Saint Paul, Saint George, and Saint Thomas for a slant of wind which would put them alongside their enemy. He was silent; but his hot heart was simmering within him. His spirit had risen even above the discomfort of the sea, and his mind was too absorbed in his mission to have a thought for that which had laid Aylward flat upon the deck. He had never doubted that Cock Badding in one way or another would accomplish his end, but when he heard his speech of despair he bounded off the bulwark and stood before the seaman with his face flushed and all his soul afire.

"By Saint Paul! master-shipman," he cried, "we should never hold up our heads in honor if we did not go further into the matter! Let us do some small deed this night upon the water, or let us never see land again, for indeed we could not wish fairer prospect of winning honorable advancement."

"With your leave, little master, you speak like a fool," said the gruff seaman. "You and all your kind are as children when once the blue water is beneath you. Can you not see that there is no wind, and that the Frenchman can warp her as swiftly as we? What then would you do?"

Nigel pointed to the boat which towed astern. "Let us venture forth in her," said he, "and let us take this ship or die worshipful in the attempt."

His bold and fiery words found their echo in the brave rough hearts around him. There was a deep-chested shout from both archers and seamen. Even Aylward sat up, with a wan smile upon his green face.

But Cock Badding shook his head. "I have never met the man who could lead where I would not follow," said he; "but by Saint Leonard! this is a mad business, and I should be a fool if I were to risk my men and my ship. Bethink you, little master, that the skiff can hold only five, though you load her to the water's edge. If there is a man yonder, there are fourteen, and you have to climb their side from the boat. What chance would you have? Your boat stove and you in the water—there is the end of it. No man of mine goes on such a fool's errand, and so I swear!"

"Then, Master Badding, I must crave the loan of your skiff, for by Saint Paul! the good Lord Chandos' papers are not to be so lightly lost. If no one else will come, then I will go alone."

The shipman smiled at the words; but the smile died away from his lips when Nigel, with features set like ivory and eyes as hard as steel, pulled on the rope so as to bring the skiff under the counter. It was very clear that he would do even as he said. At the same time Aylward raised his bulky form from the deck, leaned for a moment against the bulwarks, and then tottered aft to his master's side.

"Here is one that will go with you," said he, "or he would never dare show his face to the girls of Tilford again. Come, archers, let us leave these salt herrings in their pickle tub and try our luck out on the water."

The three archers at once ranged themselves on the same side as their comrade. They were bronzed, bearded men, short in stature, as were most Englishmen of that day, but hardy, strong, and skilled with their weapons. Each drew his string from its waterproof case and bent the huge arc of his war-bow as he fitted it into the nocks.

"Now, master, we are at your back," said they, as they pulled and tightened their sword-belts.

But already Cock Badding had been carried away by the hot lust of battle, and had thrown aside every fear and doubt which had clouded him. To see a fight and not to be in it was more than he could bear.

"Nay, have it your own way!" he cried, "and may Saint Leonard help us, for a madder venture I have never seen! And yet it may be worth the trial. But if it be done let me have the handling of it, little master, for you know no more of a boat than I do of a war-horse. The skiff can bear five and not a man more. Now, who will come?"

They had all caught fire, and there was not one who would be left out.

Badding picked up his hammer. "I will come myself," said he, "and you also, little master, since it is your hot head that has planned it. Then there is Black Simon, the best sword of the Cinque Ports. Two archers can pull on the oars, and it may be that they can pick off two or three of these Frenchmen before we close with them. Hugh Baddlesmere, and you, Dicon of Rye—into the boat with you!"

"What?" cried Aylward. "Am I to be left behind? I, who am the squire's own man? Ill fare the bowman who comes between me and yonder boat!"

"Nay, Aylward," said his master, "I order that you stay, for indeed you are a sick man."

"But now that the waves have sunk I am myself again. Nay, fair sir, I pray that you will not leave me behind."

"You must needs take the space of a better man; for what do you know of the handling of a boat?" said Badding, shortly. "No more fool's talk, I pray you, for the night will soon fall. Stand aside!"

Aylward looked hard at the French boat. "I could swim ten times up and down Frensham pond," said he, "and it will be strange if I cannot go as far as that. By these finger-bones, Samkin Aylward may be there as soon as you!"

The little boat with its five occupants pushed off from the side of the schooner, and dipping and rising, made its slow way toward the Frenchman. Badding and one archer had single oars, the second archer was in the prow, while Black Simon and Nigel huddled into the stern with the water lapping and hissing at their very elbows. A shout of defiance rose from the Frenchmen, and they stood in a line along the side of their vessel shaking their fists and waving their weapons. Already the sun was level with Dungeness, and the gray of evening was blurring sky and water into one dim haze. A great silence hung over the broad expanse of nature, and no sound broke it save the dip and splash of the oars and the slow deep surge of the boat upon the swell. Behind them their comrades of the *Marie Rose* stood motionless and silent, watching their progress with eager eyes.

They were near enough now to have a good look at the Frenchmen. One was a big swarthy man with a long black beard. He had a red cap and an ax over his shoulder. There were ten other hardy-looking fellows, all of them well armed, and there were three who seemed to be boys.

"Shall we try a shaft upon them?" asked Hugh Baddlesmere. "They are well within our bowshot."

"Only one of you can shoot at a time, for you have no footing," said Badding. "With one foot in the prow and one over the thwart you will get your stance. Do what you may, and then we will close in upon them."

The archer balanced himself in the rolling boat with the deftness of a man who has been trained upon the sea, for he was born and bred in the Cinque Ports. Carefully he nocked his arrow, strongly he drew it, steadily he loosed it, but the boat swooped at the instant, and it buried itself in the waves. The second passed over the little ship, and the third struck in her black side. Then in quick succession—so quick that two shafts were often in the air at the same instant—he discharged a dozen arrows, most of which just cleared the bulwarks and dropped upon the deck. There was a cry on the Frenchman, and the heads vanished from the side.

"Enough!" cried Badding. "One is down, and it may be two. Close in, close in, in God's name, before they rally!"

He and the other bent to their oars; but at the same instant there was a sharp zip in the air and a hard clear sound like a stone striking a wall. Baddlesmere clapped his hand to his head, groaned and fell forward out of the boat, leaving a swirl of blood upon the surface. A moment later the same fierce hiss ended in a loud wooden crash, and a short, thick crossbow-bolt was buried deep in the boat.

"Close in, close in!" roared Badding, tugging at his oar. "Saint George for England! Saint Leonard for Winchelsea! Close in!"

But again that fatal crossbow twanged. Dicon of Rye fell back with a shaft through his shoulder. "God help me, I can no more!" said he.

Badding seized the oar from his hand; but it was only to sweep the boat's head round and pull her back to the *Marie Rose*. The attack had failed.

"What now, master-shipman?" cried Nigel. "What has befallen to stop us? Surely the matter does not end here?"

"Two down out of five," said Badding, "and twelve at the least against us. The odds are too long, little master. Let us at least go back, fill up once more, and raise a mantelet against the bolts, for they have an arbalest which shoots both straight and hard. But what we do we must do quickly, for the darkness falls apace."

Their repulse had been hailed by wild yells of delight from the Frenchmen, who danced with joy and waved their weapons madly over their heads. But before their rejoicings had finished they saw the little boat creeping out once more from the shadow of the *Marie Rose*, a great wooden screen in her bows to protect her from the arrows. Without a pause she came straight and fast for her enemy. The wounded archer had been put on board, and Aylward would have had his place had Nigel been able to see him upon the deck. The third archer, Hal Masters, had sprung in, and one of the seamen, Wat Finnis of Hythe. With their hearts hardened to conquer or to die, the five ran alongside the Frenchman and sprang upon her deck. At the same instant a great iron weight crashed through the bottom of their skiff, and their feet had hardly left her before she was gone. There was no hope and no escape save victory.

The crossbowman stood under the mast, his terrible weapon at his shoulder, the steel string stretched taut, the heavy bolt shining upon the nut. One life at least he would claim out of this little band. Just for one instant too long did he dwell upon his aim, shifting from the seaman to Cock Badding, whose formidable appearance showed him to be the better prize. In that second of time Hal Masters' string twanged and his long arrow sped through the arbalester's throat. He dropped on the deck, with blood and curses pouring from his mouth.

A moment later Nigel's sword and Badding's hammer had each claimed a victim and driven back the rush of assailants. The five were safe upon the deck, but it was hard for them to keep a footing there. The French seamen, Bretons and Normans, were stout, powerful fellows, armed with axes and swords, fierce fighters and brave men. They swarmed round the little band, attacking them from all sides. Black Simon felled the black-bearded French captain, and at the same instant was cut over the head and lay with his scalp open upon the deck. The seaman Wat of Hythe was killed by a crashing blow from an axe. Nigel was struck down, but was up again like a flash, and drove his sword through the man who had felled him.

But Badding, Masters the archer, and he had been hustled back to the bulwark and were barely holding their own from minute to minute against the fierce crowd who assailed them, when an arrow coming apparently from the sea struck the foremost Frenchman to the heart. A moment later a boat dashed up alongside and four more men from the *Marie Rose* scrambled on to the blood-stained deck. With one fierce rush the remaining Frenchmen were struck down or were seized by their assailants. Nine prostrate men upon the deck showed how fierce had been the attack, how desperate the resistance.

Badding leaned panting upon his blood-clotted hammer. "By Saint Leonard!" he cried. "I thought that this little master had been the death of us all. God wot you were but just in time, and how you came I know not. This archer has had a hand in it, by the look of him."

Aylward, still pale from his sea-sickness and dripping from head to foot with water, had been the first man in the rescue party.

Nigel looked at him in amazement. "I sought you aboard the ship, Aylward, but I could not lay eyes on you," said he.

"It was because I was in the water, fair sir, and by my hilt! it suits my stomach better than being on it," he answered. "When you first set forth I swam behind you, for I saw that the Frenchman's boat hung by a rope, and I thought that while you kept him in play I might gain it. I had reached it when you were driven back, so I hid behind it in the water and said my prayers as I have not said them for many a day. Then you came again, and no one had an eye for me, so I clambered into it, cut the rope, took the oars which I found there, and brought her back for more men."

"By Saint Paul! you have acted very wisely and well," said Nigel, "and I think that of all of us it is you who have won most honor this day. But of all these men dead and alive I see none who resembles that Red Ferret whom my Lord Chandos has described and who has worked such despite upon us in the past. It would indeed be an evil chance if he has, in spite of all our pains, made his way to France in some other boat."

"That we shall soon find out," said Badding. "Come with me, and we will search the ship from truck to keel ere he escapes us."

There was a scuttle at the base of the mast which led down into the body of the vessel, and the Englishmen were approaching this when a strange sight brought them to a stand. A round brazen head had appeared in the square dark opening. An instant afterward a pair of shining shoulders followed. Then slowly the whole figure of a man in complete plate-armor emerged on the deck. In his gauntleted hand he carried a heavy steel mace. With this uplifted he moved toward his enemies, silent save for the ponderous clank of his footfall. It was an inhuman, machine-like figure, menacing and terrible, devoid of all expression, slow-moving, inexorable, and awesome.

A sudden wave of terror passed over the English seamen. One of them tried to pass and get behind the brazen man, but he was pinned against the side by a quick movement and his brains dashed out by a smashing blow from the heavy mace. Wild panic seized the others, and they rushed back to the boat. Aylward strung an arrow, but his bowstring was damp and the shaft rang loudly upon the shining breastplate and glanced off into the sea. Masters struck the brazen head with a sword, but

"Then slowly the whole figure of a man in complete plate-armor emerged on the deck." [*page 176*]

the blade snapped without injuring the helmet, and an instant later the bowman was stretched senseless on the deck. The seamen shrank from this terrible silent creature and huddled in the stern, all the fight gone out of them.

Again he raised his mace and was advancing on the helpless crowd where the brave were encumbered and hampered by the weaklings, when Nigel shook himself clear and bounded forward into the open, his sword in his hand and a smile of welcome upon his lips.

The sun had set, and one long pink gash across the western Channel was closing swiftly into the dull grays of early night. Above, a few stars began to faintly twinkle; yet the twilight was still bright enough for an observer to see every detail of the scene; the *Marie Rose,* dipping and rising on the long rollers astern; the broad French boat with its white deck blotched with blood and littered with bodies; the group of men in the stern, some trying to advance and some seeking to escape—all a confused, disorderly, struggling rabble.

Then between them and the mast the two figures: the armed shining man of metal, with hand upraised, watchful, silent, motionless, and Nigel, bareheaded and crouching, with quick foot, eager eyes, and fearless, happy face, moving this way and that, in and out, his sword flashing like a gleam of light as he sought at all points for some opening in the brazen shell before him.

It was clear to the man in armor that if he could but pen his antagonist in a corner he would beat him down without fail. But it was not to be done. The unhampered man had the advantage of speed. With a few quick steps he could always glide to either side and escape the clumsy rush. Aylward and Badding had sprung out to Nigel's assistance; but he shouted to them to stand back, with such authority and anger in his voice that their weapons dropped to their sides. With staring eyes and set features they stood watching that unequal fight.

Once it seemed that all was over with the squire, for in springing back from his enemy he tripped over one of the bodies which strewed the deck and fell flat upon his back, but with a swift wriggle he escaped the heavy blow which thundered down upon him, and springing to his feet he bit deeply into the

Frenchman's helmet with a sweeping cut in return. Again the mace fell, and this time Nigel had not quite cleared himself. His sword was beaten down and the blow fell partly upon his left shoulder. He staggered, and once more the iron club whirled upward to dash him to the ground.

Quick as a flash it passed through his mind that he could not leap beyond its reach. But he might get within it. In an instant he had dropped his sword, and springing in he had seized the brazen man round the waist. The mace was shortened and the handle jobbed down once upon the bare flaxen head. Then, with a sonorous clang, and a yell of delight from the spectators, Nigel, with one mighty wrench, tore his enemy from the deck and hurled him down upon his back. His own head was whirling and he felt that his senses were slipping away, but already his hunting-knife was out and pointing through the slit in the brazen helmet.

"Give yourself up, fair sir!" said he.

"Never to fishermen and to archers! I am a gentleman of coat-armor. Kill me!"

"I also am a gentleman of coat-armor. I promise you quarter."

"Then, sir, I surrender myself to you."

The dagger tinkled down upon the deck. Seamen and archers ran forward, to find Nigel half senseless upon his face. They drew him off, and a few deft blows struck off the helmet of his enemy. A head, sharp-featured, freckled and foxy-red, disclosed itself beneath it. Nigel raised himself on his elbow for an instant.

"You are the Red Ferret?" said he.

"So my enemies call me," said the Frenchman, with a smile. "I rejoice, sir, that I have fallen to so valiant and honorable a gentleman."

"I thank you, fair sir," said Nigel, feebly. "I also rejoice that I have encountered so debonair a person, and I shall ever bear in mind the pleasure which I have had from our meeting."

So saying he laid his bleeding head upon his enemy's brazen front and sank into a dead faint.

XV. HOW THE RED FERRET
CAME TO COSFORD

THE OLD CHRONICLER in his "*Gestes du Sieur Nigel*" has bewailed his broken narrative, which rose from the fact that out of thirty-one years of warfare no less than seven were spent by his hero at one time or another in the recovery from his wounds or from those illnesses which arose from privation and fatigue. Here at the very threshold of his career, on the eve of a great enterprise, this very fate befell him.

Stretched upon a couch in a low-roofed and ill-furnished chamber, which looks down from under the machicolated corner turret upon the inner court of the Castle of Calais, he lay half-unconscious and impotent, while great deeds were doing under his window. Wounded in three places, and with his head splintered by the sharp pommel of the Ferret's mace, he hovered between life and death, his shattered body drawing him downward, his youthful spirit plucking him up.

As in some strange dream he was aware of that deed of arms within the courtyard below. Dimly it came back to his memory afterwards, the sudden startled shout, the crash of metal, the slamming of great gates, the roar of many voices, the clang, clang, clang, as of fifty lusty smiths upon their anvils, and then at last the dwindling of the hubbub, the low groans and sudden shrill cries to the saints, the measured murmur of many voices, the heavy clanking of armored feet.

Sometime in that fell struggle he must have drawn his weakened body as far as the narrow window, and hanging to the iron bars have looked down on the wild scene beneath him. In the red glare of torches held from windows and from roof he saw the rush and swirl of men below, the ruddy light shining back from glowing brass and gleaming steel. As a wild vision it came to him afterward, the beauty and the splendor, the flying lambrequins, the jeweled crests, the blazonry and richness of surcoat and of shield, where sable and gules, argent and vair, in every pattern of saltire, bend or chevron, glowed beneath him like a drift of many-colored blossoms, tossing, sinking, stooping into shadow, springing into light. There glared the blood-red gules of Chandos, and he saw the tall figure of his master, a thunderbolt of war, raging in the van. There too were the three black chevrons on the golden shield which marked the noble Manny. That strong swordsman must surely be the royal Edward himself, since only he and the black-armored swift-footed youth at his side were marked by no symbol of heraldry.

"Manny! Manny! George for England!" rose the deep-throated bay, and ever the gallant counter-cry: "A Chargny! A Chargny! Saint Denis for France!" thundered amid the clash and thudding of the battle.

Such was the vague whirling memory still lingering in Nigel's mind when at last the mists cleared away from it and he found himself weak but clear on the low couch in the corner turret. Beside him, crushing lavender between his rough fingers and strewing it over floor and sheets, was Aylward the archer. His longbow leaned at the foot of the bed, and his steel cap was balanced on the top of it, while he himself, sitting in his shirt sleeves, fanned off the flies and scattered the fragrant herbs over his helpless master.

"By my hilt!" he cried, with a sudden shout, every tooth in his head gleaming with joy, "I thank the Virgin and all the saints for this blessed sight! I had not dared to go back to Tilford had I lost you. Three weeks have you lain there and babbled like a babe, but now I see in your eyes that you are your own man again."

"I have indeed had some small hurt," said Nigel, feebly; "but it is shame and sorrow that I should lie here if there is work for my hands. Whither go you, archer?"

"To tell the good Sir John that you are mending."

"Nay, bide with me a little longer, Aylward. I can call to mind all that has passed. There was a bickering of small boats, was there not, and I chanced upon a most worthy person and exchanged handstrokes with him? He was my prisoner, was he not?"

"He was, fair sir."

"And where is he now?"

"Below in the castle."

A smile stole over Nigel's pale face. "I know what I will do with him," said he.

"I pray you to rest, fair sir," said Aylward anxiously. "The king's own leech saw you this morning, and he said that if the bandage was torn from your head you would surely die."

"Nay, good archer, I will not move. But tell me what befell upon the boat?"

"There is little to tell, fair sir. Had this Ferret not been his own squire and taken so long a time to don his harness it is likely that they would have had the better of us. He did not reach the battle till his comrades were on their backs. Him we took to the *Marie Rose*, because he was your man. The others were of no worth, so we threw them into the sea."

"The quick and the dead?"

"Every man of them."

"It was an evil deed."

Aylward shrugged his shoulders. "I tried to save one boy," said he; "but Cock Badding would not have it, and he had Black Simon and the others at his back. 'It is the custom of the Narrow Seas,' said they: 'To-day for them; to-morrow for us.' Then they tore him from his hold and cast him screaming over the side. By my hilt! I have no love for the sea and its customs, so I care not if I never set foot on it again when it has once borne me back to England."

"Nay, there are great happenings upon the sea, and many worthy people to be found upon ships," said Nigel. "In all parts, if one goes far enough upon the water, one would find those whom it would be joy to meet. If one crosses over the Narrow Sea, as we have done, we come on the French who are so needful to us; for how else would we win worship? Or if you go south, then in time one may hope to come to the land of the unbelievers, where there is fine skirmishing and much honor for him who will venture his person. Bethink you, archer, how fair a life it must be when one can ride forth in search of advancement with some hope of finding many debonair cavaliers upon the same quest, and then if one be overborne one has died for the faith, and the gates of heaven are open before you. So also the sea to the north is a help to him who seeks honor, for it leads to the country of the Eastlanders and to those parts where the heathen still dwell who turn their faces from the blessed Gospel. There also a man might find some small deeds to do, and by Saint Paul! Aylward, if the French hold the truce and the good Sir John permits us, I would fain go down into those parts. The sea is a good friend to the cavalier, for it takes him where he may fulfil his vows."

Aylward shook his head, for his memories were too recent; but he said nothing, because at this instant the door opened and Chandos entered. With joy in his face he stepped forward to the couch and took Nigel's hand in his. Then he whispered a word in Aylward's ear, who hurried from the room.

"*Pardieu!* this is a good sight," said the knight. "I trust that you will soon be on your feet again."

"I crave your pardon, my honored lord, that I have been absent from your side," said Nigel.

"In truth my heart was sore for you, Nigel; for you have missed such a night as comes seldom in any man's life. All went even as we had planned. The postern gate was opened, and a party made their way in; but we awaited them, and all were taken or slain. But the greater part of the French had remained without upon the plain of Nieullet, so we took horse and went out against them. When we drew near them they were surprised, but they made good cheer among themselves, calling out to each other: 'If we fly we lose all. It is better to fight on, in the hopes that the day may be ours.' This was heard by our people in the van, who cried out to them: 'By Saint George! you speak truth. Evil befall him who thinks of flying!' So they held their ground like worthy people for the space of an hour, and there were many there whom it is always good to meet: Sir Geoffrey himself, and Sir Pepin de Werre, with Sir John de Landas, old Ballieul of the Yellow Tooth, and his brother Hector the Leopard. But above all Sir Eustace de Ribeaumont was at great pains to meet us worthily, and he was at handstrokes with the king for a long time. Then, when we had slain or taken them, all the prisoners were brought to a feast which was ready for them, and the knights of

England waited upon them at the table and made good cheer with them. And all this, Nigel, we owe to you."

The squire flushed with pleasure at the words. "Nay, most honored lord, it was but a small thing which I have been able to do. But I thank God and our Lady that I have done some service, since it has pleased you to take me with you to the wars. Should it chance——"

But the words were cut short upon Nigel's lips, and he lay back with amazed eyes staring from his pallid face. The door of his little chamber had opened, and who was this, the tall, stately man with the noble presence, the high forehead, the long, handsome face, the dark, brooding eyes—who but the noble Edward of England?

"Ha, my little cock of Tilford Bridge, I still bear you in mind," said he. "Right glad I was to hear that you had found your wits again, and I trust that I have not helped to make you take leave of them once more."

Nigel's stare of astonishment had brought a smile to the king's lips. Now the squire stammered forth some halting words of gratitude at the honor done to him.

"Nay, not a word," said the king. "But in sooth it is a joy to my heart to see the son of my old comrade Eustace Loring carrying himself so bravely. Had this boat got before us with news of our coming, then all our labor had been in vain, and no Frenchman ventured to Calais that night. But above all, I thank you for that you have delivered into my hands one whom I had vowed to punish in that he has caused us more scathe by fouler means than any living man. Twice have I sworn that Peter the Red Ferret shall hang, for all his noble blood and coat-armor, if ever he should fall into my hands. Now at last his time has come; but I would not put him to death until you, who had taken him, could be there to see it done. Nay, thank me not, for I could do no less, seeing that it is to you that I owe him."

But it was not thanks which Nigel was trying to utter. It was hard to frame his words, and yet they must be said.

"Sire," he murmured, "it ill becomes me to cross your royal will——"

The dark Plantagenet wrath gathered upon the king's high brow and gloomed in his fierce deep-set eyes.

"By God's dignity! no man has ever crossed it yet and lived unscathed. How now, young sir, what mean such words, to which we are little wont? Have a care, for this is no light thing which you venture."

"Sire," said Nigel, "in all matters in which I am a free man I am ever your faithful liege, but some things there are which may not be done."

"How?" cried the king. "In spite of my will?"

"In spite of your will, sire," said Nigel, sitting up on his couch, with white face and blazing eyes.

"By the Virgin!" the angry king thundered, "we are come to a pretty pass! You have been held too long at home, young man. The overstabled horse will kick. The unweathered hawk will fly at check. See to it, Master Chandos! He is thine to break, and I hold you to it that you break him. And what is it that Edward of England may not do, Master Loring?"

Nigel faced the king with a face as grim as his own. "You may not put to death the Red Ferret."

"*Pardieu!* And why?"

"Because he is not thine to slay, sire. Because he is mine. Because I promised him his life, and it is not for you, king though you be, to constrain a man of gentle blood to break his plighted word and lose his honor."

Chandos laid his soothing hand upon his squire's shoulder.

"Excuse him, sire; he is weak from his wounds," said he. "Perhaps we have stayed over-long, for the leech has ordered repose."

But the angry king was not easily to be appeased. "I am not wont to be so browbeat," said he, hotly. "This is your squire, Master John. How comes it that you can stand there and listen to his pert talk, and say no word to chide him? Is this how you guide your household? Have you not taught him that every promise given is subject to the king's consent, and that with him only lie the springs of life and death? If he is sick, you, at least, are hale. Why stand you there in silence?"

"My liege," said Chandos gravely, "I have served you for over a score of years, and have shed my blood through as many wounds in your cause, so that you should not take my words amiss. But, indeed, I should feel myself to be no true man if I did not tell you that my Squire Nigel, though perchance he has spoken more bluntly than becomes him, is none the less right in this matter, and that you are wrong. For bethink you, sire——"

"Enough!" cried the king, more furious than ever. "Like master, like man, and I might have known why it is that this saucy squire dares to bandy words with his sovereign lord. He does but give out what he hath taken in. John, John, you grow overbold. But this I tell you, and you also, young man, that as God is my help, ere the sun has set this night the Red Ferret will hang as a warning to all spies and traitors from the highest tower of Calais, that every ship upon the Narrow Seas, and every man for ten miles round may see him as he swings and know how heavy is the hand of the English king. Do you bear it in mind, lest you also may feel its weight!" With a glare like an angry lion he walked from the room, and the iron-clamped door clanged loudly behind him.

Chandos and Nigel looked ruefully at each other. Then the knight patted his squire upon his bandaged head.

"You have carried yourself right well, Nigel. I could not wish for better. Fear not. All will be well."

"My fair and honored lord," cried Nigel, "I am heavy at heart, for indeed I could do no other, and yet I have brought trouble upon you."

"Nay, the clouds will soon pass. If he does indeed slay this Frenchman, you have done all that lay within your power, and your mind may rest easy."

"I pray that it will rest easy in Paradise," said Nigel; "for at the hour that I hear that I am dishonored and my prisoner slain, I tear this bandage from my head and so end all things. I will not live when once my word is broken."

"Nay, fair son, you take this thing too heavily," said Chandos, with a grave face. "When a man has done all he may there remains no dishonor; but the king hath a kind heart for all his hot head, and it may be that if I see him I will prevail upon him. Bethink you how he swore to hang the six burghers of this very town, and yet he pardoned them. So keep a high heart, fair son, and I will come with good news ere evening."

For three hours, as the sinking sun traced the shadow higher and ever higher upon the chamber wall, Nigel tossed feverishly upon his couch, his ears straining for the footfall of Aylward or of Chandos, bringing news of the fate of the prisoner. At last the door flew open, and there before him stood the one man whom he least expected, and yet would most gladly have seen. It was the Red Ferret himself, free and joyous.

With swift furtive steps he was across the room and on his knees beside the couch, kissing the pendent hand.

"You have saved me, most noble sir!" he cried. "The gallows was fixed and the rope slung, when the good Lord Chandos told the king that you would die by your own hand if I were slain. 'Curse this mule-headed squire!' he cried. 'In God's name let him have his prisoner, and let him do what he will with him so long as he troubles me no more!' So here I have come, fair sir, to ask you what I shall do."

"I pray you to sit beside me and be at your ease," said Nigel. "In a few words I will tell you what I would have you do. Your armor I will keep that I may have some remembrance of my good fortune in meeting so valiant a gentleman. We are of a size, and I make little doubt that I can wear it. Of ransom I would ask a thousand crowns."

"Nay, nay!" cried the Ferret. "It would be a sad thing if a man of my position was worth less than five thousand."

"A thousand will suffice, fair sir, to pay my charges for the war. You will not again play the spy, nor do us harm until the truce is broken."

"That I will swear."

"And lastly there is a journey that you shall make."

The Frenchman's face lengthened. "Where you order I must go," said he; "but I pray you that it is not to the Holy Land."

"Nay," said Nigel; "but it is to a land which is holy to me. You will make your way back to Southampton."

"I know it well. I helped to burn it down some years ago."

"I rede you to say nothing of that matter when you get there. You will then journey as though to London until you come to a fair town named Guildford."

"I have heard of it. The king hath a hunt there."

"The same. You will then ask for a house named Cosford, two leagues from the town on the side of a long hill."

"I will bear it in mind."

"At Cosford you will see a good knight named Sir John Buttesthorn, and you will ask to have speech with his daughter, the Lady Mary."

"I will do so; and what shall I say to the Lady Mary, who lives at Cosford on the slope of a long hill two leagues from the fair town of Guildford?"

"Say only that I sent my greeting, and that Saint Catharine has been my friend—only that and nothing more. And now leave me, I pray you, for my head is weary and I would fain have sleep."

Thus it came about that a month later on the eve of the Feast of Saint Matthew, the Lady Mary, as she walked from Cosford gates, met with a strange horseman, richly clad, a serving-man behind him, looking shrewdly about him with quick blue eyes, which twinkled from a red and freckled face. At sight of her he doffed his hat and reined his horse.

"This house should be Cosford," said he. "Are you by chance the Lady Mary who dwells there?"

The lady bowed her proud dark head.

"Then," said he, "Squire Nigel Loring sends you greeting and tells you that Saint Catharine has been his friend." Then turning to his servant, he cried: "Heh, Raoul, our task is done! Your master is a free man once more. Come, lad, come, the nearest port to France! Hola! Hola! Hola!" And so without a word more the two, master and man, set spurs to their horses and galloped like madmen down the long slope of Hindhead, until as she looked after them they were but two dark dots in the distance, waist high in the ling and the bracken.

She turned back to the house, a smile upon her face. Nigel had sent her greeting. A Frenchman had brought it. His bringing it had made him a freeman. And Saint Catherine had been Nigel's friend. It was at her shrine that he had sworn that three deeds should be done ere he should set eyes upon her again. In the privacy of her room the Lady Mary sank upon her prie-dieu and poured forth the thanks of her heart to the Virgin that one deed was accomplished; but even as she did so her joy was overcast by the thought of those two others which lay before him.

XVI. HOW THE KING'S COURT
FEASTED IN CALAIS CASTLE

IT WAS A bright sunshiny morning when Nigel found himself at last able to leave his turret chamber and to walk upon the rampart of the castle. There was a brisk northern wind, heavy and wet with the salt of the sea, and he felt, as he turned his face to it, fresh life and strength surging in his blood and bracing his limbs. He took his hand from Aylward's supporting arm and stood with his cap off, leaning on the rampart and breathing in the cool strong air. Far off upon the distant sky-line, half hidden by the heave of the waves, was the low white fringe of cliffs which skirted England. Between him and them lay the broad blue Channel, seamed and flecked with flashing foam, for a sharp sea was running and the few ships in sight were laboring heavily. Nigel's eyes traversed the wide-spread view, rejoicing in the change from the gray wall of his cramped chamber. Finally they settled upon a strange object at his very feet.

It was a long trumpet-shaped engine of leather and iron bolted into a rude wooden stand and fitted with wheels. Beside it lay a heap of metal slugs and lumps of stone. The end of the machine was raised and pointed over the battlement. Behind it stood an iron box which Nigel opened. It was filled with a black coarse powder, like gritty charcoal.

"By Saint Paul!" said he, passing his hands over the engine, "I have heard men talk of these things, but never before have I seen one. It is none other than one of those wondrous new-made bombards."

"In sooth it is even as you say," Aylward answered, looking at it with contempt and dislike in his face. "I have seen them here upon the ramparts, and have also exchanged a buffet or two with

189

him who had charge of them. He was jack-fool enough to think that with this leather pipe he could outshoot the best archer in Christendom. I lent him a cuff on the ear that laid him across his foolish engine."

"It is a fearsome thing," said Nigel, who had stooped to examine it. "We live in strange times when such things can be made. It is loosed by fire, is it not, which springs from the black dust?"

"By my hilt! fair sir, I know not. And yet I call to mind that ere we fell out this foolish bombardman did say something of the matter. The fire-dust is within and so also is the ball. Then you take more dust from this iron box and place it in the hole at the farther end—so. It is now ready. I have never seen one fired, but I wot that this one could be fired now."

"It makes a strange sound, archer, does it not?" said Nigel, wistfully.

"So I have heard, fair sir—even as the bow twangs, so it also has a sound when you loose it."

"There is no one to hear, since we are alone upon the rampart, nor can it do scathe, since it points to sea. I pray you to loose it and I will listen to the sound." He bent over the bombard with an attentive ear, while Aylward, stooping his earnest brown face over the touch-hole, scraped away diligently with a flint and steel. A moment later both he and Nigel were seated some distance off upon the ground, while amid the roar of the discharge and the thick cloud of smoke they had a vision of the long black snake-like engine shooting back upon the recoil. For a minute or more they were struck motionless with astonishment, while the reverberations died away and the smoke-wreaths curled slowly up to the blue heavens.

"Good lack!" cried Nigel at last, picking himself up and looking round him. "Good lack, and Heaven be my aid! I thank the Virgin that all stands as it did before. I thought that the castle had fallen."

"Such a bull's bellow I have never heard," cried Aylward, rubbing his injured limbs. "One could hear it from Frensham Pond to Guildford Castle. I would not touch one again—not for a hide of the best land in Puttenham!"

"It may fare ill with your own hide, archer, if you do," said an angry voice behind them. Chandos had stepped from the open door of the corner turret and stood looking at them with a harsh gaze. Presently, as the matter was made clear to him, his face relaxed into a smile.

"Hasten to the warden, archer, and tell him how it befell. You will have the castle and the town in arms. I know not what the king may think of so sudden an alarm. And you, Nigel, how in the name of the saints came you to play the child like this?"

"I knew not its power, fair lord."

"By my soul, Nigel, I think that none of us know its power. I can see the day when all that we delight in, the splendor and glory of war, may all go down before that which beats through the plate of steel as easily as the leathern jacket. I have bestrode my war-horse in my armor and have looked down at the sooty, smoky bombardman beside me, and I have thought that perhaps I was the last of the old and he the first of the new; that there would come a time when he and his engines would sweep you and me and the rest of us from the field."

"But not yet, I trust, honored sir?"

"No, not yet, Nigel. You are still in time to win your spurs even as your fathers did. How is your strength?"

"I am ready for any task, my good and honored lord."

"It is well, for work awaits us—good work, pressing work, work of peril and of honor. Your eyes shine and your face flushes, Nigel. I live my own youth over again as I look at you. Know then that though there is truce with the French here, there is not truce in Brittany, where the houses of Blois and of Montfort still struggle for the dukedom. Half Brittany fights for one, and half for the other. The French have taken up the cause of Blois, and we of Montfort, and it is such a war that many a great leader, such as Sir Walter Manny, has first earned his name there. Of late the war has gone against us, and the bloody hands of the Rohans, of Gap-tooth Beaumanoir, of Oliver the Flesher and others have been heavy upon our people. The last tidings have been of disaster, and the king's soul is dark with wrath for that his friend and comrade Gilles de St. Pol has been done to death in the Castle of La Brohinière. He will send succors to the country, and we go at their head. How like you that, Nigel?"

"My honored lord, what could I ask for better?"

"Then have your harness ready, for we start within the week. Our path by land is blocked by the French, and we go by sea. This night the king gives a banquet ere he returns to England, and your place is behind my chair. Be in my chamber that you may help me to dress, and so we will to the hall together."

With satin and with samite, with velvet and with fur, the noble Chandos was dressed for the king's feast, and Nigel too had donned his best silk jupon, faced with the five scarlet roses, that he might wait upon him. In the great hall of Calais Castle the tables were set, a high table for the lords, a second one for the less distinguished knights, and a third at which the squires might feast when their masters were seated.

Never had Nigel in his simple life at Tilford pictured a scene of such pomp and wondrous luxury. The grim gray walls were covered from ceiling to floor with priceless tapestry of Arras, where hart, hounds and huntsmen circled the great hall with one long living image of the chase. Over the principal table drooped a line of banners, and beneath them rows of emblazoned shields upon the wall carried the arms of the high noblemen who sat beneath. The red light of cressets and of torches burned upon the badges of the great captains of England. The lions and lilies shone over the high dorseret chair in the center, and the same august device marked with the cadency label indicated the seat of the prince, while glowing to right and to left were the long lines of noble insignia, honored in peace and terrible in war. There shone the gold and sable of Manny, the engrailed cross of Suffolk, the red chevron of Stafford, the scarlet and gold of Audley, the blue lion rampant of the Percies, the silver swallows of Arundel, the red roebuck of the Montacutes, the star of the de Veres, the silver scallops of Russell, the purple lion of de Lacy, and the black crosses of Clinton.

A friendly squire at Nigel's elbow whispered the names of the famous warriors beneath.

"You are young Loring of Tilford, the squire of Chandos, are you not?" said he. "My name is Delves, and I come from

Doddington in Cheshire. I am the squire of Sir James Audley, yonder round-backed man with the dark face and close-cropped beard, who hath the Saracen head as a crest above him."

"I have heard of him as a man of great valor," said Nigel, gazing at him with interest.

"Indeed, you may well say so, Master Loring. He is the bravest knight in England, and in Christendom also, as I believe. No man hath done such deeds of valor."

Nigel looked at his new acquaintance with hope in his eyes.

"You speak as it becomes you to speak when you uphold your own master," said he. "For the same reason, Master Delves, and in no spirit of ill-will to you, it behooves me to tell you that he is not to be compared in name or fame with the noble knight on whom I wait. Should you hold otherwise, then surely we can debate the matter in whatever way or time may please you best."

Delves smiled good-humoredly. "Nay, be not so hot," said he. "Had you upheld any other knight, save perhaps Sir Walter Manny, I had taken you at your word, and your master or mine would have had place for a new squire. But indeed it is only truth that no knight is second to Chandos, nor would I draw my sword to lower his pride of place. Ha, Sir James' cup is low! I must see to it!" He darted off, a flagon of Gascony in his hand. "The king hath had good news to-night," he continued when he returned. "I have not seen him in so merry a mind since the night when we took the Frenchmen and he laid his pearl chaplet upon the head of de Ribeaumont. See how he laughs, and the prince also. That laugh bodes some one little good, or I am the more mistaken. Have a care! Sir John's plate is empty."

It was Nigel's turn to dart away; but ever in the intervals he returned to the corner whence he could look down the hall and listen to the words of the older squire. Delves was a short, thickset man past middle age, weather-beaten and scarred, with a rough manner and bearing which showed that he was more at his ease in a tent than a hall. But ten years of service had taught him much, and Nigel listened eagerly to his talk.

"Indeed the king hath some good tidings," he continued. "See now, he has whispered it to Chandos and to Manny. Manny spreads it on to Sir Reginald Cobham, and he to Robert Knolles, each smiling like the devil over a friar."

"Which is Sir Robert Knolles?" asked Nigel with interest. "I have heard much of him and his deeds."

"He is the tall hard-faced man in yellow silk, he with the hairless cheeks and the split lip. He is little older than yourself, and his father was a cobbler in Chester, yet he has already won the golden spurs. See how he dabs his great hand in the dish and hands forth the gobbets. He is more used to a camp-kettle than a silver plate. The big man with the black beard is Sir Bartholomew Berghersh, whose brother is the Abbot of Beaulieu. Haste, haste! for the boar's head is come and the plate's to be cleaned."

The table manners of our ancestors at this period would have furnished to the modern eye the strangest mixture of luxury and of barbarism. Forks were still unknown, and the courtesy fingers, the index and the middle of the left hand, took their place. To use any others was accounted the worst of manners. A crowd of dogs lay among the rushes growling at each other and quarreling over the gnawed bones which were thrown to them by the feasters. A slice of coarse bread served usually as a plate, but the king's own high table was provided with silver platters, which were wiped by the squire or page after each course. On the other hand, the table-linen was costly, and the courses, served with a pomp and dignity now unknown, comprised such a variety of dishes and such complex marvels of cookery as no modern banquet could show. Besides all our domestic animals and every kind of game, such strange delicacies as hedgehogs, bustards, porpoises, squirrels, bitterns, and cranes lent variety to the feast.

Each new course, heralded by a flourish of silver trumpets, was borne in by liveried servants walking two and two, with rubicund marshals strutting in front and behind, bearing white wands in their hands, not only as badges of their office, but also as weapons with which to repel any impertinent inroad upon the dishes in the journey from the kitchen to the hall. Boars' heads, enarmed and endored with gilt tusks and flaming mouths, were followed by wondrous pasties molded to the shape of ships, castles and other devices, with sugar seamen or soldiers who lost their own bodies in their fruitless defense against the hungry attack. Finally came the great nef, a silver vessel upon wheels laden with fruit and sweetmeats which rolled with its luscious cargo down the line of guests. Flagons of Gascony, of Rhine wine, of Canary and of Rochelle were held in readiness by the attendants; but the age, though luxurious, was not drunken, and the sober habits of the Norman had happily prevailed over the license of those Saxon banquets, where no guest might walk from the table without a slur upon his host. Honor and hardi-hood go ill with a shaking hand or a blurred eye.

While wine, fruit, and spices were handed round the high tables the squires had been served in turn at the farther end of the hall. Meanwhile round the king there had gathered a group of statesmen and soldiers, talking eagerly among themselves. The Earl of Stafford, the Earl of Warwick, the Earl of Arundel, Lord Beauchamp and Lord Neville were assembled at the back of his chair, with Lord Percy and Lord Mowbray at either side. The little group blazed with golden chains and jeweled chaplets, flame-colored paltocks and purple tunics.

Of a sudden the king said something over his shoulder to Sir William de Pakyngton the herald, who advanced and stood by the royal chair. He was a tall and noble-featured man, with long grizzled beard which rippled down to the gold-linked belt gir-dling his many-colored tabard. On his head he had placed the heraldic barret-cap which bespoke his dignity, and he slowly raised his white wand high in the air, while a great hush fell upon the hall.

"My lords of England," said he, "knight bannerets, knights, squires, and all others here present of gentle birth and coat-armor, know that your dread and sovereign lord, Edward, King of England and of France, bids me give you greeting and com-mands you to come hither that he may have speech with you."

In an instant the tables were deserted and the whole company had clustered in front of the king's chair. Those who had sat on either side of him crowded inward, so that his tall dark figure upreared itself amid the dense circle of his guests.

With a flush upon his olive cheeks and with pride smoldering in his dark eyes, he looked round him at the eager faces of the men who had been his comrades from Sluys and Cadsand to Crécy and Calais. They caught fire from that warlike gleam in his masterful gaze, and a sudden wild, fierce shout pealed up to the vaulted ceiling, a soldierly thanks for what was passed and a promise for what was to come. The king's teeth gleamed in a quick smile, and his large white hand played with the jeweled dagger in his belt.

"By the splendor of God!" said he in a loud clear voice, "I have little doubt that you will rejoice with me this night, for such tidings have come to my ears as may well bring joy to every one of you. You know well that our ships have suffered great scathe from the Spaniards, who for many years have slain without grace or ruth all of my people who have fallen into their cruel hands. Of late they have sent their ships into Flanders, and thirty great cogs and galleys lie now at Sluys well-filled with archers and men-at-arms and ready in all ways for battle. I have it to-day from a sure hand that, having taken their merchandise aboard, these ships will sail upon the next Sunday, and will make their way through our Narrow Sea. We have for a great time been long-suffering to these people, for which they have done us many contraries and despites, growing ever more arrogant as we grow more patient. It is in my mind therefore that we hie us to-morrow to Winchelsea, where we have twenty ships, and make ready to sally out upon them as they pass. May God and Saint George defend the right!"

A second shout, far louder and fiercer than the first, came like a thunderclap after the king's words. It was the bay of a fierce pack to their trusted huntsman.

Edward laughed again as he looked round at the gleaming eyes, the waving arms, and the flushed joyful faces of his liege-men.

"Who hath fought against these Spaniards?" he asked. "Is there any one here who can tell us what manner of men they be?"

A dozen hands went up into the air; but the king turned to the Earl of Suffolk at his elbow.

"You have fought them, Thomas?" said he.

"Yes, sire, I was in the great sea-fight eight years ago at the Island of Guernsey, when Lord Lewis of Spain held the sea against the Earl of Pembroke."

"How found you them, Thomas?"

"Very excellent people, sire, and no man could ask for better. On every ship they have a hundred crossbowmen of Genoa, the best in the world, and their spearmen also are very hardy men. They would throw great cantles of iron from the tops of the masts, and many of our people met their death through it. If we can bar their way in the Narrow Sea, then there will be much hope of honor for all of us."

"Your words are very welcome, Thomas," said the king, "and I make no doubt that they will show themselves to be very worthy of what we prepare for them. To you I give a ship, that you may have the handling of it. You also, my dear son, shall have a ship, that evermore honor may be thine."

"I thank you, my fair and sweet father," said the prince, with joy flushing his handsome boyish face.

"The leading ship shall be mine. But you shall have one, Walter Manny, and you, Stafford, and you, Arundel, and you, Audley, and you, Sir Thomas Holland, and you, Brocas, and you, Berkeley, and you, Reginald. The rest shall be awarded at Winchelsea, whither we sail to-morrow. Nay, John, why do you pluck so at my sleeve?"

Chandos was leaning forward, with an anxious face. "Surely, my honored lord, I have not served you so long and so faithfully that you should forget me now. Is there, then, no ship for me?"

The king smiled, but shook his head. "Nay, John, have I not given you two hundred archers and a hundred men-at-arms to take with you into Brittany? I trust that your ships will be lying in Saint Malo Bay ere the Spaniards are abreast of Winchelsea. What more would you have, old war-dog? Wouldst be in two battles at once?"

"I would be at your side, my liege, when the lion banner is in the wind once more. I have ever been there. Why should you cast me now? I ask little, dear lord—a galley, a balinger, even a pinnace, so that I may only be there."

"Nay, John, you shall come. I cannot find it in my heart to say you nay. I will find you place in my own ship, that you may indeed be by my side."

Chandos stooped and kissed the king's hand. "My squire?" he asked.

The king's brows knotted into a frown. "Nay, let him go to Brittany with the others," said he harshly. "I wonder, John, that you should bring back to my memory this youth whose pertness is too fresh that I should forget it. But some one must go to Brittany in your stead, for the matter presses and our people are hard put to it to hold their own." He cast his eyes over the assembly, and they rested upon the stern features of Sir Robert Knolles.

"Sir Robert," he said, "though you are young in years you are already old in war, and I have heard that you are as prudent in council as you are valiant in the field. To you I commit the charge of this venture to Brittany in place of Sir John Chandos, who will follow thither when our work has been done upon the waters. Three ships lie in Calais port and three hundred men are ready to your hand. Sir John will tell you what our mind is in the matter. And now, my friends and good comrades, you will haste you each to his own quarters, and you will make swiftly such preparations as are needful, for, as God is my aid, I will sail with you to Winchelsea to-morrow!"

Beckoning to Chandos, Manny and a few of his chosen leaders, the king led them away to an inner chamber, where they might discuss the plans for the future. At the same time the assembly broke up, the knights in silence and dignity, the squires in mirth and noise, but all joyful at heart for the thought of the great days which lay before them.

XVII. THE SPANIARDS ON THE SEA

DAY HAD NOT yet dawned when Nigel was in the chamber of Chandos preparing him for his departure and listening to the last cheery words of advice and direction from his noble master. That same morning, before the sun was halfway up the heaven, the king's great nef *Philippa,* bearing within it the most of those present at his banquet the night before, set its huge sail, adorned with the lions and the lilies, and turned its brazen beak for England. Behind it went five smaller cogs crammed with squires, archers and men-at-arms.

Nigel and his companions lined the ramparts of the castle and waved their caps as the bluff, burly vessels, with drums beating and trumpets clanging, a hundred knightly pennons streaming from their decks and the red cross of England over all, rolled slowly out to the open sea. Then, when they had watched them until they were hull down, they turned, with hearts heavy at being left behind, to make ready for their own more distant venture.

It took them four days of hard work ere their preparations were complete, for many were the needs of a small force sailing to a strange country. Three ships had been left to them—the cog *Thomas* of Romney, the *Grace Dieu* of Hythe, and the *Basilisk* of Southampton, into each of which one hundred men were stowed, besides the thirty seamen who formed the crew. In the hold were forty horses, among them Pommers, much wearied by his long idleness, and homesick for the slopes of Surrey, where his great limbs might find the work he craved. Then the food and the water, the bow-staves and the sheaves of arrows, the horseshoes, the nails, the hammers, the knives, the axes, the ropes, the vats of hay, the green fodder, and a score of other things were packed aboard. Always by the side of the ships stood the stern young knight Sir Robert, checking, testing, watching, and controlling, saying little, for he was a man of few words, but with his eyes, his hands, and if need be his heavy dog-whip, wherever they were wanted.

The seamen of the *Basilisk,* being from a free port, had the old feud against the men of the Cinque Ports, who were looked upon by the other mariners of England as being unduly favored by the king. A ship of the West Country could scarce meet with one from the Narrow Seas without blood flowing. Hence sprang sudden broils on the quay side, when with yell and blow the *Thomases* and *Grace Dieus,* Saint Leonard on their lips and murder in their hearts, would fall upon the *Basilisks*. Then amid the whirl of cudgels and the clash of knives would spring the tiger figure of the young leader, lashing mercilessly to right and left like a tamer among his wolves, until he had beaten them howling back to their work. Upon the morning of the fourth day all was ready, and the ropes being cast off, the three little ships were warped down the harbor by their own pinnaces until they were swallowed up in the swirling folds of a Channel mist.

Though small in numbers, it was no mean force which Edward had dispatched to succor the hard-pressed English garrisons in Brittany. There was scarce a man among them who was not an old soldier, and their leaders were men of note in council and in war. Knolles flew his flag of the black raven aboard the *Basilisk*. With him were Nigel and his own squire, John Hawthorn. Of his hundred men, forty were Yorkshire dalesmen and forty were men of Lincoln, all noted archers, with old Wat of Carlisle, a grizzled veteran of border warfare, to lead them.

Already Aylward by his skill and strength had won his way to an under-officership among them, and shared with Long Ned Widdington, a huge north countryman, the reputation of coming next to famous Wat Carlisle in all that makes an archer. The men-at-arms, too, were war-hardened soldiers, with Black Simon of Norwich, the same who had sailed from Winchelsea, to lead them. With his heart filled with hatred for the French who had slain all who were dear to him, he followed like a bloodhound over land and sea to any spot where he might glut his vengeance. Such also were the men who sailed in the other ships—Cheshire men from the Welsh borders in the cog *Thomas,* and Cumberland men, used to Scottish warfare, in the *Grace Dieu.*

Sir James Astley hung his shield of cinquefoil ermine over the quarter of the *Thomas.* Lord Thomas Percy, a cadet of Alnwick, famous already for the high spirit of that house which for ages was the bar upon the landward gate of England, showed his blue lion rampant as leader of the *Grace Dieu.* Such was the goodly company Saint Malo bound, who warped from Calais harbor to plunge into the thick reek of a Channel mist.

A slight breeze blew from the eastward, and the highended, round-bodied craft rolled slowly down the Channel. The mist rose a little at times, so that they had sight of each other dipping and rising upon a sleek, oily sea, but again it would sink down, settling over the top, shrouding the great yard, and finally frothing over the deck until even the water alongside had vanished from their view and they were afloat on a little raft in an ocean of vapor. A thin cold rain was falling, and the archers were crowded under the shelter of the overhanging poop and forecastle where some spent the hours at dice, some in sleep, and many in trimming their arrows or polishing their weapons.

At the farther end, seated on a barrel as a throne of honor, with trays and boxes of feathers around him, was Bartholomew the bowyer and fletcher, a fat, bald-headed man, whose task it was to see that every man's tackle was as it should be, and who had the privilege of selling such extras as they might need. A group of archers with their staves and quivers filed before him with complaints or requests, while half a dozen of the seniors gathered at his back and listened with grinning faces to his comments and rebukes.

"Canst not string it?" he was saying to a young bowman. "Then surely the string is overshort or the stave overlong. It could not by chance be the fault of thy own baby arms more fit to draw on thy hosen than to dress a warbow. Thou lazy lurdan, thus is it strung!" He seized the stave by the center in his right hand, leaned the end on the inside of his right foot, and then, pulling the upper nock down with the left hand, slid the eye of the string easily into place. "Now I pray thee to unstring it again," handing it to the bowman.

The youth, with an effort, did so; but he was too slow in disengaging his fingers, and the string sliding down with a snap from the upper nock caught and pinched them sorely against the stave. A roar of laughter, like the clap of a wave, swept down the deck as the luckless bowman danced and wrung his hand.

"Serve thee well right, thou redeless fool!" growled the old bowyer. "So fine a bow is wasted in such hands. How now, Samkin? I can teach you little of your trade, I trow. Here is a bow dressed as it should be; but it would, as you say, be the better for a white band to mark the true nocking point in the center of this red wrapping of silk. Leave it and I will tend to it anon. And you, Wat? A fresh head on yonder stele? Lord, that a man should carry four trades under one hat, and be bowyer, fletcher, stringer, and head-maker! Four men's work for old Bartholomew and one man's pay!"

"Nay, say no more about that," growled an old wizened bowman, with a brown parchment skin and little beady eyes. "It is better in these days to mend a bow than to bend one. You who never looked a Frenchman in the face are pricked off for ninepence a day, and I who have fought five stricken fields, can earn but fourpence."

"It is in my mind, John of Tuxford, that you have looked in the face more pots of mead than Frenchmen," said the old bowyer. "I am swinking from dawn to night, while you are guzzling in an ale-stake. How now, youngster? Overbowed? Put your bow in the tiller. It draws at sixty pounds—not a pennyweight too much for a man of your inches. Lay more body to it, lad, and it will come to you. If your bow be not stiff, how can you hope for a twenty-score flight. Feathers? Aye, plenty and of the best. Here are peacock at a groat each. Surely a dandy archer like you, Tom Beverley, with gold earrings in your ears, would have no feathering but peacocks?"

"So the shaft fly straight, I care not of the feather," said the bowman, a tall young Yorkshireman, counting out pennies on the palm of his horny hand.

"Gray goose-feathers are but a farthing. These on the left are a half-penny, for they are of the wild-goose, and the second feather of a fenny goose is worth more than the pinion of a tame one. These in the brass tray are dropped feathers, and a dropped feather is better than a plucked one. Buy a score of these, lad, and cut them saddle-backed or swine-backed, the one for a dead shaft and the other for a smooth flyer, and no man in the company will swing a better-fletched quiver over his shoulder."

It chanced that the opinion of the bowyer on this and other points differed from that of Long Ned of Widdington, a surly straw-bearded Yorkshireman, who had listened with a sneering face to his counsel. Now he broke in suddenly upon the bowyer's talk.

"You would do better to sell bows than to try to teach others how to use them," said he; "for indeed, Bartholomew, that head of thine has no more sense within it than it has hairs without. If you had drawn string for as many months as I have years you would know that a straight-cut feather flies smoother than a swine-backed, and pity it is that these young bowmen have none to teach them better!"

This attack upon his professional knowledge touched the old bowyer on the raw. His fat face became suffused with blood and his eyes glared with fury as he turned upon the archer.

"You seven-foot barrel of lies!" he cried. "All-hallows be my aid, and I will teach you to open your slabbing mouth against me! Pluck forth your sword and stand out on yonder deck, that we may see who is the man of us twain. May I never twirl a shaft over my thumb-nail if I do not put Bartholomew's mark upon your thick head!"

A score of rough voices joined at once in the quarrel, some upholding the bowyer and others taking the part of the north countryman. A red-headed dalesman snatched up a sword, but was felled by a blow from the fist of his neighbor. Instantly, with a buzz like a swarm of angry hornets, the bowmen were out on the deck; but ere a blow was struck Knolles was among them with granite face and eyes of fire.

"Stand apart, I say! I will warrant you enough fighting to cool your blood ere you see England once more. Loring, Hawthorn, cut any man down who raises his hand. Have you aught to say, you fox-haired rascal?" He thrust his face within two inches of that of the red man who had first seized his sword. The fellow shrank back, cowed, from his fierce eyes. "Now stint your noise, all of you, and stretch your long ears. Trumpeter, blow once more!"

A bugle call had been sounded every quarter of an hour so as to keep in touch with the other two vessels, who were invisible in the fog. Now the high clear note rang out once more, the call of a fierce sea-creature to its mates, but no answer came back from the thick wall which pent them in. Again and again they called, and again and again with bated breath they waited for an answer.

"Where is the shipman?" asked Knolles. "What is your name, fellow? Do you dare call yourself master-mariner?"

"My name is Nat Dennis, fair sir," said the gray-bearded old seaman. "It is thirty years since first I showed my cartel and blew trumpet for a crew at the water-gate of Southampton. If any man may call himself master-mariner, it is surely I."

"Where are our two ships?"

"Nay, sir, who can say in this fog?"

"Fellow, it was your place to hold them together."

"I have but the eyes God gave me, fair sir, and they cannot see through a cloud."

"Had it been fair, I, who am a soldier, could have kept them in company. Since it was foul, we looked to you, who are called a mariner, to do so. You have not done it. You have lost two of my ships ere the venture is begun."

"Nay, fair sir, I pray you to consider——"

"Enough words!" said Knolles sternly. "Words will not give me back my two hundred men. Unless I find them before I come to Saint Malo, I swear by Saint Wilfrid of Ripon that it will be an evil day for you! Enough! Go forth and do what you may!"

For five hours, with a light breeze behind them, they lurched through the heavy fog, the cold rain still matting their beards and shining on their faces. Sometimes they could see a circle of tossing water for a bow-shot or so in each direction, and then the wreaths would crawl in upon them once more and bank them thickly round. They had long ceased to blow the trumpet for their missing comrades, but had hopes when clear weather came to find them still in sight. By the shipman's reckoning they were now about midway between the two shores.

Nigel was leaning against the bulwarks, his thoughts away in the dingle at Cosford and out on the heather-clad slopes of Hindhead, when something struck his ear. It was a thin clear clang of metal, pealing out high above the dull murmur of the sea, the creak of the boom, and the flap of the sail. He listened, and again it was borne to his ear.

"Hark, my lord!" said he to Sir Robert. "Is there not a sound in the fog?"

They both listened together with sidelong heads. Then it rang clearly forth once more, but this time in another direction. It had been on the bow; now it was on the quarter. Again it sounded, and again. Now it had moved to the other bow; now back to the quarter again; now it was near; and now so far that it was but a faint tinkle on the ear. By this time every man on board, seamen, archers, and men-at-arms, were crowding the sides of the vessel. All round them there were noises in the darkness, and yet the wall of fog lay wet against their very faces. And the noises were such as were strange to their ears, always the same high musical clashing.

The old shipman shook his head and crossed himself.

"In thirty years upon the waters I have never heard the like," said he. "The Devil is ever loose in a fog. Well is he named the Prince of Darkness."

A wave of panic passed over the vessel, and these rough and hardy men, who feared no mortal foe, shook with terror at the shadows of their own minds. They stared into the cloud with blanched faces and fixed eyes, as though each instant some fearsome shape might break in upon them. And as they stared there came a gust of wind. For a moment the fog-bank rose and a circle of ocean lay before them.

It was covered with vessels. On all sides they lay thick upon its surface. They were huge caracks, high-ended and portly, with red sides and bulwarks carved and crusted with gold. Each had one great sail set, and was driving down channel on the same course as the *Basilisk*. Their decks were thick with men, and from their high poops came the weird clashing which filled the air. For one moment they lay there, this wondrous fleet, surging slowly forward, framed in gray vapor. The next the clouds closed in and they had vanished from view. There was a long hush, and then a buzz of excited voices.

"The Spaniards!" cried a dozen bowmen and sailors.

"I should have known it," said the shipman. "I call to mind on the Biscay coast how they would clash their cymbals after the fashion of the heathen Moor with whom they fight; but what would you have me do, fair sir? If the fog rises we are all dead men."

"There were thirty ships at the least," said Knolles, with a moody brow. "If we have seen them I trow that they have also seen us. They will lay us aboard."

"Nay, fair sir, it is in my mind that our ship is lighter and faster than theirs. If the fog hold another hour we should be through them."

"Stand to your arms!" yelled Knolles. "Stand to your arms! They are on us!"

The *Basilisk* had indeed been spied from the Spanish Admiral's ship before the fog closed down. With so light a breeze, and such a fog, he could not hope to find her under sail. But by an evil chance not a bowshot from the great Spanish carack was a low galley, thin and swift, with oars which could speed her against wind or tide. She also had seen the *Basilisk,* and it was to her that the Spanish leader shouted his orders. For a few minutes she hunted through the fog, and then sprang out of it like a lean and stealthy beast upon its prey. It was the sight of the long dark shadow gliding after them which had brought that wild shout of alarm from the lips of the English knight. In another instant the starboard oars of the galley had been shipped, the sides of the two vessels grated together, and a stream of swarthy, red-capped Spaniards were swarming up the sides of the *Basilisk* and dropped with yells of triumph upon her deck.

For a moment it seemed as if the vessel was captured without a blow being struck, for the men of the English ship had run wildly in all directions to look for their arms. Scores of archers might be seen under the shadow of the forecastle and the poop bending their bowstaves to string them with the cords from their leathern cases. Others were scrambling over saddles, barrels and cases in wild search of their quivers. Each as he came upon his arrows pulled out a few to lend to his less fortunate comrades. In mad haste the men-at-arms also were feeling and grasping in the dark corners, picking up steel caps which would not fit them, hurling them down on the deck, and snatching eagerly at any swords or spears that came their way.

The center of the ship was held by the Spaniards, and having slain all who stood before them, they were pressing up to either end before they were made to understand that it was no fat sheep but a most fierce old wolf which they had taken by the ears.

If the lesson was late, it was the more thorough. Attacked on both sides and hopelessly outnumbered, the Spaniards, who had never doubted that this little craft was a merchant-ship, were cut off to the last man. It was no fight, but a butchery. In vain the survivors ran screaming prayers to the saints and threw themselves down into the galley alongside. It also had been riddled with arrows from the poop of the *Basilisk,* and both the crew on the deck and the galley-slaves in the outriggers at either side lay dead in rows under the overwhelming shower from above. From stem to rudder every foot of her was furred with arrows. It was but a floating coffin piled with dead and dying men, which wallowed in the waves behind them as the *Basilisk* lurched onward and left her in the fog.

In their first rush on to the *Basilisk,* the Spaniards had seized six of the crew and four unarmed archers. Their throats had been cut and their bodies tossed overboard. Now the Spaniards who littered the deck, wounded and dead, were thrust over the side in the same fashion. One ran down into the hold and had to be hunted and killed squealing under the blows like a rat in the darkness. Within half an hour no sign was left of this grim meeting in the fog save for the crimson splashes upon bulwarks and deck. The archers, flushed and merry, were unstringing their bows once more, for in spite of the water glue the damp air took the strength from the cords. Some were hunting about for arrows which might have stuck inboard, and some tying up small injuries received in the scuffle. But an anxious shadow still lingered upon the face of Sir Robert, and he peered fixedly about him through the fog.

"Go among the archers, Hawthorne," said he to his squire. "Charge them on their lives to make no sound! You also, Loring. Go to the afterguard and say the same to them. We are lost if one of these great ships should spy us."

For an hour with bated breath they stole through the fleet, still hearing the cymbals clashing all round them, for in this way the Spaniards held themselves together. Once the wild music came from above their very prow, and so warned them to change their course. Once also a huge vessel loomed for an instant upon their quarter, but they turned two points away from her, and she blurred and vanished. Soon the cymbals were but a distant tinkling, and at last they died gradually away.

"It is none too soon," said the old shipman, pointing to a yellowish tint in the haze above them. "See yonder! It is the sun which wins through. It will be here anon. Ah! said I not so?"

A sickly sun, no larger and far dimmer than the moon, had indeed shown its face, with cloud-wreaths smoking across it. As they looked up it waxed larger and brighter before their eyes—a yellow halo spread round it, one ray broke through, and then a funnel of golden light poured down upon them, widening swiftly at the base. A minute later they were sailing on a clear blue sea with an azure cloud-flecked sky above their heads, and such a scene beneath it as each of them would carry in his memory while memory remained.

They were in mid-Channel. The white and green coasts of Picardy and of Kent lay clear upon either side of them. The wide Channel stretched in front, deepening from the light blue beneath their prow to purple on the far sky-line. Behind them was that thick bank of cloud from which they had just burst. It lay like a gray wall from east to west, and through it were breaking the high shadowy forms of the ships of Spain. Four of them had already emerged, their red bodies, gilded sides and painted sails shining gloriously in the evening sun. Every instant a fresh golden spot grew out of the fog, which blazed like a star for an instant, and then surged forward to show itself as the brazen beak of the great red vessel which bore it. Looking back, the whole bank of cloud was broken by the widespread line of noble ships which were bursting through it. The *Basilisk* lay a mile or more in front of them and two miles clear of their wing. Five miles farther off, in the direction of the French coast, two other small ships were running down Channel. A cry of joy from Robert Knolles and a hearty prayer of gratitude to the saints from the old shipman hailed them as their missing comrades, the cog *Thomas* and the *Grace Dieu*.

But fair as was the view of their lost friends, and wondrous the appearance of the Spanish ships, it was not on those that the eyes of the men of the *Basilisk* were chiefly bent. A greater sight lay before them—a sight which brought them clustering to the forecastle with eager eyes and pointing fingers. The English fleet was coming forth from the Winchelsea Coast. Already before the fog lifted a fast galleass had brought the news down Channel that the Spanish were on the sea, and the king's fleet was under way. Now their long array of sails, gay with the coats and colors of the towns which had furnished them, lay bright against the Kentish coast from Dungeness Point to Rye. Nine and twenty ships were there from Southampton, Shoreham, Winchelsea, Hastings, Rye, Hythe, Romney, Folkestone, Deal, Dover, and Sandwich. With their great sails slued round to catch the wind they ran out, while the Spanish, like the gallant foes that they have ever been, turned their heads landward to meet them. With flaunting banners and painted sails, blaring trumpets and clashing cymbals, the two glittering fleets, dipping and rising on the long Channel swell, drew slowly together.

King Edward had been lying all day in his great ship the *Philippa*, a mile out from the Camber Sands, waiting for the coming of the Spaniards. Above the huge sail which bore the royal arms flew the red cross of England. Along the bulwarks were shown the shields of forty knights, the flower of English chivalry, and as many pennons floated from the deck. The high ends of the ship glittered with the weapons of the men-at-arms, and the waist was crammed with the archers. From time to time a crash of nakers and blare of trumpets burst from the royal ship, and was answered by her great neighbors, the *Lion* on which the Black Prince flew his flag, the *Christopher* with the Earl of Suffolk, the *Salle du Roi* of Robert of Namur, and the *Grace Marie* of Sir Thomas Holland. Farther off lay the *White Swan,* bearing the arms of Mowbray, the *Palmer of Deal,* flying the Black Head of Audley, and the *Kentish Man* under the Lord Beauchamp. The rest lay, anchored but ready, at the mouth of Winchelsea Creek.

The king sat upon a keg in the fore part of his ship, with little John of Richmond, who was no more than a school-boy, perched upon his knee. Edward was clad in the black velvet jacket which was his favorite garb, and wore a small brown beaver hat with a white plume at the side. A rich cloak of fur turned up with miniver drooped from his shoulders. Behind him were a score of his knights, brilliant in silks and sarcenets, some seated on an upturned boat and some swinging their legs from the bulwark.

In front stood John Chandos in a party-colored jupon, one foot raised upon the anchor-stock, picking at the strings of his guitar and singing a song which he had learned at Marienburg when last he helped the Teutonic knights against the heathen. The king, his knights, and even the archers in the waist below them, laughed at the merry lilt and joined lustily in the chorus, while the men of the neighboring ships leaned over the side to hearken to the deep chant rolling over the waters.

But there came a sudden interruption to the song. A sharp, harsh shout came down from the lookout stationed in the circular top at the end of the mast.

"I spy a sail—two sails!" he cried.

John Bunce, the king's shipman, shaded his eyes and stared at the long fog-bank which shrouded the northern channel. Chandos, with his fingers over the strings of his guitar, the king, the knights, all gazed in the same direction. Two small dark shapes had burst forth, and then, after some minutes, a third.

"Surely they are the Spaniards?" said the king.

"Nay, sire," the seaman answered, "the Spaniards are greater ships and are painted red. I know not what these may be."

"But I could hazard a guess!" cried Chandos. "Surely they are the three ships with my own men on their way to Brittany."

"You have hit it, John," said the king. "But look, I pray you! What in the name of the Virgin is that?"

Four brilliant stars of flashing light had shone out from different points of the cloud-bank. The next instant as many tall ships had swooped forth into the sunshine. A fierce shout rang from the king's ship, and was taken up all down the line, until the whole coast from Dungeness to Winchelsea echoed the warlike greeting. The king sprang up with a joyous face.

"The game is afoot, my friends!" said he. "Dress, John! Dress, Walter! Quick, all of you! Squires, bring the harness! Let each tend to himself, for the time is short."

A strange sight it was to see these forty nobles tearing off their clothes, and littering the deck with velvets and satins, while the squire of each, as busy as an ostler before a race, stooped and pulled, and strained and riveted, fastening the bassinets, the leg-pieces, the front and the back plates, until the silken courtier had become the man of steel. When their work was finished, there stood a stern group of warriors where the light dandies had sung and jested round Sir John's guitar. Below in orderly silence the archers were mustering under their officers, and taking their allotted stations. A dozen had swarmed up to their hazardous post in the little tower in the tops.

"Bring wine, Nicholas!" cried the king. "Gentlemen, ere you close your visors I pray you to take a last rouse with me. You will be dry enough, I promise you, before your lips are free once more. To what shall we drink, John?"

"To the men of Spain," said Chandos, his sharp face peering like a gaunt bird through the gap in his helmet. "May their hearts be stout and their spirits high this day!"

"Well said, John!" cried the king, and the knights laughed joyously as they drank. "Now, fair sirs, let each to his post! I am warden here on the forecastle. Do you, John, take charge of the afterguard. Walter, James, William, Fitzallan, Goldesborough, Reginald—you will stay with me! John, you may pick whom you will, and the others will bide with the archers. Now, bear straight at the center, master shipman. Ere yonder sun sets we will bring a red ship back as a gift to our ladies, or never look upon a lady's face again."

The art of sailing into a wind had not yet been invented, nor was there any fore-and-aft canvas, save for small head sails with which a vessel could be turned. Hence the English fleet had to take a long slant down Channel to meet their enemies; but as the Spaniards coming before the wind were equally anxious to engage there was the less delay. With stately pomp and dignity the two great fleets approached.

It chanced that one fine carack had outstripped its consorts and came sweeping along, all red and gold, with a fringe of twinkling steel, a good half-mile before the fleet. Edward looked at her with a kindling eye, for indeed she was a noble sight, with the blue water creaming under her gilded prow.

"This is a most worthy and debonair vessel, Master Bunce," said he, to the shipman beside him. "I would fain have a tilt with her. I pray you to hold us straight that we may bear her down."

"If I hold her straight, then one or other must sink, and it may be both," the seaman answered.

"I doubt not that with the help of our lady we shall do our part," said the king. "Hold her straight, master-shipman, as I have told you."

Now the two vessels were within arrow flight, and the bolts from the crossbowmen pattered upon the English ship. These short, thick, devil's darts were everywhere humming like great wasps through the air, crashing against the bulwarks, beating upon the deck, ringing loudly on the armor of the knights, or with a soft, muffled thud sinking to the socket in a victim.

The bowmen along either side of the *Philippa* had stood motionless waiting for their orders, but now there was a sharp shout from their leader, and every string twanged together. The air was full of their harping, together with the swish of the arrows, the long-drawn keening of the bowmen, and the short, deep bark of the under-officers. "Steady, steady! Loose steady! Shoot wholly together! Twelve score paces! Ten score! Now eight! Shoot wholly together!" Their gruff shouts broke through the high shrill cry like the deep roar of a wave through the howl of the wind.

As the two great ships hurtled together the Spaniard turned away a few points so that the blow should be a glancing one. None the less it was terrific. A dozen men in the tops of the carack were balancing a huge stone with the intention of dropping it over on the English deck. With a scream of horror they saw the mast cracking beneath them. Over it went, slowly at first, then faster, until with a crash it came down on its side, sending them flying like stones from a sling far out into the sea. A swath of crushed bodies lay across the deck where the mast had fallen. But the English ship had not escaped unscathed. Her mast held, it is true, but the mighty shock not only stretched every man flat upon the deck, but had shaken a score of those who lined her sides into the sea. One bowman was hurled from the top, and his body fell with a dreadful crash at the very side of the prostrate king upon the forecastle. Many were thrown down with broken arms and legs from the high castles at either end into the waist of the ship. Worst of all, the seams had been opened by the crash, and the water was gushing in at a dozen places.

But these were men of experience and of discipline, men who had already fought together by sea and by land, so that each knew his place and his duty. Those who could staggered to their feet, and helped up a score or more of knights who were rolling and clashing in the scuppers, unable to rise for the weight of their armor. The bowmen formed up as before. The seamen ran to the gaping seams with oakum and with tar. In ten minutes order had been restored, and the *Philippa,* though shaken and weakened, was ready for battle once more. The king was glaring round him like a wounded boar.

"Grapple my ship with that," he cried, pointing to the crippled Spaniard, "for I would have possession of her!"

But already the breeze had carried them past it, and a dozen Spanish ships were bearing down full upon them.

"We cannot win back to her, lest we show our flank to these others," said the shipman.

"Let her go her way!" cried the knights. "You shall have better than her."

"By Saint George! you speak the truth," said the king, "for she is ours when we have time to take her. These also seem very worthy ships which are drawing up to us, and I pray you, master-shipman, that you will have a tilt with the nearest."

A great carack was within a bowshot of them and crossing their bows. Bunce looked up at his mast, and he saw that already it was shaken and drooping. Another blow and it would be over the side, and his ship a helpless log upon the water. He jammed his helm round, therefore, and ran his ship alongside the Spaniard, throwing out his hooks and iron chains as he did so.

They, no less eager, grappled the *Philippa* both fore and aft, and the two vessels, linked tightly together, surged slowly over the long, blue rollers. Over their bulwarks hung a cloud of men locked together in a desperate struggle, sometimes surging forward on to the deck of the Spaniard, sometimes recoiling back on to the king's ship, reeling this way and that, with the swords flickering like silver flames above them, while the long-drawn cry of rage and agony swelled up like a wolf's howl to the calm, blue heaven above them.

But now ship after ship of the English had come up, each throwing its iron over the nearest Spaniard and striving to board her high red sides. Twenty ships were drifting in furious single combat after the manner of the *Philippa,* until the whole surface of the sea was covered with a succession of these desperate duels. The dismasted carack, which the king's ship had left behind it, had been carried by the Earl of Suffolk's *Christopher,* and the water was dotted with the heads of her crew. An English ship had been sunk by a huge stone discharged from an engine, and her men also were struggling in the waves, none having leisure to lend them a hand. A second English ship was caught between two of the Spanish vessels and overwhelmed by a rush of boarders, so that not a man of her was left alive. On the other hand, Mowbray and Audley had each taken the caracks which were opposed to them, and the battle in the center, after swaying this way and that, was turning now in favor of the Islanders.

The Black Prince, with the *Lion,* the *Grace Marie* and four other ships, had swept round to turn the Spanish flank; but the movement was seen, and the Spaniards had ten ships with which to meet it, one of them their great carack, the *St. Iago di Compostella*. To this ship the prince had attached his little cog, and strove desperately to board her; but her side was so high and the defense so desperate that his men could never get beyond her bulwarks, but were hurled down again and again with a clang and clash to the deck beneath. Her side bristled with crossbowmen, who shot straight down on to the packed waist of the *Lion,* so that the dead lay there in heaps. But the most dangerous of all was a swarthy, black-bearded giant in the tops, who crouched so that none could see him, but rising every now and then with a huge lump of iron between his hands, hurled it down with such force that nothing could stop it. Again and again these ponderous bolts crashed through the deck and hurtled down into the bottom of the ship, starting the planks and shattering all that came in their way.

The prince, clad in that dark armor which gave him his name, was directing the attack from the poop when the shipman rushed wildly up to him with fear on his face.

"Sire!" he cried. "The ship may not stand against these blows. A few more will sink her! Already the water floods inboard!"

The prince looked up, and as he did so the shaggy beard showed once more, and two brawny arms swept downward. A great slug, whizzing down, beat a gaping hole in the deck, and fell rending and riving into the hold below. The master-mariner tore his grizzled hair.

"Another leak!" he cried. "I pray to Saint Leonard to bear us up this day! Twenty of my shipmen are bailing with buckets, but the water rises on them fast. The vessel may not float another hour."

The prince had snatched a crossbow from one of his attendants and leveled it at the Spaniard's tops. At the very instant when the seaman stood erect with a fresh bar in his hands, the bolt took him full in the face, and his body fell forward over the parapet, hanging there head downward. A howl of exultation burst from the English at the sight, answered by a wild roar of anger from the Spaniards. A seaman had run from the *Lion*'s hold and whispered in the ear of the shipman. He turned an ashen face upon the prince.

"It is even as I say, sire. The ship is sinking beneath our feet!" he cried.

"The more need that we should gain another," said he. "Sir Henry Stokes, Sir Thomas Stourton, William, John of Clifton, here lies our road! Advance my banner, Thomas de Mohun! On, and the day is ours!"

By a desperate scramble, a dozen men, the prince at their head, gained a footing on the edge of the Spaniard's deck. Some slashed furiously to clear a space, others hung over, clutching the rail with one hand and pulling up their comrades from below. Every instant that they could hold their own their strength increased, till twenty had become thirty, and thirty forty, when of a sudden the newcomers, still reaching forth to their comrades below, saw the deck beneath them reel and vanish in a swirling sheet of foam. The prince's ship had foundered.

A yell went up from the Spaniards as they turned furiously upon the small band who had reached their deck. Already the prince and his men had carried the poop, and from that high station they beat back their swarming enemies. But crossbow darts pelted and thudded among their ranks, till a third of their number were stretched upon the planks. Lined across the deck, they could hardly keep an unbroken front to the leaping, surging crowd who pressed upon them. Another rush, or another after that, must assuredly break them, for these dark men of Spain, hardened by an endless struggle with the Moors, were fierce and stubborn fighters. But hark to this sudden roar upon the further side of them—

"Saint George! Saint George! A Knolles to the rescue!"

A small craft had run alongside, and sixty men had swarmed on the deck of the *St. Iago*. Caught between two fires, the Spaniards wavered and broke. The fight became a massacre. Down from the poop sprang the prince's men. Up from the waist rushed the newcorners. There were five dreadful minutes of blows and screams and prayers, with struggling figures clinging to the bulwarks and sullen splashes into the water below. Then it was over, and a crowd of weary, overstrained men leaned panting upon their weapons, or lay breathless and exhausted upon the deck of the captured carack.

The prince had pulled up his visor and lowered his beaver. He smiled proudly as he gazed around him and wiped his streaming face.

"Where is the shipman?" he asked. "Let him lead us against another ship."

"Nay, sire, the shipman and all his men have sunk in the *Lion,*" said Thomas de Mohun, a young knight of the west country, who carried the standard. "We have lost our ship and the half of our following. I fear that we can fight no more."

"It matters the less since the day is already ours," said the prince, looking over the sea. "My noble father's royal banner flies upon yonder Spaniard. Mowbray, Audley, Suffolk, Beauchamp, Namur, Tracey, Stafford, Arundel, each has his flag over a scarlet carack, even as mine floats over this. See, yonder squadron is already far beyond our reach. But surely we owe thanks to you who came at so perilous a moment to our aid. Your face I have seen, and your coat-armor also, young sir, though I cannot lay my tongue to your name. Let me know it, that I may thank you."

He had turned to Nigel, who stood flushed and joyous at the head of the boarders from the *Basilisk.*

"I am but a squire, sire, and can claim no thanks, for there is nothing that I have done. Here is our leader."

The prince's eyes fell upon the shield charged with the Black Raven and the stern young face of him who bore it.

"Sir Robert Knolles," said he, "I had thought you were on your way to Brittany."

"I was so, sire, when I had the fortune to see this battle as I passed."

The prince laughed. "It would indeed be to ask too much, Robert, that you should keep on your course when much honor was to be gathered so close to you. But now I pray you that you will come back with us to Winchelsea, for well I know that my father would fain thank you for what you have done this day."

But Robert Knolles shook his head. "I have your father's command, sire, and without his order I may not go against it. Our people are hard-pressed in Brittany, and it is not for me to linger on the way. I pray you, sire, if you must needs mention me to the king, to crave his pardon that I should have broken my journey thus."

"You are right, Robert. God-speed you on your way! And I would that I were sailing under your banner, for I see clearly that you will take your people where they may worshipfully win worship. Perchance I also may be in Brittany before the year is past."

The prince turned to the task of gathering his weary people together, and the *Basilisks* passed over the side once more and dropped down on to their own little ship. They poled her off from the captured Spaniard, and set their sail with their prow for the south. Far ahead of them were their two consorts, beating towards them in the hope of giving help, while down Channel were a score of Spanish ships, with a few of the English vessels hanging upon their skirts. The sun lay low on the water, and its level beams glowed upon the scarlet and gold of fourteen great caracks, each flying the cross of Saint George, and towering high above the cluster of English ships which, with brave waving of flags and blaring of music, were moving slowly towards the Kentish coast.

XVIII. HOW BLACK SIMON CLAIMED
FORFEIT FROM THE KING OF SARK

FOR A DAY and a half the small fleet made good progress, but
on the second morning, after sighting Cape de la Hague, there
came a brisk land wind which blew them out to sea. It grew into
a squall with rain and fog so that they were two more days beating back. Next morning they found themselves in a dangerous
rock-studded sea with a small island upon their starboard quarter. It was girdled with high granite cliffs of a reddish hue, and
slopes of bright green grassland lay above them. A second
smaller island lay beside it. Dennis the shipman shook his head
as he looked.

"That is Brechou," said he, "and the larger one is the Island
of Sark. If ever I be cast away, I pray the saints that I may not
be upon yonder coast!"

Knolles gazed across at it. "You say well, master-shipman,"
said he. "It does appear to be a rocky and perilous spot."

"Nay, it is the rocky hearts of those who dwell upon it that I
had in my mind," the old sailor answered. "We are well safe in
three goodly vessels, but had we been here in a small craft I
make no doubt that they would have already had their boats out
against us."

"Who, then, are these people, and how do they live upon so
small and windswept an island?" asked the soldier.

"They do not live from the island, fair sir, but from what they
can gather upon the sea around it. They are broken folk from all
countries, justice-fliers, prison-breakers, reavers, escaped bondsmen, murderers and staff-strikers who have made their way to
this outland place and hold it against all comers. There is one
here who could tell you of them and of their ways, for he was

long time prisoner amongst them." The seaman pointed to Black Simon, the dark man from Norwich, who was leaning against the side lost in moody thought and staring with a brooding eye at the distant shore.

"How now, fellow?" asked Knolles. "What is this I hear? Is it indeed sooth that you have been a captive upon this island?"

"It is true, fair sir. For eight months I have been servant to the man whom they call their king. His name is La Muette, and he comes from Jersey, nor is there under God's sky a man whom I have more desire to see."

"Has he, then, mishandled you?"

Black Simon gave a wry smile and pulled off his jerkin. His lean sinewy back was waled and puckered with white scars.

"He has left his sign of hand upon me," said he. "He swore that he would break me to his will, and thus he tried to do it. But most I desire to see him because he hath lost a wager to me and I would fain be paid."

"This is a strange saying," said Knolles. "What is this wager, and why should he pay you?"

"It is but a small matter," Simon answered; "but I am a poor man and the payment would be welcome. Should it have chanced that we stopped at this island I should have craved your leave that I go ashore and ask for that which I have fairly won."

Sir Robert Knolles laughed. "This business tickleth my fancy," said he. "As to stopping at the island, this shipman tells me that we must needs wait a day and a night, for that we have strained our planks. But if you should go ashore, how will you be sure that you will be free to depart, or that you will see this king of whom you speak?"

Black Simon's dark face was shining with a fierce joy. "Fair sir, I will ever be your debtor if you will let me go. Concerning what you ask, I know this island even as I know the streets of Norwich, as you may well believe, seeing that it is but a small place and I upon it for near a year. Should I land after dark, I could win my way to the king's house, and if he be not dead or distraught with drink I could have speech with him alone, for I know his ways and his hours and how he may be found. I would ask only that Aylward the archer may go with me, that I may have one friend at my side if things should chance to go awry."

Knolles thought awhile. "It is much that you ask," said he, "for by God's truth I reckon that you and this friend of yours are two of my men whom I would be least ready to lose. I have seen you both at grips with the Spaniards and I know you. But I trust you, and if we must indeed stop at this accursed place, then you may do as you will. If you have deceived me, or if this is a trick by which you design to leave me, then God be your friend when next we meet, for man will be of small avail!"

It proved that not only the seams had to be calked but that the cog *Thomas* was out of fresh water. The ships moored therefore near the Isle of Brechou, where springs were to be found. There were no people upon this little patch, but over on the farther island many figures could be seen watching them, and the twinkle of steel from among them showed that they were armed men. One boat had ventured forth and taken a good look at them, but had hurried back with the warning that they were too strong to be touched.

Black Simon found Aylward seated under the poop with his back against Bartholomew the bowyer. He was whistling merrily as he carved a girl's face upon the horn of his bow.

"My friend," said Simon, "will you come ashore to-night—for I have need of your help?"

Aylward crowed lustily. "Will I come, Simon? By my hilt, I shall be right glad to put my foot on the good brown earth once more. All my life I have trod it, and yet I would never have learned its worth had I not journeyed in these cursed ships. We will go on shore together, Simon, and we will seek out the women, if there be any there, for it seems a long year since I heard their gentle voices, and my eyes are weary of such faces as Bartholomew's or thine."

Simon's grim features relaxed into a smile. "The only face that you will see ashore, Samkin, will bring you small comfort," said he, "and I warn you that this is no easy errand, but one which may be neither sweet nor fair, for if these people take us our end will be a cruel one."

"By my hilt," said Aylward, "I am with you, gossip, wherever you may go! Say no more, therefore, for I am weary of living like a cony in a hole, and I shall be right glad to stand by you in your venture."

That night, two hours after dark, a small boat put forth from the *Basilisk*. It contained Simon, Aylward and two seamen. The soldiers carried their swords, and Black Simon bore a brown biscuit-bag over his shoulder. Under his direction the rowers skirted the dangerous surf which beat against the cliffs until they came to a spot where an outlying reef formed a breakwater. Within was a belt of calm water and a shallow cover with a sloping beach. Here the boat was dragged up and the seamen were ordered to wait, while Simon and Aylward started on their errand.

With the assured air of a man who knows exactly where he is and whither he is going, the man-at-arms began to clamber up a narrow fern-lined cleft among the rocks. It was no easy ascent in the darkness, but Simon climbed on like an old dog hot upon a scent, and the panting Aylward struggled after as best he might. At last they were at the summit and the archer threw himself down upon the grass.

"Nay, Simon, I have not enough breath to blow out a candle," said he. "Stint your haste for a minute, since we have a long night before us. Surely this man is a friend indeed, if you hasten so to see him."

"Such a friend," Simon answered, "that I have often dreamed of our next meeting. Now before that moon has set it will have come."

"Had it been a wench I could have understood it," said Aylward. "By these ten finger-bones, if Mary of the mill or little Kate of Compton had waited me on the brow of this cliff, I should have come up it and never known it was there. But surely I see houses and hear voices over yonder in the shadow?"

"It is their town," whispered Simon. "There are a hundred as bloody-minded cut-throats as are to be found in Christendom beneath those roofs. Hark to that!"

A fierce burst of laughter came out of the darkness, followed by a long cry of pain.

"All-hallows be with us!" cried Aylward. "What is that?"

"As like as not some poor devil has fallen into their clutches, even as I did. Come this way, Samkin, for there is a peat-cutting where we may hide. Aye, here it is, but deeper and broader than of old. Now, follow me close, for if we keep within it we shall find ourselves a stone cast off the king's house."

Together they crept along the dark cutting. Suddenly Simon seized Aylward by the shoulder and pushed him into the shadow of the bank. Crouching in the darkness, they heard footsteps and voices upon the farther side of the trench. Two men sauntered along it and stopped almost at the very spot where the comrades were lying. Aylward could see their dark figures outlined against the starry sky.

"Why should you scold, Jacques," said one of them, speaking a strange half-French, half-English lingo. "*Le diable t'emporte* for a grumbling rascal. You won a woman and I got nothing. What more would you have?"

"You will have your chance off the next ship, *mon garçon,* but mine is passed. A woman, it is true—an old peasant out of the fields, with a face as yellow as a kite's claw. But Gaston, who threw a nine against my eight, got as fair a little Normandy lass as ever your eyes have seen. Curse the dice, I say! And as to my woman, I will sell her to you for a firkin of Gascony."

"I have no wine to spare, but I will give you a keg of apples," said the other. "I had it out of the *Peter and Paul,* the Falmouth boat that struck in Creux Bay."

"Well, well your apples may be the worse for keeping, but so is old Marie, and we can cry quits on that. Come round and drink a cup over the bargain."

They shuffled onward in the darkness.

"Heard you ever such villainy?" cried Aylward, breathing fierce and hard. "Did you hear them, Simon? A woman for a keg of apples! And my heart's root is sad for the other one, the girl of Normandy. Surely we can land to-morrow and burn all these water-rats out of their nest."

"Nay, Sir Robert will not waste time or strength ere he reach Brittany."

"Sure I am that if my little master Squire Loring had the handling of it, every woman on this island would be free ere another day had passed."

"I doubt it not," said Simon. "He is one who makes an idol of woman, after the manner of those crazy knight errants. But Sir Robert is a true soldier and hath only his purpose in view."

"Simon," said Aylward, "the light is not overgood and the place is cramped for sword-play, but if you will step out into the open I will teach you whether my master is a true soldier or not."

"Tut, man! you are as foolish yourself," said Simon. "Here we are with our work in hand, and yet you must needs fall out with me on our way to it. I say nothing against your master save that he hath the way of his fellows, who follow dreams and fancies. But Knolles looks neither to right nor left, and walks forward to his mark. Now, let us on, for the time passes."

"Simon, your words are neither good nor fair. When we are back on shipboard we will speak further of this matter. Now lead on, I pray you, and let us see some more of this ten-devil island."

For half a mile Simon led the way until they came to a large house which stood by itself. Peering at it from the edge of the cutting, Aylward could see that it was made from the wreckage of many vessels, for at each corner a prow was thrust out. Lights blazed within, and there came the sound of a strong voice singing a gay song which was taken up by a dozen others in the chorus.

"All is well, lad!" whispered Simon, in great delight. "That is the voice of the king. It is the very song he used to sing. '*Les deux filles de Pierre.*' 'Fore God, my back tingles at the very sound of it. Here we will wait until his company take their leave."

Hour after hour they crouched in the peat-cutting, listening to the noisy songs of the revelers within, some French, some English, and all growing fouler and less articulate as the night wore on. Once a quarrel broke out and the clamor was like a cageful of wild beasts at feeding-time. Then a health was drunk and there was much stamping and cheering.

Only once was the long vigil broken. A woman came forth from the house and walked up and down, with her face sunk upon her breast. She was tall and slender, but her features could not be seen for a wimple over her head. Weary sadness could be read in her bowed back and dragging steps. Once only they saw her throw her two hands up to Heaven as one who is beyond human aid. Then she passed slowly into the house again. A moment later the door of the hall was flung open, and a shouting stumbling throng came crowding forth, with whoop and yell, into the silent night. Linking arms and striking up a chorus, they marched past the peat-cutting, their voices dwindling slowly away as they made for their homes.

"Now, Samkin, now!" cried Simon, and jumping out from the hiding-place, he made for the door. It had not yet been fastened. The two comrades sprang inside. Then Simon drew the bolts so that none might interrupt them.

A long table littered with flagons and beakers lay before them. It was lit up by a line of torches, which flickered and smoked in their iron sconces. At the farther end a solitary man was seated. His head rested upon his two hands, as if he were befuddled with wine, but at the harsh sound of the snapping bolts he raised his face and looked angrily around him. It was a strange, powerful head, tawny and shaggy like a lion's, with a tangled beard and a large, harsh face, bloated and blotched with vice. He laughed as the newcomers entered, thinking that two of his boon companions had returned to finish a flagon. Then he stared hard, and he passed his hand over his eyes like one who thinks he may be dreaming.

"*Mon Dieu!*" he cried. "Who are you, and whence come you at this hour of the night? Is this the way to break into our royal presence?"

Simon approached up one side of the table and Aylward up the other. When they were close to the king, the man-at-arms plucked a torch from its socket and held it to his own face. The king staggered back with a cry, as he gazed at that grim visage.

"*Le diable noir!*" he cried. "Simon, the Englishman! What make you here?"

Simon put his hand upon his shoulder. "Sit here!" said he, and he forced the king into his seat. "Do you sit on the farther side of him, Aylward. We make a merry group, do we not? Often have I served at this table, but never did I hope to drink at it. Fill your cup, Samkin, and pass the flagon."

The king looked from one to the other with terror in his bloodshot eyes.

"What would you do?" he asked. "Are you mad, that you should come here. One shout and you are at my mercy."

"Nay, my friend, I have lived too long in your house not to know the ways of it. No man-servant ever slept beneath your roof, for you feared lest your throat would be cut in the night-time. You may shout and shout, if it so please you. It chanced that I was passing on my way from England in those ships which lie off La Brechou, and I thought I would come in and have speech with you."

"Indeed, Simon, I am right glad to see you," said the king, cringing away from the fierce eyes of the soldier. "We were good friends in the past, were we not, and I cannot call to mind that I have ever done you injury. When you made your way to England by swimming to the Levantine there was none more glad in heart than I."

"If I cared to doff my doublet I could show you the marks of what your friendship has done for me in the past," said Simon. "It is printed on my back as clearly as on my memory. Why, you foul dog, there are the very rings upon the wall to which my hands were fastened, and there the stains upon the boards on which my blood has dripped! Is it not so, you king of butchers?"

The pirate chief turned whiter still. "It may be that life here was somewhat rough, Simon, but if I have wronged you in any way, I will surely make amends. What do you ask?"

"I ask only one thing, and I have come hither that I may get it. It is that you pay me forfeit for that you have lost your wager."

"My wager, Simon! I call to mind no wager."

"But I will call it to your mind, and then I will take my payment. Often have you sworn that you would break my courage. 'By my head!' you have cried to me. 'You will crawl at my feet!' and again: 'I will wager my head that I will tame you!' Yes, yes, a score of times you have said so. In my heart, as I listened, I have taken up your gage. And now, dog, you have lost, and I am here to claim the forfeit."

His long heavy sword flew from its sheath. The king, with a howl of despair, flung his arms round him, and they rolled together under the table. There was a sound like the worrying of dogs ending in a scream. Aylward sat with a ghastly face, and his toes curled with horror at the sight, for he was still new to scenes of strife and his blood was too cold for such a deed. When Simon rose he tossed something into his bag and sheathed his bloody sword.

"Come, Samkin, our work is well done," said he.

"By my hilt, if I had known what it was I would have been less ready to come with you," said the archer. "Could you not have clapped a sword in his fist and let him take his chance in the hall?"

"Nay, Samkin, if you had such memories as I, you would have wished that he should die like a sheep and not like a man. What chance did he give me when he had the power? And why should I treat him better? But, Holy Virgin, what have we here?"

At the farther end of the table a woman was standing. An open door behind her showed that she had come from the inner room of the house. By her tall figure the comrades knew that she was the same that they had already seen. Her face had once been fair, but now was white and haggard, with wild dark eyes full of a hopeless terror and despair. Slowly she paced up the room, her gaze fixed not upon the comrades, but upon the dreadful thing beneath the table. Then as she stooped and was sure, she burst into loud laughter and clapped her hands.

"Who shall say there is no God?" she cried. "Who shall say that prayer is unavailing? Great sir, brave sir, let me kiss that conquering hand!"

"Nay, nay, dame, stand back! Well, if you must needs have one of them, take this which is the clean one."

"It is the other I crave—that which is red with his blood! Oh! joyful night when my lips have been wet with it! Now I can die in peace!"

"We must go, Aylward," said Simon. "In another hour the

dawn will have broken. In daytime a rat could not cross this island and pass unseen. Come, man, and at once!"

But Aylward was at the woman's side. "Come with us, fair dame," said he. "Surely we can, at least, take you from this island, and no such change can be for the worse."

"Nay," said she, "the saints in Heaven cannot help me now until they take me to my rest. There is no place for me in the world beyond, and all my friends were slain on the day I was taken. Leave me, brave men, and let me care for myself. Already it lightens in the east, and black will be your fate if you are taken. Go, and may the blessing of one who was once a holy nun go with you and guard you from danger!"

Sir Robert Knolles was pacing the deck in the early morning, when he heard the sound of oars, and there were his two night-birds climbing up the side.

"So, fellow," said he, "have you had speech with the king of Sark?"

"Fair sir, I have seen him."

"And he has paid his forfeit?"

"He has paid it, sir!"

Knolles looked with curiosity at the bag which Simon bore.

"What carry you there?" he asked.

"The stake that he has lost."

"What was it, then? A goblet? A silver plate?"

For answer Simon opened his bag and shook it on the deck.

Sir Robert turned away with a whistle. "'Fore God!" said he, "it is in my mind that I carry some hard men with me to Brittany."

XIX. HOW A SQUIRE OF ENGLAND
MET A SQUIRE OF FRANCE

SIR ROBERT KNOLLES with his little fleet had sighted the
Breton coast near Cancale; they had rounded the Point du
Grouin, and finally had sailed past the port of St. Malo and
down the long narrow estuary of the Rance until they were close
to the old walled city of Dinan, which was held by that Montfort
faction whose cause the English had espoused. Here the horses
had been disembarked, the stores were unloaded, and the whole
force encamped outside the city, while the leaders waited for
news as to the present state of affairs, and where there was most
hope of honor and profit.

The whole of France was feeling the effects of that war with
England which had already lasted some ten years, but no prov-
ince was in so dreadful a condition as this unhappy land of
Brittany. In Normandy or Picardy the inroads of the English
were periodical with intervals of rest between; but Brittany was
torn asunder by constant civil war apart from the grapple of the
two great combatants, so that there was no surcease of her sufferings. The struggle had begun in 1341 through the rival claims
of Montfort and of Blois to the vacant dukedom. England had
taken the part of Montfort, France that of Blois. Neither faction
was strong enough to destroy the other, and so after ten years of
continual fighting, history recorded a long ineffectual list of
surprises and ambushes, of raids and skirmishes, of towns taken
and retaken, of alternate victory and defeat, in which neither
party could claim a supremacy. It mattered nothing that
Montfort and Blois had both disappeared from the scene, the
one dead and the other taken by the English. Their wives caught

up the red swords which had dropped from the hands of their lords, and the long struggle went on even more savagely than before.

In the south and east the Blois faction held the country, and Nantes the capital was garrisoned and occupied by a strong French army. In the north and west the Montfort party prevailed, for the island kingdom was at their back, and always fresh sails broke the northern sky-line bearing adventurers from over the channel.

Between these two there lay a broad zone comprising all the center of the country which was a land of blood and violence, where no law prevailed save that of the sword. From end to end it was dotted with castles, some held for one side, some for the other, and many mere robber strongholds, the scenes of gross and monstrous deeds, whose brute owners, knowing that they could never be called to account, made war upon all mankind, and wrung with rack and with flame the last shilling from all who fell into their savage hands. The fields had long been untilled. Commerce was dead. From Rennes in the east to Hennebon in the west, and from Dinan in the north to Nantes in the south, there was no spot where a man's life or a woman's honor was safe. Such was the land, full of darkness and blood, the saddest, blackest spot in Christendom, into which Knolles and his men were now advancing.

But there was no sadness in the young heart of Nigel, as he rode by the side of Knolles at the head of a clump of spears, nor did it seem to him that Fate had led him into an unduly arduous path. On the contrary, he blessed the good fortune which had sent him into so delightful a country, and it seemed to him as he listened to dreadful stories of robber barons, and looked round at the black scars of war which lay branded upon the fair faces of the hills, that no hero or romancer or trouveur had ever journeyed through such a land of promise, with so fair a chance of knightly venture and honorable advancement.

The Red Ferret was one deed toward his vow. Surely a second, and perhaps a better, was to be found somewhere upon this glorious countryside. He had borne himself as the others had in the sea-fight, and could not count it to his credit where he had done no more than mere duty. Something beyond this was needed for such a deed as could be laid at the feet of the Lady Mary. But surely it was to be found here in fermenting war-distracted Brittany. Then with two done it would be strange if he could not find occasion for that third one, which would complete his service and set him free to look her in the face once more. With the great yellow horse curveting beneath him, his Guildford armor gleaming in the sun, his sword clanking against his stirrup-iron, and his father's tough ash-spear in his hand, he rode with a light heart and a smiling face, looking eagerly to right and to left for any chance which his good Fate might send.

The road from Dinan to Caulnes, along which the small army was moving, rose and dipped over undulating ground, with a bare marshy plain upon the left where the river Rance ran down to the sea, while upon the right lay a wooded country with a few wretched villages, so poor and sordid that they had nothing with which to tempt the spoiler. The peasants had left them at the first twinkle of a steel cap, and lurked at the edges of the woods, ready in an instant to dive into those secret recesses known only to themselves. These creatures suffered sorely at the hands of both parties, but when the chance came they revenged their wrongs on either in a savage way which brought fresh brutalities upon their heads.

The newcomers soon had a chance of seeing to what lengths they would go, for in the roadway near to Caulnes they came upon an English man-at-arms who had been waylaid and slain by them. How they had overcome him could not be told, but how they had slain him within his armor was horribly apparent, for they had carried such a rock as eight men could lift, and had dropped it upon him as he lay, so that he was spread out in his shattered case like a crab beneath a stone. Many a fist was shaken at the distant woods and many a curse hurled at those who haunted them, as the column of scowling soldiers passed the murdered man whose badge of the Molene cross showed him to have been a follower of that House of Bentley, whose head, Sir Walter, was at that time leader of the British forces in the country.

Sir Robert Knolles had served in Brittany before, and he marshaled his men on the march with the skill and caution of the veteran soldier, the man who leaves as little as possible to chance, having too steadfast a mind to heed the fool who may think him overcautious. He had recruited a number of bowmen and men-at-arms at Dinan; so that his following was now close upon five hundred men. In front under his own leadership were fifty mounted lancers, fully armed and ready for any sudden attack. Behind them on foot came the archers, and a second body of mounted men closed up the rear. Out upon either flank moved small bodies of cavalry, and a dozen scouts, spread fanwise, probed every gorge and dingle in front of the column. So for three days he moved slowly down the Southern Road.

Sir Thomas Percy and Sir James Astley had ridden to the head of the column, and Knolles conferred with them as they marched concerning the plan of their campaign. Percy and Astley were young and hot-headed, with wild visions of dashing deeds and knight errantry, but Knolles with cold, clear brain and purpose of iron, held ever his object in view.

"By the holy Dunstan and all the saints of Lindisfarne!" cried the fiery borderer, "it goes to my heart to ride forward when there are such honorable chances on either side of us. Have I not heard that the French are at Evran beyond the river, and is it not sooth that yonder castle, the towers of which I see above the woods, is in the hands of a traitor, who is false to his liege lord of Montford. There is little profit to be gained upon this road, for the folk seem to have no heart for war. Had we ventured as far over the marches of Scotland as we now are in Brittany, we should not have lacked some honorable venture or chance of winning worship."

"You say truth, Thomas," cried Astley, a red-faced and choleric young man. "It is well certain that the French will not come to us, and surely it is the more needful that we go to them. In sooth, any soldier who sees us would smile that we should creep for three days along this road as though a thousand dangers lay before us, when we have but poor broken peasants to deal with."

But Robert Knolles shook his head. "We know not what are in these woods, or behind these hills," said he, "and when I know nothing it is my wont to prepare for the worst which may befall. It is but prudence so to do."

"Your enemies might find some harsher name for it," said Astley, with a sneer. "Nay, you need not think to scare me by glaring at me, Sir Robert, nor will your ill-pleasure change my thoughts. I have faced fiercer eyes than thine, and I have not feared."

"Your speech, Sir James, is neither courteous nor good," said Knolles, "and if I were a free man I would cram your words down your throat with the point of my dagger. But I am here to lead these men in profit and honor, not to quarrel with every fool who has not the wit to understand how soldiers should be led. Can you not see that if I make attempts here and there, as you would have me do, I shall have weakened my strength before I come to that part where it can best be spent?"

"And where is that?" asked Percy. "'Fore God, Astley, it is in my mind that we ride with one who knows more of war than you or I, and that we would be wise to be guided by his rede. Tell us then what is in your mind."

"Thirty miles from here," said Knolles, "there is, as I am told, a fortalice named Ploermel, and within it is one Bambro, an Englishman, with a good garrison. No great distance from him is the Castle of Josselin, where dwells Robert of Beaumanoir with a great following of Bretons. It is my intention that we should join Bambro, and so be in such strength that we may throw ourselves upon Josselin, and by taking it become the masters of all mid-Brittany, and able to make head against the Frenchmen in the south."

"Indeed I think that you can do no better," said Percy, heartily, "and I swear to you on jeopardy of my soul that I will stand by you in the matter! I doubt not that when we come deep into their land they will draw together and do what they may to make head against us; but up to now I swear by all the saints of Lindisfarne that I should have seen more war in a summer's day in Liddesdale or at the Forest of Jedburgh than any that Brittany has shown us. But see, yonder horsemen are riding in. They are our own hobbellers, are they not? And who are these who are lashed to their stirrups?"

A small troop of mounted bowmen had ridden out of an oak grove upon the left of the road. They trotted up to where the three knights had halted. Two wretched peasants whose wrists had been tied to their leathers came leaping and straining beside the horses in their effort not to be dragged off their feet. One was a tall, gaunt, yellow-haired man, the other short and swarthy, but both so crusted with dirt, so matted and tangled and ragged, that they were more like beasts of the wood than human beings.

"What is this?" asked Knolles. "Have I not ordered you to leave the countryfolk at peace?"

The leader of the archers, old Wat of Carlisle, held up a sword, a girdle and a dagger. "If it please you, fair sir," said he, "I saw the glint of these, and I thought them no fit tools for hands which were made for the spade and the plow. But when we had ridden them down and taken them, there was the Bentley cross upon each, and we knew that they had belonged to yonder dead Englishman upon the road. Surely then, these are two of the villains who have slain him, and it is right that we do justice upon them."

Sure enough, upon sword, girdle and dagger shone the silver Molene cross which had gleamed on the dead man's armor. Knolles looked at them and then at the prisoners with a face of stone. At the sight of those fell eyes they had dropped with inarticulate howls upon their knees, screaming out their protests in a tongue which none could understand.

"We must have the roads safe for wandering Englishmen," said Knolles. "These men must surely die. Hang them to yonder tree."

He pointed to a live-oak by the roadside, and rode onward upon his way in converse with his fellow-knights. But the old bowman had ridden after him.

"If it please you, Sir Robert, the bowmen would fain put these men to death in their own fashion," said he.

"So that they die, I care not how," Knolles answered carelessly, and looked back no more.

Human life was cheap in those stern days, when the foot-men of a stricken army or the crew of a captured ship were slain without any question or thought of mercy by the victors. War was a rude game, with death for the stake, and the forfeit was always claimed on the one side and paid on the other without doubt or hesitation. Only the knight might be spared, since his ransom made him worth more alive than dead. To men trained in such a school, with death for ever hanging over their own heads, it may well be believed that the slaying of two peasant murderers was a small matter.

And yet there was special reason why upon this occasion the bowmen wished to keep the deed in their own hands. Ever since their dispute aboard the *Basilisk,* there had been ill-feeling between Bartholomew, the old bald-headed bowyer, and long Ned Widdington the dalesman, which had ended in a conflict at Dinan, in which not only they, but a dozen of their friends, had been laid upon the cobble-stones. The dispute raged round their respective knowledge and skill with the bow, and now some quick wit among the soldiers had suggested a grim fashion in which it should be put to the proof, once for all, which could draw the surer shaft.

A thick wood lay two hundred paces from the road upon which the archers stood. A stretch of smooth grassy sward lay between. The two peasants were led out fifty yards from the road, with their faces toward the wood. There they stood, held on a leash, and casting many a wondering frightened glance over their shoulders at the preparations which were being made behind them.

Old Bartholomew and the big Yorkshireman had stepped out of the ranks and stood side by side, each with his strung bow in his left hand and a single arrow in his right. With care they had drawn on and greased their shooting-gloves and fastened their bracers. They plucked and cast up a few blades of grass to measure the wind, examined every small point of their tackle, turned their sides to the mark, and widened their feet in a firmer stance. From all sides came chaff and counsel from their comrades.

"A three-quarter wind, bowyer!" cried one. "Aim a body's breadth to the right!"

"But not thy body's breadth, bowyer," laughed another. "Else may you be overwide."

"Nay, this wind will scarce turn a well-drawn shaft," said a third. "Shoot dead upon him and you will be clap in the clout."

"Steady, Ned, for the good name of the dales," cried a Yorkshireman. "Loose easy and pluck not, or I am five crowns the poorer man."

"A week's pay on Bartholomew!" shouted another. "Now, old fat-pate, fail me not!"

"Enough, enough! Stint your talk!" cried the old bowman, Wat of Carlisle. "Were your shafts as quick as your tongues there would be no facing you. Do you shoot upon the little one, Bartholomew, and you, Ned, upon the other. Give them law until I cry the word, then loose in your own fashion and at your own time. Are you ready! Hola, there, Hayward, Beddington, let them run!"

The leashes were torn away, and the two men, stooping their heads, ran madly for the shelter of the wood amid such a howl from the archers as beaters may give when the hare starts from its form. The two bowmen, each with his arrow drawn to the pile, stood like russet statues, menacing, motionless, their eager eyes fixed upon the fugitives, their bow-staves rising slowly as the distance between them lengthened. The Bretons were half-way to the wood, and still Old Wat was silent. It may have been mercy or it may have been mischief, but at least the chase should have a fair chance of life. At six score paces he turned his grizzled head at last.

"Loose!" he cried.

At the word the Yorkshireman's bow-string twanged. It was not for nothing that he had earned the name of being one of the deadliest archers of the North, and had twice borne away the silver arrow of Selby. Swift and true flew the fatal shaft and buried itself to the feather in the curved back of the long yellow-haired peasant. Without a sound he fell upon his face and lay stone-dead upon the grass, the one short white plume between his dark shoulders to mark where Death had smote him.

The Yorkshireman threw his bowstave into the air and danced in triumph, while his comrades roared their fierce delight in a shout of applause, which changed suddenly into a tempest of hooting and of laughter.

The smaller peasant, more cunning, than his comrade, had run more slowly, but with many a backward glance. He had marked his companion's fate and had waited with keen eyes until he saw the bowyer loose his string. At the moment he had thrown himself flat upon the grass and had heard the arrow scream above him, and seen it quiver in the turf beyond. Instantly he had sprung to his feet again, and amid wild whoops and halloos from the bowmen had made for the shelter of the wood. Now he had reached it, and ten score good spaces separated him from the nearest of his persecutors. Surely they could not reach him here. With the tangled brushwood behind him he was as safe as a rabbit at the mouth of his burrow. In the joy of his heart he must needs dance in derision and snap his fingers at the foolish men who had let him slip. He threw back his head, howling at them like a dog, and at the instant an arrow struck him full in the throat and laid him dead among the bracken. There was a hush of surprised silence and then a loud cheer burst from the archers.

"By the rood of Beverley!" cried old Wat, "I have not seen a finer roving shaft this many a year. In my own best day I could not have bettered it. Which of you loosed it?"

"It was Aylward of Tilford—Samkin Aylward," cried a score of voices, and the bowman, flushed at his own fame, was pushed to the front.

"Indeed I would that it had been at a nobler mark," said he. "He might have gone free for me, but I could not keep my fingers from the string when he turned to jeer at us."

"I see well that you are indeed a master-bowman," said old Wat, "and it is comfort to my soul to think that if I fall I leave such a man behind me to hold high the credit of our craft. Now gather your shafts and on, for Sir Robert awaits us on the brow of the hill."

All day Knolles and his men marched through the same wild and deserted country, inhabited only by these furtive creatures, hares to the strong and wolves to the weak, who hovered in the shadows of the wood. Ever and anon upon the tops of the hills they caught a glimpse of horsemen who watched them from a distance and vanished when approached. Sometimes bells rang an alarm from villages among the hills, and twice they passed castles which drew up their drawbridges at their approach, and lined their walls with hooting soldiers as they passed. The Englishmen gathered a few oxen and sheep from the pastures of each, but Knolles had no mind to break his strength upon stone walls, and so he went upon his way.

Once at St. Meen they passed a great nunnery, girt with a high gray lichened wall, an oasis of peace in this desert of war, the black-robed nuns basking in the sun or working in the gardens, with the strong gentle hand of Holy Church shielding them ever from evil. The archers doffed caps to them as they passed, for the boldest and roughest dared not cross that line guarded by the dire ban and blight which was the one only force in the whole steel-ridden earth which could stand between the weakling and the spoiler.

The little army halted at St. Meen and cooked its midday meal. It had gathered into its ranks again and was about to start, when Knolles drew Nigel to one side.

"Nigel," said he, "it seems to me that I have seldom set eyes upon a horse which hath more power and promise of speed than this great beast of thine."

"It is indeed a noble steed, fair sir," said Nigel. Between him and his young leader there had sprung up great affection and respect since the day that they set foot in the *Basilisk*.

"It will be the better if you stretch his limbs, for he grows overheavy," said the knight. "Now mark me, Nigel! Yonder betwixt the ash-tree and the rock what do you see on the side of the far hill?"

"There is a white dot upon it. Surely it is a horse."

"I have marked it all morning, Nigel. This horseman has kept ever upon our flank, spying upon us or waiting to make some attempt upon us. Now I should be right glad to have a prisoner, for it is my wish to know something of this countryside, and these peasants can speak neither French nor English. I would have you linger here in hiding when we go forward. This man will still follow us. When he does so, yonder wood will lie betwixt you and him. Do you ride round it and come upon him from behind. There is broad plain upon his left, and we will cut him off upon the right. If your horse be indeed the swifter, then you cannot fail to take him."

Nigel had already sprung down and was tightening Pommers' girth.

"Nay, there is no need of haste, for you cannot start until we are two miles upon our way. And above all I pray you, Nigel, none of your knight-errant ways. It is this roan that I want, him and the news that he can bring me. Think little of your own advancement and much of the needs of the army. When you get him, ride westwards upon the sun, and you cannot fail to find the road."

Nigel waited with Pommers under the shadow of the nunnery wall, horse and man chafing with impatience, while above them six round-eyed, innocent nun-faces looked down on this strange and disturbing vision from the outer world. At last the long column wound itself out of sight round a curve of the road, and the white dot was gone from the bare green flank of the hill. Nigel bowed his steel head to the nuns, gave his bridle a shake, and bounded off upon his welcome mission. The round-eyed sisters saw yellow horse and twinkling man sweep round the skirt of the wood, caught a last glimmer of him through the tree-trunks, and paced slowly back to their pruning and their planting, their minds filled with the beauty and the terror of that outer world beyond the high gray lichen-mottled wall.

Everything fell out even as Knolles had planned. As Nigel rounded the oak forest, there upon the farther side of it, with only good greensward between, was the rider upon the white horse. Already he was so near that Nigel could see him clearly, a young cavalier, proud in his bearing, clad in purple silk tunic with a red curling feather in his low black cap. He wore no armor, but his sword gleamed at his side. He rode easily and carelessly, as one who cares for no man, and his eyes were for ever fixed upon the English soldiers on the road. So intent was he upon them that he gave no thought to his own safety, and it was only when the low thunder of the great horse's hoofs broke upon his ears that he turned in his saddle, looked very coolly and steadily at Nigel, then gave his own bridle a shake and darted off, swift as a hawk, toward the hills upon the left.

Pommers had met his match that day. The white horse, two parts Arab, bore the lighter weight, since Nigel was clad in full armor. For five miles over the open neither gained a hundred yards upon the other. They had topped the hill and flew down the farther side, the stranger continually turning in his saddle to have a look at his pursuer. There was no panic in his flight, but rather the amused rivalry with which a good horseman who is proud of his mount contends with one who has challenged him. Below the hill was a marshy plain, studded with great Druidic stones, some prostrate, some erect, some bearing others across their tops like the huge doors of some vanished building. A path ran through the marsh, with green rushes as a danger signal on either side of it. Across this path many of the huge stones were lying, but the white horse cleared them in its stride, and Pommers followed close upon his heels. Then came a mile of soft ground where the lighter weight again drew to the front, but it ended in a dry upland, and once again Nigel gained. A sunken road crossed it, but the white cleared it with a mighty spring, and again the yellow followed. Two small hills lay before them with a narrow gorge of deep bushes between. Nigel saw the white horse bounding chest-deep amid the underwood.

Next instant its hind legs were high in the air, and the rider had been shot from its back. A howl of triumph rose from amid the bushes, and a dozen wild figures, armed with club and with spear, rushed upon the prostrate man.

"*A moi, Anglais, moi!*" cried a voice, and Nigel saw the young rider stagger to his feet, strike round him with his sword, and then fall once more before the rush of his assailants.

There was a comradeship among men of gentle blood and bearing which banded them together against all ruffianly or unchivalrous attack. These rude fellows were no soldiers. Their dress and arms, their uncouth cries and wild assault, marked them as banditti—such men as had slain the Englishman upon the road. Waiting in narrow gorges with a hidden rope across the path, they watched for the lonely horseman as a fowler waits by his bird-trap, trusting that they could overthrow the steed and then slay the rider ere he had recovered from his fall.

Such would have been the fate of the stranger, as of so many cavaliers before him, had Nigel not chanced to be close upon his heels. In an instant Pommers had burst through the group who struck at the prostrate man, and in another two of the robbers had fallen before Nigel's sword. A spear rang on his breastplate, but one blow shore off its head, and a second that of the man who held it. In vain they thrust at the steel-girt man. His sword played round them like lightning, and the fierce horse ramped and swooped above them with pawing iron-shod hoofs and eyes of fire. With cries and shrieks they flew off to right and left amid the bushes, springing over boulders and darting under branches where no horseman could follow them. The foul crew had gone as swiftly and suddenly as it had come, and save for four ragged figures littered among the trampled bushes, no sign remained of their passing.

Nigel tethered Pommers to a thorn-bush and then turned his attention to the injured man. The white horse had regained his feet, and stood whinnying gently as he looked down on his prostrate master. A heavy blow, half broken by his sword, had beaten him down and left a great raw bruise upon his forehead. But a stream gurgled through the gorge, and a capful of water dashed over his face brought the senses back to the injured man. He was a mere stripling, with the delicate features of a woman, and a pair of great violet-blue eyes, which looked up presently with a puzzled stare into Nigel's face.

"Who are you?" he asked. "Ah yes! I call you to mind. You are the young Englishman who chased me on the great yellow horse. By our Lady of Rocamadour, whose vernicle is round my neck! I could not have believed that any horse could have kept at the heels of Charlemagne so long. But I will wager you a hundred crowns, Englishman, that I lead you over a five-mile course."

"Nay," said Nigel, "we will wait till you can back a horse ere we talk of racing it. I am Nigel of Tilford, of the family of Loring, a squire by rank, and the son of a knight. How are you called, young sir?"

"I also am a squire by rank, and the son of a knight. I am Raoul de la Roche Pierre de Bras, whose father writes himself Lord of Grosbois, a free vavasor of the noble Count of Toulouse, with the right of fossa and of furca, the high justice, the middle and the low." He sat up and rubbed his eyes. "Englishman, you have saved my life, as I would have saved yours, had I seen such yelping dogs set upon a man of blood and of coat-armor. But now I am yours, and what is your sweet will?"

"When you are fit to ride, you will come back with me to my people."

"Alas! I feared that you would say so. Had I taken you, Nigel—that is your name, is it not?—had I taken you, I would not have acted thus."

"How, then, would you have ordered things?" asked Nigel, much taken with the frank and debonair manner of his captive.

"I would not have taken advantage of such a mischance as has befallen me which has put me in your power. I would give you a sword and beat you in fair fight, so that I might send you to give greeting to my dear lady and show her the deeds which I do for her fair sake."

"Indeed, your words are both good and fair," said Nigel. "By Saint Paul! I cannot call to mind that I have ever met a man who bore himself better. But since I am in my armor and you without, I see not how we can debate the matter."

"Surely, gentle Nigel, you could doff your armor."

"Then have I only my underclothes."

"Nay, there shall be no unfairness there, for I also will very gladly strip to my underclothes."

Nigel looked wistfully at the Frenchman; but he shook his head. "Alas! it may not be," said he. "The last words that Sir Robert said to me were that I was to bring you to his side, for he would have speech with you. Would that I could do what you ask, for I also have a fair lady to whom I would fain send you. What use are you to me, Raoul, since I have gained no honor in the taking of you? How is it with you now?"

The young Frenchman had risen to his feet. "Do not take my sword," he said. "I am yours, rescue or no rescue. I think now that I could mount my horse, though indeed my head still rings like a cracked bell."

Nigel had lost all traces of his comrades; but he remembered Sir Robert's words that he should ride upon the sun with the certainty that sooner or later he would strike upon the road. As they jogged slowly along over undulating hills, the Frenchman shook off his hurt, and the two chatted merrily together.

"I had but just come from France," said he, "and I had hoped to win honor in this country, for I have ever heard that the English are very hardy men and excellent people to fight with. My mules and my baggage are at Evran; but I rode forth to see what I could see, and I chanced upon your army moving down the road, so I coasted it in the hopes of some profit or adventure. Then you came after me, and I would have given all the gold goblets upon my father's table if I had my harness so that I could have turned upon you. I have promised the Countess Beatrice that I will send her an Englishman or two to kiss her hands."

"One might perchance have a worse fate," said Nigel. "Is this fair dame your betrothed?"

"She is my love," answered the Frenchman. "We are but waiting for the Count to be slain in the wars, and then we mean to marry. And this lady of thine, Nigel? I would that I could see her."

"Perchance you shall, fair sir," said Nigel, "for all that I have seen of you fills me with desire to go further with you. It is in my mind that we might turn this thing to profit and to honor, for when Sir Robert has spoken with you, I am free to do with you as I will."

"And what will you do, Nigel?"

"We shall surely try some small deed upon each other, so that either I shall see the Lady Beatrice, or you the Lady Mary. Nay, thank me not, for like yourself, I have come to this country in search of honor, and I know not where I may better find it than at the end of your sword-point. My good lord and master, Sir John Chandos, has told me many times that never yet did he meet French knight nor squire that he did not find great pleasure and profit from their company, and now I very clearly see that he has spoken the truth."

For an hour these two friends rode together, the Frenchman pouring forth the praises of his lady, whose glove he produced from one pocket, her garter from his vest, and her shoe from his saddle-bag. She was blond, and when he heard that Mary was dark, he would fain stop then and there to fight the question of color. He talked too of his great château at Lauta, by the head waters of the pleasant Garonne; of the hundred horses in the stables, the seventy hounds in the kennels, the fifty hawks in the mews. His English friend should come there when the wars were over, and what golden days would be theirs! Nigel too, with his English coldness thawing before this young sunbeam of the South, found himself talking of the heather slopes of Surrey, of the forest of Woolmer, even of the sacred chambers of Cosford.

But as they rode onward toward the sinking sun, their thoughts far away in their distant homes, their horses striding together, there came that which brought their minds back in an instant to the perilous hillsides of Brittany.

It was the long blast of a trumpet blown from somewhere on the farther side of a ridge toward which they were riding. A second long-drawn note from a distance answered it.

"It is your camp," said the Frenchman.

"Nay," said Nigel; "we have pipes with us and a naker or two, but I have heard no trumpet-call from our ranks. It behoves us to take heed, for we know not what may be before us. Ride this way, I pray you, that we may look over and yet be ourselves unseen."

Some scattered boulders crowned the height, and from behind them the two young squires could see the long rocky valley beyond. Upon a knoll was a small square building with a battlement round it. Some distance from it towered a great dark castle, as massive as the rocks on which it stood, with one strong keep at the corner, and four long lines of machicolated walls. Above, a great banner flew proudly in the wind, with some device which glowed red in the setting sun. Nigel shaded his eyes and stared with wrinkled brow.

"It is not the arms of England, nor yet the lilies of France, nor is it the ermine of Brittany," said he. "He who holds this castle fights for his own hand, since his own device flies above it. Surely it is a head gules on an argent field."

"The bloody head on a silver tray!" cried the Frenchman.

"Was I not warned against him? This is not a man, friend Nigel. It is a monster who wars upon English, French and all Christendom. Have you not heard of the Butcher of La Brohinière?"

"Nay, I have not heard of him."

"His name is accursed in France. Have I not been told also that he put to death this very year Giles de St. Pol, a friend of the English King?"

"Yes, in very truth it comes back to my mind now that I heard something of this matter in Calais before we started."

"Then there he dwells, and God guard you if ever you pass under yonder portal, for no prisoner has ever come forth alive! Since these wars began he hath been a king to himself, and the plunder of eleven years lies in yonder cellars. How can justice come to him, when no man knows who owns the land? But when we have packed you all back to your island, by the Blessed Mother of God, we have a heavy debt to pay to the man who dwells in yonder pile!"

But even as they watched, the trumpet-call burst forth once more. It came not from the castle but from the farther end of the valley. It was answered by a second call from the walls. Then in a long, straggling line there came a wild troop of marauders streaming homeward from some foray. In the van, at the head of a body of spearmen, rode a tall and burly man, clad in brazen armor, so that he shone like a golden image in the slanting rays of the sun. His helmet had been loosened from his gorget and was held before him on his horse's neck. A great tangled beard flowed over his breastplate, and his hair hung down as far behind. A squire at his elbow bore high the banner of the bleeding head. Behind the spearmen were a line of heavily laden mules, and on either side of them a drove of poor country folk, who were being herded into the castle. Lastly came a second strong troop of mounted spearmen, who conducted a score or more of prisoners who marched together in a solid body.

Nigel stared at them, and then springing on his horse, he urged it along the shelter of the ridge so as to reach unseen a spot which was close to the castle gate. He had scarce taken up his new position when the cavalcade reached the drawbridge, and amid yells of welcome from those upon the wall, filed in a thin line across it. Nigel stared hard once more at the prisoners in the rear, and so absorbed was he by the sight that he had passed the rocks and was standing sheer upon the summit.

"By Saint Paul!" he cried, "it must indeed be so. I see their russet jackets. They are English archers!"

As he spoke, the hindmost one, a strongly built, broad-shouldered man, looked round and saw the gleaming figure above him upon the hill, with open helmet, and the five roses glowing upon his breast. With a sweep of his hands he had thrust his guardians aside, and for a moment was clear of the throng.

"Squire Loring! Squire Loring!" he cried. "It is I, Aylward the archer! It is I, Samkin Aylward!" The next minute a dozen hands had seized him, his cries were muffled with a gag, and he was hurled, the last of the band, through the black and threatening archway of the gate. Then with a clang the two iron wings came together, the portcullis swung upward, and captives and captors, robbers and booty, were all swallowed up within the grim and silent fortress.

XX. HOW THE ENGLISH ATTEMPTED THE CASTLE OF LA BROHINIÈRE

FOR SOME MINUTES Nigel remained motionless upon the crest of the hill, his heart, like lead within him, and his eyes fixed upon the huge gray walls which contained his unhappy henchman. He was roused by a sympathetic hand upon his shoulder, and the voice of his young prisoner in his ear.

"*Peste!*" said he. "They have some of your birds in their cage, have they not? What then, my friend? Keep your heart high! Is it not the chance of war, to-day to them, to-morrow to thee, and death at last for us all? And yet I had rather they were in any hands than those of Oliver the Butcher."

"By Saint Paul, we cannot suffer it!" cried Nigel, distractedly. "This man has come with me from my own home. He has stood between me and death before now. It goes to my very heart that he should call upon me in vain. I pray you, Raoul, to use your wits, for mine are all curdled in my head. Tell me what I should do, and how I may bring him help."

The Frenchman shrugged his shoulders. "As easy to get a lamb unscathed out of a wolves' lair as a prisoner safe from La Brohinière. Nay, Nigel, whither do you go? Have you, indeed, taken leave of your wits?"

The squire had spurred his horse down the hillside, and never halted until he was within a bowshot of the gate. The French prisoner followed hard behind him with a buzz of reproaches and expostulations.

"You are mad, Nigel!" he cried. "What do you hope to do then? Would you carry the castle with your own hands? Halt, man, halt, in the name of the Virgin!"

But Nigel had no plan in his head, and only obeyed the

fevered impulse to do something to ease his thoughts. He paced his horse up and down, waving his spear, and shouting insults and challenges to the garrison. Over the high wall a hundred jeering faces looked down upon him. So rash and wild was his action that it seemed to those within to mean some trap, so the drawbridge was still held high, and none ventured forth to seize him. A few long-range arrows pattered on the rocks, and then, with a deep booming sound, a huge stone, hurled from a mangonel, sang over the head of the two squires, and crushed into splinters among the boulders behind them. The Frenchman seized Nigel's bridle, and forced him farther from the gateway.

"By the dear Virgin!" he cried, "I care not to have those pebbles about my ears, yet I cannot go back alone, so it is very clear, my crazy comrade, that you must come also. Now we are beyond their reach! But see, my friend Nigel, who are those who crown the height?"

The sun had sunk behind the western ridge, but the glowing sky was fringed at its lower edge by a score of ruddy, twinkling points. A body of horsemen showed hard and black upon the bare hill. Then they dipped down the slope into the valley, while a band of footmen followed behind.

"They are my people," cried Nigel, joyously. "Come, my friend, hasten, that we may take counsel what we shall do."

Sir Robert Knolles rode a bowshot in front of his men, and his brow was as black as night. Beside him, with crestfallen face, his horse bleeding, his armor dinted and soiled, was the hot-headed knight, Sir James Astley. A fierce discussion raged between them.

"I have done my devoir as best I might," said Astley. "Alone I had ten of them at my sword point. I know not how I have lived to tell it."

"What is your devoir to me? Where are my thirty bowmen?" cried Knolles in bitter wrath. "Ten lie dead upon the ground, and twenty are worse than dead in yonder castle. And all because you must needs show all men how bold you are, and ride into a bushment such as a child could see. Alas for my own folly that ever I should have trusted such a one as you with the handling of men!"

"By God, Sir Robert, you shall answer to me for those words!" cried Astley with a choking voice. "Never has a man dared to speak to me as you have done this day."

"As long as I hold the king's order I shall be master, and by the Lord I will hang you, James, on a near tree if I have further cause of offense! How now, Nigel? I see by yonder white horse that you, at least, have not failed me. I will speak with you anon. Percy, bring up your men, and let us gather round this castle, for, as I hope for my soul's salvation, I win not leave it until I have my archers, or the head of him who holds them."

That night the English lay thick round the fortress of La Brohinière, so that none might come forth from it. But if none could come forth it was hard to see how any could win their way in, for it was full of men, the walls were high and strong, and a deep, dry ditch girt it round. But the hatred and fear which its master had raised over the whole countryside could now be plainly seen, for during the night the brushwood men and the villagers came in from all parts with offers of such help as they could give for the intaking of the castle. Knolles set them cutting bushes and tying them into faggots. When morning came he rode out before the wall, and he held counsel with his knights and squires as to how he should enter in.

"By noon," said he, "we shall have so many faggots that we may make our way over the ditch. Then we will beat in the gates and so win a footing."

The young Frenchman had come with Nigel to the conference, and now, amid the silence which followed the leader's proposal, he asked if he might be heard. He was clad in the brazen armor which Nigel had taken from the Red Ferret.

"It may be that it is not for me to join in your counsel," said he, "seeing that I am a prisoner and a Frenchman. But this man is the enemy of all, and we of France owe him a debt even as you do, since many a good Frenchman has died in his cellars. For this reason I crave to be heard."

"We will hear you," said Knolles.

"I have come from Evran yesterday," said he. "Sir Henry Spinnefort, Sir Peter La Roye, and many other brave knights and squires lie there, with a good company of men, all of whom would very gladly join with you to destroy this butcher and his castle, for it is well known amongst us that his deeds are neither good nor fair. There are also bombards which we could drag over the hills, and so beat down this iron gate. If you so order it, I will ride to Evran and bring my companions back with me."

"Indeed, Robert," said Percy, "it is in my mind that this Frenchman speaks very wisely and well."

"And when we have taken the castle—what then?" asked Knolles.

"Then you could go upon your way, fair sir, and we upon ours. Or if it please you better you could draw together on yonder hill and we on this one, so that the valley lies between us. Then, if any cavalier wished to advance himself, or to shed a vow and exalt his lady, an opening might be found for him. Surely it would be shame if so many brave men drew together, and no small deed were to come of it."

Nigel clasped his captive's hand to show his admiration and esteem, but Knolles shook his head.

"Things are not ordered thus, save in the tales of the minstrels," said he. "I have no wish that your people at Evran should know our numbers or our plans. I am not in this land for knight errantry, but I am here to make head against the king's enemies. Has no one aught else to say?"

Percy pointed to the small outlying fortalice upon the knoll, on which also flew the flag of the bloody head.

"This smaller castle, Robert, is of no great strength, and cannot hold more than fifty men. It is built, as I conceive it, that no one should seize the high ground, and shoot down into the other. Why should we not turn all our strength upon it, since it is the weaker of the twain?"

But again the young leader shook his head. "If I should take it," said he, "I am still no nearer to my desire, nor will it avail me in getting back my bowmen. It may cost a score of men, and what profit shall I have from it? Had I bombards, I might place them on yonder hill, but having none it is of little use to me."

"It may be," said Nigel, "that they have scant food or water, and so must come forth to fight us."

"I have made inquiry of the peasants," Knolles answered,

"and they are of one mind that there is a well within the castle, and good store of food. Nay, gentlemen, there is no way before us save to take it by arms, and no spot where we can attempt it save through the great gate. Soon we will have so many faggots that we can cast them down into the ditch, and so win our way across. I have ordered them to cut a pine-tree on the hill and shear the branches, so that we may beat down the gate with it. But what is now amiss, and why do they run forward to the castle?"

A buzz had risen from the soldiers in the camp, and they all crowded in one direction, rushing toward the castle wall. The knights and squires rode after them, and when in view of the main gate, the cause of the disturbance lay before them. On the tower above the portal three men were standing in the garb of English archers, ropes round their necks and their hands bound behind them. Their comrades surged below them with cries of recognition and of pity.

"It is Ambrose!" cried one. "Surely it is Ambrose of Ingleton."

"Yes, in truth, I see his yellow hair. And the other, him with the beard, it is Lockwood of Skipton. Alas for his wife who keeps the booth by the bridge-head of Ribble! I wot not who the third may be."

"It is little Johnny Alspaye, the youngest man in the company," cried old Wat, with the tears running down his cheeks. "'Twas I who brought him from his home. Alas! Alas! Foul fare the day that ever I coaxed him from his mother's side that he might perish in a far land."

There was a sudden flourish of a trumpet, and the drawbridge fell. Across it strode a portly man with a faded herald's coat. He halted warily upon the farther side and his voice boomed like a drum.

"I would speak with your leader," he cried.

Knolles rode forward.

"Have I your knightly word that I may advance unscathed with all courteous entreaty as befits a herald?"

Knolles nodded his head.

The man came slowly and pompously forward. "I am the messenger and liege servant," said he, "of the high baron, Oliver de St. Yvon, Lord of La Brohinière. He bids me to say that if you continue your journey and molest him no further, he will engage upon his part to make no further attack upon you. As to the men whom he holds, he will enroll them in his own honorable service, for he has need of longbowmen, and has heard much of their skill. But if you constrain him or cause him further displeasure by remaining before his castle, he hereby gives you warning that he will hang these three men over his gateway, and every morning another three, until all have been slain. This he has sworn upon the rood of Calvary, and as he has said so he will do upon jeopardy of his soul."

Robert Knolles looked grimly at the messenger. "You may thank the saints that you have had my promise," said he, "else would I have stripped that lying tabard from thy back and the skin beneath it from thy bones, that thy master might have a fitting answer to his message. Tell him that I hold him and all that are within his castle as hostage for the lives of my men, and that should he dare to do them scathe, he and every man that is with him shall hang upon his battlements. Go, and go quickly, lest my patience fail."

There was that in Knolles' cold gray eyes and in his manner of speaking those last words which sent the portly envoy back at a quicker gait than he had come. As he vanished into the gloomy arch of the gateway, the drawbridge swung up with creak and rattle behind him.

A few minutes later a rough-bearded fellow stepped out over the portal where the condemned archers stood, and seizing the first by the shoulders he thrust him over the wall. A cry burst from the man's lips, and a deep groan from those of his comrades below, as he fell with a jerk which sent him halfway up to the parapet again, and then, after dancing like a child's toy, swung slowly backward and forward with limp limbs and twisted neck.

The hangman turned and bowed in mock reverence to the spectators beneath him. He had not yet learned in a land of puny archers how sure and how strong is the English bow. Half a dozen men, old Wat among them, had run forward toward the wall. They were too late to save their comrades, but at least their deaths were speedily avenged. The man was in the act of pushing off the second prisoner when an arrow crashed through his head, and he fell stone dead upon the parapet. But even in falling he had given the fatal thrust, and a second russet figure swung beside the first against the dark background of the castle wall.

There only remained the young lad, Johnny Alspaye, who stood shaking with fear, an abyss below him, and the voices of those who would hurl him over it behind. There was a long pause before any one would come forth to dare those deadly arrows. Then a fellow, crouching double, ran forward from the shelter, keeping the young archer's body as a shield between him and danger.

"Aside, John! Aside!" cried his comrades from below.

The youth sprang as far as the rope would allow him, and slipped it half over his face in the effort. Three arrows flashed past his side, and two of them buried themselves in the body of the man behind. A howl of delight burst from the spectators as he dropped first upon his knees and then upon his face. A life for a life was no bad bargain.

But it was only a short respite which the skill of his comrades had given to the young archer. Over the parapet there appeared a ball of brass, then a pair of great brazen shoulders, and lastly the full figure of an armored man. He walked to the edge, and they heard his hoarse guffaw of laughter as the arrows clanged and clattered against his impenetrable mail. He slapped his breastplate as he jeered at them. Well he knew that at the distance no dart ever sped by mortal hands could cleave through his plates of metal. So he stood, the great burly Butcher of La Brohinière, with head uptossed, laughing insolently at his foes. Then, with slow and ponderous tread, he walked toward his boy victim, seized him by the ear, and dragged him across so that the rope might be straight. Seeing that the noose had slipped across the face, he tried to push it down, but the mail glove hampering him, he pulled it off, and grasped the rope above the lad's head with his naked hand.

Quick as a flash old Wat's arrow had sped, and the Butcher

sprang back with a howl of pain, his hand skewered by a cloth-yard shaft. As he shook it furiously at his enemies a second grazed his knuckles. With a brutal kick of his metal-shod feet he hurled young Alspaye over the edge, looked down for a few moments at his death agonies, and then walked slowly from the parapet, nursing his dripping hand, the arrows still ringing loudly upon his backpiece as he went.

The archers below, enraged at the death of their comrades, leaped and howled like a pack of ravening wolves.

"By Saint Dunstan," said Percy, looking round at their flushed faces, "if ever we are to carry it, now is the moment, for these men will not be stopped if hate can take them forward."

"You are right, Thomas!" cried Knolles. "Gather together twenty men-at-arms, each with his shield to cover him. Astley, do you place the bowmen so that no head may show at window or parapet. Nigel, I pray you to order the countryfolk forward with their fardels of faggots. Let the others bring up the lopped pine-tree, which lies yonder behind the horse-lines. Ten men-at-arms can bear it on the right, and ten on the left, having shields over their heads. The gate once down, let every man rush in. And God help the better cause!"

Swiftly, and yet quietly, the dispositions were made, for these were old soldiers whose daily trade was war. In little groups the archers formed in front of each slit or crevice in the walls, while others scanned the battlements with wary eyes, and sped an arrow at every face which gleamed for an instant above them. The garrison shot forth a shower of crossbow bolts and an occasional stone from their engine, but so deadly was the hail which rained upon them that they had no time to dwell upon their aim, and their discharges were wild and harmless. Under cover of the shafts of the bowmen, a line of peasants ran unscathed to the edge of the ditch, each hurling in the bundle which he bore in his arms, and then hurrying back for another one. In twenty minutes a broad pathway of faggots lay level with the ground upon one side and the gate upon the other. With the loss of two peasants slain by bolts and one archer crushed by a stone, the ditch had been filled up. All was ready for the battering-ram.

With a shout, twenty picked men rushed forward with the pine-tree under their arms, the heavy end turned toward the gate. The arbalesters on the tower leaned over and shot into the midst of them, but could not stop their advance. Two dropped, but the others raising their shields ran onward still shouting, crossed the bridge of faggots, and came with a thundering crash against the door. It splintered from base to arch, but kept its place.

Swinging their mighty weapon, the storming party thudded and crashed upon the gate, every blow loosening and widening the cracks which rent it from end to end. The three knights, with Nigel, the Frenchman Raoul, and the other squires, stood beside the ram, cheering on the men, and chanting to the rhythm of the swing with a loud "Ha!" at every blow. A great stone loosened from the parapet roared through the air and struck Sir James Astley and another of the attackers, but Nigel and the Frenchman had taken their places in an instant, and the ram thudded and smashed with greater energy than ever. Another blow and another! the lower part was staving inward, but the great central bar still held firm. Surely another minute would beat it from its sockets.

But suddenly from above there came a great deluge of liquid. A hogshead of it had been tilted from the battlement until soldiers, bridge, and ram were equally drenched in yellow slime. Knolles rubbed his gauntlet in it, held it to his visor, and smelled it.

"Back, back!" he cried. "Back before it is too late!"

There was a small barred window above their heads at the side of the gate. A ruddy glare shone through it, and then a blazing torch was tossed down upon them. In a moment the oil had caught and the whole place was a sheet of flame. The fir-tree that they carried, the faggots beneath them, their very weapons, were all in a blaze.

To right and left the men sprang down into the dry ditch, rolling with screams upon the ground in their endeavor to extinguish the flames. The knights and squires protected by their armor strove hard, stamping and slapping, to help those who had but leather jacks to shield their bodies. From above a cease-

"Swinging their mighty weapon, the storming party thudded and crashed upon the gate." [*page 255*]

less shower of darts and of stones were poured down upon them, while on the other hand the archers, seeing the greatness of the danger, ran up to the edge of the ditch, and shot fast and true at every face which showed above the wall.

Scorched, wearied and bedraggled, the remains of the storming party clambered out of the ditch as best they could, clutching at the friendly hands held down to them, and so limped their way back amid the taunts and howls of their enemies. A long pile of smoldering cinders was all that remained of their bridge, and on it lay Astley and six other red-hot men glowing in their armor.

Knolles clinched his hands as he looked back at the ruin that was wrought, and then surveyed the group of men who stood or lay around him nursing their burned limbs and scowling up at the exultant figures who waved on the castle wall. Badly scorched himself, the young leader had no thought for his own injuries in the rage and grief which racked his soul.

"We will build another bridge," he cried. "Set the peasants binding faggots once more."

But a thought had flashed through Nigel's mind. "See, fair sir," said he. "The nails of yonder door are red-hot and the wood as white as ashes. Surely we can break our way through it."

"By the Virgin, you speak truly!" cried the French squire. "If we can cross the ditch the gate will not stop us. Come, Nigel, for our fair ladies' sakes, I will race you who will reach it first, England or France."

Alas for all the wise words of the good Chandos! Alas for all the lessons in order and discipline learned from the wary Knolles. In an instant, forgetful of all things but this noble challenge, Nigel was running at the top of his speed for the burning gate. Close at his heels was the Frenchman, blowing and gasping, as he rushed along in his brazen armor. Behind came a stream of howling archers and men-at-arms, like a flood which has broken its dam. Down they slipped into the ditch, rushed across it, and clambered on each other's backs up the opposite side. Nigel, Raoul, and two archers gained a foothold in front of the burning gate at the same moment. With blows and kicks they burst it to pieces, and dashed with a yell of triumph through the dark archway beyond. For a moment they thought with mad rapture that the castle was carried. A dark tunnel lay before them, down which they rushed. But alas! at the farther end it was blocked by a second gateway as strong as that which had been burned. In vain they beat upon it with their swords and axes. On each side the tunnel was pierced with slits, and the crossbow bolts discharged at only a few yards' distance crashed through armor as if it were cloth and laid man after man upon the stones. They raged and leaped before the great iron-clamped barrier, but the wall itself was as easy to tear down.

It was bitter to draw back; but it was madness to remain. Nigel looked round and saw that half his men were down. At the same moment Raoul sank with a gasp at his feet, a bolt driven to its socket through the links of the camail which guarded his neck. Some of the archers, seeing that certain death awaited them, were already running back to escape from the fatal passage.

"By Saint Paul!" cried Nigel hotly. "Would you leave our wounded where this butcher may lay his hands upon them? Let the archers shoot inwards and hold them back from the slits. Now let each man raise one of our comrades, lest we leave our honor in the gate of this castle."

With a mighty effort he had raised Raoul upon his shoulders and staggered with him to the edge of the ditch. Several men were waiting below where the steep bank shielded them from the arrows, and to them Nigel handed down his wounded friend, and each archer in turn did the same. Again and again Nigel went back, until no one lay in the tunnel save seven who had died there. Thirteen wounded were laid in the shelter of the ditch, and there they must remain until night came to cover them. Meanwhile the bowmen on the farther side protected them from attack, and also prevented the enemy from all attempts to build up the outer gate. The gaping smoke-blackened arch was all that they could show for a loss of thirty men, but that at least Knolles was determined to keep.

Burned and bruised, but unconscious of either pain or fatigue for the turmoil of his spirit within him, Nigel knelt by the Frenchman and loosened his helmet. The girlish face of the young squire was white as chalk, and the haze of death was gathering over his violet eyes, but a faint smile played round his lips as he looked up at his English comrade.

"I shall never see Beatrice again," he whispered. "I pray you, Nigel, that when there is a truce you will journey as far as my father's château and tell him how his son died. Young Gaston will rejoice, for to him come the land and the coat, the war-cry and the profit. See them, Nigel, and tell them that I was as forward as the others."

"Indeed, Raoul, no man could have carried himself with more honor or won more worship than you have done this day. I will do your behest when the time comes."

"Surely you are happy, Nigel," the dying squire murmured, "for this day has given you one more deed which you may lay at the feet of your lady-love."

"It might have been so had we carried the gate," Nigel answered sadly; "but, by Saint Paul! I cannot count it a deed where I have come back with my purpose unfulfilled. But this is no time, Raoul, to talk of my small affairs. If we take the castle, and I bear a good part in it, then perchance all this may indeed avail."

The Frenchman sat up with that strange energy which comes often as the harbinger of death.

"You will win your Lady Mary, Nigel, and your great deeds will be not three but a score, so that in all Christendom there shall be no man of blood and coat-armor who has not heard your name and your fame. This I tell you—I, Raoul de la Roche Pierre de Bras, dying upon the field of honor. And now kiss me, sweet friend, and lay me back, for the mists close round me and I am gone!"

With tender hands the squire lowered his comrade's head, but even as he did so there came a choking rush of blood, and the soul had passed. So died a gallant cavalier of France, and Nigel, as he knelt in the ditch beside him, prayed that his own end might be as noble and as debonair.

XXI. HOW THE SECOND MESSENGER WENT TO COSFORD

UNDER COVER OF night the wounded men were lifted from the ditch and carried back, while pickets of archers were advanced to the very gate so that none should rebuild it. Nigel, sick at heart over his own failure, the death of his prisoner, and his fears for Aylward, crept back into the camp, but his cup was not yet full, for Knolles was waiting for him with a tongue which cut like a whip-lash. Who was he, a raw squire, that he should lead an attack without orders? See what his crazy knight errantry had brought about. Twenty men had been destroyed by it and nothing gained. Their blood was on his head. Chandos should hear of his conduct. He should be sent back to England when the castle had fallen.

Such were the bitter words of Knolles, the more bitter because Nigel felt in his heart that he had indeed done wrong, and that Chandos would have said the same, though, perchance, in kinder words. He listened in silent respect, as his duty was, and then, having saluted his leader, he withdrew apart, threw himself down among the bushes, and wept the hottest tears of his life, sobbing bitterly with his face between his hands. He had striven hard, and yet everything had gone wrong with him. He was bruised, burned, and aching from head to foot. Yet so high is the spirit above the body that all was nothing compared to the sorrow and shame which racked his soul.

But a little thing changed the current of his thoughts and brought some peace to his mind. He had slipped off his mail gauntlets, and as he did so his fingers lighted upon the tiny bangle which Mary had fastened there when they stood together upon St. Catharine's Hill on the Guildford Road. He remembered the motto curiously worked in filigree of gold. It ran: *"Fais ce que dois, adviegne que pourra—c'est commandé au chevalier."*

The words rang in his weary brain. He had done what seemed right, come what might. It had gone awry, it is true; but all things human may do that. If he had carried the castle, he felt that Knolles would have forgiven and forgotten all else. If he had not carried it, it was no fault of his. No man could have done more. If Mary could see she would surely have approved. Dropping into sleep, he saw her dark face, shining with pride and with pity, stooping over him as he lay. She stretched out her hand in his dream and touched him on the shoulder. He sprang up and rubbed his eyes, for fact had woven itself into dream in the strange way that it does, and some one was indeed leaning over him in the gloom, and shaking him from his slumbers. But the gentle voice and soft touch of the Lady Mary had changed suddenly to the harsh accents and rough grip of Black Simon, the fierce Norfolk man-at-arms.

"Surely you are the Squire Loring," he said, peering close to his face in the darkness.

"I am he. What then?"

"I have searched through the camp for you, but when I saw the great horse tethered near these bushes, I thought you would be found hard by. I would have a word with you."

"Speak on."

"This man Aylward the bowman was my friend, and it is the nature that God has given me to love my friends even as I hate my foes. He is also thy servant, and it has seemed to me that you love him also."

"I have good cause so to do."

"Then you and I, Squire Loring, have more reason to strive on his behalf than any of these others, who think more of taking the castle than of saving those who are captives within. Do you not see that such a man as this robber lord would, when all else had failed him, most surely cut the throats of his prisoners at the last instant before the castle fell, knowing well that come what might, he would have short shrift himself? Is that not certain?"

"By Saint Paul! I had not thought of it."

"I was with you, hammering at the inner gate," said Simon, "and yet once when I thought that it was giving way, I said in my heart, 'Good-bye, Samkin! I shall never see you more.' This Baron has gall in his soul, even as I have myself, and do you think that I would give up my prisoners alive, if I were constrained so to do? No, no; had we won our way this day, it would have been the death-stroke for them all."

"It may be that you are right, Simon," said Nigel, "and the thought of it should assuage our grief. But if we cannot save them by taking the castle, then surely they are lost indeed."

"It may be so, or it may not," Simon answered slowly. "It is in my mind that if the castle were taken very suddenly, and in such a fashion that they could not foresee it, then perchance we might get the prisoners before they could do them scathe."

Nigel bent forward eagerly, his hand on the soldier's arm.

"You have some plan in your mind, Simon. Tell me what it is."

"I had wished to tell Sir Robert, but he is preparing the assault for to-morrow, and will not be turned from his purpose. I have indeed a plan, but whether it be good or not I cannot say, until I have tried it. But first I will tell you what put it into my thoughts. Know, then, that this morning when I was in yonder ditch I marked one of their men upon the wall. He was a big man with a white face, red hair, and a touch of Saint Anthony's fire upon the cheek."

"But what has this to do with Aylward?"

"I will show you. This evening after the assault, I chanced to walk with some of my fellows round yonder small fort upon the knoll to see if we could spy a weak spot in it. Some of them came to the wall to curse us, and among them whom should I see but a big man with a white face, red hair, and a touch of Anthony's fire upon his cheek! What make you of that, Squire Nigel?"

"That this man had crossed from the castle to the fort."

"In good sooth, it must indeed be so. There are not two such ken-speckled men in the world. But if he crossed from the castle to the fort, it was not above the ground, for our own people were between."

"By Saint Paul! I see your meaning!" cried Nigel. "It is in your mind that there is a passage under the earth from one to the other."

"I am well sure of it."

"Then if we should take the small fort we may pass down this tunnel, and so carry the great castle also."

"Such a thing might happen," said Simon, "and yet it is dangerous also, for surely those in the castle would hear our assault upon the fort and so be warned to bar the passage against us, and to slay the prisoners before we could come."

"What, then, is your rede?"

"Could we find where the tunnel lay, Squire Nigel, I know not what is to prevent us from digging down upon it and breaking into it so that both fort and castle are at our mercy before either knows that we are there."

Nigel clapped his hands with joy. "'Fore God!" he cried. "It is a most noble plan! But alas! Simon, I see not how we can tell the course of this passage or where we should dig."

"I have peasants yonder with spades," said Simon. "There are two of my friends, Harding of Barnstable and West-country John, who are waiting for us with their gear. If you will come to lead us, Squire Nigel, we are ready to venture our bodies in the attempt."

What would Knolles say in case they failed? The thought flashed through Nigel's mind, but another came swiftly behind it. He would not venture further unless he found hopes of success. And if he did venture further he would put his life upon it. Giving that, he made amends for all errors. And if, on the other hand, success crowned their efforts, then Knolles would forgive his failure at the gateway. A minute later, every doubt banished from his mind, he was making his way through the darkness under the guidance of Black Simon.

Outside the camp the two other men-at-arms were waiting for them, and the four advanced together. Presently a little group of figures loomed up in the darkness. It was a cloudy night, and a thin rain was falling, which obscured both the castle and the fort; but a stone had been placed by Simon in the daytime which assured that they were between the two.

"Is blind Andreas there?" asked Simon.

"Yes, kind sir, I am here," said a voice.

"This man," said Simon, "was once rich and of good repute, but he was beggared by this robber lord, who afterwards put out his eyes so that he has lived for many years in darkness at the charity of others."

"How can he help us in our enterprise if he be indeed blind?" asked Nigel.

"It is for that very reason, fair lord, that he can be of greater service than any other man," Simon answered; "for it often happens that when a man has lost a sense the good God will strengthen those that remain. Hence it is that Andreas has such ears that he can hear the sap in the trees or the cheep of the mouse in its burrow. He has come to help us to find the tunnel."

"And I have found it," said the blind man, proudly. "Here I have placed my staff upon the line of it. Twice as I lay there with my ear to the ground I have heard footsteps pass beneath me."

"I trust you make no mistake, old man," said Nigel.

For answer the blind man raised his staff and smote twice upon the ground, once to the right and once to the left. The one gave a dull thud, the other a hollow boom.

"Can you not hear that?" he asked. "Will you ask me now if I make a mistake?"

"Indeed, we are much beholden to you!" cried Nigel. "Let the peasants dig, then, and as silently as they may. Do you keep your ear upon the ground, Andreas, so that if any one pass beneath us we shall be warned."

So, amid the driving rain, the little group toiled in the darkness. The blind man lay silent, flat upon his face, and twice they heard his warning hiss and stopped their work, while some one passed beneath. In an hour they had dug down to a stone arch which was clearly the outer side of the tunnel roof. Here was a sad obstacle, for it might take long to loosen a stone, and if their work was not done by the break of day then their enterprise was indeed hopeless. They loosened the mortar with a dagger, and at last dislodged one small stone which enabled them to get at the others. Presently a dark hole blacker than the night around them yawned at their feet, and their swords could touch no bottom to it. They had opened the tunnel.

"I would fain enter it first," said Nigel. "I pray you to lower me down." They held him to the full length of their arms, and then letting him drop they heard him land safely beneath them. An instant later the blind man started up with a low cry of alarm.

"I hear steps coming," said he. "They are far off, but they draw nearer."

Simon thrust his head and neck down the hole. "Squire Nigel," he whispered, "can you hear me?"

"I can hear you, Simon."

"Andreas says that some one comes."

"Then cover over the hole," came the answer. "Quick, I pray you, cover it over!"

A mantle was stretched across it, so that no glimmer of light should warn the newcomer. The fear was that he might have heard the sound of Nigel's descent. But soon it was clear that he had not done so, for Andreas announced that he was still advancing. Presently Nigel could hear the distant thud of his feet. If he bore a lantern all was lost. But no gleam of light appeared in the black tunnel, and still the footsteps drew nearer.

Nigel breathed a prayer of thanks to all his guardian saints as he crouched close to the slimy wall and waited breathless, his dagger in his hand. Nearer yet and nearer came the steps. He could hear the stranger's coarse breathing in the darkness. Then as he brushed past Nigel bounded upon him with a tiger spring. There was one gasp of astonishment, and not a sound more, for the squire's grip was on the man's throat and his body was pinned motionless against the wall.

"Simon! Simon!" cried Nigel, loudly.

The mantle was moved from the hole.

"Have you a cord? Or your belts linked together may serve."

One of the peasants had a rope, and Nigel soon felt it dangling against his hand. He listened and there was no sound in the passage. For an instant he released his captive's throat. A torrent of prayers and entreaties came forth. The man was shaking like a leaf in the wind. Nigel pressed the point of his dagger against his face and dared him to open his lips. Then he slipped the rope beneath his arms and tied it.

"Pull him up!" he whispered, and for an instant the gray glimmer above him was obscured.

"We have him, fair sir," said Simon.

"Then drop me the rope and hold it fast."

A moment later Nigel stood among the group of men who had gathered round their captive. It was too dark to see him, and they dare not strike flint and steel.

Simon passed his hand roughly over him and felt a fat cleanshaven face, and a cloth gabardine which hung to the ankles. "Who are you?" he whispered. "Speak the truth and speak it low, if you would ever speak again."

The man's teeth chattered in his head with cold and fright.

"I speak no English," he murmured.

"French, then," said Nigel.

"I am a holy priest of God. You court the ban of holy Church when you lay hands upon me. I pray you let me go upon my way, for there are those whom I would shrive and housel. If they should die in sin, their damnation is upon you."

"How are you called, then?"

"I am Dom Peter de Cervolles."

"De Cervolles, the arch-priest, he who heated the brazier when they burned out my eyes," cried old Andreas. "Of all the devils in hell there is none fouler than this one. Friends, friends, if I have done aught for you this night, I ask but one reward, that ye let me have my will of this man."

But Nigel pushed the old man back. "There is no time for this," he said. "Now hark you, priest—if priest indeed you be—your gown and tonsure will not save you if you play us false, for we are here of a set purpose, and we will go forward with it, come what may. Answer me and answer me truly or it will be an ill night for you. In what part of the castle does this tunnel enter?"

"In the lower cellar."

"What is at the end?"

"An oaken door."

"Is it barred?"

"Yes, it is barred."

"How would you have entered?"

"I would have given the password."

"Who then would have opened?"

"There is a guard within."

"And beyond him?"

"Beyond him are the prison cells and the jailers."

"Who else would be afoot?"

"No one save a guard at the gate and another on the battlement."

"What, then, is the password?"

The man was silent.

"The password, fellow!"

The cold points of two daggers pricked his throat, but still he would not speak.

"Where is the blind man?" asked Nigel. "Here, Andreas, you can have him and do what you will with him."

"Nay, nay," the priest whimpered. "Keep him off me. Save me from blind Andreas! I will tell you everything."

"The password, then, this instant?"

"It is *'Benedicite!'*"

"We have the password, Simon," cried Nigel. "Come then, let us on to the farther end. These peasants will guard the priest, and they will remain here lest we wish to send a message."

"Nay, fair sir, it is in my mind that we can do better," said Simon. "Let us take the priest with us, so that he who is within may know his voice."

"It is well thought of," said Nigel, "and first let us pray together, for indeed this night may well be our last."

He and the three men-at-arms knelt in the rain and sent up their simple orisons, Simon still clutching tight to his prisoner's wrist.

The priest fumbled in his breast, and drew something forth.

"It is the heart of the blessed confessor Saint Enogat," said he. "It may be that it will ease and assoil your souls if you would wish to handle it."

The four Englishmen passed the flat silver case from hand to hand, each pressing his lips devoutly upon it. Then they rose to their feet. Nigel was the first to lower himself down the hole; then Simon; then the priest, who was instantly seized by the other two. The men-at-arms followed them. They had scarcely moved away from the hole when Nigel stopped.

"Surely some one else came after us," said he.

They listened, but no whisper or rustle came from behind them. For a minute they paused and then resumed their journey through the dark. It seemed a long, long way, though in truth it was but a few hundred yards before they came to a door with a glimmer of yellow light around it, which barred their passage. Nigel struck upon it with his hand.

There was the rasping of a bolt and then a loud voice: "Is that you, priest?"

"Yes, it is I," said the prisoner, in a quavering voice. "Open, Arnold!"

The voice was enough. There was no question of passwords. The door swung inward, and in an instant the janitor was cut down by Nigel and Simon. So sudden and so fierce was the attack that save for the thud of his body no sound was heard. A flood of light burst outward into the passage, and the Englishmen stood with blinking eyes in its glare.

In front of them lay a stone-flagged corridor, across which lay the dead body of the janitor. It had doors on either side of it, and another grated door at the farther end. A strange hubbub, a kind of low droning and whining filled the air. The four men were standing listening, full of wonder as to what this might mean, when a sharp cry came from behind them. The priest lay in a shapeless heap upon the ground, and the blood was rushing from his gaping throat. Down the passage, a black shadow in the yellow light, there fled a crouching man, who clattered with a stick as he went.

"It is Andreas," cried West-country Will. "He has slain him."

"Then it was he that I heard behind us," said Nigel. "Doubtless he was at our very heels in the darkness. I fear that the priest's cry has been heard."

"Nay," said Simon, "there are so many cries that one more may well pass. Let us take this lamp from the wall and see what sort of devil's den we have around us."

They opened the door upon the right, and so horrible a smell issued from it that they were driven back from it. The lamp which Simon held forward showed a monkey-like creature mowing and grimacing in a corner, man or woman none could tell, but driven crazy by loneliness and horror. In the other cell was a gray-bearded man fettered to the wall, looking blankly before him, a body without a soul, yet with life still in him, for his dull eyes turned slowly in their direction. But it was from behind the central door at the end of the passage that the chorus of sad cries came which filled the air.

"Simon," said Nigel, "before we go farther we will take this outer door from its hinges. With it we will block this passage so that at the worst we may hold our ground here until help comes. Do you back to the camp as fast as your feet can bear you. The peasants will draw you upward through the hole. Give my greetings to Sir Robert and tell him that the castle is taken without fail if he comes this way with fifty men. Say that we have made a lodgment within the walls. And tell him also, Simon, that I would counsel him to make a stir before the gateway so that the guard may be held there whilst we make good our footing behind them. Go, good Simon, and lose not a moment!"

But the man-at-arms shook his head. "It is I who have brought you here, fair sir, and here I bide through fair and foul. But you speak wisely and well, for Sir Robert should indeed be told what is going forward now that we have gone so far. Harding, do you go with all speed and bear the gentle Nigel's message."

Reluctantly the man-at-arms sped upon his errand. They could hear the racing of his feet and the low jingle of his harness until they died away in the tunnel. Then the three companions approached the door at the end. It was their intention to wait where they were until help should come, but suddenly amid the babel of cries within there broke forth an English voice, shouting in torment.

"My God!" it cried, "I pray you, comrades, for a cup of water, as you hope for Christ's mercy!"

A shout of laughter and the thud of a heavy blow followed the appeal.

All the hot blood rushed to Nigel's head at the sound, buzzing in his ears and throbbing in his temples. There are times when the fiery heart of a man must overbear the cold brain of a soldier. With one bound he was at the door, with another he was through it, the men-at-arms at his heels. So strange was the scene before them that for an instant all three stood motionless with horror and surprise.

It was a great vaulted chamber, brightly lit by many torches. At the farther end roared a great fire. In front of it three naked men were chained to posts in such a way that, flinch as they might, they could never get beyond the range of its scorching heat. Yet they were so far from it that no actual burn would be inflicted if they could but keep turning and shifting so as continually to present some fresh portion of their flesh to the flames. Hence they danced and whirled in front of the fire, tossing ceaselessly this way and that within the compass of their chains, wearied to death, their protruding tongues cracked and blackened with thirst, but unable for one instant to rest from their writhings and contortions.

Even stranger was the sight at each side of the room, whence came that chorus of groans which had first struck upon the ears of Nigel and his companions. A line of great hogsheads were placed alongside the walls, and within each sat a man, his head protruding from the top. As they moved within there was a constant splashing and washing of water. The white wan faces all turned together as the door flew open, and a cry of amazement and of hope took the place of those long-drawn moans of despair.

At the same instant two fellows clad in black, who had been seated with a flagon of wine between them at a table near the fire, sprang wildly to their feet, staring with blank amazement at this sudden inrush. That instant of delay deprived them of their last chance of safety. Midway down the room was a flight of stone steps which led to the main door.

Swift as a wild cat Nigel bounded toward it and gained the steps a stride or two before the jailers. They turned and made for the other which led to the passage, but Simon and his comrades were nearer to it than they. Two sweeping blows, two dagger thrusts into writhing figures, and the ruffians who worked the will of the Butcher lay dead upon the floor of their slaughter-house.

Oh, the buzz of joy and of prayer from all those white lips! Oh, the light of returning hope in all those sunken weary eyes! One wild shout would have gone up had not Nigel's outstretched hands and warning voice hushed them to silence.

He opened the door behind him. A curving newel staircase wound upward into the darkness. He listened, but no sound came down. There was a key in the outer lock of the iron door. He whipped it out and turned it on the inner side. The ground that they had gained was safe. Now they could turn to the relief of these poor fellows beside them. A few strong blows struck off the irons and freed the three dancers before the fire. With a husky croak of joy, they rushed across to their comrades' water-barrels, plunged their heads in like horses, and drank and drank and drank. Then in turn the poor shivering wretches were taken out of the barrels, their skins bleached and wrinkled with long soaking. Their bonds were torn from them; but, cramped and fixed, their limbs refused to act, and they tumbled and twisted upon the floor in their efforts to reach Nigel and to kiss his hand.

In a corner lay Aylward, dripping from his barrel and exhausted with cold and hunger. Nigel ran to his side and raised his head. The jug of wine from which the two jailers had drunk still stood upon their table. The squire placed it to the archer's lips, and he took a hearty pull at it.

"How is it with you now, Aylward?"

"Better, squire, better, but may I never touch water again as long as I live! Alas! poor Dicon has gone, and Stephen also—the life chilled out of them. The cold is in the very marrow of my bones. I pray you, let me lean upon your arm as far as the fire, that I may warm the frozen blood and set it running in my veins once more."

A strange sight it was to see these twenty naked men crouching in a half-circle round the fire with their trembling hands extended to the blaze. Soon their tongues at least were thawed, and they poured out the story of their troubles, with many a prayer and ejaculation to the saints for their safe delivery. No food had crossed their lips since they had been taken. The Butcher had commanded them to join his garrison and to shoot upon their comrades from the wall. When they refused he had set aside three of them for execution.

The others had been dragged to the cellar, whither the leering tyrant had followed them. Only one question he had asked them, whether they were of a hot-blooded nature or of a cold. Blows were showered upon them until they answered. Three had said cold, and had been condemned to the torment of the fire. The rest who had said hot were delivered up to the torture of the water-cask. Every few hours this man or fiend had come down to exult over their sufferings and to ask them whether they were ready yet to enter his service. Three had consented and were gone. But the others had all of them stood firm, two of them even to their death.

Such was the tale to which Nigel and his comrades listened while they waited impatiently for the coming of Knolles and his men. Many an anxious look did they cast down the black tunnel, but no glimmer of light and no clash of steel came from its depths. Suddenly, however, a loud and measured sound broke upon their ears. It was a dull metallic clang, ponderous and slow, growing louder and ever louder—the tread of an armored man. The poor wretches round the fire, all unnerved by hunger and suffering, huddled together with wan, scared faces, their eyes fixed in terror on the door.

"It is he!" they whispered. "It is the Butcher himself!"

Nigel had darted to the door and listened intently. There were no footfalls save those of one man. Once sure of that, he softly turned the key in the lock. At the same instant there came a bull's bellow from without.

"Ives! Bertrand!" cried the voice. "Can you not hear me coming, you drunken varlets? You shall cool your own heads in the water-casks, you lazy rascals! What, not even now! Open, you dogs. Open, I say!"

He had thrust down the latch, and with a kick he flung the door wide and rushed inward. For an instant he stood motionless, a statue of dull yellow metal, his eyes fixed upon the empty casks and the huddle of naked men. Then, with the roar of a trapped lion, he turned, but the door had slammed behind him, and Black Simon, with grim figure and sardonic face, stood between.

The Butcher looked round him helplessly, for he was unarmed save for his dagger. Then his eyes fell upon Nigel's roses.

"You are a gentleman of coat-armor," he cried. "I surrender myself to you."

"I will not take your surrender, you black villain," said Nigel. "Draw and defend yourself. Simon, give him your sword."

"Nay, this is madness," said the blunt man-at-arms. "Why should I give the wasp a sting?"

"Give it him, I say. I cannot kill him in cold blood."

"But I can!" yelled Aylward, who had crept up from the fire. "Come, comrades! By these ten finger-bones! has he not taught us how cold blood should be warmed?"

Like a pack of wolves they were on him, and he clanged upon the floor with a dozen frenzied naked figures clutching and clinging above him. In vain Nigel tried to pull them off. They were mad with rage, these tortured starving men, their eyes fixed and glaring, their hair on end, their teeth gnashing with fury, while they tore at the howling, writhing man. Then, with a rattle and clatter, they pulled him across the room by his two ankles and dragged him into the fire.

Nigel shuddered and turned away his eyes as he saw the brazen figure roll out and stagger to his knees, only to be hurled once more into the heart of the blaze. His prisoners screamed with joy and clapped their hands as they pushed him back with their feet until the armor was too hot for them to touch. Then at last he lay still and glowed darkly red, while the naked men danced in a wild half-circle round the fire.

But now at last the supports had come. Lights flashed and armor gleamed down the tunnel. The cellar filled with armed men, while from above came the cries and turmoil of the feigned assault upon the gate. Led by Knolles and Nigel, the storming party rushed upward and seized the courtyard. The guard of the gate taken in the rear threw down their weapons and cried for mercy. The gate was thrown open and the assailants rushed in, with hundreds of furious peasants at their heels. Some of the robbers died in hot blood, many in cold; but all died, for Knolles had vowed to give no quarter. Day was just breaking when the last fugitive had been hunted out and slain. From all sides came the yells and whoops of the soldiers, with the rending and riving of doors as they burst into the store-rooms and treasure-chambers. There was a joyous scramble among them, for the plunder of eleven years, gold and jewels, satins and velvets, rich plate and noble hangings were all to be had for the taking.

The rescued prisoners, their hunger appeased and their clothes restored, led the search for booty. Nigel, leaning on his sword by the gateway, saw Aylward totter past, a huge bundle under each arm, another slung over his back, and a smaller packet hanging from his mouth. He dropped it for a moment as he passed his young master.

"By these ten finger-bones! I am right glad that I came to the war, and no man could ask for a more goodly life," said he. "I have a present here for every girl in Tilford, and my father need never fear the frown of the Sacrist of Waverley again. But how of you, Squire Loring? It standeth not aright that we should gather the harvest whilst you, who sowed it, go forth empty-handed. Come, gentle sir, take these things that I have gathered, and I will go back and find more."

But Nigel smiled and shook his head. "You have gained what your heart desired, and perchance I have done so also," said he.

An instant later Knolles strode up to him with outstretched hand.

"I ask your pardon, Nigel," said he. "I have spoken too hotly in my wrath."

"Nay, fair sir, I was at fault."

"If we stand here now within this castle, it is to you that I owe it. The king shall know of it, and Chandos also. Can I do aught else, Nigel, to prove to you the high esteem in which I hold you?"

The squire flushed with pleasure. "Do you send a messenger home to England, fair sir, with news of these doings?"

"Surely, I must do so. But do not tell me, Nigel, that you would be that messenger. Ask me some other favor, for indeed I cannot let you go."

"Now, God forbid!" cried Nigel. "By Saint Paul! I would not be so caitiff and so thrall as to leave you when some small deed might still be done. But I would fain send a message by your messenger."

"To whom?"

"It is to the Lady Mary, daughter of old Sir John Buttesthorn, who dwells near Guildford."

"But you will write the message, Nigel. Such greetings as a cavalier sends to his lady-love should be under seal."

"Nay, he can carry my message by word of mouth."

"Then I shall tell him, for he goes this morning. What message, then, shall he say to the lady?"

"He will give her my very humble greeting, and he will say to her that for the second time Saint Catharine has been our friend."

XXII. HOW ROBERT OF BEAUMANOIR CAME TO PLOERMEL

SIR ROBERT KNOLLES and his men passed onward that day, looking back many a time to see the two dark columns of smoke, one thicker and one more slender, which arose from the castle and from the fort of La Brohinière. There was not an archer nor a man-at-arms who did not bear a great bundle of spoil upon his back, and Knolles frowned darkly as he looked upon them. Gladly would he have thrown it all down by the roadside, but he had tried such matters before, and he knew that it was as safe to tear a half-gnawed bone from a bear as their blood-won plunder from such men as these. In any case it was but two days' march to Ploermel, where he hoped to bring his journey to an end.

That night they camped at Mauron, where a small English and Breton garrison held the castle. Right glad were the bowmen to see some of their own countrymen once more, and they spent the night over wine and dice, a crowd of Breton girls assisting, so that next morning their bundles were much lighter, and most of the plunder of La Brohinière was left with the men and women of Mauron. Next day their march lay with a fair sluggish river upon their right, and a great rolling forest upon their left, which covered the whole country. At last, toward evening, the towers of Ploermel rose before them, and they saw against a darkening sky the Red Cross of England waving in the wind. So blue was the river Duc which skirted the road, and so green its banks, that they might indeed have been back beside their own homely streams, the Oxford Thames or the Midland Trent, but ever as the darkness deepened there came in wild gusts the howling of wolves from the forest to remind them that they were in a land of war. So busy had men been for many years in hunting one another that the beasts of the chase had grown to a monstrous degree, until the streets of the towns were no longer safe from the wild inroads of the fierce creatures, the wolves and the bears, who swarmed around them.

It was nightfall when the little army entered the outer gate of the Castle of Ploermel and encamped in the broad bailey-yard. Ploermel was at that time the center of British power in Mid-Brittany, as Hennebon was in the West, and it was held by a garrison of five hundred men under an old soldier, Richard of Bambro, a rugged Northumbrian, trained in that great school of warriors, the border wars. He who had ridden the marches of the most troubled frontier in Europe, and served his time against the Liddlesdale and Nithsdale raiders, was hardened for a life in the field.

Of late, however, Bambro had been unable to undertake any enterprise, for his reinforcements had failed him, and amid his following he had but three English knights and seventy men. The rest were a mixed crew of Bretons, Hainaulters, and a few German mercenary soldiers, brave men individually, as those of that stock have ever been, but lacking interest in the cause, and bound together by no common tie of blood or tradition.

On the other hand, the surrounding castles, and especially that of Josselin, were held by strong forces of enthusiastic Bretons, inflamed by a common patriotism, and full of warlike ardor. Robert of Beaumanoir, the fierce seneschal of the house of Rohan, pushed constant forays and excursions against Ploermel, so that town and castle were both in daily dread of being surrounded and besieged. Several small parties of the English faction had been cut off and slain to a man, and so straitened were the others that it was difficult for them to gather provisions from the country round.

Such was the state of Bambro's garrison when on that March evening Knolles and his men streamed into the bailey-yard of his castle.

In the glare of the torches at the inner gate Bambro was waiting to receive them, a dry, hard, wizened man, small and fierce, with beady black eyes and quick, furtive ways. Beside him, a strange contrast, stood his squire, Croquart, a German, whose name and fame as a man-at-arms were widespread, though like Robert Knolles himself, he had begun as a humble page. He was a very tall man, with an enormous spread of shoulders, and a pair of huge hands with which he could crack a horse-shoe. He was slow and lethargic, save in moments of excitement, and his calm blond face, his dreamy blue eyes, and his long fair hair gave him so gentle an appearance that none save those who had seen him in his berserk mood, raging, an iron giant, in the forefront of the battle, could ever guess how terrible a warrior he might be. Little knight and huge squire stood together under the arch of the donjon and gave welcome to the newcomers, while a swarm of soldiers crowded round to embrace their comrades and to lead them off where they might feed and make merry together.

Supper had been set in the hall of Ploermel, wherein the knights and squires assembled. Bambro and Croquart were there with Sir Hugh Calverly, an old friend of Knolles and a fellow-townsman, for both were men of Chester. Sir Hugh was a middle-sized flaxen man, with hard gray eyes and fierce, large-nosed face, sliced across with the scar of a sword-cut. There, too, were Geoffrey D'Ardaine, a young Breton seigneur; Sir Thomas Belford, a burly thick-set Midland Englishman; Sir Thomas Walton, whose surcoat of scarlet martlets showed that he was of the Surrey Waltons; James Marshall and John Russell, young English squires; and the two brothers, Richard and Hugh Le Galliard, who were of Gascon blood. Besides these were several squires unknown to fame, and of the newcomers, Sir Robert Knolles, Sir Thomas Percy, Nigel Loring, and two other squires, Allington and Parsons. These were the company who gathered in the torchlight round the table of the Seneschal of Ploermel, and kept high revel with joyous hearts because they thought that much honor and noble deeds lay before them.

But one sad face there was at the board, and that belonged to him at the head of it. Sir Robert Bambro sat with his chin leaning upon his hand and his eyes downcast upon the cloth, while all round him rose the merry clatter of voices, every one planning some fresh enterprise which might now be attempted. Sir Robert Knolles was for an immediate advance upon Josselin. Calverly thought that a raid might be made into the South, where the main French power lay. Others spoke of an attack upon Vannes.

To all these eager opinions Bambro listened in a moody silence, which he broke at last by a fierce execration which drew a hushed attention from the company.

"Say no more, fair sirs," he cried; "for indeed your words are like so many stabs in my heart. All this and more we might indeed have done. But of a truth you are too late."

"Too late?'" cried Knolles. "What mean you, Richard?"

"Alas that I should have to say it, but you and all these fair soldiers might be back in England once more for all the profit that I am like to have from your coming. Saw you a rider on a white horse ere you reached the castle?"

"Nay, I saw him not."

"He came by the western road from Hennebon. Would that he had broken his neck ere he came here. Not an hour ago he left his message, and now hath ridden on to warn the garrison of Malestroit. A truce has been proclaimed for a year betwixt the French king and the English, and he who breaks it forfeits life and estate."

"A truce!" Here was an end to all their fine dreams. They looked blankly at each other all round the table, while Croquart brought his great fist down upon the board until the glasses rattled again. Knolles sat with clenched hands as if he were a figure of stone, while Nigel's heart turned cold and heavy within him. A truce! Where, then, was his third deed, and how might he return without it?

Even as they sat in moody silence there was the call of a bugle from somewhere out in the darkness.

Sir Richard looked up with surprise. "We are not wont to be summoned after once the portcullis is down," said he. "Truce or no truce, we must let no man within our walls until we have proved him. Croquart, see to it!"

The huge German left the room. The company were still seated in despondent silence when he returned.

"Sir Richard," said he, "the brave knight Robert of Beaumanoir and his Squire William de Montaubon are without the gate, and would fain have speech with you."

Bambro started in his chair. What could the fierce leader of the Bretons, a man who was red to the elbow with English blood, have to say to them? On what errand had he left his castle of Josselin to pay this visit to his deadly enemies?

"Are they armed?" he asked.

"They are unarmed."

"Then admit them and bring them hither, but double the guards, and take all heed against surprise."

Places were set at the farther end of the table for these most unexpected guests. Presently the door was swung open, and Croquart, with all form and courtesy, announced the two Bretons, who entered with the proud and lofty air of gallant warriors and high-bred gentlemen.

Beaumanoir was a tall, dark man, with raven hair and long, swarthy beard. He was strong and straight as a young oak, with fiery black eyes, and no flaw in his comely features, save that his front teeth had been dashed from their sockets. His squire, William of Montaubon, was also tall, with a thin, hatchet face, and two small gray eyes set very close upon either side of a long, fierce nose. In Beaumanoir's expression one read only gallantry and frankness; in Montaubon's there was gallantry also, but it was mixed with the cruelty and cunning of the wolf. They bowed as they entered, and the little English seneschal advanced with outstretched hand to meet them.

"Welcome, Robert, so long as you are beneath this roof," said he. "Perhaps the time may come in another place when we may speak to each other in another fashion."

"So I hope, Richard," said Beaumanoir; "but, indeed, we of Josselin bear you in high esteem, and are much beholden to you and to your men for all that you have done for us. We could not wish better neighbors, nor any from whom more honor is to be gained. I learn that Sir Robert Knolles and others have joined you, and we are heavy hearted to think that the orders of our kings should debar us from attempting a venture."

He and his squire sat down at the places set for them, and, filling their glasses, drank to the company.

"What you say is true, Robert," said Bambro, "and before you came we were discussing the matter among ourselves, and grieving that it should be so. When heard you of the truce?"

"Yester evening a messenger rode from Nantes."

"Our news came to-night from Hennebon. The king's own seal was on the order. So I fear that for a year, at least, you will bide at Josselin and we at Ploermel, and kill time as we may. Perchance we may hunt the wolf together in the great forest, or fly our hawks on the banks of the Duc."

"Doubtless we shall do all this, Richard," said Beaumanoir; "but by Saint Cadoc it is in my mind that with good-will upon both sides, we may please ourselves and yet stand excused before our kings."

Knights and squires leaned forward in their chairs, their eager eyes fixed upon him. He broke into a gap-toothed smile as he looked round at the circle, the wizened seneschal, the blond giant, Nigel's fresh young face, the grim features of Knolles, and the yellow, hawk-like Calverly, all burning with the same desire.

"I see that I need not doubt the good-will," said he, "and of that I was very certain before I came upon this errand. Bethink you, then, that this order applies to war but not to challenges, spear-runnings, knightly exchanges, or the like. King Edward is too good a knight, and so is King John, that either of them should stand in the way of a gentleman who desires to advance himself, or to venture his body for the exaltation of his lady. Is this not so?"

A murmur of eager assent rose from the table.

"If you as the garrison of Ploermel, march upon the garrison of Josselin, then it is very plain that we have broken the truce, and upon our heads be it. But if there be a private bickering betwixt me, for example, and this young squire whose eyes show that he is very eager for honor, and if, thereafter, others on each side join in and fight upon the quarrel, it is in no sense war, but rather our own private business which no king can alter."

"Indeed, Robert," said Bambro, "all that you say is very good and fair."

Beaumanoir leaned forward toward Nigel, his brimming glass in his hand.

"Your name, squire?" said he.

"My name is Nigel Loring."

"I see that you are young and eager, so I choose you, as I would fain have been chosen when I was of your age."

"I thank you, fair sir," said Nigel. "It is great honor that one so famous as yourself should condescend to do some small deed upon me."

"But we must have cause for quarrel, Nigel. Now, here I drink to the ladies of Brittany, who of all ladies upon this earth, are the most fair and the most virtuous, so that the least worthy amongst them is far above the best of England. What say you to that, young sir?"

Nigel dipped his finger in his glass, and, leaning over, he placed its wet impress on the Breton's hand.

"This in your face!" said he.

Beaumanoir swept off the red drop of moisture and smiled his approval.

"It could not have been better done," said he. "Why spoil my velvet paltock, as many a hot-headed fool would have done. It is in my mind, young sir, that you will go far. And now, who follows up this quarrel?"

A growl ran round the table.

Beaumanoir ran his eye round and shook his head.

"Alas!" said he, "there are but twenty of you here, and I have thirty at Josselin who are so eager to advance themselves that, if I return without hope for all of them, there will be sore hearts amongst them. I pray you, Richard, since we have been at these pains to arrange matters, that you in turn will do what you may. Can you not find ten more men?"

"But not of gentle blood."

"Nay, it matters not, if they will only fight."

"Of that there can be no doubt, for the castle is full of archers and men-at-arms who would gladly play a part in the matter."

"Then choose ten," said Beaumanoir.

But for the first time the wolf-like squire opened his thin lips.

"Surely, my lord, you will not allow archers," said he.

"I fear not any man."

"Nay, fair sir, consider that this is a trial of weapons betwixt us, where man faces man. You have seen these English archers, and you know how fast and how strong are their shafts. Bethink you that if ten of them were against us, it is likely that half of us would be down before ever we came to handstrokes."

"By Saint Cadoc, William, I think that you are right," cried the Breton. "If we are to have such a fight as will remain in the memories of men, you will bring no archers and we no cross-bows. Let it be steel upon steel. How say you, then?"

"Surely we can bring ten men-at-arms to make up the thirty that you desire, Robert. It is agreed, then, that we fight on no quarrel of England and France, but over this matter of the ladies in which you and Squire Loring have fallen out. And now the time?"

"At once."

"Surely at once, or perchance a second messenger may come and this also be forbidden. We will be ready with to-morrow's sunrise."

"Nay, a day later," cried the Breton squire. "Bethink you, my lord, that the three lances of Radenac would take time to come over."

"They are not of our garrison, and they shall not have a place."

"But, fair sir, of all the lances of Brittany——"

"Nay, William, I will not have it an hour later. To-morrow it shall be, Richard."

"And where?"

"I marked a fitting place even as I rode here this evening. If you cross the river and take the bridle-path through the fields which leads to Josselin you come midway upon a mighty oak standing at the corner of a fair and level meadow. There let us meet at midday to-morrow."

"Agreed!" cried Bambro. "But I pray you not to rise, Robert! The night is still young, and the spices and hippocras will soon be served. Bide with us, I pray you, for if you would fain hear the latest songs from England, these gentlemen have doubtless brought them. To some of us perchance it is the last night, so we would make it a full one."

But the gallant Breton shook his head. "It may indeed be the last night for many," said he, "and it is but right that my com-rades should know it. I have no need of monk or friar, for I can-not think that harm will ever come beyond the grave to one who has borne himself as a knight should, but others have other thoughts upon these matters, and would fain have time for prayer and penitence. Adieu, fair sirs, and I drink a last glass to a happy meeting at the midway oak."

XXIII. HOW THIRTY OF JOSSELIN
ENCOUNTERED THIRTY OF PLOERMEL

ALL NIGHT THE Castle of Ploermel rang with warlike preparations, for the smiths were hammering and filing and riveting,
preparing the armor for the champions. In the stable yard hostlers were testing and grooming the great war-horses, while in
the chapel knights and squires were easing their souls at the
knees of old Father Benedict.

Down in the courtyard, meanwhile, the men-at-arms had
been assembled, and the volunteers weeded out until the best
men had been selected. Black Simon had obtained a place, and
great was the joy which shone upon his grim visage. With him
were chosen young Nicholas Dagsworth, a gentleman adven-
turer who was nephew to the famous Sir Thomas, Walter the
German, Hulbitée—a huge peasant whose massive frame gave
promise which his sluggish spirit failed to fulfil—John Alcock,
Robin Adey and Raoul Provost. These with three others made
up the required thirty. Great was the grumbling and evil the talk
among the archers when it was learned that none of them were
to be included, but the bow had been forbidden on either side.
It is true that many of them were expert fighters both with axe
and with sword, but they were unused to carry heavy armor, and
a half-armed man would have short shrift in such a hand-to-
hand struggle as lay before them.

It was two hours after tierce, or one hour before noon, on the
fourth Wednesday of Lent, in the year of Christ 1351, that the
men of Ploermel rode forth from their castle-gate and crossed
the bridge of the Due. In front was Bambro with his squire,
Croquart, the latter on a great roan horse bearing the banner of
Ploermel, which was a black rampant lion holding a blue flag

284

upon a field of ermine. Behind him came Robert Knolles and
Nigel Loring, with an attendant at their side, who carried the
pennon of the black raven. Then rode Sir Thomas Percy, with
his blue lion flaunting above him, and Sir Hugh Calverly, whose
banner bore a silver owl, followed by the massive Belford, who
carried a huge iron club, weighing sixty pounds, upon his saddle-
bow, and Sir Thomas Walton, the knight of Surrey. Behind them
were four brave Anglo-Bretons, Perrot de Commelain, Le
Gaillart, d'Aspremont and d'Ardaine, who fought against their
own countrymen because they were partisans of the Countess of
Montfort. Her engrailed silver cross upon a blue field was carried at their head. In the rear were five German or Hainault
mercenaries, the tall Hulbitée, and the men-at-arms. Altogether
of these combatants twenty were of English birth, four were
Breton, and six were of German blood.

So, with glitter of armor and flaunting of pennons, their war-
horses tossing and pawing, the champions rode down to the
midway oak. Behind them streamed hundreds of archers and
men-at-arms, whose weapons had been wisely taken from them,
lest a general battle should ensue. With them also went the
townsfolk, men and women, together with wine-sellers, provision merchants, armorers, grooms, and heralds, with surgeons to
tend the wounded and priests to shrive the dying. The path was
blocked by this throng, but all over the face of the country,
horsemen and footmen, gentle and simple, men and women,
could be seen speeding their way to the scene of the encounter.

The journey was not a long one, for presently, as they
threaded their way through the fields, there appeared before
them a great gray oak which spread its gnarled leafless branches
over the corner of a green and level meadow. The tree was black
with the peasants who had climbed into it, and all round it was
a huge throng, chattering and calling like a rookery at sunset. A
storm of hooting broke out from them at the approach of the
English, for Bambro was hated in the country, where he raised
money for the Montfort cause by putting every parish to ransom, and maltreating those who refused to pay. There was little
amenity in the warlike ways which had been learned upon the
Scottish border. The champions rode onward without deigning

to take notice of the taunts of the rabble, but the archers turned that way and soon beat the mob to silence. Then they resolved themselves into the keepers of the ground, and pressed the people back until they formed a dense line along the edge of the field, leaving the whole space clear for the warriors.

The Breton champions had not yet arrived, so the English tethered their horses at one side of the ground, and then gathered round their leader. Every man had his shield slung round his neck, and had cut his spear to the length of five feet, so that it might be more manageable for fighting on foot. Besides the spear, a sword or a battle-axe hung at the side of each. They were clad from head to foot in armor, with devices upon the crests and surcoats to distinguish them from their antagonists. At present their visors were still up, and they chatted gaily with each other.

"By Saint Dunstan!" cried Percy, slapping his gauntleted hands together and stamping his steel feet, "I shall be right glad to get to work, for my blood is chilled."

"I warrant you will be warm enough ere you get through," said Calverly.

"Or cold for ever. Candle shall burn and bell toll at Alnwick Chapel if I leave this ground alive; but come what may, fair sirs, it should be a famous joust, and one which will help us forward. Surely each of us will have worshipfully won worship, if we chance to come through."

"You say truth, Thomas," said Knolles, bracing his girdle. "For my own part I have no joy in such encounters when there is warfare to be carried out, for it standeth not aright that a man should think of his own pleasure and advancement rather than of the king's cause and the weal of the army. But in times of truce I can think of no better way in which a day may be profitably spent. Why so silent, Nigel?"

"Indeed, fair sir, I was looking toward Josselin, which lies, as I understand, beyond those woods. I see no sign of this debonair gentleman and of his following. It would be indeed grievous pity if any cause came to hold them back."

Hugh Calverly laughed at the words. "You need have no fear, young sir," said he. "Such a spirit lies in Robert de Beaumanoir that if he must come alone he would ride against us none the less. I warrant that if he were on a bed of death he would be borne here and die on the green field."

"You say truly, Hugh," said Bambro. "I know him and those who ride behind him. Thirty stouter men or more skilled in arms are not to be found in Christendom. It is in my mind that, come what may, there will be much honor for all of us this day. Ever in my head I have a rhyme which the wife of a Welsh archer gave me when I crossed her hand with a golden bracelet after the intaking of Bergerac. She was of the old blood of Merlin with the power of sight. Thus she said—

> " 'Twixt the oak-tree and the river
> Knightly fame and brave endeavor
> Make an honored name for ever.'

"Methinks I see the oak-tree, and yonder is the river. Surely this should betide some good to us."

The huge German squire betrayed some impatience during this speech of his leader. Though his rank was subordinate, no man present had more experience of warfare or was more famous as a fighter than he. He now broke brusquely into the talk.

"We should be better employed in ordering our line and making our plans than in talking of the rhymes of Merlin or such old wives' tales," said he. "It is to our own strong arms and good weapons that we must trust this day. And first I would ask you, Sir Richard, what is your will if perchance you should fall in the midst of the fight?"

Bambro turned to the others. "If such should be the case, fair sirs, I desire that my squire, Croquart, should command."

There was a pause, while the knights looked with some chagrin at each other. The silence was broken by Knolles.

"I will do what you say, Richard," said he, "though indeed it is bitter that we who are knights should serve beneath a squire. Yet it is not for us to fall out among ourselves now at this last moment, and I have ever heard that Croquart is a very worthy and valiant man. Therefore, I will pledge you on jeopardy of my soul that I will accept him as leader if you fall."

"So will I also, Richard," said Calverly.

"And I too!" cried Belford. "But surely I hear music, and yonder are their pennons amid the trees."

They all turned, leaning upon their short spears, and watched the advance of the men of Josselin, as their troop wound its way out from the woodlands. In front rode three heralds with tabards of the ermine of Brittany, blowing loudly upon silver trumpets. Behind them a great man upon a white horse bore the banner of Josselin, which carries nine golden bezants upon a scarlet field. Then came the champions riding two and two, fifteen knights and fifteen squires, each with his pennon displayed. Behind them on a litter was borne an aged priest, the Bishop of Rennes, carrying in his hands the viaticum and the holy oils that he might give the last aid and comfort of the Church to those who were dying. The procession was terminated by hundreds of men and women from Josselin, Guegon, and Helleon, and by the entire garrison of the fortress, who came, as the English had done, without their arms. The head of this long column had reached the field before the rear were clear of the wood, but as they arrived the champions picketed their horses on the farther side, behind which their banner was planted, and the people lined up until they had inclosed the whole lists with a dense wall of spectators.

With keen eyes the English party had watched the armorial blazonry of their antagonists, for those fluttering pennons and brilliant surcoats carried a language which all men could read. In front was the banner of Beaumanoir, blue with silver frets. His motto, *"J'ayme qui m'ayme,"* was carried on a second flag by a little page.

"Whose is the shield behind him—silver with scarlet drops?" asked Knolles.

"It is his squire, William of Montaubon," Calverly answered. "And there are the golden lion of Rochefort and the silver cross of Du Bois the Strong. I would not wish to meet a better company than are before us this day. See, there are the blue rings of young Tintiniac, who slew my squire, Hubert, last Lammastide. With the aid of Saint George I will avenge him ere nightfall."

"By the three kings of Almain," growled Croquart, "we will

need to fight hard this day, for never have I seen so many good soldiers gathered together. Yonder is Yves Cheruel, whom they call the man of iron; Caro de Bodegat also, with whom I have had more than one bickering—that is he with the three ermine circles on the scarlet shield. There too is left-handed Alain de Karanais; bear in mind that his stroke comes on the side where there is no shield."

"Who is the small stout man," asked Nigel—"he with the black and silver shield? By Saint Paul! he seems a very worthy person and one from whom much might be gained, for he is nigh as broad as he is long."

"It is Sir Robert Raguenel," said Calverly, whose long spell of service in Brittany had made him familiar with the people. "It is said that he can lift a horse upon his back. Beware a full stroke of that steel mace, for the armor is not made that can abide it. But here is the good Beaumanoir, and surely it is time that we came to grips."

The Breton leader had marshaled his men in a line opposite to the English, and now he strode forward and shook Bambro by the hand.

"By Saint Cadoc! this is a very joyous meeting, Richard," said he, "and we have certainly hit upon a very excellent way of keeping a truce."

"Indeed, Robert," said Bambro, "we owe you much thanks, for I can see that you have been at great pains to bring a worthy company against us this day. Surely if all should chance to perish there will be few noble houses in Brittany who will not mourn."

"Nay, we have none of the highest of Brittany," Beaumanoir answered. "Neither a Blois, nor a Leon, nor a Rohan, nor a Conan, fights in our ranks this day. And yet we are all men of blood and coat-armor, who are ready to venture our persons for the desire of our ladies and the love of the high order of knighthood. And now, Richard, what is your sweet will concerning this fight?"

"That we continue until one or other can endure no longer, for since it is seldom that so many brave men draw together it is fitting that we see as much as is possible of each other."

"Richard, your words are fair and good. It shall be even as you say. For the rest, each shall fight as pleases him best from the time that the herald calls the word. If any man from without shall break in upon us he shall be hanged on yonder oak."

With a salute he drew down his visor and returned to his own men, who were kneeling in a twinkling, many colored group, while the old bishop gave them his blessing.

The heralds rode round with a warning to the spectators. Then they halted at the side of the two bands of men, who now stood in a long line facing each other with fifty yards of grass between. The visors had been closed, and every man was now cased in metal from head to foot, some few glowing in brass, the greater number shining in steel. Only their fierce eyes could be seen smoldering in the dark shadow of their helmets. So for an instant they stood glaring and crouching.

Then, with a loud cry of "*Allez!*" the herald dropped his upraised hand, and the two lines of men shuffled as fast as their heavy armor would permit, until they met with a sharp clang of metal in the middle of the field. There was a sound as of sixty smiths working upon their anvils. Then the babel of yells and shouts from the spectators, cheering on this party or that, rose and swelled, until even the uproar of the combat was drowned in that mighty surge.

So eager were the combatants to engage that in a few moments all order had been lost and the two bands were mixed up in one furious scrambling, clattering throng, each man tossed hither and thither, thrown against one adversary and then against another, beaten and hustled and buffeted, with only the one thought in his mind to thrust with his spear or to beat with his axe against anyone who came within the narrow slit of vision left by his visor.

But alas for Nigel and his hopes of some great deed! His was at least the fate of the brave, for he was the first to fall. With a high heart, he had placed himself in the line as nearly opposite to Beaumanoir as he could, and had made straight for the Breton leader, remembering that in the outset the quarrel had been so ordered that it lay between them. But ere he could reach his goal he was caught in the swirl of his own comrades, and, being the lighter man, was swept aside and dashed into the arms of Alain de Karanais, the left-handed swordsman, with such a crash that the two rolled upon the ground together. Light-footed as a cat, Nigel had sprung up first, and was stooping over the Breton squire, when the powerful dwarf Raguenel brought his mace thudding down upon the exposed back of his helmet. With a groan Nigel fell upon his face, blood gushing from his mouth, nose, and ears. There he lay, trampled over by either party, while that great fight for which his fiery soul had panted was swaying back and forward above his unconscious form.

But Nigel was not long unavenged. The huge iron club of Belford struck the dwarf Raguenel to the ground, while Belford in turn was felled by a sweeping blow from Beaumanoir. Sometimes a dozen were on the ground at one time, but so strong was the armor, and so deftly was the force of a blow broken by guard and shield, that the stricken men were often pulled to their feet once more by their comrades, and were able to continue the fight.

Some, however, were beyond all aid. Croquart had cut at a Breton knight named Jean Rousselot, and had shorn away his shoulder-piece, exposing his neck and the upper part of his arm. Vainly he tried to cover this vulnerable surface with his shield. It was his right side, and he could not stretch it far enough across, nor could he get away on account of the press of men around him. For a time he held his foemen at bay, but that bare patch of white shoulder was a mark for every weapon, until at last a hatchet sank up to the socket in the knight's chest. Almost at the same moment a second Breton, a young squire named Geoffrey Mellon, was slain by a thrust from Black Simon, which found the weak spot beneath the armpit. Three other Bretons, Evan Cheruel, Caro de Bodegat, and Tristan de Pestivien, the first two knights and the latter a squire, became separated from their comrades, and were beaten to the ground with English all around them, so that they had to choose between instant death and surrender. They handed their swords to Bambro, and stood apart, each of them sorely wounded, watching with hot and bitter hearts the *mêlée* which still surged up and down the field.

But now the combat had lasted half an hour without stint or

rest, until the warriors were so exhausted with the burden of their armor, the loss of blood, the shock of blows, and their own furious exertions, that they could scarce totter or raise their weapons. There must be a pause if the combat was to have any decisive end.

"Cessez! Cessez! Retirez!" cried the heralds, as they spurred their horses between the exhausted men.

Slowly the gallant Beaumanoir led the twenty-five men who were left to their original station, where they opened their visors and threw themselves down upon the grass, panting like weary dogs, and wiping the sweat from their bloodshot eyes. A pitcher of wine of Anjou was carried round by a page, and each in turn drained a cup, save only Beaumanoir, who kept his Lent with such strictness that neither food nor drink might pass his lips before sunset. He paced slowly among his men, croaking forth encouragement from his parched lips, and pointing out to them that among the English there was scarce a man who was not wounded, and some so sorely that they could hardly stand. If the fight so far had gone against them, there were still five hours of daylight, and much might happen before the last of them was laid upon his back.

Varlets had rushed forth to draw away the two dead Bretons, and a brace of English archers had carried Nigel from the field. With his own hands, Aylward had unlaced the crushed helmet, and had wept to see the bloodless and unconscious face of his young master. He still breathed, however, and stretched upon the grass by the riverside the bowman tended him with rude surgery, until the water upon his brow and the wind upon his face had coaxed back the life into his battered frame. He breathed with heavy gasps, and some tinge of blood crept hack into his cheeks, but still he lay unconscious of the roar of the crowd and of that great struggle which his comrades were now waging once again.

The English had lain for a space, bleeding and breathless, in no better case than their rivals, save that they were still twenty-nine in number. But of this muster there were not nine who were hale men, and some were so weak from loss of blood that they could scarce keep standing. Yet, when the signal was at last given to re-engage, there was not a man upon either side who did not totter to his feet and stagger forward toward his enemies.

But the opening of this second phase of the combat brought one great misfortune and discouragement to the English. Bambro, like the others, had undone his visor, but with his mind full of many cares, he had neglected to make it fast again. There was an opening an inch broad between it and the beaver. As the two lines met, the left-handed Breton squire, Alain de Karanais, caught sight of Bambro's face, and in an instant thrust his short spear through the opening. The English leader gave a cry of pain and fell on his knees, but staggered to his feet again, too weak to raise his shield. As he stood exposed, the Breton knight, Geoffrey Dubois the Strong, struck him such a blow with his axe that he beat in the whole breast-plate with the breast behind it. Bambro fell dead upon the ground, and for a few minutes a fierce fight raged round his body.

Then the English drew back, sullen and dogged, bearing Bambro with them, and the Bretons, breathing hard, gathered again in their own quarter. At the same instant the three prisoners picked up such weapons as were scattered upon the grass and ran over to join their own party.

"Nay, nay!" cried Knolles, raising his visor and advancing. "This may not be. You have been held to mercy when we might have slain you, and by the Virgin, I will hold you dishonored, all three, if you stand not back."

"Say not so, Robert Knolles," Evan Cheruel answered. "Never yet has the word dishonor been breathed with my name; but I should count myself *fainéant* if I did not fight beside my comrades when chance has made it right and proper that I should do so."

"By Saint Cadoc! he speaks truly," croaked Beaumanoir, advancing in front of his men. "You are well aware, Robert, that it is the law of war and the usage of chivalry that if the knight to whom you have surrendered is himself slain, the prisoners thereby become released."

There was no answer to this, and Knolles, weary and spent, returned to his comrades.

"I would that we had slain them," said he. "We have lost our leader, and they have gained three men by the same stroke."

"If any more lay down their arms, it is my order that you slay them forthwith," said Croquart, whose bent sword and bloody armor showed how manfully he had borne himself in the fray. "And now, comrades, do not be heavy hearted because we have lost our leader. Indeed, his rhymes of Merlin have availed him little. By the three kings of Almain! I can teach you what is better than an old woman's prophecies, and that is that you should keep your shoulders together and your shields so close that none can break between them. Then you will know what is on either side of you, and you can fix your eyes upon the front. Also, if any be so weak or wounded that he must sink his hands, his comrades on right and left can bear him up. Now advance all together in God's name, for the battle is still ours if we bear ourselves like men."

In a solid line the English advanced, while the Bretons ran forward as before to meet them. The swiftest of these was a certain squire, Geoffrey Poulart, who bore a helmet which was fashioned as a cock's head, with high comb above, and long pointed beak in front pierced with the breathing-holes. He thrust with his sword at Calverly, but Belford, who was the next in the line, raised his giant club and struck him a crushing blow from the side. He staggered, and then pushing forth from the crowd, he ran round and round in circles as one whose brain is stricken, the blood dripping from the holes of his brazen beak. So for a long time he ran, the crowd laughing and cock-crowing at the sight, until at last he stumbled and fell stone dead upon his face. But the fighters had seen nothing of his fate, for desperate and unceasing was the rush of the Bretons and the steady advance of the English line.

For a time it seemed as if nothing would break it, but gap-toothed Beaumanoir was a general as well as a warrior. While his weary, bleeding, hard-breathing men still flung themselves upon the front of the line, he himself with Raguenel, Tentiniac, Alain de Karanais, and Dubois, rushed round the flank and attacked the English with fury from behind. There was a long and desperate *mêlée*, until once more the heralds, seeing the com-

batants stand gasping and unable to strike a blow, rode in and
called yet another interval of truce.

But in those few minutes while they had been assaulted upon
both sides the losses of the English party had been heavy. The
Anglo-Breton D'Ardaine had fallen before Beaumanoir's sword,
but not before he had cut deeply into his enemy's shoulder. Sir
Thomas Walton, Richard of Ireland one of the squires, and
Hulbitée the big peasant had all fallen before the mace of the
dwarf Raguenel or the swords of his companions. Some twenty
men were still left standing upon either side, but all were in the
last state of exhaustion, gasping, reeling, hardly capable of striking a blow.

It was strange to see them as they staggered, with many a
lurch and stumble, toward each other once again, for they
moved like drunken men, and the scales of their neck-armor
and joints were as red as fishes' gills when they raised them
They left foul wet footprints behind them on the green grass as
they moved forward once more to their endless contest.

Beaumanoir, faint with the drain of his blood and with a
tongue of leather, paused as he advanced.

"I am fainting, comrades," he cried. "I must drink."

"Drink your own blood, Beaumanoir!" cried Dubois, and the
weary men all croaked together in dreadful laughter.

But now the English had learned from experience, and under
the guidance of Croquart they fought no longer in a straight
line, but in one so bent that at last it became a circle. As the
Bretons still pushed and staggered against it they thrust it back
on every side, until they had turned it into the most dangerous
formation of all, a solid block of men, their faces turned outward, their weapons bristling forth to meet every attack. Thus
the English stood, and no assault could move them. They could
lean against each other back to back while they waited and allowed their foemen to tire themselves out. Again and again the
gallant Bretons tried to make a way through. Again and again
they were beaten back by a shower of blows.

Beaumanoir, his head giddy with fatigue, opened his helmet
and gazed in despair at this terrible, unbreakable circle. Only
too clearly he could see the inevitable result. His men were

wearing themselves out. Already many of them could scarce stir hand or foot, and might be dead for any aid which they could give him in winning the fight. Soon all would be in the same plight. Then these cursed English would break their circle to swarm over his helpless men and to strike them down. Do what he might, he could see no way by which such an end might be prevented. He cast his eyes round in his agony, and there was one of his Bretons slinking away to the side of the lists. He could scarce credit his senses when he saw by the scarlet and silver that the deserter was his own well-tried squire, William of Montaubon.

"William! William!" he cried. "Surely you would not leave me?"

But the other's helmet was closed and he could hear nothing. Beaumanoir saw that he was staggering away as swiftly as he could. With a cry of bitter despair, he drew into a knot as many of his braves as could still move, and together they made a last rush upon the English spears. This time he was firmly resolved, deep in his gallant soul, that he would come no foot back, but would find his death there among his foemen or carve a path into the heart of their ranks. The fire in his breast spread from man to man of his followers, and amid the crashing of blows they still locked themselves against the English shields and drove hard for an opening in their ranks.

But all was vain! Beaumanoir's head reeled. His senses were leaving him. In another minute he and his men would have been stretched senseless before this terrible circle of steel, when suddenly the whole array fell in pieces before his eyes; his enemies, Croquart, Knolles, Calverly, Belford, all were stretched upon the ground together, their weapons dashed from their hands and their bodies too exhausted to rise. The surviving Bretons had but strength to fall upon them dagger in hand, and to wring from them their surrender with the sharp point stabbing through their visors. Then victors and vanquished lay groaning and panting in one helpless and blood-smeared heap.

To Beaumanoir's simple mind it had seemed that at the supreme moment the Saints of Brittany had risen at their country's call. Already, as he lay gasping, his heart was pouring forth

its thanks to his patron Saint Cadoc. But the spectators had
seen clearly enough the earthly cause of this sudden victory,
and a hurricane of applause from one side, with a storm of hooting from the other, showed how different was the emotion
which it raised in minds which sympathized with the victors or
the vanquished.

William of Montaubon, the cunning squire, had made his way
across to the spot where the steeds were tethered, and had
mounted his own great roussin. At first it was thought that he
was about to ride from the field, but the howl of execration from
the Breton peasants changed suddenly to a yell of applause and
delight as he turned the beast's head for the English circle and
thrust his long prick spurs into its side. Those who faced him
saw this sudden and unexpected appearance. Time was when
both horse and rider must have winced away from the shower of
their blows. But now they were in no state to meet such a rush.
They could scarce raise their arms. Their blows were too feeble
to hurt this mighty creature. In a moment it had plunged
through the ranks, and seven of them were on the grass. It
turned and rushed through them again, leaving five others helpless beneath its hoofs. No need to do more! Already Beaumanoir
and his companions were inside the circle, the prostrate men
were helpless, and Josselin had won.

That night a train of crest-fallen archers, bearing many a prostrate figure, marched sadly into Ploermel Castle. Behind them
rode ten men, all weary, all wounded, and all with burning
hearts against William of Montaubon for the foul trick that he
had served them.

But over at Josselin, yellow gorse-blossoms in their helmets,
the victors were borne in on the shoulders of a shouting mob,
amid the fanfare of trumpets and the beating of drums. Such
was the combat of the Midway Oak, where brave men met brave
men, and such honor was gained that from that day he who had
fought in the Battle of the Thirty was ever given the highest
place and the post of honor, nor was it easy for any man to pre-
tend to have been there, for it has been said by that great
chronicler who knew them all, that not one on either side failed
to carry to his grave the marks of that stern encounter.

XXIV. HOW NIGEL WAS CALLED
TO HIS MASTER

"MY SWEET LADYE," wrote Nigel in a script which it would take
the eyes of love to read, "there hath been a most noble meeting
in the fourth sennight of Lent betwixt some of our own people
and sundry most worthy persons of this country, which ended,
by the grace of our lady, in so fine a joust that no man living can
call to mind so fair an occasion. Much honor was gained by the
Sieur de Beaumanoir and also by an Almain named Croquart,
with whom I hope to have some speech when I am hale again,
for he is a most excellent person and very ready to advance himself or to relieve another from a vow. For myself I had hoped,
with Godde's help, to venture that third small deed which might
set me free to haste to your sweet side, but things have gone
awry with me, and I early met with such scathe and was of so
small comfort to my friends that my heart is heavy within me,
and in sooth I feel that I have lost honor rather than gained it.
Here I have lain since the Feast of the Virgin, and here I am like
still to be, for I can move no limb, save only my hand; but grieve
not, sweet lady, for Saint Catharine hath been our friend since
in so short a time I had two such ventures as the Red Ferret and
the intaking of the Reaver's fortalice. It needs but one more
deed, and sickerly when I am hale once more it will not be long
ere I seek it out. Till then, if my eyes may not rest upon you, my
heart at least is ever at thy feet."

So he wrote from his sick-room in the Castle of Ploermel late
in the summer, but yet another summer had come before his
crushed head had mended and his wasted limbs had gained
their strength once more. With despair he heard of the breaking
of the truce, and of the fight at Mauron, in which Sir Robert

Knolles and Sir Walter Bentley crushed the rising power of Brittany—a fight in which many of the thirty champions of Josselin met their end. Then, when with renewed strength and high hopes in his heart he went forth to search for the famous Croquart, who proclaimed himself ever ready night or day to meet any man with any weapon, it was only to find that, in trying the paces of his new horse, the German had been cast into a ditch and had broken his neck. In the same ditch perished Nigel's last chance of soon accomplishing that deed which should free him from his vow.

There was truce once more over all Christendom, and mankind was sated with war, so that only in far-off Prussia, where the Teutonic knights waged ceaseless battle with the Lithuanian heathen, could he hope to find his heart's desire. But money and high knightly fame were needed ere a man could go upon the northern crusade, and ten years were yet to pass ere Nigel should look from the battlements of Marienberg on the waters of the Frische Haff, or should endure the torture of the hot plate when bound to the Holy Woden stone of Memel. Meanwhile, he chafed his burning soul out through the long seasons of garrison life in Brittany, broken only by one visit to the chateau of the father of Raoul, when he carried to the Lord of Grosbois the news of how his son had fallen like a gallant gentleman under the gateway of La Brohinière.

And then, then at last, when all hope was well-nigh dead in his heart, there came one glorious July morning which brought a horseman bearing a letter to the Castle of Vannes, of which Nigel now was seneschal. It contained but few words, short and clear as the call of a war-trumpet. It was Chandos who wrote. He needed his squire at his side, for his pennon was in the breeze once more. He was at Bordeaux. The prince was starting at once for Bergerac, whence he would make a great raid into France. It would not end without a battle. They had sent word of their coming, and the good French king had promised to be at great pains to receive them. Let Nigel hasten at once. If the army had left, then let him follow after with all speed. Chandos had three other squires, but would very gladly see his fourth once again, for he had heard much of him since he parted, and nothing which he might not have expected to hear of his father's son. Such was the letter which made the summer sun shine brighter and the blue sky seem of a still fairer blue upon that happy morning in Vannes.

It is a weary way from Vannes to Bordeaux. Coast-wise ships are hard to find, and winds blow north when all brave hearts would fain be speeding south. A full month has passed from the day when Nigel received his letter before he stood upon the quay-side of the Garonne amid the stacked barrels of Gascon wine and helped to lead Pommers down the gang-planks. Not Aylward himself had a worse opinion of the sea than the great yellow horse, and he whinnied with joy as he thrust his muzzle into his master's outstretched hand, and stamped his ringing hoofs upon the good firm cobblestones. Beside him, slapping his tawny shoulder in encouragement, was the lean spare form of Black Simon who had remained ever under Nigel's pennon.

But Aylward, where was he? Alas! two years before he and the whole of Knolles' company of archers had been drafted away on the king's service to Guienne, and since he could not write the squire knew not whether he was alive or dead. Simon, indeed, had thrice heard of him from wandering archers, each time that he was alive and well and newly married, but as the wife in one case was a fair maid, and in another a dark, while in the third she was a French widow, it was hard to know the truth.

Already the army had been gone a month, but news of it came daily to the town, and such news as all men could read, for through the landward gates there rolled one constant stream of wagons, pouring down the Libourne Road, and bearing the booty of southern France. The town was full of foot soldiers, for none but mounted men had been taken by the prince. With sad faces and longing eyes they watched the passing of the train of plunder-laden carts, piled high with rich furniture, silks, velvets, tapestries, carvings, and precious metals, which had been the pride of many a lordly home in fair Auvergne or the wealthy Bourbonnais.

Let no man think that in these wars England alone was face to face with France alone. There is glory and to spare without trifling with the truth. Two provinces in France, both rich and

warlike, had become English through a royal marriage, and
these, Guienne and Gascony, furnished many of the most valiant soldiers under the island flag. So poor a country as England
could not afford to keep a great force overseas, and so must
needs have lost the war with France through want of power to
uphold the struggle. The feudal system enabled an army to be
drawn rapidly together with small expense, but at the end of a
few weeks it dispersed again as swiftly, and only by a well-filled
money-chest could it be held together. There was no such chest
in England, and the king was forever at his wits' end how to
keep his men in the field.

But Guienne and Gascony were full of knights and squires
who were always ready to assemble from their isolated castles
for a raid into France, and these with the addition of those
English cavaliers who fought for honor, and a few thousand of
the formidable archers, hired for fourpence a day, made an
army with which a short campaign could be carried on. Such
were the materials of the prince's force, some eight thousand
strong, who were now riding in a great circle through southern
France, leaving a broad wale of blackened and ruined country
behind them.

But France, even with her south western corner in English
hands, was still a very warlike power, far richer and more popu-
lous than her rival. Single provinces were so great that they were
stronger than many a kingdom. Normandy in the north,
Burgundy in the east, Brittany in the west, and Languedoc in
the south were each capable of fitting out a great army of their
own. Therefore the brave and spirited John, watching from
Paris this insolent raid into his dominions, sent messengers in
hot haste to all these great feudatories as well as to Lorraine,
Picardy, Auvergne, Hainault, Vermandois, Champagne, and to
the German mercenaries over his eastern border, bidding all of
them to ride hard, with bloody spur, day and night, until they
should gather to a head at Chartres.

There a great army had assembled early in September, while
the prince, all unconscious of its presence, sacked towns and
besieged castles from Bourges to Issodun, passing Romorantin,
and so onward to Vierzon and to Tours. From week to week

there were merry skirmishes at barriers, brisk assaults of for-
tresses in which much honor was won, knightly meetings with
detached parties of Frenchmen and occasional spear-runnings,
where noble champions deigned to venture their persons.
Houses, too, were to be plundered, while wine and women were
in plenty. Never had either knights or archers had so pleasant
and profitable an excursion, so that it was with high heart and
much hope of pleasant days at Bordeaux with their pockets full
of money that the army turned south from the Loire and began
to retrace its steps to the seaboard city.

But now its pleasant and martial promenade changed suddenly to very serious work of war. As the prince moved south he
found that all supplies had been cleared away from in front of
him and that there was neither fodder for the horses nor food
for the men. Two hundred wagons laden with spoil rolled at the
head of the army, but the starving soldiers would soon have
gladly changed it all for as many loads of bread and of meat. The
light troops of the French had preceded them, and burned or
destroyed everything that could be of use. Now also for the first
time the prince and his men became aware that a great army
was moving upon the eastern side of them, streaming southward
in the hope of cutting off their retreat to the sea. The sky glowed
with their fires at night, and the autumn sun twinkled and
gleamed from one end of the horizon to the other upon the steel
caps and flashing weapons of a mighty host.

Anxious to secure his plunder, and conscious that the levies of
France were far superior in number to his own force, the prince
redoubled his attempts to escape; but his horses were exhausted
and his starving men were hardly to be kept in order. A few
more days would unfit them for battle. Therefore, when he
found near the village of Maupertuis a position in which a small
force might have a chance to hold its own, he gave up the attempt to outmarch his pursuers, and he turned at bay, like a
hunted boar, all tusks and eyes of flame.

While these high events had been in progress, Nigel with
Black Simon and four other men-at-arms from Bordeaux were
hastening northward to join the army. As far as Bergerac they
were in a friendly land, but thence onward they rode over a

blackened landscape with many a roofless house, its two bare gable-ends sticking upward—a "Knolles' miter," as it was afterwards called, when Sir Robert worked his stern will upon the country. For three days they rode northward, seeing many small parties of French in all directions, but too eager to reach the army to ease their march in the search of adventures.

Then at last after passing Lusignan they began to come in touch with English foragers, mounted bowmen for the most part, who were endeavoring to collect supplies either for the army or for themselves. From them Nigel learned that the prince, with Chandos ever at his side, was hastening south and might be met within a short day's march. As he still advanced these English stragglers became more and more numerous, until at last he overtook a considerable column of archers moving in the same direction as his own party. These were men whose horses had failed them and who had therefore been left behind on the advance, but were now hastening to be in time for the impending battle. A crowd of peasant girls accompanied them upon their march, and a whole train of laden mules were led beside them.

Nigel and his little troop of men-at-arms were riding past the archers when Black Simon, with a sudden exclamation, touched his leader upon the arm.

"See yonder, fair sir," he cried, with gleaming eyes, "there where the wastrel walks with the great fardel upon his back! Who is he who marches behind him?"

Nigel looked, and was aware of a stunted peasant who bore upon his rounded back an enormous bundle very much larger than himself. Behind him walked a burly broad-shouldered archer, whose stained jerkin and battered headpiece gave token of long and hard service. His bow was slung over his shoulder, and his arms were round the waists of two buxom Frenchwomen, who tripped along beside him with much laughter and many saucy answers flung back over their shoulders to a score of admirers behind them.

"Aylward!" cried Nigel, spurring forward.

The archer turned his bronzed face, stared for an instant with wild eyes, and then, dropping his two ladies, who were instantly carried off by his comrades, he rushed to seize the hand which his young master held down to him.

"Now, by my hilt, Squire Nigel, this is the fairest sight of my lifetime!" he cried. "And you, old leather-face! Nay, Simon, I would put my arms round your dried herring of a body, if I could but reach you. Here is Pommers too, and I read in his eye that he knows me well, and is as ready to put his teeth into me as when he stood in my father's stall."

It was like a whiff of the heather-perfumed breezes of Hankley to see his homely face once more. Nigel laughed with sheer joy as he looked at him.

"It was an ill day when the king's service called you from my side," said he, "and by Saint Paul! I am right glad to set eyes upon you once more! I see well that you are in no wise altered, but the same Aylward that I have ever known. But who is this varlet with the great bundle who waits upon your movements?"

"It is no less than a feather-bed, fair sir, which he bears upon his back, for I would fain bring it to Tilford, and yet it is over-large for me when I take my place with my fellows in the ranks. But indeed this war has been a most excellent one, and I have already sent half a wagonload of my gear back to Bordeaux to await my homecoming. Yet I have my fears when I think of all the rascal foot-archers who are waiting there, for some folk have no grace or honesty in their souls, and cannot keep their hands from that which belongs to another. But if I may throw my leg over yonder spare horse I will come on with you, fair sir, for indeed it would be joy to my heart to know that I was riding under your banner once again."

So Aylward, having given instructions to the bearer of his feather-bed, rode away in spite of shrill protests from his French companions, who speedily consoled themselves with those of his comrades who seemed to have most to give.

Nigel's party was soon clear of the column of archers and riding hard in the direction of the prince's army. They passed by a narrow and winding track, through the great wood of Nouaille, and found before them a marshy valley down which ran a sluggish stream. Along its farther bank hundreds of horses were being watered, and beyond was a dense block of wagons. Through these the comrades passed, and then topped a small mound, from which the whole strange scene lay spread before them.

Down the valley the slow stream meandered, with marshy meadows on either side. A mile or two lower a huge drove of horses were to be seen assembled upon the bank. They were the steeds of the French cavalry, and the blue haze of a hundred fires showed where King John's men were camping. In front of the mound upon which they stood the English line was drawn, but there were few fires, for indeed, save their horses, there was little for them to cook. Their right rested upon the river, and their array stretched across a mile of ground, until the left was in touch with a tangled forest which guarded it from flank attack. In front was a long thick hedge and much broken ground, with a single deeply rutted country road cutting through it in the middle. Under the hedge and along the whole front of the position lay swarms of archers upon the grass, the greater number slumbering peacefully with sprawling limbs in the warm rays of the September sun. Behind were the quarters of the various knights, and from end to end flew the banners and pennons marked with the devices of the chivalry of England and Guienne.

With a glow in his heart Nigel saw those badges of famous captains and leaders, and knew that now at last he also might show his coat-armor in such noble company. There was the flag of Jean Grailly, the Captal de Buch, five silver shells on a black cross, which marked the presence of the most famous soldier of Gascony, while beside it waved the red lion of the noble Knight of Hainault, Sir Eustace d'Ambreticourt. These two coats Nigel knew, as did every warrior in Europe, but a dense grove of pennoned lances surrounded them, bearing charges which were strange to him, from which he understood that these belonged to the Guienne division of the army. Farther down the line the famous English ensigns floated on the wind, the scarlet and gold of Warwick, the silver star of Oxford, the golden cross of Suffolk, the blue and gold of Willoughby, and the gold-fretted scarlet of Audley. In the very center of them all was one which caused all others to pass from his mind, for close to the royal banner of England, crossed with the label of the prince, there waved the war-worn flag with the red wedge upon the golden field which marked the quarters of the noble Chandos.

At the sight Nigel set spurs to his horse, and a few minutes later had reached the spot. Chandos, gaunt from hunger and want of sleep, but with the old fire lurking in his eye, was standing by the prince's tent, gazing down at what could be seen of the French array, and heavy with thought. Nigel sprang from his horse and was within touch of his master when the silken hanging of the royal tent was torn violently aside and Edward rushed out.

He was without his armor and clad in a sober suit of black, but the high dignity of his bearing and the imperious anger which flushed his face proclaimed the leader and the prince. At his heels was a little white-haired ecclesiastic in a flowing gown of scarlet sendal, expostulating and arguing in a torrent of words.

"Not another word, my Lord Cardinal," cried the angry prince. "I have listened to you overlong, and by God's dignity! that which you say is neither good nor fair in my ears. Hark you, John, I would have your counsel. What think you is the message which my Lord Cardinal of Perigord has carried from the king of France? He says that of his clemency he will let my army pass back to Bordeaux if we will restore to him all that we have taken, remit all ransoms, and surrender my own person with that of a hundred nobles of England and Guienne to be held as prisoners. What think you, John?"

Chandos smiled. "Things are not done in that fashion," said he.

"But, my Lord Chandos," cried the Cardinal, "I have made it clear to the prince that indeed it is a scandal to all Christendom and a cause of mocking to the heathen, that two great sons of the Church should turn their swords thus upon each other."

"Then bid the king of France keep clear of us," said the prince.

"Fair son, you are aware that you are in the heart of his country, and that it standeth not aright that he should suffer you to go forth as you came. You have but a small army, three thousand bowmen and five thousand men-at-arms at the most, who seem in evil case for want of food and rest. The king has thirty thousand men at his back, of which twenty thousand are expert men-at-arms. It is fitting therefore that you make such terms as you may, lest worse befall."

"Give my greetings to the king of France and tell him that England will never pay ransom for me. But it seems to me, my Lord Cardinal, that you have our numbers and condition very ready upon your tongue, and I would fain know how the eye of a Churchman can read a line of battle so easily. I have seen that these knights of your household have walked freely to and fro within our camp, and I much fear that when I welcomed you as envoys I have in truth given my protection to spies. How say you, my Lord Cardinal?"

"Fair prince, I know not how you can find it in your heart or conscience to say such evil words."

"There is this red-bearded nephew of thine, Robert de Duras. See where he stands yonder, counting and prying. Hark hither, young sir! I have been saying to your uncle the Cardinal that it is in my mind that you and your comrades have carried news of our dispositions to the French king. How say you?"

The knight turned pale and sank his eyes. "My lord," he murmured, "it may be that I have answered some questions."

"And how will such answers accord with your honor, seeing that we have trusted you since you came in the train of the Cardinal?"

"My lord, it is true that I am in the train of the Cardinal, and yet I am liege man of King John and a knight of France, so I pray you to assuage your wrath against me."

The prince ground his teeth and his piercing eyes blazed upon the youth.

"By my father's soul! I can scarce forbear to strike you to the earth! But this I promise you, that if you show that sign of the Red Griffin in the field and if you be taken alive in to-morrow's battle, your head shall most assuredly be shorn from your shoulders."

"Fair son, indeed you speak wildly," cried the Cardinal. "I pledge you my word that neither my nephew Robert nor any of my train will take part in the battle. And now I leave you, sire, and may God assoil your soul, for indeed in all this world no men stand in greater peril than you and those who are around you, and I rede you that you spend the night in such ghostly exercises as may best prepare you for that which may befall." So saying the Cardinal bowed, and with his household walking behind him set off for the spot where they had left their horses, whence they rode to the neighboring abbey.

The angry prince turned upon his heel and entered his tent once more, while Chandos, glancing round, held out a warm welcoming hand to Nigel.

"I have heard much of your noble deeds," said he. "Already your name rises as a squire errant. I stood no higher, nor so high, at your age."

Nigel flushed with pride and pleasure. "Indeed, my dear lord, it is very little that I have done. But now that I am back at your side I hope that in truth I shall learn to bear myself in worthy fashion, for where else should I win honor if it be not under your banner?"

"Truly, Nigel, you have come at a very good time for advancement. I cannot see how we can leave this spot without a great battle which will live in men's minds for ever. In all our fights in France I cannot call to mind any in which they have been so strong or we so weak as now, so that there will be the more honor to be gained. I would that we had two thousand more archers. But I doubt not that we shall give them much trouble ere they drive us out from amidst these hedges. Have you seen the French?"

"Nay, fair sir, I have but this moment arrived."

"I was about to ride forth myself to coast their army and observe their countenance, so come with me ere the night fall, and we shall see what we can of their order and dispositions."

There was a truce between the two forces for the day, on account of the ill-advised and useless interposition of the Cardinal of Perigord. Hence when Chandos and Nigel had pushed their horses through the long hedge which fronted the position they found that many small parties of the knights of either army were riding up and down on the plain outside. The greater number of these groups were French, since it was very necessary for them to know as much as possible of the English defenses; and many of their scouts had ridden up to within a hundred yards of the hedge, where they were sternly ordered back by the pickets of archers on guard.

Through these scattered knots of horsemen Chandos rode, and as many of them were old antagonists it was "Ha, John!" on the one side, and "Ha, Raoul!" "Ha, Nicholas!" "Ha, Guichard!" upon the other, as they brushed past them. Only one cavalier greeted them amiss, a large, red-faced man, the Lord Clermont, who by some strange chance bore upon his surcoat a blue virgin standing amid golden sunbeams, which was the very device which Chandos had donned for the day. The fiery Frenchman dashed across their path and drew his steed back on to its haunches.

"How long is it, my Lord Chandos," said he, hotly, "since you have taken it upon yourself to wear my arms?"

Chandos smiled. "It is surely you who have mine," said he, "since this surcoat was worked for me by the good nuns of Windsor a long year ago."

"If it were not for the truce," said Clermont, "I would soon show you that you have no right to wear it."

"Look for it then in the battle to-morrow, and I also will look for yours," Chandos answered. "There we can very honorably settle the matter."

But the Frenchman was choleric and hard to appease.

"You English can invent nothing," said he, "and you take for your own whatever you see handsome belonging to others." So, grumbling and fuming, he rode upon his way, while Chandos, laughing gaily, spurred onward across the plain.

The immediate front of the English line was shrouded with scattered trees and bushes which hid the enemy; but when they had cleared these a fair view of the great French army lay before them. In the center of the huge camp was a long and high pavilion of red silk, with the silver lilies of the king at one end of it, and the golden oriflamme, the battle-flag of old France, at the other. Like the reeds of a pool from side to side of the broad array, and dwindling away as far as their eyes could see, were the banners and pennons of high barons and famous knights, but above them all flew the ducal standards which showed that the feudal muster of all the warlike provinces of France was in the field before them.

With a kindling eye Chandos looked across at the proud ensigns of Normandy, of Burgundy, of Auvergne, of Champagne, of Vermandois, and of Berry, flaunting and gleaming in the rays of the sinking sun. Riding slowly down the line he marked with attentive gaze the camp of the cross-bowmen, the muster of the German mercenaries, the numbers of the foot-soldiers, the arms of every proud vassal or vavasor which might give some guide as to the power of each division. From wing to wing and round the flanks he went, keeping ever within crossbow-shot of the army, and then at last having noted all things in his mind he turned his horse's head and rode slowly back, heavy with thought, to the English lines.

XXV. HOW THE KING OF FRANCE HELD COUNSEL AT MAUPERTUIS

THE MORNING OF Sunday, the nineteenth of September, in the year of our Lord 1356, was cold and fine. A haze which rose from the marshy valley of Muisson covered both camps and set the starving Englishmen shivering, but it cleared slowly away as the sun rose. In the red silken pavilion of the French king—the same which had been viewed by Nigel and Chandos the evening before—a solemn mass was held by the Bishop of Chalons, who prayed for those who were about to die, with little thought in his mind that his own last hour was so near at hand. Then, when communion had been taken by the king and his four young sons the altar was cleared away, and a great red-covered table placed lengthwise down the tent, round which John might assemble his council and determine how best he should proceed. With the silken roof, rich tapestries of Arras round the walls and eastern rugs beneath the feet, his palace could furnish no fairer chamber.

King John, who sat upon the canopied daïs at the upper end, was now in the sixth year of his reign and the thirty-sixth of his life. He was a short burly man, ruddy-faced and deep-chested, with dark kindly eyes and a most noble bearing. It did not need the blue cloak sewed with silver lilies to mark him as the king. Though his reign had been short, his fame was already widespread over all Europe as a kindly gentleman and a fearless soldier—a fit leader for a chivalrous nation. His elder son, the Duke of Normandy, still hardly more than a boy, stood beside him, his hand upon the king's shoulder, and John half turned from time to time to fondle him. On the right, at the same high daïs, was the king's younger brother, the Duke of Orleans, a pale heavy-featured man, with a languid manner and intolerant eyes. On the left was the Duke of Bourbon, sad-faced and absorbed, with that gentle melancholy in his eyes and bearing which comes often with the premonition of death. All these were in their armor, save only for their helmets, which lay upon the board before them.

Below, grouped around the long red table, was an assembly of the most famous warriors in Europe. At the end nearest the king was the veteran soldier the Duke of Athens, son of a banished father, and now high constable of France. On one side of him sat the red-faced and choleric Lord Clermont, with the same blue virgin in golden rays upon his surcoat which had caused his quarrel with Chandos the night before. On the other was a noble-featured grizzly-haired soldier, Arnold d'Andreghen, who shared with Clermont the honor of being Marshal of France. Next to them sat Lord James of Bourbon, a brave warrior who was afterwards slain by the White Company at Brignais, and beside him a little group of German noblemen, including the Earl of Salzburg and the Earl of Nassau, who had ridden over the frontier with their formidable mercenaries at the bidding of the French king. The ridged armor and the hanging nasals of their bassinets were enough in themselves to tell every soldier that they were from beyond the Rhine. At the other side of the table were a line of proud and war-like Lords, Fiennes, Chatillon, Nesle, de Landas, de Beaujeu, with the fierce knight errant de Chargny, he who had planned the surprise of Calais, and Eustace de Ribeaumont, who had upon the same occasion won the prize of valor from the hands of Edward of England. Such were the chiefs to whom the king now turned for assistance and advice.

"You have already heard, my friends," said he, "that the Prince of Wales has made no answer to the proposal which we sent by the Lord Cardinal of Perigord. Certes this is as it should be, and though I have obeyed the call of Holy Church I had no fears that so excellent a prince as Edward of England would refuse to meet us in battle. I am now of opinion that we should fall upon them at once, lest perchance the Cardinal's cross should again come betwixt our swords and our enemies."

A buzz of joyful assent arose from the meeting, and even from the attendant men-at-arms who guarded the door. When it had died away the Duke of Orleans rose in his place beside the king.

"Sire," said he, "you speak as we would have you do, and I for one am of opinion that the Cardinal of Perigord has been an ill friend of France, for why should we bargain for a part when we have but to hold out our hand in order to grasp the whole? What need is there for words? Let us spring to horse forthwith and ride over this handful of marauders who have dared to lay waste your fair dominions. If one of them go hence save as our prisoner we are the more to blame."

"By Saint Denis, brother!" said the king, smiling, "if words could slay you would have had them all upon their backs ere ever we left Chartres. You are new to war, but when you have had experience of a stricken field or two you know that things must be done with forethought and in order or they may go awry. In our father's time we sprang to horse and spurred upon these English at Crécy and elsewhere as you advise, but we had little profit from it, and now we are grown wiser. How say you, Sieur de Ribeaumont? You have coasted their lines and observed their countenance. Would you ride down upon them, as my brother has advised, or how would you order the matter?"

De Ribeaumont, a tall dark-eyed, handsome man, paused ere he answered.

"Sire," he said at last, "I have indeed ridden along their front and down their flanks in company with Lord Landas and Lord de Beaujeu, who are here at your council to witness to what I say. Indeed, sire, it is in my mind that though the English are few in number yet they are in such a position amongst these hedges and vines that you would be well-advised if you were to leave them alone, for they have no food and must retreat, so that you will be able to follow them and to fight them to better advantage."

A murmur of disapproval rose from the company and the Lord Clermont, marshal of the army, sprang to his feet, his face red with anger.

"Eustace; Eustace," said he, "I bear in mind the days when

you were of great heart and high enterprise, but since King Edward gave you yonder chaplet of pearls you have ever been backward against the English!"

"My Lord Clermont," said de Ribeaumont, sternly, "it is not for me to brawl at the king's council and in the face of the enemy, but we will go further into this matter at some other time. Meanwhile, the king has asked me for my advice and I have given it as best I might."

"It had been better for your honor, Sir Eustace, had you held your peace," said the Duke of Orleans. "Shall we let them slip from our fingers when we have them here and are fourfold their number? I know not where we should dwell afterwards, for I am very sure that we should be ashamed to ride back to Paris, or to look our ladies in the eyes again."

"Indeed, Eustace, you have done well to say what is in your mind," said the king; "but I have already said that we shall join battle this morning, so that there is no room here for further talk. But I would fain have heard from you how it would be wisest and best that we attack them?"

"I will advise you, sire, to the best of my power. Upon their right is a river with marshes around it, and upon their left a great wood, so that we can advance only upon the center. Along their front is a thick hedge, and behind it I saw the green jerkins of their archers, as thick as the sedges by the river. It is broken by one road where only four horsemen could ride abreast, which leads through the position. It is clear, then, that if we are to drive them back we must cross the great hedge, and I am very sure that the horses will not face it with such a storm of arrows beating from behind it. Therefore, it is my council that we fight upon foot, as the English did at Crécy, for indeed we may find that our horses will be more hindrance than help to us this day."

"The same thought was in my own mind, sire," said Arnold d'Andreghen, the veteran marshal. "At Crécy the bravest had to turn their backs, for what can a man do with a horse which is mad with pain and fear? If we advance upon foot we are our own masters, and if we stop the shame is ours."

"The counsel is good," said the Duke of Athens, turning his

"'Indeed, Eustace, you have done well to say what is in your mind.'"
[*page 314*]

shrewd wizened face to the king; "but one thing only I would add to it. The strength of these people lies in their archers, and if we could throw them into disorder, were it only for a short time, we should win the hedge; else they will shoot so strongly that we must lose many men before we reach it, for indeed we have learned that no armor will keep out their shafts when they are close."

"Your words, fair sir, are both good and wise," said the king, "but I pray you to tell us how you would throw these archers into disorder?"

"I would choose three hundred horsemen, sire, the best and most forward in the army. With these I would ride up the narrow road, and so turn to right and left, falling upon the archers behind the hedge. It may be that the three hundred would suffer sorely, but what are they among so great a host, if a road may be cleared for their companions?"

"I would say a word to that, sire," cried the German Count of Nassau, "I have come here with my comrades to venture our persons in your quarrel; but we claim the right to fight in our own fashion, and we would count it dishonor to dismount from our steeds out of fear of the arrows of the English. Therefore, with your permission, we will ride to the front, as the Duke of Athens has advised, and so clear a path for the rest of you."

"This may not be!" cried the Lord Clermont, angrily. "It would be strange indeed if Frenchmen could not be found to clear a path for the army of the king of France. One would think to hear you talk, my Lord Count, that your hardihood was greater than our own, but by our Lady of Rocamadour you will learn before nightfall that it is not so. It is for me, who am a marshal of France, to lead these three hundred, since it is an honorable venture."

"And I claim the same right for the same reason," said Arnold of Andreghen.

The German count struck the table with his mailed fist.

"Do what you like!" said he. "But this only I can promise you, that neither I nor any of my German riders will descend from our horses so long as they are able to carry us, for in our country it is only people of no consequence who fight upon their feet."

The Lord Clermont was leaning angrily forward with some hot reply when King John intervened.

"Enough, enough!" he said. "It is for you to give your opinions, and for me to tell you what you will do. Lord Clermont, and you, Arnold, you will choose three hundred of the bravest cavaliers in the army and you will endeavor to break these archers. As to you and your Germans, my Lord Nassau, you will remain upon horseback, since you desire it, and you will follow the marshals and support them as best you may. The rest of the army will advance upon foot, in three other divisions as arranged: yours, Charles," and he patted his son, the Duke of Normandy, affectionately upon the hand; "yours, Philip," he glanced at the Duke of Orleans; "and the main battle which is my own. To you, Geoffrey de Chargny, I intrust the oriflamme this day. But who is this knight and what does he desire?"

A young knight, ruddy-bearded and tall, a red griffin upon his surcoat, had appeared in the opening of the tent. His flushed face and disheveled dress showed that he had come in haste.

"Sire," said he, "I am Robert de Duras, of the household of the Cardinal de Perigord. I have told you yesterday all that I have learned of the English camp. This morning I was again admitted to it, and I have seen their wagons moving to the rear. Sire, they are in flight for Bordeaux."

"'Fore God, I knew it!" cried the Duke of Orleans, in a voice of fury. "Whilst we have been talking they have slipped through our fingers. Did I not warn you?"

"Be silent, Philip!" said the king angrily. "But you, sir, have you seen this with your own eyes?"

"With my own eyes, sire, and I have ridden straight from their camp."

King John looked at him with a stern gaze. "I know not how it accords with your honor to carry such tidings in such a fashion," said he; "but we cannot choose but take advantage of it. Fear not, brother Philip, it is in my mind that you will see all that you would wish of the Englishmen before nightfall. Should we fall upon them whilst they cross the ford it will be to our advantage. Now, fair sirs, I pray you to hasten to your posts and to carry out all that we have agreed. Advance the oriflamme,

Geoffrey, and do you marshal the divisions, Arnold. So may God and Saint Denis have us in their holy keeping this day!"

The Prince of Wales stood upon that little knoll where Nigel had halted the day before. Beside him were Chandos, and a tall sunburned warrior of middle age, the Gascon Captal de Buch. The three men were all attentively watching the distant French lines, while behind them a column of wagons wound down to the ford of the Muisson.

Close in the rear four knights in full armor with open visors sat their horses and conversed in undertones with each other. A glance at their shields would have given their names to any soldier, for they were all men of fame who had seen much warfare. At present they were awaiting their orders, for each of them commanded the whole or part of a division of the army. The youth upon the left, dark, slim, and earnest, was William Montacute, Earl of Salisbury, only twenty-eight years of age, and yet a veteran of Crécy. How high he stood in reputation is shown by the fact that the command of the rear, the post of honor in a retreating army, had been given to him by the prince. He was talking to a grizzled harsh-faced man, somewhat over middle age, with lion features and fierce light-blue eyes which gleamed as they watched the distant enemy. It was the famous Robert de Ufford, Earl of Suffolk, who had fought without a break from Cadsand onward through the whole Continental War. The other tall silent soldier, with the silver star gleaming upon his surcoat, was John de Vere, Earl of Oxford, and he listened to the talk of Thomas Beauchamp, a burly, jovial, ruddy nobleman and a tried soldier, who leaned forward and tapped his mailed hand upon the other's steel-clad thigh. They were old battle-companions, of the same age and in the very prime of life, with equal fame and equal experience of the wars. Such was the group of famous English soldiers who sat their horses behind the prince and waited for their orders.

"I would that you had laid hands upon him," said the prince angrily, continuing his conversation with Chandos, "and yet, perchance, it was wiser to play this trick and make them think that we were retreating."

"He has certainly carried the tidings," said Chandos, with a smile. "No sooner had the wagons started than I saw him gallop down the edge of the wood."

"It was well thought of, John," the prince remarked, "for it would indeed be great comfort if we could turn their own spy against them. Unless they advance upon us, I know not how we can hold out another day, for there is not a loaf left in the army; and yet if we leave this position, where shall we hope to find such another?"

"They will stoop, fair sir, they will stoop to our lure. Even now Robert de Duras will be telling them that the wagons are on the move, and they will hasten to overtake us lest we pass the ford. But who is this, who rides so fast? Here perchance may be tidings."

A horseman had spurred up to the knoll. He sprang from the saddle, and sank on one knee before the prince.

"How now, my Lord Audley," said Edward. "What would you have?"

"Sir," said the knight, still kneeling with bowed head before his leader, "I have a boon to ask of you."

"Nay, James, rise! Let me hear what I can do."

The famous knight errant, pattern of chivalry for all time, rose and turned his swarthy face and dark earnest eyes upon his master.

"Sir," said he, "I have ever served most loyally my lord your father and yourself, and shall continue so to do so long as I have life. Dear sir, I must now acquaint you that formerly I made a vow if ever I should be in any battle under your command that I would be foremost or die in the attempt. I beg therefore that you will graciously permit me to honorably quit my place among the others, that I may post myself in such wise as to accomplish my vow."

The prince smiled, for it was very sure that vow or no vow, permission or no permission, Lord James Audley would still be in the van.

"Go, James," said he, shaking his hand, "and God grant that this day you may shine in valor above all knights. But hark, John, what is that?"

Chandos cast up his fierce nose like the eagle which smells slaughter afar.

"Surely, sir, all is forming even as we had planned it."

From far away there came a thunderous shout. Then another and yet another.

"See, they are moving!" cried the Captal de Buch.

All morning they had watched the gleam of the armed squadrons who were drawn up in front of the French camp. Now, while a great blare of trumpets was borne to their ears, the distant masses flickered and twinkled in the sunlight.

"Yes, yes, they are moving!" cried the prince.

"They are moving! They are moving!" Down the line the murmur ran. And then, with a sudden impulse, the archers at the hedge sprang to their feet and the knights behind them waved their weapons in the air, while one tremendous shout of warlike joy carried their defiance to the approaching enemy. Then there fell such a silence that the pawing of the horses or the jingle of their harness struck loud upon the ear, until amid the hush there rose a low deep roar like the sound of the tide upon the beach, ever growing and deepening as the host of France drew near.

XXVI. HOW NIGEL FOUND
HIS THIRD DEED

FOUR ARCHERS LAY behind a clump of bushes ten yards in front of the thick hedge which shielded their companions. Amid the long line of bowmen those behind them were their own company, and in the main the same who were with Knolles in Brittany. The four in front were their leaders: old Wat of Carlisle, Ned Widdington the red-headed dalesman, the bald bowyer Bartholomew, and Samkin Alyward, newly rejoined after a week's absence. All four were munching bread and apples, for Aylward had brought in a full haversack, and divided them freely amongst his starving comrades. The old borderer and the Yorkshireman were gaunt and hollow-eyed with privation, while the bowyer's round face had fallen in so that the skin hung in loose pouches under his eyes and beneath his jaws.

Behind them lines of haggard, wolfish men glared through the underwood, silent and watchful save that they burst into a fierce yelp of welcome when Chandos and Nigel galloped up, sprang from their horses and took their station beneath them. All along the green fringe of bowmen might be seen the steel-clad figures of knights and squires who had pushed their way into the front line to share the fortune of the archers.

"I call to mind that I once shot six ends with a Kentish woldsman at Ashford——" began the bowyer.

"Nay, nay, we have heard that story!" said old Wat, impatiently. "Shut thy clap, Bartholomew, for it is no time for redeless gossip! Walk down the line, I pray you, and see if there be no frayed string, nor broken nock nor loosened whipping to be mended."

The stout bowyer passed down the fringe of bowmen, amid a

running fire of rough wit. Here and there a bow was thrust out at him through the hedge for his professional advice.

"Wax your heads!" he kept crying. "Pass down the wax-pot and wax your heads. A waxed arrow will pass where a dry will be held. Tom Beverley, you jack-fool! where is your bracer-guard? Your string will flay your arm ere you reach your up-shot this day. And you, Watkin, draw not to your mouth, as is your wont, but to your shoulder. You are so used to the wine-pot that the string must needs follow it. Nay, stand loose, and give space for your drawing arms, for they will be on us anon."

He ran back and joined his comrades in the front, who had now risen to their feet. Behind them a half-mile of archers stood behind the hedge, each with his great war-bow strung, half a dozen shafts loose behind him, and eighteen more in the quiver slung across his front. With arrow on string, their feet firm-planted, their fierce eager faces peering through the branches, they awaited the coming storm.

The broad flood of steel, after oozing slowly forward, had stopped about a mile from the English front. The greater part of the army had then descended from their horses, while a crowd of varlets and hostlers led them to the rear. The French formed themselves now into three great divisions, which shimmered in the sun like silvery pools, reed-capped with many a thousand of banners and pennons. A space of several hundred yards divided each. At the same time two bodies of horsemen formed themselves in front. The first consisted of three hundred men in one thick column, the second of a thousand, riding in a more extended line.

The prince had ridden up to the line of archers. He was in dark armor, his visor open, and his handsome aquiline face all glowing with spirit and martial fire. The bowmen yelled at him, and he waved his hands to them as a huntsman cheers his hounds.

"Well, John, what think you now?" he asked. "What would my noble father not give to be by our side this day? Have you seen that they have left their horses?"

"Yes, my fair lord, they have learned their lesson," said Chandos. "Because we have had good fortune upon our feet at

Crécy and elsewhere, they think that they have found the trick of it. But it is in my mind that it is very different to stand when you are assailed, as we have done, and to assail others when you must drag your harness for a mile and come weary to the fray."

"You speak wisely, John. But these horsemen who form in front and ride slowly toward us, what make you of them?"

"Doubtless they hope to cut the strings of our bowmen and so clear a way for the others. But they are indeed a chosen band, for mark you, fair sir, are not those the colors of Clermont upon the left, and of d'Andreghen upon the right, so that both marshals ride with the vanguard?"

"By God's soul, John!" cried the prince, "it is very sure that you can see more with one eye than any man in this army with two. But it is even as you say. And this larger band behind?"

"They should be Germans, fair sir, by the fashion of their harness."

The two bodies of horsemen had moved slowly over the plain, with a space of nearly a quarter of a mile between them. Now, having come two bowshots from the hostile line, they halted. All that they could see of the English was the long hedge, with an occasional twinkle of steel through its leafy branches, and behind that the spear-heads of the men-at-arms rising from amid the brushwood and the vines. A lovely autumn countryside with changing many-tinted foliage lay stretched before them, all bathed in peaceful sunshine, and nothing save those flickering fitful gleams to tell of the silent and lurking enemy who barred their way. But the bold spirit of the French cavaliers rose the higher to the danger. The clamor of their war-cries filled the air, and they tossed their pennoned spears over their heads in menace and defiance. From the English line it was a noble sight, the gallant, pawing, curveting horses, the many-colored twinkling riders, the swoop and wave and toss of plume and banner.

Then a bugle rang forth. With a sudden yell every spur struck deep, every lance was laid in rest, and the whole gallant squadron flew like a glittering thunderbolt for the center of the English line.

A hundred yards they had crossed, and yet another hundred, but there was no movement in front of them, and no sound save their own hoarse battle-cries and the thunder of their horses. Ever swifter and swifter they flew. From behind the hedge it was a vision of horses, white, bay and black, their necks stretched, their nostrils distended, their bellies to the ground, while of the rider one could but see a shield with a plume-tufted visor above it, and a spear-head twinkling in front.

Then of a sudden the prince raised his hand and gave a cry. Chandos echoed it, it swelled down the line, and with one mighty chorus of twanging strings and hissing shafts the long-pent storm broke at last.

Alas for the noble steeds! Alas for the gallant men! When the lust of battle is over who would not grieve to see that noble squadron break into red ruin before the rain of arrows beating upon the faces and breasts of the horses? The front rank crashed down, and the others piled themselves upon the top of them, unable to check their speed, or to swerve aside from the terrible wall of their shattered comrades which had so suddenly sprung up before them. Fifteen feet high was that blood-spurting mound of screaming, kicking horses and writhing, struggling men. Here and there on the flanks a horseman cleared himself and dashed for the hedge, only to have his steed slain under him and to be hurled from his saddle. Of all the three hundred gallant riders, not one ever reached that fatal hedge.

But now in a long rolling wave of steel the German battalion roared swiftly onward. They opened in the center to pass that terrible mound of death, and then spurred swiftly in upon the archers. They were brave men, well led, and in their open lines they could avoid the clubbing together which had been the ruin of the vanguard; yet they perished singly even as the others had perished together. A few were slain by the arrows. The greater number had their horses killed under them, and were so shaken and shattered by the fall that they could not raise their limbs, overweighted with iron, from the spot where they lay.

Three men riding together broke through the bushes which sheltered the leaders of the archers, cut down Widdington the dalesman, spurred onward through the hedge, dashed over the bowmen behind it, and made for the prince. One fell with an arrow through his head, a second was beaten from his saddle by

Chandos, and the third was slain by the prince's own hand. A second band broke through near the river, but were cut off by Lord Audley and his squires, so that all were slain. A single horseman whose steed was mad with pain, an arrow in its eye and a second in its nostril, sprang over the hedge and clattered through the whole army, disappearing amid whoops and laughter into the woods behind. But none others won as far as the hedge. The whole front of the position was fringed with a litter of German wounded or dead, while one great heap in the center marked the downfall of the gallant French three hundred.

While these two waves of the attack had broken in front of the English position, leaving this blood-stained wreckage behind them, the main divisions had halted and made their last preparations for their own assault. They had not yet begun their advance, and the nearest was still half a mile distant, when the few survivors from the forlorn hope, their maddened horses bristling with arrows, flew past them on either flank.

At the same moment the English archers and men-at-arms dashed through the hedge, and dragged all who were living out of that tangled heap of shattered horses and men. It was a mad wild rush, for in a few minutes the fight must be renewed, and yet there was a rich harvest of wealth for the lucky man who could pick a wealthy prisoner from amid the crowd. The nobler spirits disdained to think of ransoms while the fight was still unsettled; but a swarm of needy soldiers, Gascons and English, dragged the wounded out by the leg or the arm, and with daggers at their throats demanded their names, title, and means. He who had made a good prize hurried him to the rear where his own servants could guard him, while he who was disappointed too often drove the dagger home and then rushed once more into the tangle in the hope of better luck. Clermont, with an arrow through the sky-blue virgin on his surcoat, lay dead within ten paces of the hedge; d'Andreghen was dragged by a penniless squire from under a horse and became his prisoner. The Earls of Salzburg and of Nassau were both found helpless on the ground and taken to the rear. Aylward cast his thick arms round Count Otto von Langenbeck, and laid him, helpless from a broken leg, behind his bush. Black Simon had made prize of

Bernard, Count of Ventadour, and hurried him through the hedge. Everywhere there was rushing and shouting, brawling and buffeting, while amid it all a swarm of archers were seeking their shafts, plucking them from the dead, and sometimes even from the wounded. Then there was a sudden cry of warning. In a moment every man was back in his place once more, and the line of the hedge was clear.

It was high time; for already the first division of the French was close upon them. If the charge of the horsemen had been terrible from its rush and its fire, this steady advance of a huge phalanx of armored footmen was even more fearsome to the spectator. They moved very slowly, on account of the weight of their armor, but their progress was the more regular and inexorable. With elbows touching—their shields slung in front, their short five-foot spears carried in their right hands, and their maces or swords ready at their belts, the deep column of men-at-arms moved onward. Again the storm of arrows beat upon them clinking and thudding on the armor. They crouched double behind their shields as they met it. Many fell, but still the slow tide lapped onward. Yelling, they surged up to the hedge, and lined it for half a mile, struggling hard to pierce it.

For five minutes the long straining ranks faced each other with fierce stab of spear on one side and heavy beat of axe or mace upon the other. In many parts the hedge was pierced or leveled to the ground, and the French men-at-arms were raging among the archers, hacking and hewing among the lightly armed men. For a moment it seemed as if the battle was on the turn.

But John de Vere, Earl of Oxford, cool, wise, and crafty in war, saw and seized his chance. On the right flank a marshy meadow skirted the river. So soft was it that a heavily-armed man would sink to his knees. At his order a spray of light bowmen was thrown out from the battle-line and forming upon the flank of the French poured their arrows into them. At the same moment Chandos, with Audley, Nigel, Bartholomew Burghersh, the Captal de Buch, and a score of other knights sprang upon their horses, and charging down the narrow lane rode over the

French line in front of them. Once through it they spurred to left and right, trampling down the dismounted men-at-arms.

A fearsome sight was Pommers that day, his red eyes rolling, his nostrils gaping, his tawny mane tossing, and his savage teeth gnashing in fury, as he tore and smashed and ground beneath his ramping hoofs all that came before him. Fearsome too was the rider, ice-cool, alert, concentrated of purpose, with heart of fire and muscles of steel. A very angel of battle he seemed as he drove his maddened horse through the thickest of the press; but, strive as he would, the tall figure of his master upon his coal-black steed was ever half a length before him.

Already the moment of danger was passed. The French line had given back. Those who had pierced the hedge had fallen like brave men amid the ranks of their foemen. The division of Warwick had hurried up from the vineyards to fill the gaps of Salisbury's battle line. Back rolled the shining tide, slowly at first, even as it had advanced, but quicker now as the bolder fell and the weaker shredded out and shuffled with ungainly speed for a place of safety. Again there was a rush from behind the hedge. Again there was a reaping of that strange crop of bearded arrows which grew so thick upon the ground, and again the wounded prisoners were seized and dragged in brutal haste to the rear. Then the line was restored, and the English, weary, panting and shaken, awaited the next attack.

But a great good fortune had come to them—so great that as they looked down the valley they could scarce credit their own senses. Behind the division of the dauphin, which had pressed them so hard, stood a second division hardly less numerous, led by the Duke of Orleans. The fugitives from in front, blood-smeared and bedraggled, blinded with sweat and with fear, rushed amid its ranks in their flight, and in a moment, without a blow being struck, had carried them off in their wild rout. This vast array, so solid and so martial, thawed suddenly away like a snow-wreath in the sun. It was gone, and in its place thousands of shining dots scattered over the whole plain as each man made his own way to the spot where he could find his horse and bear himself from the field. For a moment it seemed that the battle was won, and a thundershout of joy pealed up from the English line.

But as the curtain of the duke's division was drawn away it was only to disclose stretching far behind it, and spanning the valley from side to side, the magnificent array of the French king, solid, unshaken, and preparing its ranks for the attack. Its numbers were as great as those of the English army; it was unscathed by all that was past, and it had a valiant monarch to lead it to the charge. With the slow deliberation of the man who means to do or to die, its leader marshaled its ranks for the supreme effort of the day.

Meanwhile during that brief moment of exultation when the battle appeared to be won, a crowd of hot-headed young knights and squires swarmed and clamored round the prince, beseeching that he would allow them to ride forth.

"See this insolent fellow who bears three martlets upon a field gules!" cried Sir Maurice Berkeley. "He stands betwixt the two armies as though he had no dread of us."

"I pray you, sir, that I may ride out to him, since he seems ready to attempt some small deed," pleaded Nigel.

"Nay, fair sirs, it is an evil thing that we should break our line, seeing that we still have much to do," said the prince. "See! he rides away, and so the matter is settled."

"Nay, fair prince," said the young knight who had spoken first. "My gray horse, Lebryte, could run him down ere he could reach shelter. Never since I left Severn side have I seen steed so fleet as mine. Shall I not show you?" In an instant he had spurred the charger and was speeding across the plain.

The Frenchman, John de Helennes, a squire of Picardy, had waited with a burning heart, his soul sick at the flight of the division in which he had ridden. In the hope of doing some redeeming exploit, or of meeting his own death, he had loitered between the armies, but no movement had come from the English lines. Now he had turned his horse's head to join the king's array, when the low drumming of hoofs sounded behind him, and he turned to find a horseman hard upon his heels. Each had drawn his sword, and the two armies paused to view the fight. In the first bout Sir Maurice Berkeley's lance was struck from

his hand, and as he sprang down to recover it the Frenchman
ran him through the thigh, dismounted from his horse, and received his surrender. As the unfortunate Englishman hobbled
away at the side of his captor a roar of laughter burst from both
armies at the spectacle.

"By my ten finger-bones!" cried Aylward, chuckling behind
the remains of his bush, "he found more on his distaff that time
than he knew how to spin. Who was the knight?"

"By his arms," said old Wat, "he should either be a Berkeley
of the West or a Popham of Kent."

"I call to mind that I shot a match of six ends once with a
Kentish woldsman——" began the fat bowyer.

"Nay, nay, stint thy talk, Bartholomew!" cried old Wat. "Here
is poor Ned with his head cloven, and it would be more fitting
if you were saying aves for his soul, instead of all this bobance
and boasting. How now, Tom of Beverley?"

"We have suffered sorely in this last bout, Wat. There are
forty of our men upon their backs, and the Dean foresters on
the right are in worse case still."

"Talking will not mend it, Tom, and if all but one were on
their backs he must still hold his ground."

While the archers were chatting, the leaders of the army were
in solemn conclave just behind them. Two divisions of the
French had been repulsed, and yet there was many an anxious
face as the older knights looked across the plain at the unbroken
array of the French king moving slowly toward them. The line
of the archers was much thinned and shredded. Many knights
and squires had been disabled in the long and fierce combat at
the hedge. Others, exhausted by want of food, had no strength
left and were stretched panting upon the ground. Some were
engaged in carrying the wounded to the rear and laying them
under the shelter of the trees, while others were replacing their
broken swords or lances from the weapons of the slain. The
Captal de Buch, brave and experienced as he was, frowned
darkly and whispered his misgivings to Chandos.

But the prince's courage flamed the higher as the shadow fell,
while his dark eyes gleamed with a soldier's pride as he glanced
round him at his weary comrades, and then at the dense masses

of the king's battle which now, with a hundred trumpets blaring and a thousand pennons waving, rolled slowly over the plain.

"Come what may, John, this has been a most noble meeting," said he. "They will not be ashamed of us in England. Take heart, my friends, for if we conquer we shall carry the glory ever with us; but if we be slain then we die most worshipfully and in high honor, as we have ever prayed that we might die, and we leave behind us our brothers and kinsmen who will assuredly avenge us. It is but one more effort, and all will be well. Warwick, Oxford, Salisbury, Suffolk, every man to the front! My banner to the front also! Your horses, fair sirs! The archers are spent, and our own good lances must win the field this day. Advance, Walter, and may God and Saint George be with England!"

Sir Walter Woodland, riding a high black horse, took station by the prince, with the royal banner resting in a socket by his saddle. From all sides the knights and squires crowded in upon it, until they formed a great squadron containing the survivors of the battalions of Warwick and Salisbury, as well as those of the prince. Four hundred men-at-arms who had been held in reserve were brought up and thickened the array, but even so Chandos's face was grave as he scanned it, and then turned his eyes upon the masses of the Frenchmen.

"I like it not, fair sir. The weight is overgreat," he whispered to the prince.

"How would you order it, John? Speak what is in your mind."

"We should attempt something upon their flank whilst we hold them in front. How say you, Jean?"

He turned to the Captal de Buch, whose dark, resolute face reflected the same misgivings.

"Indeed, John, I think as you do," said he. "The French king is a very valiant man, and so are those who are about him, and I know not how we may drive them back unless we can do as you advise. If you will give me only a hundred men I will attempt it."

"Surely the task is mine, fair sir, since the thought has come from me," said Chandos.

"Nay, John, I would keep you at my side. But you speak well,

Jean, and you shall do even as you have said. Go, ask the Earl of
Oxford for a hundred men-at-arms and as many hobbelers, that
you may ride round the mound yonder, and so fall upon them
unseen. Let all that are left of the archers gather on each side,
shoot away their arrows, and then fight as best they may. Wait
till they are past yonder thorn-bush and then, Walter, bear my
banner straight against that of the king of France. Fair sirs, may
God and the thought of your ladies hold high your hearts!"

The French monarch, seeing that his footmen had made no
impression upon the English, and also that the hedge had been
well-nigh leveled to the ground in the course of the combat, so
that it no longer presented an obstacle, had ordered his followers to remount their horses, and it was as a solid mass of cavalry
that the chivalry of France advanced to their last supreme effort.
The king was in the center of the front line, Geoffrey de
Chargny with the golden oriflamme upon his right, and Eustace
de Ribeaumont with the royal lilies upon the left. At his elbow
was the Duke of Athens, High Constable of France, and round
him were the nobles of the court, fiery and furious, yelling their
war-cries as they waved their weapons over their heads. Six
thousand gallant men of the bravest race in Europe, men whose
very names are like blasts of a battle-trumpet—Beaujeus and
Chatillons, Tancarvilles and Ventadours—pressed hard behind
the silver lilies.

Slowly they moved at first, walking their horses that they
might be the fresher for the shock. Then they broke into a trot
which was quickening into a gallop when the remains of the
hedge in front of them was beaten in an instant to the ground
and the broad line of the steel-clad chivalry of England swept
grandly forth to the final shock. With loose rein and busy spur
the two lines of horsemen galloped at the top of their speed
straight and hard for each other. An instant later they met with
a thunder-crash which was heard by the burghers on the wall of
Poictiers, seven good miles away.

Under that frightful impact horses fell dead with broken
necks, and many a rider, held in his saddle by the high pommel,
fractured his thighs with the shock. Here and there a pair met
breast to breast, the horses rearing straight upward and falling

back upon their masters. But for the most part the line had opened in the gallop, and the cavaliers, flying through the gaps, buried themselves in the enemy's ranks. Then the flanks shredded out, and the thick press in the center loosened until there was space to swing a sword and to guide a steed. For ten acres there was one wild tumultuous swirl of tossing heads, of gleaming weapons which rose and fell, of upthrown hands, of tossing plumes and of lifted shields, while the din of a thousand war-cries and the clash-clash of metal upon metal rose and swelled like the roar and beat of an ocean surge upon a rock-bound coast. Backward and forward swayed the mighty throng, now down the valley and now up, as each side in turn put forth its strength for a fresh rally. Locked in one long deadly grapple, great England and gallant France with iron hearts and souls of fire strove and strove for mastery.

Sir Walter Woodland, riding hard upon his high black horse, had plunged into the swelter and headed for the blue and silver banner of King John. Close at his heels in a solid wedge rode the prince, Chandos, Nigel, Lord Reginald Cobham, Audley, with his four famous squires, and a score of the flower of the English and Gascon knighthood. Holding together and bearing down opposition by a shower of blows and by the weight of their powerful horses, their progress was still very slow, for ever fresh waves of French cavaliers surged up against them and broke in front only to close in again upon their rear. Sometimes they were swept backward by the rush, sometimes they gained a few paces, sometimes they could but keep their foothold, and yet from minute to minute that blue and silver flag which waved above the press grew ever a little closer. A dozen furious hard-breathing French knights had broken into their ranks, and clutched at Sir Walter Woodland's banner, but Chandos and Nigel guarded it on one side, Audley with his squires on the other, so that no man laid his hand upon it and lived.

But now there was a distant crash and a roar of "Saint George for Guienne!" from behind. The Captal de Buch had charged home. "Saint George for England!" yelled the main attack, and ever the counter-cry came back to them from afar. The ranks opened in front of them. The French were giving way. A small knight with golden scroll-work upon his armor threw himself upon the prince and was struck dead by his mace. It was the Duke of Athens, Constable of France, but none had time to note it, and the fight rolled on over his body. Looser still were the French ranks. Many were turning their horses, for that ominous roar had shaken their resolution. The little English wedge poured onward, the prince, Chandos, Audley, and Nigel ever in the van.

A huge warrior in black, bearing a golden banner, appeared suddenly in a gap of the shredding ranks. He tossed his precious burden to a squire, who bore it away. Like a pack of hounds on the very haunch of a deer the English rushed yelling for the oriflamme. But the black warrior flung himself across their path. "Chargny! Chargny *à la recousse!*" he roared with a voice of thunder. Sir Reginald Cobham dropped before his battle-axe, so did the Gascon de Clisson. Nigel was beaten down on to the crupper of his horse by a sweeping blow; but at the same instant Chandos's quick blade passed through the Frenchman's camail and pierced his throat. So died Geoffrey de Chargny; but the oriflamme was saved.

Dazed with the shock, Nigel still kept his saddle, and Pommers, his yellow hide mottled with blood, bore him onward with the others. The French horsemen were now in full flight; but one stern group of knights stood firm, like a rock in a rushing torrent, beating off all, whether friend or foe, who tried to break their ranks. The oriflamme had gone, and so had the blue and silver banner, but here were desperate men ready to fight to the death. In their ranks honor was to be reaped. The prince and his following hurled themselves upon them, while the rest of the English horsemen swept onward to secure the fugitives and to win their ransoms. But the nobler spirits—Audley, Chandos, and the others—would have thought it shame to gain money while there was work to be done or honor to be won. Furious was the wild attack, desperate the prolonged defense. Men fell from their saddles for very exhaustion.

Nigel, still at his place near Chandos's elbow, was hotly attacked by a short broad-shouldered warrior upon a stout white cob, but Pommers reared with pawing forefeet and dashed the smaller horse to the ground. The falling rider clutched Nigel's arm and tore him from the saddle, so that the two rolled upon the grass under the stamping hoofs, the English squire on the top, and his shortened sword glimmered before the visor of the gasping, breathless Frenchman.

"*Je me rends! je me rends!*" he panted.

For a moment a vision of rich ransoms passed through Nigel's brain. That noble palfrey, that gold-flecked armor, meant fortune to the captor. Let others have it! There was work still to be done. How could he desert the prince and his noble master for the sake of a private gain? Could he lead a prisoner to the rear when honor beckoned him to the van? He staggered to his feet, seized Pommers by the mane, and swung himself into the saddle.

An instant later he was by Chandos' side once more and they were bursting together through the last ranks of the gallant group who had fought so bravely to the end. Behind them was one long swath of the dead and the wounded. In front the whole wide plain was covered with the flying French and their pursuers.

The prince reined up his steed and opened his visor, while his followers crowded round him with waving weapons and frenzied shouts of victory.

"What now, John!" cried the smiling prince, wiping his streaming face with his ungauntleted hand. "How fares it then?"

"I am little hurt, fair lord, save for a crushed hand and a spear-prick in the shoulder. But you, sir? I trust you have no scathe?"

"In truth, John, with you at one elbow and Lord Audley at the other, I know not how I could come to harm. But alas! I fear that Sir James is sorely stricken."

The gallant Lord Audley had dropped upon the ground and the blood oozed from every crevice of his battered armor. His four brave squires—Dutton of Dutton, Delves of Doddington, Fowlhurst of Crewe, and Hawkstone of Wainhill—wounded and weary themselves, but with no thought save for their master, unlaced his helmet and bathed his pallid blood-stained face.

He looked up at the prince with burning eyes. "I thank you, sir, for deigning to consider so poor a knight as myself," said he, in a feeble voice.

The prince dismounted and bent over him. "I am bound to honor you very much, James," said he, "for by your valor this day you have won glory and renown above us all, and your prowess has proved you to be the bravest knight."

"My Lord," murmured the wounded man, "you have a right to say what you please; but I wish it were as you say."

"James," said the prince, "from this time onward I make you a knight of my own household, and I settle upon you five hundred marks of yearly income from my own estates in England."

"Sir," the knight answered, "God make me worthy of the good fortune you bestow upon me. Your knight I will ever be, and the money I will divide with your leave amongst these four squires who have brought me whatever glory I have won this day." So saying his head fell back, and he lay white and silent upon the grass.

"Bring water!" said the prince. "Let the royal leech see to him; for I had rather lose many men than the good Sir James. Ha, Chandos, what have we here?"

A knight lay across the path with his helmet beaten down upon his shoulders. On his surcoat and shield were the arms of a red griffin.

"It is Robert de Duras the spy," said Chandos.

"Well for him that he has met his end," said the angry prince. "Put him on his shield, Hubert, and let four archers bear him to the monastery. Lay him at the feet of the Cardinal and say that by this sign I greet him. Place my flag on yonder high bush, Walter, and let my tent be raised there, that my friends may know where to seek me."

The flight and pursuit had thundered far away, and the field was deserted save for the numerous groups of weary horsemen who were making their way back, driving their prisoners before them. The archers were scattered over the whole plain, rifling the saddle-bags and gathering the armor of those who had fallen, or searching for their own scattered arrows.

Suddenly, however, as the prince was turning toward the

bush which he had chosen for his headquarters, there broke out
from behind him an extraordinary uproar and a group of knights
and squires came pouring toward him, all arguing, swearing and
abusing each other in French and English at the tops of their
voices. In the midst of them limped a stout little man in gold-
spangled armor, who appeared to be the object of the conten-
tion, for one would drag him one way and one another, as
though they would pull him limb from limb.

"Nay, fair sirs, gently, gently, I pray you!" he pleaded. "There
is enough for all, and no need to treat me so rudely."

But ever the hubbub broke out again, and swords gleamed as
the angry disputants glared furiously at each other. The prince's
eyes fell upon the small prisoner, and he staggered back with a
gasp of astonishment.

"King John!" he cried.

A shout of joy rose from the warriors around him. "The king
of France! The king of France a prisoner!" they cried in an
ecstasy.

"Nay, nay, fair sirs, let him not hear that we rejoice! Let no
word bring pain to his soul!" Running forward the prince
clasped the French king by the two hands.

"Most welcome, sire!" he cried. "Indeed it is good for us that
so gallant a knight should stay with us for some short time, since
the chance of war has so ordered it. Wine there! Bring wine for
the king!"

But John was flushed and angry. His helmet had been roughly
torn off, and blood was smeared upon his cheek. His noisy captors stood around him in a circle, eyeing him hungrily like dogs
who have been beaten from their quarry. There were Gascons
and English, knights, squires, and archers, all pushing and
straining.

"I pray you, fair prince, to get rid of these rude fellows," said
King John, "for indeed they have plagued me sorely. By Saint
Denis! my arm has been well-nigh pulled from its socket."

"What wish you then?" asked the prince, turning angrily upon
the noisy swarm of his followers.

"We took him, fair lord. He is ours!" cried a score of voices.
They closed in, all yelping together like a pack of wolves. "It was

I, fair lord!"—"Nay, it was I!"—"You lie, you rascal, it was I!" Again their fierce eyes glared and their blood-stained hands sought the hilts of their weapons.

"Nay, this must be settled here and now!" said the prince. "I crave your patience, fair and honored sir, for a few brief minutes, since indeed much ill-will may spring from this if it be not set at rest. Who is this tall knight who can scarce keep his hands from the king's shoulder?"

"It is Denis de Morbecque, my lord, a knight of St. Omer, who is in our service, being an outlaw from France."

"I call him to mind. How then, Sir Denis? What say you in this matter?"

"He gave himself to me, fair lord. He had fallen in the press, and I came upon him and seized him. I told him that I was a knight from Artois, and he gave me his glove. See here, I bear it in my hand."

"It is true, fair lord! It is true!" cried a dozen French voices.

"Nay, sir, judge not too soon!" shouted an English squire, pushing his way to the front. "It was I who had him at my mercy, and he is my prisoner, for he spoke to this man only because he could tell by his tongue that he was his own countryman. I took him, and here are a score to prove it."

"It is true, fair lord. We saw it, and it was even so," cried a chorus of Englishmen.

At all times there are growling and snapping between the English and their allies of France. The prince saw how easily this might set a light to such a flame as could not readily be quenched. It must be stamped out now ere it had time to mount.

"Fair and honored lord," he said to the king, "again I pray you for a moment of patience. It is your word and only yours which can tell us what is just and right. To whom were you graciously pleased to commit your royal person?"

King John looked up from the flagon which had been brought to him and wiped his lips with the dawnings of a smile upon his ruddy face.

"It was not this Englishman," he said, and a cheer burst from the Gascons, "nor was it this bastard Frenchman," he added. "To neither of them did I surrender."

There was a hush of surprise.

"To whom then, sir?" asked the prince.

The king looked slowly round. "There was a devil of a yellow horse," said he. "My poor palfrey went over like a skittle-pin before a ball. Of the rider I know nothing save that he bore red roses on a silver shield. Ah! by Saint Denis, there is the man himself, and there his thrice-accursed horse!"

His head swimming, and moving as if in a dream, Nigel found himself the center of the circle of armed and angry men.

The prince laid his hand upon his shoulder. "It is the little cock of Tilford Bridge," said he. "On my father's soul, I have ever said that you would win your way. Did you receive the king's surrender?"

"Nay, fair lord, I did not receive it."

"Did you hear him give it?"

"I heard, sir, but I did not know that it was the king. My master Lord Chandos had gone on, and I followed after."

"And left him lying. Then the surrender was not complete, and by the laws of war the ransom goes to Denis de Morbecque, if his story be true."

"It is true," said the king. "He was the second."

"Then the ransom is yours, Denis. But for my part I swear by my father's soul that I had rather have the honor this squire has gathered than all the richest ransoms of France."

At these words spoken before that circle of noble warriors Nigel's heart gave one great throb, and he dropped upon his knee before the prince.

"Fair lord, how can I thank you?" he murmured. "These words at least are more than any ransom."

"Rise up!" said the smiling prince, and he smote with his sword upon his shoulder. "England has lost a brave squire, and has gained a gallant knight. Nay, linger not, I pray! Rise up, Sir Nigel."

XXVII. HOW THE THIRD MESSENGER
CAME TO COSFORD

TWO MONTHS HAVE passed, and the long slopes of Hindhead are russet with the faded ferns—the fuzzy brown pelt which wraps the chilling earth. With whoop and scream the wild November wind sweeps over the great rolling downs, tossing the branches of the Cosford beeches, and rattling at the rude latticed windows. The stout old knight of Dupplin, grown even a little stouter, with whiter beard to fringe an ever redder face, sits as of yore at the head of his own board. A well-heaped platter, flanked by a foaming tankard stands before him. At his right sits the Lady Mary, her dark, plain, queenly face marked deep with those years of weary waiting, but bearing the gentle grace and dignity which only sorrow and restraint can give. On his left is Matthew, the old priest. Long ago the golden-haired beauty had passed from Cosford to Fernhurst, where the young and beautiful Lady Edith Brocas is the belle of all Sussex, a sunbeam of smiles and merriment, save perhaps when her thoughts for an instant fly back to that dread night when she was plucked from under the very talons of the foul hawk of Shalford.

The old knight looked up as a fresh gust of wind with a dash of rain beat against the window behind him.

"By Saint Hubert, it is a wild night," said he. "I had hoped to-morrow to have a flight at a heron of the pool or a mallard in the brook. How fares it with little Katherine the peregrine, Mary?"

"I have joined the wing, father, and I have imped the feathers; but I fear it will be Christmas ere she can fly again."

"This is a hard saying," said Sir John; "for indeed I have seen no bolder better bird. Her wing was broken by a heron's beak last Sabbath sennight, holy father, and Mary has the mending of it."

"I trust, my son, that you had heard mass ere you turned to worldly pleasure upon God's holy day," Father Matthew answered.

"Tut, tut!" said the old knight, laughing. "Shall I make confession at the head of my own table? I can worship the good God amongst His own works, the woods and the fields, better than in yon pile of stone and wood. But I call to mind a charm for a wounded hawk which was taught me by the fowler of Gaston de Foix. How did it run? 'The lion of the tribe of Judah, the root of David, has conquered.' Yes, those were the words to be said three times as you walk round the perch where the bird is mewed."

The old priest shook his head. "Nay, these charms are tricks of the devil," said he. "Holy Church lends them no countenance, for they are neither good nor fair. But how is it now with your tapestry, Lady Mary? When last I was beneath this roof you had half done in five fair colors the story of Theseus and Ariadne."

"It is half done still, holy father."

"How is this, my daughter? Have you then so many calls?"

"Nay, holy father, her thoughts are otherwhere," Sir John answered. "She will sit an hour at a time, the needle in her hand and her soul a hundred leagues from Cosford House. Ever since the prince's battle——"

"Good father, I beg you——"

"Nay, Mary, none can hear me, save your own confessor, Father Matthew. Ever since the prince's battle, I say, when we heard that young Nigel had won such honor, she is brain-wode, and sits ever—well, even as you see her now."

An intent look had come into Mary's eyes; her gaze was fixed upon the dark rain-splashed window. It was a face carved from ivory, white-lipped and rigid, on which the old priest looked.

"What is it, my daughter? What do you see?"

"I see nothing, father."

"What is it, then, that disturbs you?"

"I hear, father."

"What do you hear?"

"There are horsemen on the road."

The old knight laughed. "So it goes on, father. What day is there that a hundred horsemen do not pass our gate, and yet every clink of hoofs sets her poor heart a-trembling. So strong and steadfast she has ever been, my Mary, and now no sound too slight to shake her to the soul! Nay, daughter, nay, I pray you!"

She had half-risen from her chair, her hands clinched and her dark, startled eyes still fixed upon the window.

"I hear them, father! I hear them amid the wind and the rain! Yes, yes, they are turning—they have turned! My God, they are at our very door!"

"By Saint Hubert, the girl is right!" cried old Sir John, beating his fist upon the board. "Ho, varlets, out with you to the yard! Set the mulled wine on the blaze once more! There are travelers at the gate, and it is no night to keep a dog waiting at our door. Hurry, Hannekin! Hurry, I say, or I will haste you with my cudgel!"

Plainly to the ears of all men could be heard the stamping of the horses. Mary had stood up, quivering in every limb. An eager step at the threshold, the door was flung wide, and there in the opening stood Nigel, the rain gleaming upon his smiling face, his cheeks flushed with the beating of the wind, his blue eyes shining with tenderness and love. Something held her by the throat, the light of the torches danced up and down; but her strong spirit rose at the thought that others should see that inner holy of holies of her soul. There is a heroism of women to which no valor of man can attain. Her eyes only carried him her message as she held out her hand.

"Welcome, Nigel!" said she.

He stooped and kissed it.

"Saint Catharine has brought me home," said he.

A merry supper it was at Cosford Manor that night, with Nigel at the head between the jovial old knight and the Lady Mary, while at the farther end Samkin Aylward, wedged between two servant maids kept his neighbors in alternate laughter and terror as he told his tales of the French Wars. Nigel had to turn his doeskin heels and show his little golden spurs. As he spoke of what was passed Sir John clapped him on the shoulder, while Mary took his strong right hand in hers, and the good old priest, smiling, blessed them both. Nigel had drawn a little golden ring from his pocket, and it twinkled in the torchlight.

"Did you say that you must go on your way, to-morrow, father?" he asked the priest.

"Indeed, fair son, the matter presses."

"But you may bide the morning?"

"It will suffice if I start at noon."

"Much may be done in a morning." He looked at Mary, who blushed and smiled. "By Saint Paul! I have waited long enough."

"Good, good!" chuckled the old knight, with wheezy laughter. "Even so I wooed your mother, Mary. Wooers were brisk in the olden time. To-morrow is Tuesday, and Tuesday is ever a lucky day. Alas! that the good Dame Ermyntrude is no longer with us to see it done! The old hound must run us down, Nigel, and I hear its bay upon my own heels; but my heart will rejoice that before the end I may call you son. Give me your hand, Mary, and yours, Nigel. Now, take an old man's blessing, and may God keep and guard you both, and give you your desert, for I believe on my soul that in all this broad land there dwells no nobler man nor any woman more fitted to be his mate!"

There let us leave them, their hearts full of gentle joy, the golden future of hope and promise stretching out before their youthful eyes. Alas for those green spring dreamings! How often do they fade and wither until they fall and rot, a dreary sight, by the wayside of life! But here, by God's blessing, it was not so, for they burgeoned and they grew, ever fairer and more noble, until the whole wide world might marvel at the beauty of it.

It has been told elsewhere how as the years passed Nigel's name rose higher in honor; but still Mary's would keep pace with it, each helping and sustaining the other upon an ever higher path. In many lands did Nigel carve his fame, and ever as he returned spent and weary from his work he drank fresh strength and fire and craving for honor from her who glorified his home. At Twynham Castle they dwelled for many years, beloved and honored by all. Then in the fullness of time they came back to the Tilford Manor-house and spent their happy, healthy age amid those heather downs where Nigel had passed his first lusty youth, ere ever he turned his face to the wars. Thither also came Aylward when he had left the Pied Merlin where for many a year he sold ale to the men of the forest.

But the years pass; the old wheel turns and ever the thread runs out. The wise and the good, the noble and the brave, they come from the darkness, and into the darkness they go, whence, whither, and why, who may say? Here is the slope of Hindhead. The fern still glows russet in November, the heather still burns red in July; but where now is the Manor of Cosford? Where is the old house of Tilford? Where, but for a few scattered gray stones, is the mighty pile of Waverley? And yet even gnawing Time has not eaten all things away. Walk with me toward Guildford, reader, upon the busy highway. Here, where the high green mound rises before us, mark yonder roofless shrine which still stands four-square to the winds. It is St. Catharine's, where Nigel and Mary plighted their faith. Below lies the winding river, and over yonder you still see the dark Chantry woods which mount up to the bare summit, on which, roofed and whole, stands that Chapel of the Martyr where the comrades beat off the archers of the crooked Lord of Shalford. Down yonder on the flanks of the long chalk hills one traces the road by which they made their journey to the wars. And now turn hither to the north, down this sunken winding path! It is all unchanged since Nigel's day. Here is the Church of Compton. Pass under the aged and crumbling arch. Before the steps of that ancient altar, unrecorded and unbrassed, lies the dust of Nigel and of Mary. Near them is that of Maude their daughter, and of Alleyne Edricson, whose spouse she was; their children and children's children are lying by their side. Here too, near the old yew in the churchyard, is the little mound which marks where Samkin Aylward went back to that good soil from which he sprang.

So lie the dead leaves; but they and such as they nourish for ever that great old trunk of England, which still sheds forth another crop and another, each as strong and as fair as the last.

The body may lie in moldering chancel, or in crumbling vault, but the rumor of noble lives, the record of valor and truth, can never die, but lives on in the soul of the people. Our own work lies ready to our hands; and yet our strength may be the greater and our faith the firmer if we spare an hour from present toils to look back upon the women who were gentle and strong, or the men who loved honor more than life on this green stage of England where for a few short years we play our little part.